THE TENDER COCONUT TAMASHA

AN INSPECTOR CHATPATI MYSTERY

BANGALORE CIVIL NUISANCE UNIT
BOOK ONE

JOE CHACKO

PRAISE FOR JOE CHACKO

"I read the book last evening virtually non stop till I finished it. I enjoyed reading it and did not want to stop till I finished it. I would recommend it to any Police library both from the professional as well as the humorous contents."

— FORMER DIRECTOR GENERAL OF POLICE, KARNATAKA

This is a work of fiction.

Names, characters, places and incidents are either the product of the author's imagination or are used fictitiously.

Any resemblance to actual persons, living or dead, events or locales is coincidental.

Copyright © 2021 by Joe Chacko

Cover image by Glenn Jones

ISBN 978-1-8383673-1-2

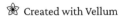 Created with Vellum

To The Ffool, the Denizens of Abjar
and my wonderful wife.

May your drums ever thunder
and your lights never dim.

CHAPTER 1

DATE OF EXPIRY

M ohan Rao hadn't expected his Tuesday morning to end the way it did. It had begun, like all his weekdays, with a run in Cubbon Park.

It was the best part of the day, the first rays of sunlight glinting off the steely glass facades of the office blocks and hotels that ensnared the city's ancient, woody heart. The avenues were cool under leaf, the obstacles a mere handful of perambulating pensioners, no real impediment to the sure-footed.

One such non-impediment, Colonel Rajvir Singh, Indian Army (retired), memory still bayonet keen, would recognise Mohan Rao from the photograph in the next day's Bangalore Herald and remark on it to his wife, who said nothing.

K. Senthil, street vendor, at his usual spot opposite the Maharajah's statue, would describe how Rao had stopped by at his usual time, paid for his usual refreshment and downed it in the usual single gulp.

The doorman at ParkVue Apartments would report that Rao had staggered, rather than walked, into the lobby.

The lift attendant would say, when asked, that Rao had looked sweaty and pale.

Dr. Anand Acharya, general practitioner, would confirm that Rao had rung for an urgent appointment at 8.13am. "Feeling unwell" read the receptionist's note. "Abdominal pain. Nausea."

An ambulance had been despatched, as per the corporate insurance policy, but the ambulance crew received no answer at Rao's door.

The apartment manager, duly summoned, had found Rao in the kitchen, face down in a pool of frothy vomit.

Had he been given the opportunity to reflect, Mohan Rao might have declared himself satisfied with the weave of his life so far. The private education his parents couldn't really afford had led to a fine job with a good salary. He had left the small town of his birth for a high-rise in the big city.

His entry into adult life had been ballistic, his arc on the ascendant.

Weightless, Rao felt not the clutch of casual circumstance that flattens many such trajectories.

Death grounds every mortal expectation.

This is what Inspector Hari Chatpati would discover some days later, thanks to the angry Austrian tourist and the travel agent who was anything but.

CHAPTER 2
NO HERO'S WELCOME

S ome weeks after Mohan Rao died, Inspector Chatpati died his own kind of death. There weren't many things that might drive Chatpati to wish for an early death but chief among them was having to meet with the Assistant Commissioner of Police.

The Headquarters of Central Division on Kasturba Road had been a drab, soot-stained villa, built during the British Raj, until the addition of a steel carbuncle five storeys tall. The ACP's office was on the top floor and commanded a fine view of the city. Had Chatpati looked out through the window, he might even have glimpsed the cause of Mohan Rao's demise in the distance. As it was, Chatpati was fully engaged trying to suppress his ire.

The ACP's PA, a matronly woman in a khaki uniform sari, had instructed Chatpati on protocol as she led him in. Her eyes were kind.

"Don't forget to salute, Inspector. And best to wait to be asked a question before speaking." She smiled at him. "He's in a good mood today, so you should be fine. Just remember to salute!"

ACP Srinivasan had been the first to speak, his greeting unexpectedly effusive.

"Ah! The hero of the hour! Come in, Inspector Chatpati."

Srinivasan had been lounging on his non-regulation sofa, his non-regulation shoes glistening with someone else's spit and polish and resting on the non-regulation coffee table. The sofa was leather, the shoes brogues and the coffee table glass. Chatpati guessed that the least of these cost half a year's salary. More tinted glass formed the far wall behind the ACP's teak desk. Another wall bore the crest and flags of the Bangalore Police Service. The floor was polished granite, the air suitably conditioned.

Srinivasan's attention had been on the huge flat-screen TV that dominated the near wall. Chatpati saluted and waited. Srinivasan glanced sidelong at him.

"Sit. Don't loiter," Srinivasan snapped, waving at a matching armchair.

Chatpati removed his hat and sat. Srinivasan had the physiognomy of a bon vivant; an improbably large nose overhung a caterpillar moustache and fleshy lips. His paunch cascaded over his Versace belt.

Srinivasan waved the remote control at the TV and turned the volume up.

"This will interest you," he said.

The Bangalore TV news was on. The screen showed a grizzled man in prison uniform and shackles being dragged out of a police van, surrounded by masked commandos wielding sub-machine guns. Chatpati recognised the High Court in the background. Anchorwoman Nita Singh's stentorian delivery cut through the hubbub of journalists swarming about the prisoner.

"Today sees the beginning of the trial of Govind Prabhu, self-styled leader of the Kissan Yudh, the self-titled Farmer's War Party. Residents of Bangalore will remember it was not four months ago that the banned terrorist organisation launched their devastating chemical attack on the Vidhana Soudha[1]. The terrorists claim they are fighting for the preservation of their traditional livelihoods against the incursion of foreign agro-tech companies. Six people died in the attack, including three schoolchildren. It was only the prompt action of the police that prevented more casualties and saw the culprits swiftly brought to justice. The trial is expected to last several days, but the outcome is likely a foregone conclusion."

The picture changed to a map of the city, shrouded in grey.

"And now, here's today's weather report. Smog in most areas-"

SRINIVASAN SWITCHED THE TV OFF. "So," he said, smiling, "how does it feel to see justice done? Eh? To be the hero at the centre of the storm?"

Chatpati pursed his lips. "It's not something I think about. Sir."

Srinivasan sat up. "Really?" he sneered. " A commendation from the Justice Minister. Cash rewards from a grateful Government. A promotion. Your face splattered all over the TV. And you don't think about it." Srinivasan shook his head in disbelief. "You are a very modest man, Inspector."

Chatpati shrugged. "I did not ask for the commendation. I refused the cash. And I avoided the media. As for the promotion—"

5

"You refused that too," Srinivasan said, nodding. "Strange man, Chatpati. Strange. Though," he wagged a finger, "some might say calculating. After all, what could be more attractive than a hero? Except a *reluctant* hero? Eh?" Srinivasan leant over and slapped Chatpati on the shoulder. "Shabash![2] Well done! Because, despite all your earnest refusals, they rewarded you. Am I wrong?"

Chatpati rubbed his shoulder. "I—"

"Oh yes," Srinivasan replied. "You refused the apartment, but they forced you to accept it. The Minister can be very persuasive. Your wife was fed up with living in Police Quarters, no doubt. Nothing like air-conditioning, a fitted kitchen, a concierge, eh? And, instead of accepting the promotion to Assistant Commissioner of Police, you chose a sideways move. Commander of the very first 'semi-autonomous police unit' in the City. Remind me what it's called again. Common Nonsense Unit, is it?"

Chatpati bristled. "Civil Nuisance Unit. Sir."

Srinivasan cackled, dispensing spittle. "Oh, yes. Civil Nuisance Unit. What a glorious name. You're at least half qualified to run that. You're not very civil, Inspector, but you're certainly a nuisance!"

Chatpati throttled his hat in his lap. "Again, sir-"

Srinivasan got to his feet and plodded over to his desk. "Yes, yes, not your choice. Victim of circumstance, blah, blah, blah. Spare me the details." He beckoned Chatpati over. "Come over here."

Behind the desk, Srinivasan looked even more the despot. Chatpati stood.

"Oh, for heaven's sake, sit, man," Srinivasan growled, flicking through papers. "Why such formality, eh? After all, we're all friends here. Now, where is that file?" He pressed a button on his phone.

"Yes, sir," the PA's voice said.

"Mina, where the bloody hell is that file? The German tourist? I thought I said to leave it on my desk."

"You did, sir," Mina replied. "But I had to update it with the medical report. Shall I bring it in?"

"Never mind," Srinivasan snapped. "You can give it to the Inspector when he leaves."

Chatpati felt a brief surge of hope. The end was in sight.

Srinivasan sat back in his chair and studied Chatpati.

"Some work for you, Inspector. To occupy you while your Unit is being set up. What is the status of your Nonsense Unit, by the way?"

"Nuisance. Sir." Chatpati replied. "The premises is being refurbished. We've recruited some staff, mostly volunteers from other divisions."

"I know about the volunteers," Srinivasan hissed, "since I'm paying their salaries for the next three months. Where is your premises? Remind me."

Chatpati swallowed. "The General Utilities building, sir. On Mahatma Gandhi Road. Top floor. The twenty-fourth."

Srinivasan scowled at him. "Utilities building? Not a police station?"

"No, sir. I thought it a better fit." And not subject to your routine interference, Chatpati did not say. "It's smack bang in the middle of our patch, the Central Business District. It's a government building, so it's rent free. The building's mostly vacant, apart from a cinema on the ground floor, a vegetarian restaurant and a few small shops."

"What was on the top floor?" Srinivasan asked. "I can't recall."

"A nightclub. Sir."

Srinivasan's jaw dropped. "A nightclub?"

"Yes, sir," Chatpati replied, matter of fact. "It was repossessed. Two bars, a restaurant, an open-air balcony and lounge and a dance floor. And a mirrored disco ball." He paused. "Parquet, sir. The dance floor. You should drop by."

CHAPTER 3
ILL-MET BY AUTO-RICKSHAW

Inspector Chatpati emerged from the ACP's office around the middle of the morning. The sun was high in the sky. The traffic surged down Kasturba Road with a full-throated, asphyxiating roar. It was hot and getting hotter.

He waited for an auto-rickshaw[1] outside the gates, in the scant shade offered by an ancient cassia tree in bloom. The tree had stood here when the road had been laid during the British Raj[2]. It had outlasted the colonial conquerors; its roots had long since reclaimed most of the narrow, fractured pavement. Pedestrians picked their way past with care, avoiding loose flagstones that might send them tumbling into the mad throng of vehicles that raced past a shirtsleeve away.

The sting of ozone made Chatpati's nose run. He fished a face-mask out of his breast pocket and slipped it on. The smoke from the swarm of teetering buses, skittering auto-rickshaws and buzzing motorcycles gave the air a blue pall. The clamour of engines, horns, brakes, and gears was deafening.

He soon realised that his chances of hailing an auto-rickshaw were small. It was peak time on one of the major arteries feeding Bangalore's buzzing heart. Factor in his being in police uniform and the probability of success approximated zero. Auto-rickshaws avoided policemen like the plague. Policemen rarely paid the fare.

Chatpati had waved at a couple of autos that puttered past, but it was as if Chatpati were a low-caste Dalit[3] hailing an upper-caste Brahmin. The auto-drivers' gaze slipped right over him as if he didn't exist.

"Shall I stop one for you, Inspector?" the gate guard had asked. The guard had slipped the rifle off his shoulder and raised it across his chest. "This usually stops them."

"Good God, no!" Chatpati said, raising an arm. "Put that thing away! What's wrong with you?"

He had visions of an auto-rickshaw skidding to a halt before a pointed gun, only to be upended from behind by a speeding Municipal Corporation bus. Buses didn't stop for anything smaller than another bus. He could see the auto-rickshaw's tin-thin skeleton cleaved in two, passengers spilling out in a tangle of limbs, sarees spooling into spinning wheels, blood on the spokes and brains on the tarmac. He shuddered. He'd been at the scene of more road traffic accidents than he cared to remember.

The guard shrugged. "It works. Usually. Or I could call for a Hoysala[4]."

"No thanks," Chatpati said, "The driving is awful. I value my life. And it'll take an hour to arrive. They'll suddenly discover some urgent parking felony to prosecute instead."

"Try down the road, sir," the gate guard said, shouldering his rifle. "There are usually some auto-rickshaws outside Cubbon Park, near the Marriott, hustling for tourists." He gave Chatpati a conspiratorial grin. "You can sneak up on them. There will be at least one driver not in uniform."

The Municipal Corporation had recently mandated khaki uniforms for all auto-drivers. Compliance had been patchy, another rich source of revenue for the police.

Chatpati walked down Kasturba Road, sticking to the shade where he could. He made it halfway down when his luck changed. There, outside the entrance to the Industrial and Technology Museum, he happened across a gaggle of auto-rickshaws, parked carelessly by the pavement.

Three auto-drivers in various approximations of uniform surrounded a tall, moustachioed man in a dress shirt and tie. The tall man had placed a defensive blue fabric suitcase between him and the auto-drivers. They were so engrossed in heated discussion that none noticed Chatpati approach.

The tall man's voice rose above the din of traffic. He raised an arm, index finger pointed at the sky.

"I protest, thou recalcitrant vagabonds!" the tall man bellowed. "Thine attempts to inflict a calumny is treasonous!"

The two auto-drivers at either side of the third laughed outright. The third, clearly the leader, gave the suitcase a kick.

"Oy! Clown!" the leader growled, shaking a fist. "Stop talking nonsense and pay up. Don't try to cheat me! Pay the fare! Or else!"

The other two chipped in like a Greek chorus. "Yes. Pay up! Don't think you can cheat him just because he is an auto-driver! Better pay quick!"

The tall man drew himself up to his full height, towering above the drivers. "Villains perpetually declara-

11

tion themselves victim. Thine remonstrations fall on mute ears, vagrant! Dost thou not comprehend that I am a deputy of the justiciary!"

"What's going on here?" Chatpati said, in his official police voice. They turned to look at him. Shock registered on the faces of the auto-drivers, relief on that of the tall man. The two peripheral drivers edged away.

"Stop!" Chatpati said. "You two stay right there. You!" He pointed at the leader, the one who had kicked the suitcase. "What's going on here? Why are you assaulting that suitcase?"

The fellow wilted, eyes to the ground. "It's nothing, sir," he mumbled. "Simple misunderstanding."

The tall man addressed Chatpati. "Penultimately! A fellow compatriot. Honourable compatriot, I entreat thee to imprison this multitude-"

Chatpati raised a hand. "You. Also stop." He stepped up to the ringleader and examined the regulation brass name-plate pinned to the auto-driver's khaki uniform top. "Nagesh. That's your name, is it?" The man nodded, mute. "I asked you what's going on here. Speak up, damn it!"

Nagesh wrung his hands. "Sir, this fellow is refusing to pay his fare, sir. He began shouting! I – I felt threatened and-"

"Let me guess," Chatpati said, "you waved these two down to assist you. Am I correct?" He turned to the other two auto-drivers. They shrugged. "Assist? Or intimidate? Which is it?"

The auto-drivers stared at their feet and said nothing.

The tall man had been concentrating intently on the conversation. He spoke again to Chatpati. "Thou hast the great measure of the matter, respected compatriot of the justiciary. These vagabonds-"

Chatpati raised a hand. The tall man stopped. Chatpati addressed the auto-drivers. "Why does he speak like that?"

Nagesh shook his head and tapped his forehead. "Mad, sir. Unbalanced."

Chatpati's face was expressionless. "Where did you pick him up?"

"Majestic, sir."

Majestic was what the locals called the area around the Majestic Theatre in the city's north, in which the Central Bus and Train stations were located.

That made sense, Chatpati thought. The man was clearly from out of town. Chatpati looked him over. The traveller did not appear in the least intimidated. He had a trim moustache and well-maintained eyebrows. His nose was proud, his lips full. He was sweating freely in his long-sleeves and tie. There were damp patches under his arms.

"Where are you from?" Chatpati asked. The tall man looked puzzled. Chatpati tried again in the literary Kannada[5] the man had used. "What is thine abode, o compatriot?"

"Ah," the man smiled, "my native place is Cochin, that shining firmament in the fair kingdom of Kerala[6]."

Chatpati nodded. "Dost thou sojourn?

The man nodded. "Verily. I am arrived to engage in an enterprise of profession."

Chatpati's head was aching. He fished out his handkerchief and wiped his face. "Hast thou the faculty of other tongues?" he asked in hope. "English, mayhaps?"

"Why, yes," the tall man replied. In English. "I speak English. Of course. Why?"

"Thank God." Chatpati said. "Where did you learn to speak Kannada, may I ask?"

The tall man looked puzzled. "Well, from a book. It came with a CD-ROM."

Chatpati nodded. "I see. Was your Kannada book published any time in the last, say, twenty years?"

"I'm not sure. I got it from a second-hand bookshop. Why? What's wrong with my Kannada?"

"No one in Bangalore speaks like that," Chatpati said. "You're speaking the literary, declarative form of Kannada. It's only ever used in traditional folk plays, like Yakshagana[7]."

The tall man looked nonplussed. "Oh. I-"

"Never mind," Chatpati said. "Let's stick to English. What's the problem here?"

"This fellow," the tall man said, pointing at the auto-driver Nagesh, "demanded five hundred rupees! For a fifteen minute journey! It's outrageous! I refused to pay! In Cochin, I would have had him arrested! I was about to ring for backup when you arrived."

"Cochin is Cochin. In Kerala State." Chatpati said. "This is Bangalore. In Karnataka State. Things are different here." The tall man bristled. "Nevertheless, that fare is excessive. Wait a moment."

He turned to the auto-drivers and pointed at the two at the periphery. He used the guttural street Kannada of a true local. "You two! Bugger off. If I see your sorry arses again, you're in for a kicking. Get it? Now get lost."

The two men ran off towards their vehicles. Chatpati turned his attention to Nagesh. "As for you," he said, "this fellow says you demanded five hundred rupees."

"No, sir!" Nagesh wailed. He folded himself into a crouch, hands raised overhead, palms together in the traditional gesture of supplication. "No, sir! I just asked for a supplement over the standard fare because of rush hour and—"

"Idiot!" Chatpati cut him off. "Do you think I was born yesterday? There is no supplement for rush hour. Let's see what the fare on your meter is." Chatpati examined the fare meter on the remaining auto-rickshaw. The meter was off. Chatpati turned back. "Well, well, Nagesh. It looks like you didn't even turn the meter on. That's an automatic fine. Five hundred rupees. Get up, you idiot."

Nagesh struggled back upright and wrung his hands. ""Sir, please, sir. I don't have that much money. I just started my day. I have only two hundred, sir. See, sir?" He produced a clutch of threadbare notes. "Please! If I don't make five hundred rupees today, I can't pay the daily rent for the auto. My family will—"

Chatpati rolled his eyes. "Oh, here we go. Your family will starve, your children will have to beg and your saintly dead mother will be refused entry to her heavenly abode. The usual excuses. Save it. Where were all your fine considerations when you summoned those two other idiots to intimidate this fellow, huh? And just around the corner from Assistant Commissioner's Office! Shameless! I should fine you just for being an idiot."

The tall man had had enough of being the observer. In English, he said, "I demand you arrest this fellow. Such individuals deserve—"

"Never mind," Chatpati replied in English. "I have dealt with the matter. For your information, the standard fare from Majestic to the city centre is fifty rupees. On this occasion, there's no charge. You are free to go. Goodbye."

Chatpati turned his back on the tall man and grabbed Nagesh by the collar. He thrust him towards his auto-rickshaw. "Get in. Start that thing up." Chatpati got in the rear passenger seat. "No fare for you for that trip, Nagesh. Serves you right. As for the fine, you can either pay it or you can take me to MG Road. Which is it to be?"

Nagesh cranked the machine to life. He turned back to Chatpati, hands folded. "Please, sir. I would be honoured to take you wherever you wish."

The tall man had picked up his suitcase. Chatpati called out to him as the auto-rickshaw pulled away.

"Have a pleasant stay in Bangalore. And buy another Kannada textbook!"

CHAPTER 4
CIVIL NUISANCES, ALL

Chatpati had barely said the words "Utilities Building" to the driver before the vehicle leapt forward. Chatpati was flung back into his seat. The presence of an Inspector of Police did not seem to deter the driver; if anything, it spurred him on to bad driving, as if Chatpati's patronage were an endorsement to rashness and a shield against misfortune.

The auto cut across three lanes of traffic like a deranged terrier. By the time they skidded to a stop at the T-junction where Kasturba Road intersected MG Road, they stood at the head of a queue of traffic poised to turn right. The junction was controlled by traffic lights but, at peak times, the lights were switched off and Traffic Division policemen took over. There was a Traffic officer there in the middle of the intersection, facing down eighteen lanes of growling traffic. The only concession to personal safety was a respirator against exhaust fumes and the guarantee of a mortal thrashing for any driver foolish enough to knock him down, said beating to be administered by his surviving colleagues.

The traffic policeman's gloved right hand was raised, indicating that Chatpati's queue should wait.

Auto-driver Nagesh seemed to take great offence at this setback. Nagesh stuck his head out and waved at the policeman to attract his attention. The policeman glared back, then took a few ill-tempered steps towards them as traffic from MG Road began flowing behind him.

"VIP!" Nagesh shouted, thumb pointing back over his shoulder at Chatpati in the passenger seat. "Inspector! Police Inspector!"

"Idiot!" Chatpati growled, sinking down in his seat. He tilted his hat down to cover his face. "Stop that!"

The traffic policeman had drawn close enough to glimpse the three stars on Chatpati's epaulettes. The policeman almost leapt into the air; he sketched a hasty salute, then ran back to his station. The gloved hand swivelled to halt the flow of traffic obstructing the auto's path. When the way was clear, the policeman waved them on. Nagesh started the vehicle and, with great pride manifest as studied indolence, cruised across the junction at a crawl. Nagesh saluted the policeman as they passed. The policeman saluted the auto. Chatpati hid as best he could and wished he had walked.

It was a clear run east down MG Road, the oldest of the city's thoroughfares. Arcades of prestigious retail to the south faced off against the untouched leafy enclave of the military parade ground to the north. The Metro railway lay overhead, it's concrete pillars forming the No-man's-land of the median that separated new and old. Their destination was clearly visible a mile in the distance. The General Utilities Building rose above everything else around it like an upraised finger from a fist.

As they drew closer, the Utilities Building poor state of

maintenance was obvious. It brought to mind Chatpati's only experience of the Taj Mahal, that as a child of ten on a family holiday. Chatpati's father had insisted they "see the north". It had taken three days on the train to get there. Agra had been hot, dirty and dusty, the three children the same with the addition of hungry. Their father had hired a tonga[1] from the train station, squeezing all five of them in for an extra charge. The tongawallah[2] had taken them down narrow, winding lanes, each more dung-stained than the last. They had dismounted at a crumbling portico, taking care to avoid cow pats. Stepping through the gateway, though, it was as if they had entered another world.

Against a perfect blue sky, the Taj Mahal had shimmered an unearthly white in the distance, symmetry and form perfect, its gardens and fountains arranged around and before the way a court might arrange itself around its king, to amplify and reflect their regent's majesty. It was only as they had neared that the defects became visible: the soot stains, the moss, the cavities where visitors had hulled out the semi-precious stone inlays as keepsakes, the crude pen-knife etchings in the marble that declared "Ravi Loves Rita".

Thus it was with the General Utilities Building. While it looked good from afar, close up it was far from good. The mustard yellow paint was peeling. Moss was in a stalemate with soot. Pigeon droppings studded the window frames. And Ravi still loved Rita.

Despite that, there was a small but steady flow of foot traffic for the cinema on the ground floor. Nagesh made to pull up under a giant billboard depicting the latest Kannada film hero in supersize neon. Chatpati waved him on.

"Go up the loading ramp. At the side."

Chatpati dismounted amidst a clutter of cardboard cartons and labourers toting hand trolleys. Nagesh, thinking his penance served, saluted, then put the vehicle in gear. Chatpati raised a hand.

"You," the Inspector said, "are a prime idiot!" Nagesh grinned. He had clearly enjoyed transporting an Inspector of Police. "If I ever see you again, Nagesh, it will be a fine. Understand?"

"Yes, sir," Nagesh said, saluting once more.

"Stop your bloody saluting! Here."

Nagesh stared at what the Inspector held out. Three ten rupee notes.

"Take it, you idiot," Chatpati said. "It's the correct fare."

Nagesh shook his head like a dog with an earache and folded his hands in a namaste[3]. "No, sir. No, sir. I won't take. It is my honour-"

"Oh, shut up," Chatpati said. He slid the notes into the man's breast pocket. "Just remember, Nagesh. Not all policemen are criminals. Not all auto-drivers either. Change your ways. Because if I ever catch you again, Nagesh-"

Nagesh wagged his head and drew a finger across his throat. "I am finished, sir?"

"Yes, you will be!"

Chatpati commandeered the freight elevator. The blind old lift operator was perched on his aluminium stool. Before Chatpati could say a word, the man pressed the button for floor 24. Chatpati hadn't quite figured out how the man always knew the correct destination.

"Thanks," Chatpati said. The man raised his rheumy eyes and wagged his head. His pupils were milky-white.

"Why don't you get your cataracts operated on, Uncle?" Chatpati asked. The man rubbed his fingers together, then shrugged. Money, he said with his hands, or the lack of.

"But treatment at the government hospital is free," Chatpati said.

The man rubbed his fingers together again. Chatpati nodded and said no more. Even though government healthcare was notionally free, nothing got done without the greasing of palms. This man had barely enough grease to line his stomach. Sight was, it seemed, an unaffordable luxury for the poor.

A few minutes later, Inspector Chatpati pushed through the gilt revolving doors into what had been the saloon bar of the now defunct Cloud 24 Nightclub and Restaurant. Cloud24 had been the very distillation of ostentation when it had opened ten years ago. Despite the cobwebs on chandeliers and the grime on bar stools, it retained something of its original grandeur.

Constable Jaswant Singh was busy wiping off the shelves of the speed rack. Stacks of blank forms had replaced the liquor bottles. Paper was as much the lifeblood of policing as liquor was to hospitality. Singh had played semi-professional hockey. With his lean physique and perfect beard, he looked very much the mixologist, khaki uniform turban notwithstanding. He looked up from his task and gave Chatpati a salute.

Chatpati waved back and pushed through the sprung saloon doors into the restaurant's dining room. Grimy floor to ceiling glass bound five hundred square feet of parquet on three sides. A sprung dance floor occupied the very centre, above which dangled a mirrored disco ball. A giant video screen covered most of the remaining bare brick. There was a mirrored DJ booth below the screen. There was another island bar in the far corner, covered in dust sheets.

21

Two separate recesses housed billiard tables, also covered. The art on the wall was abstract, garish neon frames containing streaks of gold and zig-zags of silver.

The team had made good progress. A handful of constables were rearranging restaurant tables into workstations around the periphery of the dance floor. Cabling snaked over the parquet in toe-tripping tangles. The air was full of casual conversation and ribald humour.

"Sir!" A shout hailed Chatpati. Constable Raj leapt to his feet from an island of tables in the middle of the dance floor. Heads turned, chairs slid back, silence fell. Raj saluted. The other policemen followed suit.

Chatpati waved back and walked over to join Raj. "At ease, everyone," he said to his men. "Back to your tasks." Constable Raj was young, barely twenty-one, the first volunteer to enlist in the new Civil Nuisance Unit. His eyes were bright with his usual energy. "How's it going, Raj?"

"Very well, Sir," Raj replied. "Have you met Hemanth? He is our new IT person."

Hemanth was the only one in civilian clothes. He was barely thirty, Chatpati noted, but already jowly, heavy-set and losing the hair battle to male pattern baldness. He rose to his feet and nodded at Chatpati. "Pleased to meet you, Inspector. Hemanth Sachdev. I am the private contractor assigned to help you get going with the new system."

Chatpati nodded. "And this is?" he asked, nodding at the female constable standing to attention beyond.

She answered before Raj could. "Constable Seema Nayak. Sir. Seconded from Traffic Division." She was petite, barely coming up to Hemanth's shoulder. Her hair was in the regulation bun, her smile sincere, teeth as perfect as her salute. "Sir. It is a privilege to be here. Sir."

"Welcome, both," Chatpati said. "It's good to have you onboard. Sit. What progress?"

"So far so good, Inspector," Hemanth said. "We have electricity and basic telecoms. I've rigged up a temporary internal computer network. We should be able to connect to PoliceNet soon. I've repurposed the disco video screen—that has saved us having to commission a new one and kept us within budget. I'll show you."

He tapped at his keyboard. The video screen lit up. It was the ad break before the Bangalore TV Midday News. On screen, a cartoon green coconut was bouncing down a busy street, dodging cars, pursued by a swarthy man in vest and lungi[4]. The man wielded a machete. Jaunty Caribbean calypso music played in the background, the sound booming over the nightclub sound system. The thump of the subwoofers set glassware rattling. Hands flew to cover ears.

"Coco 2 Go!" the voice-over sang. "Bringing you all the scientifically proven health benefits of TENDER COCONUT WATER in hygienic TETRAPAK packaging."

"SORRY!" Hemanth shouted. "Still need to adjust the master volume! It's accessed from the DJ booth. Excuse me." He ran off.

The coconut ricocheted off a wall, evaded the swinging machete, and knocked the pursuer out. The swarthy man lay on the tarmac, his tongue out, cartoon arrows spinning around his head.

"Why risk your health and the health of your loved ones by consuming your favourite liquid refreshment from an UNHYGIENIC street vendor? WHERE did his coconuts come from? Has he washed his hands after going to the TOILET? What BACTERIA and VIRUSES are growing on his coconut knife?"

Under a cartoon microscope, the blade of the comatose vendor's knife teemed with snag-toothed crimson microbes, frothing with berserker bacterial rage.

"Make the RIGHT CHOICE for your family! CHOOSE COCO2GO! Pasteurised in sterilised laboratory conditions! Packaged against contamination! With all the electrolytes, vitamins and minerals you know and love from YOUR TENDEREST COCONUT!"

The cartoon coconut grinned at them, holding up a packet of the product. The coconut stuck a straw into the packet and sucked hard. An aura of glowing green vitality suffused it.

"It's what the coconut wants! Available from all good retailers! Remember! THE FUTURE IS BRIGHT! THE FUTURE IS COCONUT!"

THE VOLUME REDUCED to a tolerable level. Chatpati let his hands drop. Hemanth jogged back from the booth. "Almost there, Inspector!" he shouted.

Anchorwoman Nita Singh was next on the screen. Behind her, the studio wall showed a still of two rows of diplomats facing *each other across a long conference table. The scrolling sub-title said "LANKA STALEMATE!"*

"The second day of talks between representatives of the Foreign Ministry and the Government of Sri Lanka took place today in Colombo. It's been one hundred and forty-seven days since the Indian Army's Peace-Keeping Force landed in Lanka to assist the Lankan Government after civil war broke out in the country.

Despite cessation of hostilities, the Indian Government maintains it is premature to withdraw, citing ongoing intelligence of terrorist activity.

Sri Lanka's ambassador to the UN has decried what he called a 'de facto invasion' of Sri Lanka by India, a statement denounced by India's Foreign Minister.

The Foreign Minister called the Lankan statement 'the worst form of ingratitude against a democratic nation stepping in to help a neighbour in times of need'.

The outlawed Lankan terrorist organisation, the Sinhala Freedom Front, has threatened violence against Indian troops. A curfew is in place across the island. We go live to our reporter in Colombo."

HEMANTH TAPPED at his keyboard again and the display went blank. "That's better," he said.

"Indeed," said the Inspector, "though I'm not sure what's worse. The annexation of Sri Lanka or the rebranding of coconut water. Neither seems necessary. Anyway, carry on. I'm heading up to the office. I'm expecting a call." He turned to Raj. "We need to make our way to Curzon Hospital this afternoon. What's the situation with transport?"

Raj shook his head. "Traffic Division is still being difficult, sir. They claim we haven't got the right authorisation codes for Hoysalas. Which is nonsense. I checked. They're just being obstructive."

Seema broke in. "If I may say, sir? Speaking as someone who has just transferred from Traffic, sir, I should say Traffic Division isn't happy about ferrying other Division officers back and forth. They see it as insulting. They feel as if they have become a glorified taxi service."

"It's their own fault," Chatpati replied. "Traffic Division is notorious for pocketing fines. The takings never make it onto the books. All that diesel burnt and nothing to show for it. No wonder the Commissioner ordered them to assist their non-Traffic colleagues with transport. Perhaps I should point that out to ACP (Traffic)? In person."

"Actually, sir, maybe I can solve the problem another way?" Seema said. "I still have contacts in Traffic. A quiet word in the right ear might—" She left the last sentence hanging.

Chatpati nodded. Smart. Tread softly before raising the big stick.

"See to it, Seema. You can say Inspector Chatpati expects a Hoysala here at 1.30pm sharp. Or I'll be drafting a letter to the Commissioner."

"Sir!" she saluted.

As the new 'manager', it had seemed only right that the Inspector occupy the former restaurant manager's office. To reach it, Chatpati had to ascend the steel staircase by the kitchen entrance and make his way along an elevated steel walkway suspended from the rafters by steel wire. Opening the door, Chatpati noted the cleaner had been in and rearranged the dust. The office ceiling was a riot of electrical ducts and industrial vents. A tiny soot-encrusted window begrudgingly granted some natural light. On the opposite wall, a pane of one-way glass gave onto the expanse of the restaurant below.

The office was uninspiring. It contained two locked filing cabinets (whose keys they could not find), a utilitarian metal desk and a trio of surplus restaurant dining chairs. The singular oddity stood askance in the corner, an ancient upright grandfather clock, complete with pendulum. The brass dial proclaimed it to be the work of "John Walker & Sons, 77 Cornhill & South Regent Street, London. 1887." Chatpati hadn't quite figured out how it had made it from 19th century London to 21st Century Bangalore. The clock worked but was consistently late, despite Chatpati's daily ritual of setting the correct time.

His phone buzzed as he threw the file onto the desk. He was taken aback to hear the Justice Minister's voice—he'd expected the Minister's PA.

"Hari, how are you? Things progressing well?"

"Yes, sir," Chatpati replied. "Some teething issues but, overall, we're making progress."

"Good, good. I just wanted to check in with you to make sure the Unit is on track. We will be going live next week."

"Oh? So soon? I'd thought the original date—"

"Had to be brought forward," the Minister said. "It's complicated, and it's political. As always. It suits the Chief Minister to make the announcement earlier, considering the Government's overall strategy. You understand, I'm sure. And will be ready?"

Chatpati gulped. "You can count on it, sir."

The Minister exhaled, relief audible. "Excellent. I need not impress upon you how challenging it might be. Not the policing – I'm sure you have that in hand—but there are many, in the Cabinet, in Parliament, in the Municipal

Corporation and even in your own Police Force that see the Government's approach as far too....what's the word?"

"Authoritarian?" Chatpati ventured.

The Minister chuckled. "You're clearly not a politician, Inspector. I prefer 'progressive'. They're not ready for change."

"Change is a threat, sir."

"And so it should be! It should be a threat. A threat to the old hierarchies and the cobwebs that girdle them. To cronyism! To nepotism!" The Minister had slipped into his default rhetorical mode. "The people elected us to do away with all that. This city, this state, nay, this very country, cannot embrace it's God-given destiny while shackled to the past! We need Change. And you, along with others, will be the vanguard! The skirmishers! The spear-point!"

Chatpati considered a response. "Yes, sir" seemed safest for a non-politician.

"Anyway," the Minister continued, "I'm sure you will do us proud. We need people who can not only perform but be seen to be worthy of their task. And we have them. You are one, Hari. As recent events have proved. Don't let us down."

"I won't. Sir."

"Good." The Minister's tone softened. "You have recovered from it, I hope? You feel up to the task? No flashbacks? Sleeping alright?"

"I am, sir," Chatpati lied. "How is your daughter? If I may ask?"

There was no immediate reply. Chatpati wondered whether he had overstepped the mark. The Minister's voice, when he spoke, carried the faintest tremor.

"Thank you for asking. Better. She still has nightmares. We've stopped watching the news at home—a bit of a challenge for a Cabinet Minister—but any mention of the

THE TENDER COCONUT TAMASHA

Vidhana Soudha distresses her. However, the doctors say she will recover in time. We can only hope. And trust in God."

"I'm glad to hear it, sir," Chatpati said.

"You will have seen that Govind Prabhu's trial has begun," the Minister said, all business again. "I had to order a barrister to represent him. Order, Hari. And the barrister in question refused to even look at the casework until I published the order. No lawyer wishes to be seen to be defending a mass murderer of children."

"I can imagine," Chatpati said, "though it is important that the trial be fair."

"And seen to be so! I agree. Whatever our personal stakes. And we both have stakes in that. You, me and the families of everyone who died at his hands. Yes, it will be fair. As will the outcome. They will find him guilty. And he will hang."

Chatpati heard a door open at the Minister's end. A female voice spoke to the Minister, the words indistinguishable.

"Yes, yes," the Minister said to someone else, "ask him to wait. I'll be another minute."

The Minister addressed the Inspector again, his voice low, as if he were palming the phone.

"One last thing. You will shortly be contacted by people representing, well, an organisation. Let me call it that. They are keen to work with you. They are more than they appear. And their purpose aligns with ours. Consider it a personal favour that you lend them your ear. Hear what they have to say, that's all I ask. You can, of course, decide whether you get involved. Best wishes, Inspector Chatpati. Do us proud."

Chatpati considered the Minister's brightly painted vision. The idea of being anyone's spear-point alarmed him

29

—Chatpati's visible hard edges had long since turned pulpy —but he had always known that this quiet backwater, tending to minor crime, might lead to dangerous shoals.

He might have to learn to paddle. And fast.

First, though, there was the ACP's German tourist mission to deal with. He had barely flipped the folder open when Raj knocked at the door.

"Hoysala's here, sir," he said.

Chatpati sighed. He flipped the folder shut and reached for his hat.

"Let's go, Raj. We'll update ourselves on the way."

CHAPTER 5
VIEL UNKLAR

Constable Seema clearly had influence and ability. She'd persuaded her former Division to despatch a Hoysala. More, the vehicle not only arrived on time, but it was also one of the new electric-powered, air-conditioned models. Its paintwork gleamed. Its bumpers were untarnished. Further, the driver was one of those Traffic Division rarities that both knew the rules of the road and followed them.

"Ten minutes only, sir," the driver had said as they waited at the foot of the loading ramp for a gap in traffic. "Rush is not very heavy."

With the air-conditioning on and windows up, Chatpati and Raj were spared having to shout at each other over the incessant beeping of horns.

"What's at Curzon Hospital, chief?" Raj had asked. "Assault victim?"

"No," Chatpati replied. "It's a German tourist." He raised the folder. "Actually, Austrian, according to this." He related what Mina, the ACP's PA, had told him.

"A somewhat sensitive case, Inspector," she had said.

31

"Perhaps more molehill than mountain. It involves a foreign Austrian couple. They were on a cultural tour of South India - temples, forts, palaces, that sort of thing – when the wife, a Mrs. Esther Braun, fell ill shortly after visiting Cubbon Park. Stomach upset. An errant samosa or the like. It's easily done."

"Normally, this would not be a police matter, but the husband, Mr. Günther, is alleging his wife was poisoned. Mr. Günther has had some contact with the Austrian High Commission in Delhi. Apparently, he is of an energetic disposition when it comes to complaints."

She smiled at him as she slid the folder over. "This has come to us via the Foreign Ministry in New Delhi, through the Chief Minister's Office, then the Health Ministry, then the Justice Ministry, then the Commissioner of Police to the Assistant-Commissioner."

"And finally," Chatpati said, "to me. The bottom of the pile?"

"Call it the top of the ladder."

Chatpati inclined his head. "I assume everyone else is giving it a wide berth."

She'd shrugged. "Well, no one's dead, so Murder Squad aren't interested. There's no robbery. Or fraud. It's minor crime, really, if it is a crime at all."

"A nuisance, I suppose? A civil nuisance?"

Mina spread her hands. "Precisely."

Chatpati shook his head. "How timely. And what, I wonder, is the ACP's expectation?"

Mina's face was inscrutable. "Why, investigate, I assume?" She leant in and whispered. "Actually, I think making it go away would be perfectly adequate." She sat back. "I'm sure you'll do an admirable job, Inspector.

Though, perhaps, it's not quite up to the standard of recent challenges?"

"I can do without any more challenges of that nature, Madam Mina." Chatpati had said, tucking the folder under his arm.

By the time Chatpati had finished his tale, the high-rises of the Central Business District lay behind them. They were weaving through the congested byroads of Shivaji Nagar. A million souls struggled on here in scrums of drab high-density housing, contained from outward expansion by the geograph-ical immovability of Ulsoor Lake to the east and the genteel immovability of the Golf Club to the west. Years ago, this quarter was where the lowest class had lived, those drivers, cooks and housemaids who had served the British Raj. And they still lived here, because the new Empire of Wealth that had replaced the long-departed colonial masters still needed cheap labour to wash their cars and feed their children.

Raj looked puzzled. "Well, I can't see the crime, but I suppose it is the kind of thing we might have to get used to, no, boss? We are the Civil Nuisance Unit, after all."

Chatpati frowned. "The problem begins, Raj, when our work becomes work that other people can't be bothered to do. Misdemeanours, misconduct, misbehaviour—that we can deal with. Food poisoning in the park? Tourist diplo-macy at the bedside?" He shook his head. "I sense the thin end of a long wedge. Being driven between our collective buttocks."

Whether Raj sputtered at the collective of buttocks or what was being inserted was never clear, for, within seconds, they had turned in through the gates of Lord Curzon Hospital.

A gate guard directed them to the Infectious Disease

Unit, a modern five-storey cuboid that loomed over the original colonial-era building like an heiress awaiting the demise of an ailing dowager. The old lady still stood, but she bore the stigmata of relentless time and indifferent circumstance. The brickwork was pitted. Her gables sagged. Her corridors were inhabited by the dispossessed, the pillars impaled by signs declaring "Dialysis" and "No Spitting!"

The Infectious Disease Unit, though, was bright and clean. The floor glistened under the cool fluorescent tube lighting, the air redolent with antiseptic and a hint of something altogether more organic. A trio of nurses inhabited the nursing station, looking up with interest as they approached.

"Yes?" said the oldest, a trim fifty. She wore a short-sleeved white coat over her uniform white sari. Her badge declared her to be 'Matron Annamma'. Her manner suggested that there was little on earth she had yet to see.

Raj took the lead. "Police, madam. We're here to see the Germans."

"Oh, thank God!" said a junior nurse from behind Matron. "Finally!" She turned to her equally junior colleague. "They've come to arrest Mr. Goonta!"

"Quiet, Molly!" the Matron snapped. "If you don't have any work to do, at least be quiet." Molly did so, looking wounded. Her colleague giggled behind her hands. They were neither of them older than twenty and wore the white salwar kameez uniform of nursing students. "And it's Günther, not Goonta. He's from Vienna, not Hubli[1]."

"Not arrest," Chatpati said. "We're here to—" What were they here for? "Assist?"

"Assistance will do very well," Matron replied. "If you can get him to stay in his room, stop shouting and stop taking photographs, that, at least, will be a blessing. In fact, any of those will do for a start."

"What is he photographing?" Raj asked, looking around. "It looks pretty ordinary to me."

Matron sighed. "Everything. The room. The corridor. The trolleys. The bed-pans. The nurses. Even the porters."

"Why?" Raj said.

Matron shook her head. "I have no idea. He rants in English, then gets very agitated and ends up in German. It's very difficult to make sense of. They're in Room Seven. Second on the left. Please. Be my guest."

Room Seven was utilitarian but clean. A stout, short woman with frizzy hair lay on the bed, covered up to her neck with a sheet. Had it not been for the snores rattling the iron bed frame, she might have been dead, so pale was her colouring. Mr. Günther sat in a wicker chair by the window, reading the Bangalore Herald. At the sight of the policemen, he flung the newspaper to the floor and leapt up. He was thin and pink with a shock of white hair that approximated a tonsure.

"*Ah!*" he shouted. "*Endlich! Die Polizei!* The police, yes? You are?"

Raj, for all his earlier vigour, seemed to have been struck dumb. Chatpati stepped forward. "Yes. We are the police. Mr. Braun? And this is your wife? Esther?"

"*Ja! Ja!* Yes! I am Günther Braun. You have taken long time to come, *denke ich. Aber* you are here. *Das ist gut.*"

"I am Inspector Chatpati and this is my colleague, Constable Raj. We have been sent-"

"Chapati? Chapati?" Günther frowned. "*Wie so?* Chapati *ist ein brot, nicht so?* Chapati! It is a bread. Yes. Indian bread. This I know."

"CHATPATI" said Chatpati, a little louder than necessary. "Not CHAPATI. There is a 'T' in it. I am not bread."

Günther Braun shook his head. "*Unklar. Dieses land ist viel unklar.*"

Chatpati suppressed a sigh. "What seems to be the problem?"

"Problem? I tell you. Yes. My wife, yes, she is poison, yes? Nearly dead! *Tot!* No one is taking serious. I ask the doctors, what is *diagnose*? They shrugging. My wife is recover. I say we want to leave! They shrugging! Only shrugging!" By way of illustration, Günther Braun strode back and forth, shrugging.

Chatpati resisted the urge to do likewise. "So, if I have it right, you want to know what was wrong with your wife and why you cannot leave?"

"*Genau!* Exact!" Günther said, collapsing back into his chair. "What is *diagnose*? Why we can not go?"

Chatpati looked at Raj.

"Seems reasonable to me, boss," Raj said.

Günther rummaged around in a well-travelled suitcase by his chair. When he stood back up, he had a camera in his hands. It was an expensive model with a proper lens.

"*Also!*" he said, "I take photo! *Photografieren!* I send photo to *Konsulat! Hier*, I say, *hier* you can see! Room is bad! Treatment is bad! Information is bad!" He raised the camera. "*Und jetzt—*"

"Police is bad, no doubt," Chatpati muttered. He raised a hand, mustering all the German he could remember. "Stop! *Verboten!* This is a hospital! Photograph is *nein*!"

For a moment, it looked like Günther Braun might rupture. The camera quivered. His colour went from rose to plum. His jaw clenched. Then, suddenly, the fight went out of him. He lowered the camera and sat back in the chair.

"*Entschuldigung!*" he said. "I apologise. *Entschuldigung.*"

"It's okay," Chatpati said. He could feel the heat streaming off him. His pulse pounded in his ears. "Just relax a moment. Raj, stay with him. Get him some water or something."

Inspector Chatpati stepped out into the corridor. Three faces stared out at him from the nurses' station.

"Oh!" Molly squealed. "He's alive! He's unharmed! Matron! He's—"

Matron spun around and said something low and dangerous. Molly made herself scarce.

"Matron," Chatpati said, leaning on the nurses' station. "We need to talk. Privately. Now."

She ushered him into the cubbyhole that served as her office. Their knees butted briefly below the desk.

"Are you alright, Inspector?" she asked. "I thought you would be fine, but we sent for the security guard just in case."

Chatpati waved her concerns away. "What is Mrs. Braun's status? Is she ill? What's the diagnosis? What treatment is she receiving?"

The Matron folded her arms and looked away. "You will have to ask the doctors, Inspector."

"Matron," Chatpati said slowly. "Look at me. Is Mrs. Braun receiving treatment? Is she still ill?"

She pursed her lips, then sighed. "No."

"No? To both?"

"Yes."

"So why is she still here?"

She looked over his shoulder. "Can you close the door, please, Inspector?" He leaned back in his chair and did so. She studied him, her eyes wandering to his badge. Her brows furrowed as she read the name. "Chatpati? Not that—"

"Yes," he said. "That one. Does it help?"

She placed her elbows on the table. "My apologies, Inspector Chatpati. My thinking today is slower than it should be."

"It's fine," Chatpati said, "it's been a tough day all around."

"The patient completed her treatment three days ago. She is no longer ill. She should have been discharged but—"

"But?"

"To discharge a patient with a suspected infectious disease requires a certificate stating that the patient is no longer infectious. A certificate signed by the Medical Superintendent of the hospital. Such a certificate has not been provided."

"Why not?"

She looked away again. "You'll have to ask the Medical Superintendent."

Chatpati studied her. There was some hidden meaning in what the Matron was saying. He acted on a hunch. He raised one hand and rubbed the fingers together, the gesture the old lift-operator had used. She blinked at him and remained silent.

"May I?" He picked up the telephone on her desk. "What's the Medical Superintendent's extension?"

The Medical Superintendent's secretary would not say where the Medical Superintendent was, merely that he was out of the office.

"But he's meant to be working, yes?" Chatpati asked. "He's not on leave?"

"Noooo," replied the secretary. "He's not on leave. Can I take a message? Inspector Chapati, did you say?"

"Yes," he growled, "Chapati. Like the bread." Chatpati put the phone down and turned to Matron. "Where is he?"

Matron typed something into her computer, then turned the screen towards him.

'Supreme Medical Clinic' Google said. 'Dr. Ratheesh Yadav, MD. Consulting hours: 12pm to 4pm.'

"That's the Medical Superintendent? Dr. Yadav?" Chatpati asked. She said nothing as she turned the screen away. "Thank you, Matron. Can you order some coffee for Room Seven, please? Send out for it if you must. I'll pay. And another chair. I'm not paying for that, though."

He made a phone call, then went back into Room Seven. Mrs. Braun had roused. She was propped up in bed, Günther Braun perched on the mattress beside her, holding her hand. Raj occupied the chair, hands clenched and ill at ease.

Chatpati beckoned to Raj. "Get the Hoysala. Go back to the CNU. Collect Jaswant Singh and another fierce-looking constable, perhaps that fellow Krishna." He handed Raj a slip of paper. "Go to this address. Bring me back this man. Don't take any crap."

Raj nodded, eyes wide. "Got it."

Chatpati turned to the Brauns. They stared at him expectantly.

"I'm going to try to solve your problem." he said. "Then maybe you can help me solve mine."

CHAPTER 6
THE PERILS OF TOURISM

Inspector Chatpati spent a pleasant hour drinking coffee with the Brauns. They were both retired. Günther had worked in the civil service in Vienna and his wife had been a teacher. They were staunch vegetarians and had a shared passion for all things Oriental.

"This is why," Mrs. Braun said, "we come to India. Last year, we visit north. This year, we visit south. Our travel manager organise a tour for us. We want spend three days here, in Bangalore. To see Hampi? You know this place? It is famous."

Chatpati nodded. "Yes. The old capital of the Vijaynagar Kingdom. Very picturesque. If you like ruins."

Mrs. Braun nodded. "Yes. This we must see. But, unfortunately, the day we are arrive here, I am became unwell. Then, I am admit here. Now, our tour is broken." She shrugged. "I feel OK now, but they say we cannot leave."

Günther Braun patted his wife's hand. "*Na ja, liebchen,* you are recover. That is most important. Holiday, we can make another time."

"How did you fall ill, if I may ask?" the Inspector said. "Your husband thinks you were poisoned?"

Mrs. Braun shook her head at her husband. "Günther gets very excited," she said with affection.

Günther waved a fist. "Yes!" he said, "she was poison! *Die verdammte Kokosnuss!*"

Chatpati frowned. "*Kokosnuss?* I don't know this word."

"Coconut, *Herr Inspektor*," Mrs Braun replied. She shook her head again. "Günther is convince it is the coconut. But me, I am not so sure."

"Tell me," Chatpati said. "Start from the beginning."

The Brauns had checked into their hotel, the Marriott, at Cubbon Park, just after 7am, having taken the overnight Chalukya Express from Pondicherry on the east coast.

"We have a beautiful view of the Cubbon Park from our room," Mrs. Braun said. "The sun is just rise. It is cool. We decide to go for a walk after breakfast. The breakfast is provided with the room, you know. I ask at the reception if the breakfast have the famous Benny Dosa[1]. You know this Dosa?"

Chatpati was a connoisseur of the South Indian breakfast. He could, at a pinch, debate the merits and demerits of dosa versus idli2 but, to keep Mrs. Braun talking, he just nodded.

"We are looking forward for this famous dosa," Günther said. "In Pondicherry and in Madras, we eat the other types, the rava dosa and the masala dosa. These two is nice, but we are looking forward in Bangalore to Benny Dosa."

"Anyway," Mrs. Braun continued, "the hotel breakfast does not have Benny dosa so we eat a few idlis[2] – just okay, we have had before in Pondicherry better - then we decide to go to walk in the Cubbon Park. Then, we think, after walk, we ask our travel company for best place for eat Benny Dosa."

"I know a few," Chatpati said. "Where does the coconut come in?"

That set Günther off. "*Ja! Du solltest über die Kokosnuss sprechen!* Speak to *Herr Inspektor* about the coconut!"

Mrs. Braun sighed, "I drink a coconut. You know the one? Green colour? They cut open with a big knife to drink the water."

"Tender coconut!" Chatpati said. "I understand. You had a tender coconut."

"Tender?" Günther spluttered. "*Ich kenne dieses wort nicht. Zärtlich?*"

Chatpati looked at Mrs. Braun. She smiled. "My husband translates tender into German. *Zärtlich* means loving. That is not the right meaning, no?"

Chatpati smiled. A loving coconut seemed a fine idea. "No. By tender, we mean young. A young coconut."

She translated for her husband, who approved. "*Junge Kokosnuss! Viel besser!*"

"*Also,*" she continued, "I drink this young coconut. It is very nice. I have drink this coconut before, in Madras. This one is better sweet, but not too much. Then we walk back to hotel. We are back in the room when I feel bad. Terrible." She stopped, suddenly tearful. She dabbed at her eyes. "I thought I will die."

"What happened next?"

She nodded. Her voice was stronger when she spoke. "I have a headache, suddenly. Worse headache I ever have. My head is spinning. My eyes are - blur? That is right word? In German we say *verschwommen*. Swimming? I begin vomit then I have to go to toilet. Diarrhoea. Very painful. Then I collapse. That is all I remember."

Günther continued. "I find her collapse in toilet. She is confuse, yes? I call reception. The manager comes. He telephone. The ambulance come, yes, they put her on stretcher and they bring here."

"That was, what, a week ago?" Chatpati asked. They nodded. "What did the doctors say?"

"First," Günther said, "there are many doctors. They come three times in one day. They give fluid drip and injection. They are very worry. But soon, maybe in one, two days, she is better and they do not come. I ask what is problem? No one can answer. One doctor, a *junge* doctor, she says it is food poisoning. From where? I ask. No one answer. When we can leave? Nothing. Why we cannot leave? We need *Zertifikat*. Where I must go to get *Zertifikat*? *Der Chef* must give, they say. I go to *Der Chef*. He say 'yes, no, maybe tomorrow, maybe day after'. I ask why? He does not say."

Chatpati nodded. "Then?"

Günther sprung to his feet. "I know why. *Ja?* He want money. OK, I say. I will pay. I have insurance. They will pay. But no. He is want cash. I must give him."

Chatpati's eyes narrowed. "He said this? He asked you for cash?"

Günther shook his head. "He is not stupid. No, he write on paper."

"Do you have this paper?"

Günther looked wary. "Why?"

"It could be very useful," Chatpati said, "to get you back on your tour." He was beginning to see the bones of the matter.

Günther glanced at his wife. They spoke to each other in quick-fire German, the tone anything but tender. Mrs. Braun ended the conversation with a raised hand, then turned to the Inspector.

"My husband, he is worry. He is worry that he gives you the paper, then there is no evidence."

Chatpati felt his ire rising but contained it. "I understand," he said. "What do you think?"

She smiled at him, motioned Günther to sit down, and took her husband's hands in hers.

"I say to him, look, here is a policeman. He is sit down with us. He is ask about us. He is listen to us. We must trust him. To help us. So we can leave this place."

"Thank you," Chatpati said, "for your trust."

Esther Braun said a word to Günther, who retrieved a piece of paper from the suitcase. He handed it to Chatpati. The Inspector took it between thumb and forefinger, holding it by a corner. It was a yellow Post-It note. On it, written in royal blue ink, were the numbers "50,000".

"No, I say to *Der Chef*," Günther said. "You are *korrupt*. *Kriminell*. I will not give."

"Then?"

"Then I call Austrian *Konsulat*. I take photo. For evidence. Two days, three days, nothing. Then you come."

"I will keep this, *Herr Braun*," Chatpati said. "With your permission. OK?"

Günther looked at his wife, then nodded at Chatpati. "Is OK."

Chatpati's phone buzzed. He glanced at it then rose. "Excuse me. I shall be back shortly. Stay in this room, please, until I return."

'Ten minutes out,' read Raj's message. 'Target secured.'

Chatpati walked up to the nurses' station. "You may wish to retire to your office, Matron," he said. "It might get a bit heated in here."

Matron looked up from her paperwork. "Oh? What have you done, Inspector? Have you upset Mr. Günther?"

"We have found the missing Medical Superintendent. He arrives shortly, under escort. I wouldn't want you to get into any trouble."

Matron Annamma considered this. "Actually, Inspector, if it's all the same to you, I'd rather stay. If this is going to be what I think it is, I have been waiting a long time for it."

Chatpati nodded. "As you wish. Do you, by any chance, Matron, have a Zip-Lock bag?"

"We have specimen bags, Inspector. Why? Are you planning on taking a biopsy of the Medical Superintendent?"

Chatpati smiled. "You could say that, Matron, but rest assured it will be bloodless. Probably."

They didn't have long to wait. The rescue party's arrival was preceded by a minute of shouting, the hubbub drawing closer in fits and starts. Raj crashed through the doors first. Behind him came the combined might of Constables Jaswant Singh and Krishna, each with a hand on the shoulder of a round man in a white doctor's coat and blue tie. The round man was making enough noise to rouse the mortuary. Chatpati was pleased to see that the policemen had not needed to use the handcuffs. The rescue party had attracted a tail of followers that crowded the doorway.

"Who the bloody hell is responsible for this bloody outrage?" the round man yelled. He squirmed under the Constables' grip. "Who is the senior officer? I'll have your badges, you swine! How dare you!"

Chatpati stepped forward. "Ratheesh Yadav, I presume?"

The man stopped wriggling and glared at him. "And who the hell are you? Dr. Livingstone? Yes, I am Doctor Yadav! I am the Medical Superintendent of this hospital! This is my hospital! Who the hell do you think you are?"

"Inspector Chatpati. Bangalore Police. Pleased to make your acquaintance."

Yadav's eyes bulged. "Pleased? PLEASED? I'll bloody please you! I'll flatten you! I'll-"

"Enough!" Chatpati said, softly. "It is best for all if we keep it civil. Or we can move this conversation to the back of a police van. Your choice."

Everyone knew that the back of the police van was the traditional place for the police to administer their beatings. Waiting till arrival at the police station might mean having to contend with the suspect's lawyer. Chatpati had never felt the need to use this approach – he thought violence the province of imbeciles – but he was not above using the implication to effect.

Yadav had heard of this custom because Yadav shut up.

"As I was saying," the Inspector continued, "I'm pleased to make your acquaintance. I called your office, but they didn't know where you were. Strange, that, I thought. A senior doctor, head of a large hospital, not to be found during working hours. So many things to oversee - patients, other doctors, supplies. Where were you, Dr. Yadav, if not on the premises?"

"You know where I was!" Yadav hissed. "You sent these goons. An outrage! They dragged me out! From my clinic! Where I was seeing patients, patients whose vital medical needs are now unmet because of your actions! Yes, your actions!"

"Oh, yes," Chatpati said. "Supreme Medical Clinic. As a government doctor, surely your role is to serve the needs of the people who come to this institution? Rather than practice elsewhere, for your own profit? While you are being paid by the government to be here?"

Yadav looked around. He couldn't have missed the score

of eyes studying him: policemen, nurses, onlookers, even a pair of lowly hospital porters. Disgust in some, delight in others. He met Chatpati's eyes and nodded, indicating Chatpati should approach.

Chatpati waved to the constables to release him. They had barely done so before Yadav elbowed them aside and strode towards him. Constable Singh started after Yadav, but Chatpati raised a hand.

Yadav stopped so close that Chatpati could read the seconds on the silver chronograph on Yadav's wrist. Yadav's tie was raw silk, the tie-pin gold. The fountain-pen in the Medical Superintendent's pocket was a Mont Blanc. Close-up, Yadav looked like a jackal: a long face, a twitchy nose and an over-bite. The eyes were calculating.

"What do you want?" Yadav said in a low voice. "Why do you humiliate me in this way?"

"You did that yourself," Chatpati replied. "What I want is to know why you refuse to discharge Mrs. Braun."

"Huh," Yadav sniffed. "She is receiving treatment."

"No, she is not. Her treatment stopped three days ago. She doesn't even have a drip in."

Yadav snorted. "Well, I say she is. So far as I know, the Police Academy has not turned into a medical school. I am the doctor here. I am the expert. She is not fit to leave. There is a risk to the public. From infectious disease."

"What infectious disease?"

Yadav looked down his nose at the Inspector. "Again, you are not a medical expert. I don't have to explain anything to you."

"I suggest you start," Chatpati replied. "Because my expertise relates to the Indian Penal Code. Section 368, specifically wrongfully keeping in confinement. The Brauns wish to leave. You are preventing them from doing so. Without good reason, therefore wrongfully."

"I am not!" Yadav shouted. "There is a public health risk! They cannot leave! I am the Medical Superintendent! I decide! Me! Not you!"

"Be smart. Keep your voice down," Chatpati said. "You have much to lose. Think carefully. And reconsider." Yadav made to speak. "Before you say anything, consider something else. The Prevention of Corruption Act, specifically the 2018 Amendment."

Yadav's fists clenched and unclenched. "More bullshit," he growled.

"Maybe," Chatpati said, "but the bull that passed it is the Parliament of India. I am one of its horns, so pay attention. A public servant who attempts to obtain from any person an undue advantage, intending that in consequence a public duty would be performed improperly, is guilty of an offence under Section 7 and shall be imprisoned for a term of 3 to 7 years."

"What is that to do with me?" Yadav shouted. "I have obtained no 'undue advantage'! Anyone who says otherwise is a liar! There is no proof! Nothing!"

Yadav took a step back. "I am leaving. And the Germans are staying. Until I say so. You can prevent neither of these things."

Yadav turned to his audience and raised his voice, a finger pointed back at Chatpati. "This man accuses me! Here is what I say in reply!"

He spun back to the Inspector. "First, I return to my clinic to discharge my duty to the patients who have been waiting hours for medical succour! Then, I will call the Commissioner of Police. To register an official complaint.

Then the Minister of Health. Then my lawyer. You will suffer for this indignity!"

Chatpati looked over Yadav's shoulder. Uncertainty was writ large on the faces of his men. Raj looked like he might faint. The crowd at the door had grown. The two porters were jostling for position, phones held up. Only Matron Annamma behind the nurses' station seemed unperturbed, her head up, her arms crossed.

Chatpati raised his hands, as if in apology. "I might have made a grave error, Dr. Yadav. Would you forgive me?"

"Never!" Yadav's arm shot up in the air, finger pointed at the ceiling. "You have humiliated me! Denigrated my office! I will have your badge! And," he drew breath, "after that, I will drag you through the courts until you are penniless. A civil suit! For defamation! Until you come crawling, on your hand and knees, to lick my shoes and beg me to forgive you! And you will!" he sneered. "That I promise!"

Yadav would have made a passable Bollywood villain, Chatpati thought. The only elements lacking were a roll of thunder, some lightning, and a few dramatic violins. Chatpati reached into his breast pocket and fished out the plastic sleeve. He waved it at the Medical Superintendent.

Yadav blanched. His pointed finger unpointed. His arm fell.

Chatpati spoke loud enough for his voice to carry.

"All very well, Dr. Yadav, Medical Superintendent. Except for this. It's a note. I wonder what it would show under forensic examination? Your fingerprints, perhaps? Might the ink match that of the very fine fountain-pen in your pocket? Might the handwriting be your own?"

Chatpati paused for effect. "Mr. Günther Braun might provide an affidavit saying when and where it was written. In your office. When Mr. Braun came to ask if his wife, now fully recovered, could be discharged. For which you demanded a cash payment. You wrote the amount on this." Chatpati made to examine it. "Fifty thousand. I assume you meant rupees. Or was it Euros?"

Yadav seemed thunderstruck. He put a hand out and steadied himself against the nurses' station.

Chatpati called out to his men at the door. "Clear those crowds, please, gentlemen. This is a hospital, not a play-house. Raj, lend Dr. Yadav an arm, won't you?"

The Inspector took the other. "We're going to have a little chat."

CHAPTER 7

DISHONOURABLE DISCHARGE

I t was nearly 4pm when Inspector Chatpati stepped back into Room Seven. Mrs. Braun was in the chair reading the newspaper. Mr. Braun wore circles on the linoleum.

Chatpati held up a form, complete with stamp and signature. "*Zertifikat,*" he said.

"I told you, Günther," Mrs Braun said with a broad smile. "I told you."

"That's not all," Chatpati said. "Here is a list of the top three bene dosa places in Bangalore. Personally, I recommend a small cart beside Idly Corner on Veera Pillai Street. It's called Naveen's. Ask anyone in the area. Naveen's father started that before I was born."

"Thank you," Günther said, glowing with rare joy. "Thank you."

"My pleasure," Chatpati replied. "Enjoy your tour."

He turned to go. Günther grabbed Chatpati's right hand with both of his own and wrung it bloodless.

"*Auf wiedersehen, Herr Inspektor. Vergessen Sie nicht Den Kokosnuss!* Forget not the coconut!"

Chatpati did not say that forgetting it was the very first thing he planned to do.

Matron was at her station, waiting. "So," she began, "how did you get on with the Medical Superintendent?"

Chatpati considered the question. "Let's just say Dr. Yadav realised his position was tenuous."

Raj and Chatpati had steered the stunned Medical Superintendent into an empty room and sat him on the bed. Yadav seemed in shock. Raj poured the man a glass of water, which Yadav clutched to his chest like a charm to ward off evil. There was dread in his eyes.

Chatpati sat down opposite and leaned forward, elbows on knees.

"Relax, Dr. Yadav, we will not pummel you. Here's what I propose. You will provide a stamped and signed certificate of discharge for Mrs. Braun. In return, I will forget about this other bit of paper."

Yadav's reply was a whimper. "But my reputation—" he began, "my position."

"Ruined. Regardless of your choice," Chatpati replied. "Bad luck. That's your own doing. My way, you get to stay out of jail. Oh, and to continue your lucrative private practice, where I'm sure you'll find plenty of people who you don't have to blackmail for money."

Yadav made a call. Ten minutes later, a porter arrived bearing the document, typed post-haste by the Medical Superintendent's secretary. Yadav signed it, then flung it at Chatpati.

"You policemen are no better than criminals," Yadav muttered as the policemen turned to go

Chatpati sniffed. "If you're planning to dabble in more double-timing, consider this insight from someone who deals with a lot of crooks. The difference between a good criminal and a bad one is that the good one knows when the game's up. It's time to cut your losses. Consider your position here. Goodbye."

Chatpati bade Matron farewell."Thank you for your help. Are you sure there won't be consequences for you? Dr. Yadav seems a rather vindictive sort."

"Oh, don't worry about me, Inspector," Matron replied. "I'm long enough in the tooth to take care of myself." She nodded at the ward entrance. "Better watch out for your junior colleague there, though."

Just beyond the doorway, Raj was deep in conversation with Molly. She seemed to do a lot of giggling, Raj a lot of smiling.

"Ah," Chatpati said. "That's one thing I don't intend to police." He bade Matron goodbye, took a step, then stopped. "Oh, there is one more favour you could do me. If you don't mind?"

Matron tilted her chin at him. "And how will that end?" she asked. "Another spectacle?"

Chatpati shook his head and explained.

"Consider it done," Matron replied. She scribbled on a card. "Call this number and give them the details. Mention my name. I will speak to the surgeon today. He is a decent man. There will be a wait, but not very long, I should think. They operate on hundreds of these cases every week."

"Cost?" Chatpati asked.

Matron shook her head. "None. As I said. He is a decent man."

Chatpati made the call to the ACP's office as the Hoysala negotiated its way back south. The ACP's PA picked up on the second ring.

"Madam Mina," Chatpati said, "please tell the ACP we have dealt with the matter in question with."

"That was quick, Inspector. Was it not just this morning that I gave you the folder? I will inform the ACP. Would you like me to do it now? Or perhaps tomorrow?" The emphasis suggested the second option might be better.

Chatpati took her meaning. The reward for good work was usually more work. The Inspector had plenty to be getting on with without another of the ACP's random errands.

"Tomorrow will be fine," he replied.

"Excellent. Oh, while I have you on the line, the ACP asked me to inform you he is sending over a candidate for your team. The officer in question will attend your office tomorrow at 11 am for an interview. I assume that's convenient? Of course, the final decision is yours, but the ACP thinks this man will be a good fit. Apparently, the officer requested a transfer in to the Bangalore Police from another state altogether. Specifically to join your unit. Your reputation precedes you, Inspector."

Chatpati groaned inwardly. He wished for some way of arresting his reputation's relentless progression. What fresh hell was the ACP was about to inflict on him? Regardless, Chatpati knew he couldn't very well refuse.

Mina took his silence for assent. "I will send the paperwork over directly. Have a pleasant evening, Inspector."

By the time the Hoysala had deposited them on the loading ramp of the Utilities Building, the sun was low in the sky. Down on the pavement, streams of office workers surged out of buildings as the working day drew to a close. Traffic on MG Road was a solid, immoveable grid of hot metal and rising tempers.

Chatpati turned to his men. "Well done, boys. You did a

good job today. Keep it up." They grinned back at him, pleased with their first outing. "Go up, sign out, and head home. Be in first thing tomorrow. We have a lot of work to do in the next few days. The CNU goes live next week. A little care now will ensure it doesn't die on its feet."

CHAPTER 8
ALL'S WELL THAT BEGINS WELL

At 7.17 am the next morning, Inspector Chatpati stepped off the Metro at MG Road Station. He felt as if he'd been in a wrestling match. That he'd lost.

He had arrived home the evening before to find that his wife, Nirmala, had organised an informal soiree with their neighbours. By the time he'd spent an hour with Dr. and Mrs. Prabhakar from number 172, Jacintha and Donald Rodrigues from 173 and the solitary Mr. Talwalker from 175, he had exhausted whatever reserves of civility remained.

Dr. Prabhakar turned out to be a relentless bore, his wife a relentless social climber. He dropped celebrity names like cluster bombs, the impact rippling through the gathering in "Oohs!" and "Ahs!" The Rodrigues seemed nice enough, the youngest of the three couples gathered there. They were childless but "trying", which started Dr. Prabhakar toff on an insensitive discourse on the best infertility unit in the city (his, of course). Mr. Talwalker perched in a corner, watched everything and said little. He was "in IT" and IT showed.

Chatpati had had to work hard to avoid Mrs. Prabhakar's increasingly direct questions about "The Event". He ended that interrogation with the response, "I'm afraid it's all confidential". That must have put her out, because it shut her up. For a while.

Two hours in, Chatpati had had to fake an urgent phone call and retire to the bedroom. He'd emerged only when he heard the front door opening to cries of "Goodbye! Such a wonderful evening!" and "We must have you over to ours!" The guests waved at him from the front door and he waved back at them from the bedroom door.

One did not need a degree in human behaviour to discern that Nirmala wasn't happy. The clatter of cutlery being flung into the dishwasher rang a warning knell.

"Well," she muttered, her back to him, "that was a pleasant evening!" He made no reply. She turned, a clutch of forks in her grip. "So glad you made such an effort!"

"What?" he replied. "I was here, wasn't I?"

"Why can't you try, Hari? It's always the same with you. If it doesn't interest you, it's not important to you. But what about me? What about what's important to me?"

His blood was up. "I don't know what you're complaining about," he shot back. "Here you are in a brand new luxury apartment, with all the mod cons you always wanted. Better than that dank cubbyhole in the Police Officers' Quarters, surely. Or would you prefer to return? To that?"

She'd pointed a fork at him.

"There," she hissed, "there, I had other people around me. Other wives. Other casualties of the Great Bangalore Police Force. Something to occupy my time with while I sat around waiting and wondering when the Great Inspector might deign to return." She spun around and tossed the fork in with its fellows. "Yes, this is all very wonderful, Inspector Chatpati, and thank you for the heroics that got us here, but sometimes I wish we were back in that cubbyhole, as you call it." She closed the dishwasher door, the click ominous. "At least I had a life of sorts."

They'd cleared up in silence. When he'd joined her in bed, her back had been rock rigid against his, her face turned away into her pillow. He had slept fitfully. She had been asleep when he awoke.

Usually, she would have risen before him. His breakfast would have been on the table, the TV news on, coffee steaming. Instead, he had emerged from the bedroom to a silent dawn, a blank screen and a repast that comprised three damp fingers of paneer[1] from the night before on a cold and solitary chapati.

There had been few other commuters travelling to the city at 6.45 am. This meant he could not avoid the infestation of uniformed teenagers at the Metro station. They lurked at the very centre of the concourse, manning a pop-up stall under a giant LED screen displaying a familiar green grinning coconut.

"Hello, sir!" sang one, a tiny thing in a skin-tight green jumpsuit. Her smile was noon bright. "Care to try one? Coco2Go! It's hygienic pasteurised revitalising tender coconut water." She spoke without commas, each adjective delivered with a subliminal thrust. "Just the way to start your day! Full of vitamins minerals zinc! Here!" She tossed a carton at him, straw attached. "Have a great day, sir!"

Once on the train, he'd stuck the straw into the packet and sucked at it, along with the three other people in his carriage. They'd eyed each other sidelong as if they were engaged in a collective act of public indecency.

He'd sent Nirmala a text as he neared the Utilities building.

"Sorry. Will try harder. Love, H."

He'd hoped it would be enough, but his sense of things told him it might not be as easy as all that.

He hadn't expected to see the blind old lift operator this early in the day, but the man sat on his stool as if he had never left. Just before Chatpati got off at the 24th floor, he placed a card in the man's hand. The old man started.

"There is a telephone number on that card," Chatpati said. "And a name. Do you have someone who can call for you?"

The man blinked up at Chatpati and nodded slowly.

"Call that number. Mention the name on the card. Give them your details and they will have your cataracts operated on."

The old man shook his head.

"There is no cost," Chatpati said. "It will be free. You are a government employee. It is all arranged. Just call the number today. Will you do that?"

The old man blinked at Chatpati again, then nodded.

In his office, Inspector Chatpati got through a clutch of invoices before the cleaner rattled in. Chanderpal had the uncertain vintage of a preserved mango, rendered soft and pulpy by the brining of years. His skin was wrinkled, his expression sour.

Chanderpal had simply appeared one day, weeks ago, carrying a bucket and the traditional coconut stick broom. No one could actually recall hiring the man; Chatpati assumed someone somewhere paid him. Chanderpal's dedication to work was dubious—he needed direction and direction was what he got that morning, the Inspector standing over him until the cobwebs were rendered into filaments and the grime deconstructed into dust.

The rest of the team arrived with the sun. Chatpati stood on the walkway and bade them good morning from on high. A flurry of salutes rent the air. He made his way down the steel stairs to where Hemanth from IT waited on the dance floor. Constable Seema was already at her console, headset on, hands flying over the keyboard.

"Ah, Inspector," Hemanth said. "I heard we're going live sooner than expected?"

Chatpati shrugged. "Executive decision." He gestured at the ceiling. "From on high. How's it looking?"

"We're ready to go. I'm familiarising Seema with the set-up. You can see it in action now, if you like."

The giant screen lit up, displaying an overhead map of Bangalore. From above, the city looked like the paw-print of a colossal tiger striding north-east. It lay in the centre of a V formed by the mountain ranges of the Eastern and Western Ghats. The city's limit was delineated in sunflower yellow, this the Ring Road from which the National Highways radiated out to all points of the compass: east across the Deccan Plateau to drought-struck Madras, west through the foothills to the mosquito haven of Mangalore, north to Hyderabad, City of Pearls, and south to the hills of verdant Kerala. Within the circumference of the Ring Road, the city's flat grey expanse was fissured by hundreds of smaller lines, each squiggle an urban road, rippling with colour.

"This is the default view," Hemanth said. "It combines a satellite map with real-time feeds from traffic monitors and aggregated live crime data from PoliceNet. All recorded criminal activity in the city in real time. You can filter by Division or crime or criminal. Seema enters reports into the

PoliceNet database. They appear on the map until resolved or otherwise dealt with."

"Good morning, boss," Raj appeared at Hemanth's shoulder, brimming with excitement. "The drones are spooling up!"

"Drones?" Chatpati said, alarmed. "What drones?"

"The Unit has four dedicated UASs. That's Unmanned Aerial Systems." Hemanth said. "Part of the Commissioner's equipment specification, Inspector. It's budgeted for and part of my contract. They're out there. Do have a look."

Chatpati followed Raj through the folding glass doors that led out into Cloud24's outdoor lounge. There, on the mossy decking, between the weather-beaten parasols and rusting fire pits, stood four steel cradles, each the size of a coffee table. Each cradle held a grey-black machine that might have passed for a giant upturned spider except for the spinning rotors and the cluster of lenses on its belly.

"Near military grade," Raj said at his shoulder. He sounded awed. "High-definition cameras. Infra-red heat sensors. Night vision. We've named them Garuda[2] One to Four."

Chatpati circled the machines. "They look very expensive. I'd rather have spent the money on a few more police-officers than a flying video camera."

Hemanth had joined them. "It's what the Commissioner wanted, sir. It's future proofing. They're already paid for. We're planning a test flight today. You might, perhaps, be more convinced afterwards?"

Chatpati looked sceptical. Hemanth continued in a rush. "The drones can do many things policemen can't, Inspector. Fly programmed circuits, search for particular heat signatures and return home when it's time to recharge. They're pretty near autonomous, if you choose.

Think of them like agile, moderately intelligent guard dogs. Except they don't drop turds or bark or need feeding."

"They might turn into turds if one falls on a civilian's head," Chatpati muttered. "You'll hear the barking all the way to the Commissioner's office. But, if that's what the Commissioner wants, so be it."

Seema's voice sounded over the outdoor speakers. "Sir, the Justice Minister is on TV."

They returned to the dance floor. BTV News was on the display. The Justice Minister was in the studio being interviewed by anchorwoman Nita Singh.

Minister Anand Urs had the proud nose and upright bearing of his forefathers. His bloodline could be traced back to Mysore royalty[3], a fact he had buried under a career in grass-root politics. He wore the traditional modest garb of the career politician: a grey Nehru jacket over a long-sleeved white kurta.

Nita was in strident mode. "Your programme of improvement has been strenuously decried by the opposition, Minister Urs." She flipped through her notes as if they offended her. "A waste of money, they say. Nothing will change, they say." She fixed him with a glare. "Aren't they right?"

The Minister smiled at her, a benign smile granted like an indulgence for an idiot. "They will say what they will, Nita. Need I remind you, and all your viewers, what the last five years have looked like? When the current Opposition was the Government? Five years which saw a steady decline in the standards of living for the common man. In which crime and terror ruled the land. Can anyone ever forget the attack on the Vidhana Soudha? This administration is going to change all that. We are ushering in a new age."

"All new governments say that," Nita replied. "Will words really change anything?"

Urs shook his head. "Not just words. Next week, you will see, in the capital, the launch of the Bangalore Civil Nuisance Unit, a hi-tech elite police unit dedicated to tackling the things that trouble hard-working people the most."

"Protection rackets that nibble away, like so many rats, at the meagre earnings of simple labourers. The casual molestation of women, of wives, of daughters, of sisters, on their way to work, on their way to school, on buses, on trains, on street corners. Organised beggary that feeds the trafficking of children. The anonymous defacing of public buildings. Rampant fly-tipping. Shameful public urination. Those hundreds of daily infractions that impinge on the ability of the people of this great state to truly live. Not just exist from hand to mouth but live! Bangalore will change and, from that, so too will society. I know it."

Nita looked doubtful. "Surely, surely, Minister, it is the big crimes that the government should focus on. Murder. Assault. Robbery. These are the big issues, not someone urinating against a wall!"

"You say that, Nita, but honestly, how likely are you to be murdered today?"

Nita's eyebrows rose. "Well," she said, "there are some, I'm sure, who—"

The Minister laughed. "There are always those who wish to silence the media. What I mean to say is that we already have a strong police force that is dedicated to tackling major crime. Since we came to power, we have strengthened the hand of the police. Most major crimes are successfully prosecuted already."

The Minister raised a finger. "But is MAJOR crime the major problem for the ordinary man? Is the factory worker troubled by the murder of a gangland criminal by other gang-sters? No. Does the vegetable seller care if a corrupt billionaire loses millions to fraudsters? No. What affects normal, working people are those myriad MINOR crimes that assail them from all sides, so constant, so immutable, so unavoidable that they become a part of daily life."

"Minor crime becomes the major problem. It becomes a social norm. When that happens, honest people feel powerless. That is going to change. The Civil Nuisance Unit, amongst our other innovations, is going to be a driver of that change. No crime will be so minor that it evades prosecution. No infraction will go unpunished. It starts with Bangalore, but soon it will spread outwards. With that, we will see a new Karnataka, a place where all honest people can live and work."

Nita looked sceptical. "Well, I suppose I should thank you for the assurance that I am safe from murder, if nothing else. Minister Urs, that's all we have time for." She turned to the camera. "And now it's time for a break. When we come back, we'll have the latest from the High Court trial of Govind Prabhu, leader of the outlawed Farmers' War Party."

APPLAUSE RIPPLED through the assembled policemen. Chatpati waved them back to their work and took the stairs to his office. At the office door, he glanced back. They were still watching him, their faces expectant.

He felt a pressure to speak. This was the time to say something Churchillian, words to spur them on to civil nuisance glory. His throat tightened. His mind raced. The urge to retreat into his office was strong. Instead, he took a step forward and placed his hands on the walkway railing. He took a breath.

"Much of this is new to many of you. You've come here, giving up what some might call safe jobs, to journey into uncharted waters. I thank you and I welcome you. We have much to do." There were a few nods, a few smiles. "Whatever the Minister's aspirations for society, it will not be easy. We start this journey as pariahs amongst our police colleagues. Common Nonsense Unit is what they call us."

A murmur of outrage rose into the air. He stilled it with a raised hand.

"Our best response is action. We will show them. That the Civil Nuisance Unit can be a real nuisance. A nuisance for criminals everywhere. We will prosecute those who oppress the common man. Without fear. Without favour. And that starts today, every day, by doing your job, as best you can." He took a breath. "We're all in it together. It's sink or swim. And we will not sink!"

Another round of applause. He closed the door on it before it died down. He had barely gained his desk when his phone rang.

"Call for you, sir," Seema said. "It's a doctor. From the Curzon Hospital. Said he would speak only to you."

It was not, as Chatpati had expected, the disgraced Medical Superintendent. This voice was soft and cultured.

"Is that Inspector Chatpati? I am very sorry to bother you, Inspector. My name is Dr. Saleem. I am a pathologist at Curzon Hospital." He paused. "I need to speak to you, Inspector, about something. It is quite urgent."

"What is it about, Dr. Saleem?" Chatpati said, reaching for a notepad.

The reply was almost inaudible. "It's about the

Germans, Inspector. I heard what happened yesterday. It is all over the hospital."

"Dr. Saleem, if you've called to plead for the Medical Superintendent—"

"No, no," Dr. Saleem replied. "Not at all. Quite the contrary." He paused. "I can't say much on the phone. It's not safe. Can I come and see you? They're not the only ones, you see. The German lady. She's not the only one." He paused again. "She was lucky. She's alive. Others are not. They're dead, Inspector. Quite dead."

CHAPTER 9
COMETH THE HOUR, COMETH THE NAIR

Dr. Saleem, the pathologist, would arrive at noon, which was just as well because Chatpati had forgotten about the interview at eleven o'clock. At ten minutes to the hour, Raj appeared at the door, clutching a manilla folder.

"There's a police officer here," Raj said. He looked worried. "He says he's the new Sub-Inspector."

Chatpati suppressed a curse. "Damnation. The ACP's PA said she'd send the details over. Check with Seema please, Raj."

"I have, sir." Raj placed the folder on Chatpati's desk. It had the words 'V. NAIR' on the cover. "It's all in here."

Chatpati looked at his watch. "Ask him to wait, Raj. He's a bit early. Give him a coffee or something. There must be a coffee-machine somewhere in that kitchen. Bring him up in ten minutes." Raj lingered. "Is there something else?"

"He's a bit-" Raj swallowed. "Odd, sir."

"Odd?" Chatpati said. "Odd, you say? Raj, look around you. There's a disco ball hanging from the struts. The IT guy works in the DJ booth. We have four drones on the decking." He flipped the folder open. "He should fit right in."

Sub-Inspector Vasanth Nair was, according to his CV, twenty-six years old and one hundred and seventy-eight point five centimetres tall. He had been a policeman for six years, most recently serving as liaison to the Directorate of Revenue Intelligence in the port of Cochin in the state of Kerala. His CV declared he had been "instrumental in the seizure of illicit goods worth several lakh[1] rupees and key in the arrest of notorious smugglers of said illicit goods". He was a strict vegetarian and unmarried. He described his interests as Iyengar Yoga, Royal Enfield motorcycles, and languages.

The photograph showed a slim, serious face with heavy eyelids, an angular nose and a strident moustache. There was something familiar about it.

In response to the question "Reasons for transfer:" V. Nair had written "I have been impressed by the courage demonstrated by the Bangalore police officers involved in the Vidhana Soudha incident. I aspire to personal improvement by working with these officers to be of service to the state of India."

"Future career ambitions:" received the response "Intelligence". With a capital I.

Chatpati did the maths. An inter-state transfer for someone of Nair's experience would mean a reduction in salary to the starting point of Nair's rank. This young officer was prepared to leave all that was familiar to come here at some financial cost. Such dedication worried the Inspector.

There was also no place for a Sub-Inspector in Chatpati's plan for the CNU. The idea of a second in command, especially one with such zeal, didn't sit well. It would be a pity to reject V. Nair, Chatpati thought, considering that he had travelled so far, but Chatpati was sure the ACP could make some other use of the man. Making use of men was one of the ACP's few talents.

The interview's outcome pre-determined, Inspector Chatpati closed the folder. All he would have to do would be to see this brief conversation through, then he could get back to the business of the day.

Such thoughts were dispelled when Raj opened the door. The man who followed him in was tall.

And hadn't improved his Kannada.

"Thou!" Vasanth Nair exclaimed. "It is thou! Respected comrade of the justiciary! Opponent of fraudulent chariot drivers!"

Chatpati leapt to his feet. He didn't realise he had done so. "You!" he said. "You! The auto-rickshaw! The bad Kannada! You are Sub-Inspector Nair?"

"Verily!" Nair returned, grinning, "and thou art the venerable Inspector Chatpati! Hail and well met!"

Once Chatpati had dismissed the bewildered Raj and they had seated themselves, Chatpati decided he would conduct the interview in English.

"Wherefore?" Nair had said, struggling on.

"Because," Chatpati replied, "your Kannada is giving me a headache."

Nair looked put out but shrugged. "As you wish," he said. "You're the boss." Before Chatpati could begin, Nair continued in a rush. "I would just like to say, Inspector, it's a great honour, truly, to be working with you. I have followed every detail of the Vidhana Soudha incident in the news. Your—"

Chatpati raised a hand. "We're not here to discuss that. And you haven't been appointed. Yet."

It was Nair's turn to look bewildered. "Oh? But I

requested this posting specifically. The ACP told me it was all arranged. That you needed a number two, what with all the things to do and such."

"I don't need a number two," Chatpati said. "The ACP requested I interview you, and that is what this is. An interview. So let's get to it."

It took far longer than Chatpati had hoped. Vasanth Nair was one of those fortunate individuals who had faced few obstacles in life. Raised in a prosperous high-caste Hindu household, Nair had gone to a private school ("Catholic. I know all the hymns.") and studied botany at Cochin University ("My family has lots of agricultural land. Coconuts, sugar cane, rice, that kind of thing. Acres and acres.") After graduation, he had found plant life too boring and switched to the police.

"And what did your family think of that?" Chatpati asked.

"Oh, they hated it," Nair replied. "Dirty, degrading work, my father said. My mother wailed that they would never find a good match for me. No good Hindu girl from our caste would want to marry a policeman. Long hours, evil company, disreputable workplaces. But I said I didn't care." Nair smoothed his moustache with a thumb, the third time in three minutes. The mannerism was grating on the Inspector. "I want to be of service. To the state. To India."

Nair had found routine police work jaded after his probation year ("After you've arrested the third burglar, the passion is gone."). When the opportunity to work in Excise came up, he'd jumped at it.

"Working in boats is so much more fun," Nair said, leaning back in the chair and talking to the ceiling. "And undercover work. Plain clothes, Inspector. You've done it yourself, right?" Nair did not wait for Chatpati's reply, nor did he see the expression on the Inspector's face. "I've been in many places in disguise. Disgusting brothels. Filthy dives. Gambling dens." Nair shuddered. "It required a great deal of application, if I say so myself, especially for someone to whom the body is a temple. But," he shrugged, "what is that for the greater good? I keep myself fit. Yoga. A strict vegetarian diet. No substances. I think of myself as a weapon, a bayonet of the state. It's no use if the edges are dull."

Chatpati wished he had a bayonet to thrust into V. Nair. A dull one would have been preferable.

Nair sat up in his chair. "So? Anything else you'd like to know? When do I start?"

Chatpati frowned. "I'm not sure you're the right fit for this Unit, Sub-Inspector. I don't need a second in command. This is a small set-up. We have enough people to do the job."

"Ah, yes. That may be the case. Now." Nair said. "Now, you have enough people, but once your success becomes established, why, you'll be flooded with calls. Tens of reports every day, maybe hundreds! I could deal with a lot of that. I could keep the trivialities off your desk. So you can concentrate on—"

Chatpati folded his hands and waited. "On?"

"Leadership!" Nair raised a finger in the air. "That's it. Leadership! And direction!"

Chatpati shook his head. "I don't think so. We have enough direction, as it stands. The Justice Minister, the Commissioner, the Assistant Commissioner. And leadership is best delivered direct, not through another layer of hierarchy." He slid the folder away with a finger. "No, I don't think we have a place for you here."

Nair's face fell. He looked lost. "Oh," he said in a small voice. "I would never have made the move if I hadn't been sure of working with you. I thought—"

"Wrong," Chatpati said, brutal. He regretted it instantly. Nair looked close to tears. "Look, I don't even have the budget for a Sub-Inspector. There's no money to pay your salary. Anyway, you'd be better off in some other Division. Traffic, for example, is renowned for their honesty and dynamism. You could learn the ropes, learn the language. Then, maybe, at some future time, we can look at things again."

Nair perked up. "I would work for free. A probationary period. Yes! A month. No, two months! No, three months! Anything!" He looked Chatpati in the eye. "Please, Inspector Chatpati. Give me a chance."

Chatpati could feel his resolve melting. He could not deny that the idea had merit. That the workload would increase was undeniable. An extra body for a month or two would be a help, especially if said body could be despatched to some other Division afterwards. And, truth be told, Chatpati didn't quite have the heart to send Nair packing straight away.

"Alright," Chatpati said. "Let me think about it. I need to discuss this with the ACP. I'll let you know."

"No problem," Nair said, rising. "I'll wait. It'll give me a chance to get to know the troops." He saluted. "Thank you, Inspector. You won't regret it."

Chatpati was regretting it already. He had meant he would let Nair know in a day or two, not in ten minutes. With little grace, he rang the ACP's office and spoke to Mina, hedging the proposal with as many caveats as he could muster. She rang back a bare five minutes later.

"The ACP says fine, Inspector. But not a month. Three

months minimum. It's too awkward to process salaries for a single month. Central Division will pay the Sub-Inspector's salary for that period. At the end, if you wish to dispense with his services, we will arrange a transfer to Traffic."

Nair was jubilant when he was told. "Thank you, Inspector! I won't let you down. Promise!"

"Fine, fine," Chatpati said, shooing him away. "Familiarise yourself with the place. And find a desk. There are several stacked up near the kitchen. Ask Raj if you need anything. Oh, and be back here at noon. Bring Raj with you. I'll need you to take notes. We might have some work to do."

CHAPTER 10

CASE HISTORY

Communing with cadavers seemed to have rendered Dr. Saleem cadaverous. The pathologist was thin to the point of cachexia, his clothes hanging off him like the abandoned banners that flutter over battlefields. He entered Chatpati's office clutching reams of paper to his chest like a heretic to his burning. Raj and Nair arranged themselves on either side like guards poised to prevent flight.

"It's about the cases," the pathologist began. "The poisonings."

Chatpati nodded. "Carry on, please, doctor. You said the German tourist was lucky to be alive. That there were others not so fortunate. That people have died."

Dr. Saleem nodded back. "You see, Inspector, there have been at least nine cases in the last five weeks. People with similar symptoms. Three have died." He swallowed. "I did the post-mortems on those three." He placed the papers on Chatpati's desk. "It's all in there. The hospital records." He glanced around the room. "I made copies, you see."

"Thou wearest a garment of angst," Nair said. "Wherefore?"

Dr. Saleem stared at Nair in alarm.

Chatpati spoke before Nair could continue. "My colleague, Sub-Inspector Nair, has just arrived in Bangalore, doctor. His command of the language is still evolving. Perhaps we can continue in English?"

Nair looked put out but shut up.

Dr. Saleem nodded. "If your question was, am I fearful? Then the answer is yes. What I have done is strictly forbidden. Making copies of patient records. Taking them out of the hospital. I could be disciplined. Struck off the medical register."

"Anything you say is in strict confidence," Chatpati said. "You've nothing to fear from us."

The pathologist explained what had aroused his suspicions. All three deaths had taken place the same morning. Also, the symptoms were not typical of the food poisoning to which they had been attributed.

"In all three cases, death was quick," Saleem said. "Within an hour of becoming unwell, each victim was dead. Bystanders described respiratory and central nervous system symptoms first, rather than gastrointestinal. That is unusual. Two had convulsions. Again, highly unusual."

None of the three cases had lived long enough to reach hospital alive. There had been no cases for a week, then came another three, those of milder severity.

"Those three lived," Saleem said, "though they required a lengthy hospital stay. Then, again, no cases for another week. Then, the week after, another three, milder yet. Only two days of treatment. One of those was the German tourist."

"You would have done tests for food poisoning?" Nair asked. "Cholera? Typhoid? Dysentery? That kind of thing."

"Oh yes," Saleem nodded. "All the bacterial and viral screens came back negative, blood, urine and faeces. It was not an infection, I am sure of it." He looked fearful again. "I think it was poisoning. With a substance. The most likely cause is adulteration of a foodstuff. Though I haven't been able to figure out what."

"Food adulteration's not uncommon," Raj said. "Brick dust in chilli powder. Starch added to milk. Used mineral water bottles filled with dirty tap water and resealed. Hardly anyone's ever prosecuted for it."

"You informed the public health authorities, I presume?" Chatpati said.

"Yes," Saleem replied. "I filed reports for every single case. I spoke to the local Public Health Officer thrice. I even showed the Medical Superintendent the evidence."

"And?"

Saleem shrugged. "Public Health said they would look into it but they are over-worked and under-resourced, Inspector. It might take months. The Medical Superintendent ordered me to focus on our day-to-day work and not play detective. But, Inspector, I am worried that this is not the end. That more people will die."

"The timeline is curious," Nair said. "You say the cases occurred every fortnight? And that they grew less severe from week to week? Why might that be?"

Saleem shook his head. "I couldn't make sense of it. If it was food adulteration one would expect a cluster of cases, linked in time and place All the members of one household, for example. Or all the customers of a restaurant. There was no geographical clustering. They seemed to occur in different places."

"What about the demographics of the victims?" Chatpati said. "Did they have anything in common?"

"Not that I could see," Saleem said. "The German lady was the only foreigner. All the others were Bangalore residents, either natives or immigrants from neighbouring states. Of those, most were working class. Only one middle-class professional type."

Saleem glanced at his watch, then rose to go. "I must head back, Inspector, forgive me. I am on my lunch break and there is an autopsy to do in the afternoon. Can I leave this with you?"

Chatpati got to his feet. "This is not exactly within our remit, Dr. Saleem, but I'll see what we can do. If nothing else, perhaps we can energise the public health authorities. Raj, please see the doctor out."

"Curious," Nair said when Raj returned.

"Hypotheses?" Chatpati said. "Raj?"

"A travelling salesman?" Raj ventured. "Some guy who goes from door to door selling adulterated foodstuffs. Like cooking oil already used by a restaurant that should have been disposed of but is sold on for profit? The salesman is in one spot one day, then somewhere else the next. That would explain the different sites."

Nair shook his head. "Then why a week between cases? No travelling salesman would make a living if he only sold every other week. And why only three cases a week? There should have been more."

Chatpati nodded. "Fair point. Vasanth, your alternative?"

"The tourist is the odd one out," Nair said. "Where would a tourist mix with working class patrons? Most foreign tourists are not terribly adventurous. They're all warned about the horrors of food poisoning. They tend to stay in upmarket hotels. They only eat in reputable places and drink bottled water."

Raj's face lit up. "Coconut! Mr. Günther! The park!"

"Coconut?" Nair's voice was scathing. "What's all that about?"

Chatpati described his conversation with the Brauns at Curzon Hospital.

"Günther Braun was adamant that a tender coconut his wife had drunk in Cubbon Park caused her symptoms. That might be your connection, a link between labourers and tourists. Everyone visits Cubbon Park. Everyone drinks tender coconut water."

"Ludicrous," Nair replied. "Tender coconut water is perfectly safe. I should know. My family grows coconuts. The coconut water is contained within the coconut's impermeable husk. The contents are sterile until the husk is breached. And the husk is only ever breached just before consumption. Like you would only open a soft drink can just before you drank it."

Raj looked put out. "Well, what if the shell had been accidentally breached?" he said. He sounded resentful that Nair had shot his idea down. "Or the tender coconut was old? Wouldn't that make the coconut water dangerous?"

Nair snorted. "It's clear that you, Constable Raj, have no coconut experience. It's about as easy to 'accidentally' breach a coconut as it is to accidentally breach concrete. And old coconut water is still safe. It just tastes old. You wouldn't want to drink it, but it wouldn't kill you if you did."

"Well, it's a start," Chatpati said. "Let's get to work. Raj, I want you to pull together the demographics of these cases: age, sex, occupation, address. Vasanth, focus on the timeline. Then let's put all that together and see if there's a pattern."

The Justice Minister's announcement about the Civil Nuisance Unit on TV that morning seemed to have set the world on fire. In the space of an hour, Seema fielded three calls from local newspapers with requests for interviews with Inspector Chatpati. The Bangalore Herald planned "a special feature on modern policing". The Deccan Mirror was keen on "a personal profile on the Hero of the Vidhana Soudha". Kannada Suddi was producing "an illustrated supplement on Bangalore's leading figures". Chatpati gave Seema a canned reply, along the lines of 'the Inspector will consider each request but due to pressure of work etcetera'.

The CNU's status had also been elevated in the eyes of Traffic Division. ACP (Traffic) sent a Hoysala driver to deliver a greetings card and a large box of Indian sweets.

"What's so GREAT about a customer like you?" the card's front cover asked between swirly stars. Inside was the printed answer. *"Everything! We just wanted to let you know!"* A handwritten scrawl underneath translated to *"Looking forward to close mutual future co-operation. ACP (Traffic)"*

The sweets were of the variety designed to keep dentists in business: a brace of gulab jamun[1] and handfuls of barfi[2]. Chatpati's teeth ached just looking at them. He despatched them to the post-lunch workforce downstairs and instructed Seema to send a suitable reply by return.

Soon after, Hemanth knocked at his door. "We have something for you, Inspector. If you wouldn't mind coming down?"

They joined Raj and Nair at Seema's console. All three were looking up at the city map on the giant screen. There were three red dots on the map, forming the points of a triangle, the apex pointing north.

"What's happening?" Chatpati said. "A rash of begging?"

"I asked Hemanth to plot the cases on the map," Nair said. "Have a look. The pathologist said there were three cases in the first week. There they are."

"OK," Chatpati said. "I see three red dots. So?"

"The pathologist said there was no pattern," Nair replied. "But look at the next three cases that happened a fortnight later." Three new dots appeared, each next to an existing dot. "The second cluster of cases appears at the same locations as the first. And the same for the third set." Three more dots joined their fellows.

Chatpati nodded slowly. It was suddenly obvious. "So there is a geographical pattern. All the cases appear at one of three locations. Consistently. Week to week."

"Exactly," Nair said. "Seema, zoom in on the three locations please."

Seema did so. "The northernmost point of the triangle is near Russell Market," she said. "The triangle's base connects Cubbon Park in the west and Saint Gregory's Hospital in the east."

"It's very circumscribed," Chatpati remarked. "Bangalore covers 700 square kilometres, yet these nine cases lie within two kilometres of each other. What's the commonality here? What's common to a park, a market and a hospital?"

"People," Nair said. "They're all places with lots of foot traffic."

"And criminals," Raj said. "Where there are people, there's crime."

Nair sniffed. "Oh, really? Find many criminals in hospitals, do you?"

"Actually," Raj replied, "yes. As you would know if you'd been at the Curzon Hospital yesterday. But you weren't."

Nair bristled. Chatpati could see the beginnings of a spat.

"Good work," he said, to take the heat out of the discussion. "That's useful information, even if we don't know what it means yet. Keep at it. Anything on the timelines?"

"Week one," Raj said. "The first three cases, all of which died. The first at about 7am at St. Gregory's in the east, the next at Cubbon Park in the west and the last at Russell Market in the north at 9am. All within a couple of hours."

Chatpati nodded. "Nothing in week two. We know that."

"Week three and another three cases. Same locations, same order. None of these died, but all cases were hospitalised the same morning, all between 8am and noon."

"Nothing in week four," Chatpati said.

"Correct," Raj nodded. "And week five, the geographical pattern repeats itself."

"Same order? East, west and north?"

Raj nodded again. "Exactly. Again, none died, but all hospitalised the same day. Between 9am and 2pm. There's one other thing." He paused. "All the cases happened on a Tuesday. Every single one."

Chatpati stared at him. Raj nodded vigorously. "I'm sure, sir. I double-checked. There's no doubt."

"Odd" was Nair's reply. "What's special about Tuesdays? Festival? Market day?"

"A good question," Chatpati said. "Look into those particular Tuesdays, Raj. Check for events, concerts, public meetings. Focus on those within the vicinity of the three sites. Then report back once you have something."

He'd barely made it back into his office when his phone rang. Again.

"A call for you, Inspector," Seema said.

"I'm not taking any media calls, Seema."

"Yes, sir. I know. It's not a newspaper. It's a travel agency."

"Travel agency? I haven't booked a holiday. Just deal with it."

"I would, sir, except they said you were expecting their call. That someone had mentioned they would be in touch? The lady said to say that she would consider it a personal favour to speak to you." Seema paused. "She said it twice. A personal favour."

Favour? An odd word to use. Chatpati racked his brain. It came to him in a flash – the Minister's words from their telephone call.

"You will shortly be contacted by people representing an organisation. Consider it a personal favour that you lend them your ear."

Chatpati took the call. The woman on the line sounded professional, the diction precise, not the usual effusive over-familiarity Chatpati associated with cold-calling.

"Inspector Chatpati? Good afternoon. I'm sorry to bother you at what must be a busy time. My name is Mary D'Souza, from Falcon Travels. We're a boutique travel operator newly opened in Bangalore and would appreciate the opportunity to offer you a personal overview of *what we offer*." The emphasis could not be clearer. "If we could, perhaps, meet to discuss your needs, my boss and I would consider it a *personal favour*." Again, that deliberate emphasis.

Chatpati remembered what else the Minister had said.

"They are more than they appear. And their purpose aligns with ours."

Chatpati agreed to meet.

"Wonderful," Mary D'Souza said. "We look forward to seeing you this afternoon, then. We can send a car?"

"That's unnecessary," Chatpati said. "I'll make my own way. Where are you located?"

"Langford Town," she replied. "9, Myrtle Lane. I look forward to seeing you."

Odd location for a travel agent, Chatpati thought. Langford Town was a residential area two kilometres south of the Central Business District, mostly grand old villas with rambling gardens and a smattering of newer apartment blocks. Not the first place one would have thought to set up a travel business. Who used travel agents these days, anyway? Didn't everyone book their own travel online?

The remaining hour passed without interruptions. When it was time to leave, he made his way down to the restaurant and told Seema he'd be away.

Seema nodded. "Will the Sub-Inspector be in charge while you're away?"

"Absolutely not!" Chatpati said, a little too quickly. He didn't plan to leave Nair in charge of anything. There was no telling what authority Nair might attempt to exert while Chatpati was absent. He thought quickly. "No, he's coming with me. Raj is in charge. Tell Raj to ring if anything urgent crops up." He looked around. "Where is the Sub-Inspector?"

Raj appeared as if on cue. "He's occupied one of the private suites, sir. Just next to the billiard tables. There are three suites. He's taken one." Raj and Seema shared a knowing look.

"Private suites?" Chatpati said. "I didn't know there were any."

"Oh, yes," Raj said. "Well appointed. Meant for private events and the like. That was one reason the nightclub was closed down. Too many 'private dances' taking place in there." Raj smirked. "If you know what I mean."

Chatpati pursed his lips. "Does Sub-Inspector Nair know he's occupying a space once used for 'immoral purposes'? He might feel a bit tarnished."

Raj's expression was neutral. "I was going to tell him, sir. Later. At an appropriate point. And recommend he wipe the surfaces down."

Chatpati raised a brow. "Wise. Yes, leave that for later. We don't want to overload the Sub-Inspector with too much at this stage."

"Yes, sir. The Sub-Inspector wanted to occupy the largest of the three suites, sir, but I told him the larger rooms were being repurposed. Into holding cells."

Chatpati nodded. "Ah. That's a good idea. Yes, we'll need somewhere to hold the drunkards and wastrels. Have a look at the two remaining suites and get back to me with what it will take to convert them into cells. It's unfortunate that the Sub-Inspector has chosen an office right next to the cells. He won't get much peace. But," Chatpati shrugged, feigning sadness, "I suppose we all have to compromise. Tell the Sub-Inspector to meet me downstairs in five minutes. We've got somewhere to go. You're holding the fort."

Raj positively swelled at the honour. Inspector Chatpati headed out.

CHAPTER 11

A FALCON IN TIME-

By the time Nair appeared, Chatpati had waylaid an unsuspecting auto-rickshaw. The auto had been parked outside the theatre entrance, waiting for the matinee crowd to emerge, but the driver's attention had been on watching porn on his phone and scratching his arse. The driver's face fell when he saw who his customer was. That expression changed to serious worry when Nair climbed in.

Myrtle Lane was a narrow, potholed road made near impassable by bad parking. It was dominated by drab apartment buildings with names like Myrtle Palace and Myrtle Prestige. There was nothing palatial or prestigious about them.

Falcon Travels occupied a pair of twin villas set behind the high walls of a gated compound, the grounds studded with mature mango and jacaranda trees. The sign on the gate was discreet and bore only the blue and gold insignia of a glinty-eyed bird of prey. There was a guard in a booth at the gate. The guard was not the usual underfed geriatric, but a fit-looking youth with bulging biceps. The guard studied the two policemen with extreme interest as they approached.

The guard checked the Inspector's name off a list. "And your companion?" the guard asked.

Nair puffed up. "An extraneous officer of the justiciary," Nair snarled. "Art thou blindness?"

"He's with me," Chatpati said.

"Please wait, Inspector," the guard said. He spoke into his walkie-talkie and seemed to understand the garbled reply. The guard opened the gate. "Please go ahead. Take the left fork in the path, please."

The twin villas were mirror images of each other, separated by a paved driveway. There were three black people carriers parked on the paving, each with tinted windows. All the vehicles had the blue-gold falcon logo on them. The roof of the villa on the right bore industrial air-conditioning units and three satellite dishes. The facing wall of the villa on the left, their destination, was mirrored glass instead of brick. There was no obvious door. As they came to the end of the path, a section of the glass slid away.

The young man behind the reception desk was on his feet as they entered. "Inspector Chatpati? Good afternoon. Welcome to Falcon Travels," he said. "You are slightly early. Ms. D'Souza is just in the middle of an important call. Would you mind waiting? It will be only a few minutes."

The waiting area was plush: a plasma screen TV showing live cricket, leather sofas, plants in artisan pots and a coffee machine, stocked with bone china cups and saucers. Nair fixed himself a latte. Chatpati declined the offer of a beverage.

The wall behind the reception desk was again floor to ceiling plate glass. Through it, the Inspector could see a long room with two rows of desks on either side. Agents occupied all the desks, five to a side, all wearing headsets and attending to their computer screens.

"What kind of travel agency is this?" Nair asked, settling down opposite. "It's very lavish. These sofas are real leather."

"Odd is the word I would use," Chatpati said. "Notice anything unusual?"

Nair nodded. "Three satellite dishes. Three. One, I can understand, but three? The gardens are immaculate, the kind of maintenance that costs money. The topiary is nicely done. And the pond is full of koi carp."

"And the vehicles," Chatpati said. "Presumably to ferry clients around in. Each has a pair of radio antennae. Quite discreet."

Nair shrugged. "Well, maybe high-end tourists require broadband Internet access wherever they go. You know, Netflix on the three-hour drive to the coast, that sort of thing. Rich people don't understand the difference between luxuries and essentials."

The receptionist reappeared. He was accompanied by a pretty young girl with a dazzling white smile. "Inspector Chatpati, Ms. D'Souza would be happy to see you now." He turned to Nair with an apologetic smile. "I'm afraid this will be a private meeting, but perhaps Sub-Inspector Nair would like to accompany Miss Asha here, who would be delighted to take him through what we offer here at Falcon. Asha, please get the Sub-Inspector a fresh coffee."

Asha smiled at Vasanth Nair. "This way, please, sir." Nair followed dumbstruck, the Inspector entirely forgotten.

The receptionist lead Chatpati between the rows of desks to a meeting room, a long wood-panelled space with recessed lighting, a conference table and a wall of TV screens. Mary D'Souza rose to greet him.

D'Souza had emerald green eyes and a milky complexion that spoke of the Portuguese ancestor her name suggested. Her eyes matched her sari, draped in the Dhangad style typical of Goa[1]. The sari blouse was sleeveless, her shoulders bare. She wore no jewellery except for a simple silver-banded wristwatch.

Her companion, a man in a linen suit and tie, had also got to his feet. He was in his fifties, slim and clean shaven, with silvery hair in a comb-over. The suit was dark-grey, the cufflinks gold.

"Welcome, Inspector," D'Souza said. "May I introduce my boss, Director Rajan?"

Chatpati nodded. "Pleased to meet you both. Is Mr. Rajan the director of this branch? Or the whole firm?"

Rajan smiled. "I'm the Regional Director for south India, Inspector. A pleasure."

Chatpati nodded. "Excellent. And Ms. D'Souza is the head of this branch, I assume? Do you have many other travel agencies?"

"Yes and no," Rajan replied. "We have many branches across India, Inspector, but travel is not our sole area of interest. We have others."

"Interesting," Chatpati said. "You're a national firm, then."

Rajan nodded. "Exactly. We're a relatively new venture, though our base business is decades old. We're expanding. Into new markets."

"Of course," Chatpati said. "Though I'm a little curious who exactly uses travel agents these days? It's a bit of a throwback, isn't it? I mean, you can even book bus travel from a smartphone."

D'Souza replied. "We focus on the top end of the travel market, Inspector. Our customers are corporates and those individuals with high net worth. We provide a curated, personal experience for the discerning. Bespoke, if you like."

"Oh, well, then you've come to the right place," Chatpati said. "There's plenty of money in Bangalore. We have the only Lamborghini showroom in South India, did you know? But I expect you did."

Rajan smiled. "Yes. Bangalore, The Silicon Valley of India. A booming middle-class. Upwardly mobile. Confident. With high expectations. That's what our market research suggests."

Chatpati nodded. "So what can a humble Inspector of Police do for you? My clientele is unlikely to be in your target market. Mine are beggars and vagrants. If it's illicit wealth you're after, the Fraud Squad is your best bet. They know all the people with ill-gotten gains to offload."

D'Souza leaned forward. "It's a matter of some sensitivity, Inspector. May I count on your confidence?"

Chatpati sat back in his chair. "Ms. D'Souza, I should be delighted if you would speak plainly. I am intrigued by your set-up here. There's more to it than meets the eye."

"Oh," Rajan replied, sitting forward. His eyes glinted. "How so?"

Chatpati folded his hands. "You have bulletproof plate glass behind the reception desk. Your vehicles have high-bandwidth antennae. The building next door has a satellite comms cluster on its roof and the cooling apparatus needed to run lots of expensive big computers. And the gate guard looks like he could break me in half bare-handed." He smiled. "Get many dissatisfied customers, do you?"

There was the merest flicker of gaze between D'Souza and the Director.

"You could say that, Inspector," D'Souza said. "We're not just a travel agency. We're an agency of another sort."

The statement hung in the air for a moment until the Director spoke.

"The Minister said you were smart, Inspector. I'm pleased to see he was right. Perhaps it might be easier if we cut to the chase. Mary, would you do the honours?"

D'Souza nodded. "You will know the Humayun's Tomb Incident, Inspector?"

Chatpati was. It had been in the papers some months ago. Security forces manning a checkpoint near the tomb of the Emperor Humayun in New Delhi had discovered a bomb in a bullock cart. The story had been that the bomb was a dud, designed to incite panic amongst the populace.

"What you may not know, Inspector, is that the bomb was fully functional. It was what we call a dirty bomb. Radio-active material wrapped around conventional explosive. The target was Safdarjung[2], two kilometres down the road. The aim was to render the whole of central New Delhi a no-go zone, effectively paralysing the government. And with it, the state security apparatus."

"I see," Chatpati said. "And the perpetrators? Terrorists, I presume. The usual suspects? Kashmiri separatists funded by Pakistan?"

D'Souza glanced at the Director again. Rajan nodded. She turned back to Chatpati.

"The Sinhala Freedom Front. We suspect. Backed by the Chinese. The fissile material contained trace elements that acted like a physical fingerprint. Traced to a Chinese reactor thought long extinguished, near the Juyan Lake Basin, just south of the Mongolian Gobi desert. "

Chatpati nodded. "Lanka, then. Retribution for the Indian invasion."

"*Peace-keeping mission*, Inspector," Rajan said. "The Lanka government invited India to *assist*, remember?"

"And," Chatpati replied, "as I recall, they invited us to leave. But we have not done so."

Rajan shrugged. "Politics, Inspector. Beyond my pay grade. And yours."

"Regardless," D'Souza continued, "the Humayun's Tomb incident led to much thinking. One of the ensuing recommendations was that the military and intelligence services be re-organised. Rather than have one visible headquarters - a head, if you like, that could be decapitated - the services should become cellular, mimicking the terrorist networks. Decentralised discrete units distributed across the nation, working semi-autonomously with a common purpose."

"Fight fire with fire," Chatpati said. "It makes sense. But where do I come in?"

Rajan spoke next. "Part of the new brief, Inspector, is to link up with local law enforcement. The intelligence services have been too far removed from much of what happens on the ground. There is a lot of cross-pollination between crime and terrorism. It's a new age. We need new partners."

Chatpati scratched his head. "You may not have noticed, but my Unit has not even got off the ground yet. It has a very narrow remit. Minor crime. We don't do terrorism or weapons trafficking. I can't see what we offer that might be of use to you."

"On the contrary," Rajan replied, "you'll be plugged in to what's happening on the streets. You will develop informants. Your Unit is lean, relatively unburdened by hierarchy. You can respond quickly. And you in particular, Inspector, have showed a talent for thinking on your feet. You are the kind of person we need on our side."

Chatpati nodded. "I can see why you don't want to get tangled up with the existing law enforcement infrastructure. Too riddled with holes, perhaps? Difficult to know who to trust?"

Rajan shrugged and waited.

Chatpati considered all that had been said, then shook his head. "No, thank you. My unit will have plenty on our plate without having to chase down dirty bombs in the bazaars of Sultangunta[3]. Besides, Bangalore's not a terrorist hotspot. There's no reason for this city to be a target for the Chinese. Or the SFF."

"I disagree," Rajan said. "With respect. Our analysis suggests all major Indian cities are at risk. Bangalore is no different. You have multiple races and creeds living together. In relative harmony at present, but there have been flash-points in the past. Those tensions are easily re-ignited with the right kindling. Karnataka is embroiled in a running war of words with neighbouring states of Kerala and Tamil Nadu over access to scarce Cauvery River water. The native Kannadigas resent the immigrants from those states. Hindus fear Muslims, and vice versa. The Vidhana Soudha Incident was not that long ago. Our very own home-grown eco-terrorists, once harmless farmers. As I'm sure you remember. All terror needs to flourish is purpose and means."

"Think of what we can offer you, Inspector," D'Souza said, her gaze intense. "We have access to a lot of intelligence you don't. We have super-computer processing power at our disposal. We don't need to wait three days for a facial ID to creak through your police system or a week for the Fraud Squad to do a preliminary forensic analysis of bank accounts. We can be a valuable asset to you."

Chatpati pursed his lips. "It's the 'in return' that worries me. Frankly, I can't see that we will ever need that kind of help, Ms. D'Souza. We've got more than enough technology and most of our work will be old-fashioned policing down on the streets. If it's all the same to you, I would like to keep it that way." He paused. "Unless, of course, this is an order?"

The Director shook his head. "No. Not at all. Call it networking. An offer of friendship, of mutual assistance." Rajan paused. "I can see why you might have misgivings, Inspector. We have no intention of forcing you to work with us, though we could. That was the old way of doing things. All that does is rub people up the wrong way. No, what we are saying is that we are here if you need us. And perhaps you might consider the odd request from us as and when the situation arises? You will always be free to refuse."

"If that's all," Chatpati said, retrieving his hat, "I'll take my leave. Good luck with your new enterprise."

"And with yours, Inspector," D'Souza said, rising. She handed him a card at the door. "My mobile number. A call from your number, mobile or landline, will have priority. Please, ring if we can help."

Chatpati inclined his head. "Thank you. And something in return, if I may?" She raised her eyebrows. "You may wish to tell your agent at reception not to greet people by their names if he's not supposed to know who they are. I don't think the Sub-Inspector noticed—he was too entranced by Miss Asha—but others might."

D'Souza's face betrayed no emotion. "Thank you, Inspector," she said. "Every successful enterprise thrives on feedback. I will pass it on. Goodbye."

Nair was still deeply ensconced with Miss Asha, so Chatpati waited for the Sub-Inspector in the waiting area. Nair arrived ten minutes later, clutching a brochure.

"A profitable meeting?" Chatpati asked, getting to his feet.

Nair's expression was glazed, like someone who has gorged himself on too many laddus and needed a lie down. He shook his head in slow motion.

"No," he said, "their packages are far above what a humble Sub-Inspector of Police can afford. But," he brightened, "they say they have special introductory discounts."

Chatpati pointed at the brochure. "What've you got there? Europe? Thailand?"

Nair tucked the brochure under his arm. "Oh, nothing. Just some reading material, that's all. How was your meeting? Was that profitable?"

Chatpati had considered how much to tell Nair. That Nair had been excluded from the meeting suggested to the Inspector that he shouldn't say much. So he didn't.

"Far above what a humble Inspector of Police can afford," Chatpati replied. "Let's just call it an introductory meeting. Shall we head off?"

One of Falcon's sleek vehicles was waiting outside the gate, a driver standing by the sliding door.

"Ms. D'Souza ordered a vehicle to take you back, Inspector," the gate guard said. "The driver will take you wherever you wish to go."

The vehicle was as plush as Falcon's offices. There was a tinted sunroof and four quilted leather seats in facing configuration, each with its own pop-up TV screen, folding table, drinks holder and 'individual climate control'.

"There are refreshments in the refrigerator," the driver said over the intercom as they moved off. "Please help yourselves. And please press the intercom button if you wish to speak to me, gentlemen."

Nair had already found the refrigerator. He fished out a packet with a grinning green coconut on it.

"Ooh," he said, "tender coconut water. This is new. A drink for you, boss?"

Chatpati shook his head. "Driver, please drop me off at the nearest Metro. After that, please take Sub-Inspector Nair home. Which begs the question, Vasanth. Where are you staying? Have you found some digs yet?"

Nair took a slurpy sip. "Nothing permanent," he replied. "I'm staying at a place in Koramangala as a paying guest. I'm on the lookout for somewhere to rent. It's not important. First, I need to get some wheels." Nair pressed the intercom button. "Driver, after we drop the Inspector off, I need to go to the Royal Enfield motorcycle showroom on JC Road. Do you know it?"

"No problem, sir," the driver replied.

Chatpati picked up the brochure Nair had left on a vacant seat.

The brochure was matrimonial red, silver lettering on handmade artisan paper. The cover photograph depicted the deck of a cruise ship at sunset, an azure sea in the background. Beautiful young things in formal wear lounged against the railing, some holding hands, others looking out at the islands in the distance. In the foreground, older people, equally well-dressed, lounged on sofas, watching the young people with benign indulgence.

Bespoke Matrimonial Cruises!
A FIRST in India!
"An innovation for high net worth individuals looking for that

*perfect life partner! Offered only by your bespoke travel
experience partner, FALCON TRAVELS!
We offer five-day cruise packages leaving from the port of
Cochin. Travel to the Maldives in luxury with other singles
looking for their perfect match! There is no better environment
in which to get to know your future life partner.
Every evening, we host a formal soiree where clients can mingle
and get to know one another. The table seating arrangement
changes daily for maximum intermingling. Parents are, of
course, always present to ensure all interactions remain cordial.
On arrival at Male, the beautiful capital of the Maldives, clients
can partake of the city's delights. We offer half-day outings (at
an extra cost) for couples who, having met on the cruise, wish a
little private time to get to know one another a little better. The
price includes programmed diversions for both sets of parents
and official substitute chaperones. Chaperones will maintain a
minimum personal distance. We request clients to do likewise.
Please note that dissatisfaction with your chosen outing partner
is not a valid reason for refunds.
All packages include the services of a resident astrologer who will
cast one horoscope per day per potential couple, where
applicable.
With God(s) in your favour, you could return, not just refreshed
and renewed, but with the partner of your dreams!
Don't delay! Packages are selling out fast! Enquire now with
your customer services representative!"*

CHATPATI PLACED the brochure back on the seat. Nair looked distinctly uncomfortable.

"I didn't know you were in the marriage market, Vasanth," he said, struggling to keep a straight face.

"Well," Nair said, sounding defensive, "my mother is always going on at me about marriage. I thought I might send this to her, you know, to keep her quiet."

"Looks pricey," Chatpati said, "but I daresay your parents can afford it. Acres of land, did you say? The price of coconuts being what it is, a cruise to the Maldives should be no problem at all for you."

"Metro Station, sir," the driver said over the intercom.

Inspector Chatpati waved the vehicle off. He didn't bother to hide the grin. Vasanth Nair looked straight ahead and did not wave back.

CHAPTER 12
FIRST INFORMATION RECEIVED

All seemed well with Nirmala when Chatpati returned home. Neither mentioned the events of the previous evening. Chatpati looked over some kitchen brochures with enthusiasm and complimented her on her choices. Dinner comprised the leftovers from the ill-fated soiree. When he woke the next day, breakfast was waiting for him and he was seen out the door with a hug. All seemed well with the world again.

At the Utilities Building, the blind lift-operator was absent, his replacement a smelly, callow youth who didn't look up from his phone as Chatpati got in. The lift doors opened on the fourteenth floor.

"Twenty-fourth floor! Not fourteenth!" Chatpati barked. "Wake up! Buffoon!" The youth leapt off his stool and got it right the second time.

Chatpati pushed through the revolving doors into the studio bar. There was an old Sikh gentleman hammering on the bar with his fists. Chatpati raised an eyebrow, but the desk constable Jaswant Singh was writing with such concentration that he didn't even notice the Inspector.

Activity in the restaurant was at fever pitch. There were only a few days before the Civil Nuisance Unit went live and there was a lot to do. Chatpati checked things were ticking over as they should, then headed for the stairs. A shout stopped him in his tracks.

"Sir!" It was Jaswant Singh, hurrying towards him, waving a form. "Sir! We have our first FIR[1]!"

"But we're not open yet!" Nair said, wandering over. He looked at Chatpati. "Right? We're not open?"

All activity stopped, all attention focused on the Inspector. Chatpati took the FIR and read it.

REPORT OF
FIRST INFORMATION RECEIVED (FIR)
OF A COGNISABLE OFFENCE
(Under Section 154 of the Criminal Procedure Code)

Police Station: CNU, Bangalore

- **Personal details of the Complainant/Informant:**
- **Name:** Col. Rajvir Singh
- **Father's/Husband's name:** Major Ravi Singh (deceased)
- **Address:** 3/2 Embassy Towers, Infantry Road
- **Phone/number & fax:** +91 7872332211
- **Email:** none
- **Place of occurrence:** Cubbon Park, near entrance on CK Jaffer Sharief Road
- **Date & hour of occurrence:** 3rd February, 2020, 7.45 am
- **Nature of offence:**

- Assault or criminal force to a woman with intent to outrage her modesty
- Assault or criminal force in attempt to commit theft of property carried by a person
- **Section:** 354, 356
- **Particulars of property (in case one has got stolen):** Hockey stick, mobile phone
- **Description of accused:** Indian male, mid-twenties, medium height, dark hair, dark eyes, unshaven, wearing khaki trousers and singlet. Crescent scar on neck. Smelling of alcohol.
- **Details of witnesses (if any):** Miss Gurpreet Kaur, aged 16 years (victim)
- **Complaint: briefly lay down facts regarding the incident reported in an accurate way**
- Returning from hockey practice at Chinnaswamy Stadium at approximate time of incident, victim (Miss Gurpreet Kaur) was accosted by accused inside entrance of Cubbon Park near King Edward statue. Accused appeared from behind bushes, laid hands on victim and molested her person by such laying of hands. Victim gave a shout, struck accused with hockey stick and fled, leaving behind hockey stick and mobile phone. She was found by a jogger who went with her to site of assault but accused had fled along with hockey stick and phone. Jogger accompanied her to her grandparents' house. Grandfather has come to make complaint.

CONSTABLE SINGH BROUGHT the grandfather up to Chatpati's office. Despite his seventy-four years of age, the Colonel still had the bearing of a military man, his back ramrod straight. He was furious.

"It's outrageous, Inspector! Absolutely outrageous! What is this city coming to?"

Colonel Singh continued in this vein until a tumbler of tea arrived. The drinking of it calmed him somewhat. When he resumed, his tone was more measured.

"My son and his wife are stationed in Kashmir. My son is a captain in the infantry. Gurpreet, my granddaughter, studies at college here in Bangalore and has been staying with us for the last two years."

Colonel Singh took another sip. "She is a good girl. Studious, homely, no boyfriends. She is top of her class in Economics. Thrice a week she attends morning hockey practice at Chinnaswamy Stadium. She is on the State Youth Team, you know. She usually takes a shortcut through Cubbon Park on her way back. It is light by then and should be safe for girls. It has always been so. Always! Until today!"

Nair had been reading the FIR. He set it down. "Disgraceful!" he said, shaking his head. That set the Colonel off again.

"Yes!" the Colonel shouted, slamming his tumbler down on the desk. "Exactly! That's what I thought! So I came straight here."

"How did you hear about us, Colonel?" Chatpati asked. "We aren't yet officially open for business."

"I heard the Justice Minister on the news the other day," the Colonel replied. "That's good, I said to my wife. That's exactly what this city needs! Someone to enforce the law! To crack down on this kind of rowdyism! Too much of it about these days. Though I never thought, in a thousand years, that I would have to call on you. So I took an auto. Chatpati, I said to the driver, the Inspector, the Civil Nuisance. He brought me straight here!"

Nair stifled a smirk. Chatpati shot him a warning look.

The Colonel glanced at them both. "Why? Was I wrong to come? Will you not look into this? Because, if not, I know the Comm—"

"Have no fear, Colonel," Chatpati replied. "We may not officially be open for business, but we are always open for crime."

Chatpati walked the Colonel back to the saloon bar. He handed him off to Jaswant Singh.

"Get the Colonel an auto," Chatpati said. "And make sure we have the Colonel's contact details."

The team was waiting for him under the disco ball, Hemanth twitching with excitement.

"Are we go, Inspector?" Hemanth said. "The drones are ready. Garuda One and Two are powered up."

Out on the decking, sixteen sets of rotors cleaved the air.

"Go to it," Chatpati said. "Set the search area around the Cubbon Park perimeter. If you get nothing after a few sweeps, extend south to Hudson Memorial, west to the Racecourse, and east to Trinity. Look for a man with a hockey stick."

"How about a ground patrol?" Nair said, motorcycle helmet at the ready. "A rapid response force. I can lead it. On motorbike. I've just taken delivery of my Bullet[2]. We can be ready to spring on the miscreant once you've located him."

Chatpati nodded. "Good. Take four constables, Vasanth." A number had already stepped forward.

"We can track the stolen mobile phone," Raj said. "If it's still on. Should be easy enough to triangulate the approximate location from the cell masts. That'll help narrow down the search."

"Excellent," Chatpati said. "Do it. Liaise with Vasanth's ground team. Seema, send the suspect's description to Traffic units in the vicinity. And upload the FIR to PoliceNet. Let's get it moving. Our best chance to catch him is now. He might still be in the area."

Nair and his quartet made for the lifts, strapping their batons on. The two drones rose into the air with a whine and swooped away like raptors down MG Road, heading for the park.

The atmosphere in the CNU had changed. Chatpati could feel it, that sharp, clean charge in the air just before the monsoon breaks, the promise of something live and dangerous. It infected them all; there was a new energy about the team as they set about their work.

Chatpati resisted the urge to hang about. These things took their own course and wearing the parquet down would not advance the cause any.

Back in his office, Chatpati went through Raj and Nair's analysis of the evidence in the alleged poisoning cases. There was no mistake. It was exactly as they had said. Three cases of suspected poisoning every other week, at or near the same three locations. All on a Tuesday. It was too much to be a coincidence.

He looked through the medical records of the first three cases, the ones who had died. Two had been immigrant labourers, one a street sweeper employed by the Municipal Corporation, the other a day labourer who worked at Russell Market. The street sweeper had taken ill near St. Gregory's Hospital in the east and died some minutes after being rushed into their Casualty. The day labourer was about to begin a day of moving produce about the market with his handcart. Three weeks on, it was likely their bodies would have been reclaimed by their families and taken home to be burned or buried. It would take a lot of work to find their families and probably little purpose to it.

The third death was of a junior finance executive named Mohan Rao. Rao had a Bangalore address: ParkVue Apartments, a stone's throw from Cubbon Park. Chatpati looked up the telephone number and was just about to ring when he heard shouting from the restaurant. It was a male voice. There was a lot of swearing.

He flung open the door just as Raj rushed up the stairs.

"We found him," Raj panted. "We've got him."

They watched from the walkway as the saloon doors clattered open. The ground patrol team entered with Vasanth Nair in the lead. Nair still had his motorcycle helmet on. He held a hockey stick in one hand, the heel resting on one shoulder, like the mace of some mythical warrior returning from battle.

The constables followed with less majesty, largely because they had to grapple with the sweaty lout doing his best to wriggle out of their grip. Their captive wore khaki trousers, ripped in parts, and a white singlet streaked with dirt and blood. The suspect's hands were cuffed behind him. His tongue, however, was unrestrained.

"Bastards!" he shouted. "Sons of whores! Your mothers were—"

Nair wheeled and dealt the man an open-handed slap on the cheek. The sound split the air. The captive fell to his knees. The constables dragged him to his feet again just as Nair set up for a backhand on the rebound.

"Enough!" Chatpati shouted. "That will do."

By the time Chatpati and Raj had made it down, the captive was flat on his back on the parquet. He smelt of old sweat and cheap liquor.

"This is the man," Nair said, pointing with the hockey stick. "See the scar. He was carrying this," he raised the hockey stick," and this." He produced a mobile phone. The screen was cracked.

"We triangulated the phone," Raj explained. "Still within the Cubbon Park area. The drones picked him up, sneaking through the cricket pitch behind the YMCA."

"I was just outside the stadium when Raj called," Nair continued. "I zoomed up the road and got a visual on the idiot just past St. Martha's Hospital. I hung back until the boys caught up in their auto-rickshaws. Then we nabbed him." Nair lifted the stick off his shoulder. "He had a go at Krishna there with this, but drunkards don't swing all that well."

"Process him," Chatpati said to Raj. "Then lock the idiot up. Get a photo of him so that the Colonel's granddaughter can identify him. I'll let the Colonel know."

Raj looked nonplussed.

"Well?" Chatpati said. "What is it?"

"Where?" Raj said. "Where do we lock him up?"

After much head-scratching, they laid the suspect out on his back on the conference table in one of the private suites. A handcuff was passed around each wrist and ankle, the other end secured to a table leg. Spread-eagled on a table, the suspect looked like an untidy reproduction of Vetruvian Man. It was undignified, Chatpati thought, but it would have to do. The Utilities Building carpenter was summoned from his subterranean cubbyhole to fit a bolt and padlock to the door.

The Colonel's granddaughter made a positive identification by SMS. They requested a police van to transport the miscreant to the Central Jail.

ACP Srinivasan rang soon after.

"Chikka Rajan," the ACP said, without so much as a good afternoon. "I hear you've got him in custody. It flagged up on the computer."

"Oh, is that who he is?" Chatpati said. "Is he important?"

"Part of the Raja Market crew. That's Hosur Reddy's gang," the ACP said. "The word on the street is that Reddy's thrown Chikka Rajan out. Too much womanising and drinking. Major Crimes is extremely interested in Rajan. As an informant. They've been looking for a way into the market gangs. Send him over to Central as soon as."

The ACP paused. "I thought your Unit didn't start till next week. Bit keen, aren't you, Chatpati? Out of character."

"Crime doesn't stop, sir, so neither do we."

"Humph. Good slogan. Get it printed. Put it above your door. Might inspire your men." The ACP's tone dripped with sarcasm.

"Oh, we're inspired enough, thanks."

"How's that fellow Nair working out? Any use?"

Chatpati thought for a moment. "So far, so good."

"Ha! Get that printed out for above your door as well. Might inspire you!"

Srinivasan rang off with a cackle.

Chatpati had a sour taste in his mouth. He could see that the CNU would get zero credit for this job. That rankled. However, if the Unit had showed anything today, it was that they were up to the task.

At twelve noon precisely, the lunch he had ordered arrived, borne by three sweating men in restaurant livery.

"Chicken biryani and chicken kebabs," the Inspector

announced from the walkway. "To celebrate our first successful case. Everyone dig in. I'll join you shortly. Don't look so put out, Vasanth - I haven't forgotten the token vegetarian. Vegetable pulao for you. And Gobi Manchurian[3]. I hope you like cauliflower. I've never met a vegetarian who doesn't."

Even Chikka Rajan got a plate of biryani and cleared it before the custody van arrived. He gave the Inspector an unsteady salute as they hauled him off.

Nair shook his head at the Inspector in disapproval.

"What?" Chatpati said, spearing a kebab. "Even criminals need to eat."

CHAPTER 13
LIFE INTERRUPTED

After lunch, Seema told Chatpati that Traffic Division had declined the request for a Hoysala.

"There's a dignitary in town," Seema said. "They're all deployed diverting traffic."

Chatpati looked out through the windows. It was far too hot to walk.

"No problem," Nair said. "I'll take you. The Bullet needs running in. Where are we headed?"

"Walton Road," Chatpati replied. The prospect of riding pillion behind Nair alarmed him. "But I don't have a helmet. It's fine. We'll just take an auto."

"Helmet shmelmet," Nair returned. "You're a police inspector. Your hat is your helmet. No one's going to knock us down." Nair considered what he had just said. "Well, if they do, they better kill us both because otherwise I'll thrash them silly. And I'm a skilled rider. Nothing to fear. Let's go."

Walton Road was six minutes away by auto-rickshaw, but Nair managed it in three. He split traffic like a cheetah splitting a herd of gazelles. Chatpati clung onto his hat for decorum and onto Nair for dear life. Nair was not so much a skilled motorcyclist as one no other road user dared to come near. The effect was much the same.

ParkVue apartments was one of those rare modern Bangalorean architectural developments that actually delivered what it promised; it actually had a view of the park. It was just around the corner from the Lamborghini showroom, a steel cake-slice of a building with decked balconies and a feature living wall of foliage plants. The living wall looked terminal for lack of watering. Everything else about ParkVue shouted 'prestige', from the marble foyer to the besuited receptionist, who sprang to his feet as the policemen entered.

The manager was summoned.

"Very sorry," the manager said, clutching his hands. "Inspector – Chatpati, is it?"

"Lackest thou wisdom?" Nair said. "Hast thou not heard the acclamations of the venerable Justiciary Chatpati? The Nuisance Civilian Brigade? The declarations have been heralded on the telescope."

The manager blinked several times. Once he had figured out what Nair had meant, he bobbed his head.

"Yes, yes. Of course. Very sorry. Very sorry." The head bobbing stopped when Mohan Rao was mentioned. "Ah, yes. Very sad. Very sad. It was myself on duty when he died. I let the paramedics into his apartment. He did not answer the doorbell. Because he had passed away."

They established Rao had died within approximately thirty minutes of returning to the building.

"He went jogging every morning," the receptionist said. "Always exactly on time. That day, when he came back, he looked unwell. Very pale. Shaky. He was holding his stomach. I was also here. He was a very fine man. Always said good morning to everyone. Very sad."

"We'd like to see his flat," Chatpati said. "I assume it's unoccupied."

The manager and receptionist exchanged a look.

"Well, no," the manager said after a second. "It is occupied. Currently."

"Verily?" Nair said. "By whom? The corpse was not marriage, nay?" The manager looked distinctly apprehensive. "Declaim, human! This is not the hour for bashfulness!"

"The apartment is occupied," the manager said. "It's not his wife." He paused. "Perhaps the best term is 'female friend'?"

"You mean girlfriend," Chatpati said. "Just use the word, man. It's the 21st century. Living with someone you're not married to is not a crime."

Girlfriend or fiancée, Hamna Shaikh was now a widow in all but name. She was a lawyer in the company at which Mohan Rao had worked. They had met at a team-building event.

There was a framed photograph of the couple on the sideboard, taken at Agra, the Taj Mahal in the background. They leaned into each other, laughing, shoulders touching, hands intertwined. They were due to get married in the New Year. He was Hindu, she Muslim. It had taken two years to bring their parents round to the idea.

"All for nothing," Hamna said to the air. The air made no reply. A single tear made its way down her cheek and fell into her lap. She dashed away the second.

The policemen sat on the edge of their seats, eyes on the floor, as the young woman wept.

"We are sorry to intrude on your loss," Chatpati said.

"We're trying to understand the circumstances around Mr. Rao's death. We were hoping you might help."

She shook her head. "I can't tell you anything about that. I was away on a business trip to Bombay." She looked broken. "If only I had been here."

"You couldn't have done anything," Chatpati said quickly. "You should know that. Whatever killed him killed other people that day. And it happened too quickly for anyone to do anything."

She looked shocked. "There are others? Other people died?"

Chatpati nodded. "Unfortunately, yes. Within an hour of your fiancé. There may have been more deaths that went undetected. Anything you can tell us about him might help us find out what happened."

She looked out through the open doors to the balcony and beyond. Cubbon Park shimmered in the afternoon heat. A kestrel rode its thermals, head cocked, looking for prey.

"You must understand," she said, "Mohan's family is not well off. Mohan was the first to go to university, the first in his family to move away from his hometown, the first to get a good job. Mohan made more in a month than his father ever made in a year. They were so proud of him. And he of them. They had sacrificed a great deal for him and he never forgot it. He never spoke badly of his upbringing. He never tried to hide it." She looked away. "It's what I found so attractive about him."

"His routine gave him mastery over his life. He believed it was why he had been successful in his career. Mohan woke at the same time every day. He ate at the same times. His work wardrobe was always the same. He didn't believe in wasting time on the inconsequential."

"Where would he have been coming back from at 7.30 am on a Tuesday?" Chatpati asked.

"He used to go for a run in Cubbon Park at 7am." She bit her lip. "Used to." She looked away again.

They waited for her to continue. When nothing more was forthcoming and the silence felt unbearable, Nair jumped in.

"Do you know the route he took? Did he have a running partner? Might he have met anyone else?"

She shook her head. "No, but he was meticulous about logging his runs every day on his phone. He had an app. Is it important?"

Nair nodded. "It might be."

She fetched the phone. Nair swiped through it then looked up at Hamna.

"This is very useful," he said. "May we keep this? We will return-"

"Actually," Chatpati broke in, "Sub-Inspector Nair will just copy down the times of Mr. Rao's last, um, most recent run. We don't need to take the phone away."

The policemen rose to take their leave, hats clutched to their chests.

"Please convey our condolences to Mr. Rao's parents," Chatpati said at the door. "And to yours."

She nodded absently, her gaze somewhere distant.

"I'm going to see them next week," she said. "Mohan's parents. I've never been to his hometown. I want to see the places that Mohan spoke about. I may have lost a husband, Inspector, but I don't intend to lose a family."

The policemen said nothing to each other until they were back on the street.

"We could have borrowed the phone," Nair said, half-apologetic. "We would have returned it to her."

Chatpati huffed. "Really, Vasanth. She's lost the person she held dearest in her life. Her future is shattered. Much of what she has left of him is on that phone. An imprint of their moments, their words, their dreams. How could we take that away from her?" Chatpati shook his head. "We'll just have to manage without."

Nair nodded. When he spoke, he was barely audible.

"You're right. In the rendering of things into their parts, I sometimes forget how terrible loss is." He shook himself. "What now?"

Chatpati pointed down the road. Cubbon Park glowed in the distance, the leaves of its trees iridescent in the noonday sun. "Let's go for a walk. And see if we can trace Mohan Rao's last route."

They made their way along the pavement towards the park entrance on Kasturba Road. Chatpati pointed up at the Marriott as they passed.

"That's where the Austrian couple stayed," he said. "Within a stone's throw of Rao's flat. Mohan Rao and the Brauns visited the park. There must be a connection here. Keep your eyes peeled."

No sooner had they stepped through the iron gateway than the city behind them seemed to melt away. It was like entering another world. The incessant horns and squealing brakes faded away to be replaced by birdsong. The air was instantly cool, the sunlight filtering through leaf, its brutal heat so tempered. A skittering breeze played with shrubs and earlobes. Schoolchildren scampered on the grass and grappled up tree trunks, their voices bright. Office-workers lunched on benches. A labourer dozed in the shade. A park worker tortured grass with a rake.

Nair had his notebook out, but kept getting distracted by botany.

"Rao went up this avenue at about 7am," he said, "heading towards that statue there. Oh, look, those are rain trees. Genus Samanea, I think. The leaves fold up during thunderstorms. These look at least a century old."

The avenue ended at a garden island, from which smaller paths radiated out to all corners of the park. The island was dominated by a pedestal on which stood a marble statue. Chamraja Wodiyar the Tenth, Maharajah of Mysore, gazed out over their heads with benign grace, right hand grasping the belt over his robes, the left on his walking stick.

Mohan Rao's circuit had taken in all the rulers. He had proceeded north-east through a grove of feathery Malayan Badminton Ball trees ("Parkia biglandulosa. The fruit look like shuttlecocks.") to another statue on a plinth.

A court of stately jacarandas in full bloom surrounded King Edward. By comparison to his botanical retinue, His Imperial Majesty looked ill-tempered, his marble jowls heavy, his thighs fat and unflattering in his garters. Someone had chalked 'khalnayak[1]' on the pedestal.

Queen Victoria lurked in a grove of Moreton bay chestnuts, the Sovereign's Orb in one hand. She, too, looked grumpy, perhaps because her stony gaze was fixed, immovably, on the crush of cars jousting for parking space in the solitary strip of tarmac by the gate.

Finally, Rao had run past Sheshadri Iyer, Second Dewan of Mysore State, fenced off from the hoi polloi by railings with fleur de lis embellishments. Ranks of roses stood prickly guard. The policemen completed the circuit, arriving back at the Maharajah.

"He did three circuits, the same route thrice," Nair said. "On the move the whole time. He only stopped once. Right here. At 7.30am. The app then shows him moving off again five minutes later, heading back to his apartment."

"He was dead within an hour," Chatpati said. "So he didn't stop anywhere else. What would cause a jogger to pause here?"

Facing the Maharajah was a roundabout with a blue fountain inset. Beyond the roundabout lay a paved verge, protected from traffic by concrete bollards. On the paving, a pair of enterprising fruit vendors had set up tables stacked with plastic trays of Kashmiri apples, guava and sweet lime. Business was brisk. There was a queue, the patrons retiring with their purchases to benches in the shade. The policemen walked over.

Nair showed Mohan Rao's photo to the vendors. They examined it, then shook their heads.

"7am?" one asked. "We're not here at that time, sir. There aren't many customers then. We open up here at 9 o'clock. The only vendor here that early in the morning is Senthil. He's packed up for the day. He's sold out. It's a hot day, so his business has been good."

"What does he sell?" Chatpati asked. Nair tapped the Inspector on the shoulder and pointed. The answer was obvious before the trader answered.

In one corner of the verge, near the solitary grey dustbin, lay a small pile of glistening green husks.

The trader made a chopping movement with his hand. "Tender coconuts, sir. For drinking." He followed Nair's arm. "Yes, Senthil is supposed to take the husks with him, but he had no space on his cart, so he left a small amount behind. I will tell him tomorrow the police were asking. Please don't fine him for littering, sir. He will clear any mess up tomorrow, no problem. He is a decent fellow. From Tamil Nadu."

"Actually," Chatpati said, "don't mention us, please. He is not in any trouble, but it is important we speak to him. Agreed?"

The trader nodded. "As you say, sir."

They headed back to ParkVue apartments to retrieve Nair's bike.

"It's too much of a coincidence," Nair said. "The German lady must have drunk her coconut water at that spot. From that vendor."

"And Rao," Chatpati said. "After a run in the park, what could be better? Coconut water is supposed to be full of electrolytes and stuff, good for athletes."

"And within an hour, both became unwell." Nair looked worried. "But that makes little sense. Tender coconuts don't go off. I have drunk hundreds. I have never fallen ill." He looked around. "Perhaps there's another vendor here on Tuesdays? Some unhygienic fried food fellow. Samosas or pakoras. That would make more sense. Adulterated oil. No hand-washing." Nair shuddered. "That's why I steer clear of fried snacks."

Chatpati nodded. "Even if you're right, that still doesn't explain why there was only one victim on each of those Tuesdays? If the tender coconuts were off, or the samosas or pakoras, surely there should have been an epidemic."

Nair mounted his bike and kicked the Bullet into life. The thing sounded like a herd of rutting water buffalo. Its rumble shook the air.

"Not getting on?" Nair shouted.

Chatpati shook his head. He tried to restrict close shaves to only one a day. He'd exhausted his quota. "I've a few errands to run," he lied. "You carry on. Are you up for an early start tomorrow?"

"Of course," Nair said. "What's the plan?"

"Let's meet at the Maharajah's statue. At 7am. I want to speak to this Senthil. Then we do a circuit of the other two hotspots. The hospital and Russell Market. Don't wear your uniform. We're going incognito."

"All for the sake of some coconuts," Nair said, backing the motorcycle out. He pointed it out the gates and put it in gear. "It'll be filthy pakoras. Or samosas. I'm sure of it! See you tomorrow!"

He slipped the clutch and shot off. Chatpati watched him weave through traffic and disappear round the corner. Chatpati wished he shared the Sub-Inspector's certainty.

CHAPTER 14

PARK LIFE

nspector Chatpati arrived early the next morning, getting off the Metro at the Vidhana Soudha station at 6.32am. He slipped into the park through the entrance off Dr. Ambedkar Road. The morning mist still clung to the ground. It swallowed the sound of his footsteps. There seemed to be no other living being around.

As he passed the High Court, the statue of Sir Mark Cubbon floated above the gloom, the legs of his mount lost in the haze. Against the backdrop of the red columns of the courthouse, Sir Mark appeared to be a wraith guarding the gates of Hell. Chatpati shuddered and quickened his pace. His pulse rate settled as he reached the bandstand. Just beyond stood the Maharajah's statue and further, the avenue they had walked up the day before. He hid behind a tree trunk. And watched.

The vendor had already set up on the paved verge. His cart had four bicycle wheels, a push-handle and a bright red canopy that proclaimed this to be 'Senthil Orgenik Tender Coconut Water' in English and Kannada. Senthil was thin and dark, with neatly parted hair, and unusually well turned out for a street vendor. He wore a pressed pair of beltless trousers and a plain long-sleeved shirt buttoned at the wrists.

Senthil took great care arranging his coconuts into three pyramids. In the fifteen minutes it took for sun's rays to dispel the mist, the vendor sold four: three to joggers and one to a pensioner in a flat cap walking a dog. Chatpati watched as Senthil hacked the top off a coconut with three precise blows of his machete before piercing the shell with the blade's curved tip. He inserted a straw into the hole before the coconut was handed over and payment taken.

The joggers ran off, so it was impossible for the Inspector to tell whether they had become corpses. The pensioner settled on a bench nearby to read his newspaper. He was still alive when Nair thundered up the avenue on his Bullet.

Even in plain clothes, Nair looked like a Bollywood policeman, thanks to the mirrored Aviator sunglasses and the belligerence with which he kicked the stand out from the motorcycle. He smoothed his moustache as he stalked over to the stall. Chatpati stepped out of the tree-line at the same time, catching Nair's eye as he did so. Senthil's attention was focussed entirely on the advancing Nair and so did not notice the Inspector approach from behind.

"Good morning, sir," Senthil said, in English, to Nair. "Tender coconut water, sir? One hundred per cent organic. Very best quality."

"Hmm," Nair said, playing the picky customer with no difficulty. "Organic? What does that mean?"

"No chemicals used in growing, sir. Natural. Please try."

Nair examined the three pyramids. "Very expensive. And why the difference in price?"

"Is quality, sir," Senthil replied. "Most expensive one is

from Mandya, sir, in Karnataka. Sixty-five rupees. Middle quality is from Tamil Nadu, sir. Sixty rupees. This one is Kerala, sir. Only fifty rupees. Mandya one is best, sir."

"Ridiculous!" Nair replied, scowling. "Kerala is the best quality! I should know." He jabbed a thumb at his chest. "I'm from Kerala. I grow coconuts."

Senthil wagged his head. He knew enough about business than to disagree with a customer.

"Sir is correct. Kerala is best, but in Bangalore people are thinking Mandya is best, so I am providing that one, sir. Top quality Kerala coconut is there, sir, available from wholesale market, but price is too high. Seventy-five rupees. Bangalore people are not paying that much, sir."

Chatpati had had enough of this coconut discourse. He tapped Senthil on the shoulder. The vendor spun around, startled.

Chatpati held out his ID. "Police. I want to talk to you. This," he pointed at Nair, "is Sub-Inspector Nair. I am Inspector Chatpati."

Senthil quailed. "Sir, I have licence, sir." He pulled open a drawer built into the cart and produced a laminated sheet of paper. "From Municipal Corporation, sir. All is correct."

Chatpati waved it away. "We're not here to check your licence."

"Ah!" Senthil's face brightened. "Sorry. I understand. You are thirsty, no? Policemen are so busy, walking here and there in hot sun. Please! Allow me to serve you. Mandya? One for each? Or two for each? Let me get for you. Free." He reached for a coconut. "It is my pleasure. For police."

"Stop," Chatpati said. "We're not here to extort your coconuts. We want to ask you some questions."

Nair had his phone out. "You know this man?"

Senthil studied the photograph on the screen, then

looked from Nair to Chatpati. He wrung his hands. "Sir," he began.

Nair grabbed him by the collar. "Don't play the fool. Do you know him? Or not?"

Chatpati waved a hand at Nair. Nair released the quivering Senthil.

"Listen, Mr. Senthil," Chatpati said, "just tell the truth and answer the question. Do you know this man?"

"Yes, sir," Senthil said, his voice trembling. "He is Mr. Mohan. He is always come in the morning, sir, for jog. He is always buy a coconut after jog. Very good man." Senthil paused. "He is always buying one coconut but paying for two."

Nair raised an eyebrow. "Why would he pay for two?"

Senthil smiled. "Sir, he is saying to give one to beggars. So, every day I give one. In Mr. Mohan's name. But I not seen Mr. Mohan for one or two weeks, sir. I think he is go on holiday, to his native place. Udupi, sir. He told me this. Also, he is working for big bank." Senthil wagged his head. "He is a good man, sir. Many people buy and go only. Mr. Mohan likes talking."

"Did he buy a tender coconut from you the last time you saw him?" Chatpati asked.

"Yes, sir," Senthil replied, looking from Nair to the Inspector. "Yes. Why? Is problem?"

"Yes. There is." the Inspector said. "Mr. Mohan died an hour later. An hour after drinking your tender coconut water. What do you know about that?"

After ten minutes of hard questioning, it was clear that Senthil knew very little. Senthil hailed from Vellore in the state of Tamil Nadu and had moved from to Bangalore to work in a factory. The factory had closed, and he had been laid off. One of the three other men that shared Senthil's upstairs squat in Sultangunta had a friend who was selling his pushcart. Senthil used his savings to buy the cart and learned his trade on the streets. Through another coconut vendor, he had learned which civil servants in the Municipal Corporation to pay off to get a licence.

Senthil had been operating in Cubbon Park for just over a year. He bought his produce from the wholesale market in Silkboard at 5.30am. It took him an hour to push his handcart to his patch in the park. On a good day, he made triple his expenditure. It was many times more than he had ever made from factory work.

Senthil had been able to send money home to his parents, enough for a dowry for his younger sister. He showed them her wedding photos on his phone. Now, he was saving up for his own wedding. His parents were looking for a bride for him, now that his prospects had risen. Senthil had found another room that he and his wife could live in after marriage. He was thinking of buying a second cart and hiring an apprentice. Tender coconuts had been good for him. He seemed saddened to hear of Mohan Rao's death. It all seemed genuine.

"How do you know English?" Nair asked.

"I learn, sir," Senthil replied. "Many tourists are come. From foreign. White people. Big hotel is there. Marriott Hotel, sir. They speaking English so I learn. One man is there, sir, he works for NGO[1]. It is call StreetEatz. Mr. Shaji is his good name. He is looking after us coconut sellers. He is giving advice. He is saying organic is better for tourist market, sir. Big trend. So I sell only organic. He is giving me a book for English learn. He is giving class to coconut sellers in English speaking. He is speaking to me in English only. For practice. Slowly I learn, sir. I speaking English." Senthil smiled a shy smile. "I also giving tourist help on park.

Where going. What seeing. I tell them to see roses garden, to see statue, Maharajah, Queen, King, to see Vidhana Soudha. Free, sir. I no charge. I do this for service. For Bangalore. Bangalore is good help for me. So I help Bangalore."

Chatpati felt a grudging admiration for the man. Senthil had made something of himself with very little.

"Is there a problem?" The policemen turned to see a walking stick raised at them. The wielder was the pensioner with the dog. The newspaper was now tucked under his arm. The dog, a well-fed mongrel with the scars of a street fighter, growled at them, revealing fully functional teeth. "What are you doing to that man?"

"No problem at all, sir," Chatpati replied. "We were just discussing coconuts. And, since we've taken up so much of your time and business, Mr. Senthil, it seems only fair that we buy some. Four Mandya, please. One for my colleague, one for this gentleman here and one for the dog."

Senthil reached for his machete. "And number four, sir?"

"For the beggar," Chatpati replied. "In memory of Mr. Mohan."

"Very kind," the pensioner replied. "I thought you were bullying him. Extorting money, you know. Goes on a lot around here. Bloody gangsters everywhere. So I thought I would check."

Senthil fashioned a bowl for the dog by hacking a spent coconut in half. Rex lapped the coconut water with delight and growled for a refill. This was granted.

Nair licked his lips. "Mm. Almost as good as Kerala, Senthil. Almost as good."

Chatpati handed over three hundred rupees and refused the change. The pensioner bade them a good day.

"The wife will wonder where I got to," he said, tottering off. Rex gave them a warning bark and followed his master.

Chatpati got on the Bullet behind Nair.

"Isn't it reassuring, Vasanth," he said, "that there are still people looking out for the less fortunate? That old chap over there. Just thought he'd find out what was going on. In case we were gangsters."

"Humph," Nair said, over his shoulder. "And what would he have done if we had turned out to be gangsters? Either of us could have laid him out flat."

"I think Rex would have had something to say about that."

"If Rex is still alive, you mean," Nair replied. "If the coconut did it, mongrel and master might be lying stiff at the gate."

They took care to check as they exited the park, but, happily, there were no corpses to be seen, canine or otherwise.

CHAPTER 15

BUBBLE, TOIL AND TROUBLE

They found much threat to human life at the two other locations that morning. At St. Gregory's Hospital, the perils comprised a missing manhole cover and a bare high-voltage wire on a junction box. At Russell Market, the chief hazards were packs of rats and vagrant cats that dragged the meat market's discarded offal through the vegetable market's produce.

By the end of it all, though, even Sub-Inspector Nair had to admit that the only factor common to all three locations was tender coconuts.

There were two coconut sellers outside the hospital entrance and at least eight in the maze of streets around the old market. The policemen spent the morning going from one to the other. At the end of it all, they had become far more acquainted with the tender coconut trade than they wished to be.

None of the vendors had heard of any poisonings. All denied any involvement. They shook their heads at the victim photos the policemen showed them, eyes flicking away without a second glance.

"They're afraid," Nair observed. "Of something. I wonder if they suspect who we are."

The policemen were sipping tea from clay tumblers. The chaiwallah[1] had set up shop under the single row of trees that fringed the road leading to the main square in Russell Market. Nair had parked his bike in the shade and sat side-saddle on the Bullet. Chatpati reclined against a tree trunk, one foot on a gnarled root that had clawed its way out of the tarmac.

"You're pretty bad at playing anything else," Chatpati replied. The tea was hot and sweet. "Your tender coconut aficionado role failed to pass muster. The moment you open your mouth, it's obvious you're from out of town. And a cop. And is it surprising no one said anything? Who trusts the police? I don't."

"Oh, I don't know," Nair said. "I think my coconut knowledge impressed a couple of those vendors. I struck a chord, I think."

Chatpati almost choked. "Chord? What was it you said again? 'Fellow, wherefore cometh this coconut?'"

Nair grimaced. "Well, perhaps that was a bit off-key. It's not my command of the Kannada language, though. It's almost as if the vendors knew we were coming. Guarded looks. Monosyllabic answers. I mean, just look at this place. It's teeming with people. If someone had dropped dead here, as we know at least one person did, it would have been all over the neighbourhood before the blood had congealed."

It was afternoon. The square a short distance beyond was a snarl of moving metal and swarming flesh. Stalls and shopfronts formed three sides, the pavements invisible under the stacks of cartons and household goods for sale.

The muezzin's call to prayer echoed along the alleyways from the minarets of the Juma Masjid two streets along. Foot traffic was heavy: tradesmen, housewives, wholesalers. Auto-rickshaws rattled in and out with passengers and cargo. A bullock had decided to take a nap in the middle of the road, splitting traffic. The heat surged in waves, a living thing, birthed of sunlight and fed by exhausts.

"No," Nair said, "they fear something. Or someone."

A small boy trotted up to them. The boy had been working at the very last stall they had visited, which was only a heap of coconuts under a makeshift tarpaulin canopy. The boy tugged at Chatpati's belt and held out his hand. Chatpati fished in his pocket for a coin to give him, then realised the boy had something in his palm. It was a mobile phone, the cheap kind with buttons. Chatpati took the phone. The boy ran off.

Nair watched the boy dart away through the traffic. "What was that about?"

"We'll soon find out," the Inspector said. "This is the way it's done in Sultangunta. Someone wants to talk to us. Privately."

Chatpati looked around. "This used to be my patch, you know. Back when I was a humble Sub-Inspector. It was my second posting. I learnt a lot about policing. It was like learning to firefight by being deployed to Hell."

Nair's curiosity was aroused. Before Nair could ask him questions, the phone rang. Chatpati answered, listened and rang off without saying a word. He bent down and placed the phone on the tree root by his foot.

"Let's go," he said to Nair. "We're walking."

Nair leapt off the bike. "Where? And what about the phone?"

"The phone will be picked up. Where we have to go is not far, but I promise you, you'll hate it."

Nair did. For a staunch Hindu vegetarian, the shortcut through the alleyways bordering the Beef Market was akin to a ramble through Naraka[2]. The fresh smell of hanging meat and the buzzing of flies brought out Nair's handkerchief. He clapped it to his face.

They had to thread their way along cracked pavements teeming with humanity, brushing shoulders and knocking elbows. There seemed to be a hundred tiny restaurants along the narrow streets, all open fronted with dark, smoky interiors and formica tables. Each restaurant had annexed a good portion of pavement with cooking apparatus. The smoke from charcoal fires seeped through their clothing.

Chatpati kept up a running commentary as they hurried along. "Beef biryani" to a steaming cauldron of golden rice studded with chunks of meat. "Lamb seekh kebab" to a great grill sizzling with skewers of mince. "Egg paratha" to an iron skillet the size of a carom board bearing stacks of burnished bread, glistening with butter.

By the time they turned the corner and ducked into a quieter alleyway, Nair's complexion was puce.

"We're going in here," Chatpati said.

The restaurant was only three shoulder breadths wide, its length that of three tall men laid head to toe. There was a row of tables and benches along one wall. The only other occupants were a pair of day labourers, each making rapid progress through a mound of rice and a pool of vegetable curry. The proprietor sat at the entrance behind a glass case containing cigarette packets. He watched them with a beady eye.

"Sorry about that," Chatpati said to Nair. They had sat down facing each other, Chatpati facing out into the street.

"Speed was of the essence and that was the shortest route. This place is vegetarian, you'll be pleased to know. Let me buy you lunch. Dosa OK?"

Nair's appetite, thought permanently exiled by the sight of kidneys and carcasses, returned with the arrival of his masala dosa. It was crispy and hot, the ghee glistening on its surface, the potato filling moist and yielding. Nair dug in with his fingers. A minute later, someone slipped into the seat beside him.

"I am Avicenna Yousuf," the man said, touching a hand to his chest by way of greeting. He had a ready smile, pixieish eyes and a shock of curly hair under a white Muslim prayer cap. His checked shirt and plain trousers were distinctly unfashionable. There was a ballpoint pen in the shirt pocket.

Avicenna glanced over at the labourers at their lunch before speaking again. "I hope you don't mind talking in English. It is the language least likely to be understood here if overheard."

Chatpati nodded. "Of course. What can we do for you?"

The man smiled. "You have been talking to all the tender coconut sellers in Russell Market, I hear. I was curious as to your reasons."

"I'm sure you know," Chatpati said. "You found us. You must have heard what it was all about."

Avicenna inclined his head. "You are right. I regret to say I have no direct information about the matters that concern you, but I thought it might be useful for you to know about recent connected events."

"What's your interest?" Nair asked, dosa consumption temporarily suspended.

"I own a few stalls," Avicenna replied. "A modest operation, really, but I know all the other vendors and owners in this area. We have a good relationship. It is competitive, this business, but we work together when it is in all our interests."

"Please carry on," Chatpati said. "We're all ears."

Avicenna glanced around again before speaking. "About three months ago, I heard of some people doing the rounds of Russell Market. Like yourselves. They were approaching the owners of all the coconut stalls. I heard they wanted to sign the vendors up to their new business."

"I waited and, sure enough, I, too, was approached. There were two of them. Very young. Smartly dressed. They came in a big car with a driver. They had laptops and the latest mobile phones. The ones with five camera lenses, that cost as much as a motorcycle. I expressed some interest simply to find out what they were after. They took me to a grand buffet lunch at the Taj Hotel. You know it? It is a five-star. Near the racecourse. The lunch was very fine. They showed me their graphs and spreadsheets. Then they made the offer."

"Which was?" Nair said.

"To join them. Join their franchise. A tender coconut water franchise business."

The policemen glanced at each other. "You didn't accept," Chatpati said.

Avicenna shook his head. "No. Their terms were not attractive. I already made more than I would have under their scheme, even with the bonus payment for signing up. Also, I would have had to buy a new cart from them in their livery. When I already own several. Not to mention pay for uniforms, payroll, inventory. Do training in Food Handling and Food Hygiene. A lot of nonsense. And I told them so. You are over-egging this pudding, I said. No one will pay triple to buy coconut water in a packet from a man in a uniform when they can get the same thing, fresh, from a coconut vendor on every street corner. It is a silly idea."

"How did they take that?" Nair asked.

"Not well. At first, they tried to persuade me. Another lunch. This time à la carte. With liquor. I drank juice, of course. Watermelon. Very fine. They came again. And again. But they were getting nowhere with any of the traders."

Avicenna glanced around again. "Then the threats began. At first, only verbal but, early one morning, a couple of rowdies roughed up one of our vendors as he was setting up. Then it happened again a few days later with another vendor. People were running scared."

"What did you do?" Chatpati said. "Of course, you didn't go to the police."

Avicenna chuckled. "What use would that have been? No. I merely brought it to the attention of our local—peace-keepers, shall I say?"

Chatpati nodded. "Peacekeepers. Yes, I'm familiar with the concept. Presumably you pay an 'insurance premium' for such peacekeeping."

Avicenna shrugged. "You know how it works, sir. Our people waited for them. Two days later, the toughs reap-peared. They got a mighty thrashing. They never showed their faces after that. Before our people let them go, we learned the thugs were from Hosur Reddy's gang. They had been paid to intimidate us by some outside party. A contract. They were just underlings, so they did not know who. But we could guess." Avicenna tapped on the table with a finger. "This coconut franchise operation."

"Any problems since?" Nair asked.

"Not a peep," Avicenna replied. "It is as if they have given up but, when I heard some people were asking around, I feared they had come back."

"Which is why you brought those two with you," Chatpati said, pointing with his chin. "The two well-fed fellows across the road. By the juice stall."

There was the merest flash of alarm beneath Avicenna's bonhomie before he shrugged. "It pays to take precautions, sir."

"And?" Chatpati said. "What's your conclusion? About us?"

Avicenna shook his head. "I recognised you, Inspector, when I sat down. I remember you from when you worked here many years ago. Local people called you 'that fair policeman'. They were not referring to your complexion. Which, if you don't mind my saying, is very pleasant. But not fair."

"I don't remember meeting you then," Chatpati said, "but I daresay if we had more time we might come up with a few mutual acquaintances. I might even have arrested some."

Avicenna smiled and shrugged.

"Why tell us all this?" Nair said. "Looks like you've solved your gangster problem."

Avicenna sat back. The calm manner was gone, replaced by something altogether less accommodating. He blinked once before he spoke again.

"It was when I heard what you were asking about that it occurred to me. You were asking about the man who died here. I know of this. He was a manual labourer who rented a cart and made his living moving vegetables from warehouse to market for wholesalers. A poor fellow. Harmed no one."

Avicenna leaned in and lowered his voice. "I thought to myself, if you are asking about him, it means someone killed him." He turned his palms up. "Who will be next? We

THE TENDER COCONUT TAMASHA

are small people, sir. We can look after ourselves on our own turf, but we can't fight things we can't see. I don't think our enemies have given up."

"Who were they?" Chatpati asked. "Your enemies? This franchise operation?"

Avicenna pulled a phone out of his pocket, pressed a button, and held it out. On the screen was a familiar grinning green coconut.

The policemen took a less direct, meat-free route back to Nair's bike.

"I suppose you're going to gloat," Nair said.

"Not at all," Chatpati replied. "The whole idea is quite ridiculous."

"I'm glad you think so. A turf war over coconuts is the stupidest thing I've ever heard."

"A coconut war? Yes, though there have been turf wars over many things in these parts. Ever heard of Kerosene Kumar? No, you wouldn't have. This was back in the days of the ration card system, when every poor household was supposed to receive a free monthly allocation of essentials from the government through Fair Price Shops. You turn up, present your card and collect your allocation. Kerosene Kumar made his fortune subverting that system."

"Apt," Nair said. "Diluted the kerosene, did he?"

"Oh, no," Chatpati replied. "He didn't get that moniker from diluting kerosene. He got it because of the way he disposed of his enemies. He cooked them. Alive. Anyway, with the availability of cheap LPG, the kerosene black market trade died a death."

Nair laughed. "I suppose there's a Gas Govinda running the LPG business!"

"Not Govinda," Chatpati replied, deadly serious.

"Gouda. Gas Gouda. What did you make of our informant, Mr. Avicenna?"

Nair shook his head. "A gangster, clearly. With a personal stake in this. He came to find out what we know. I don't buy his story about this coconut company muscling in. It's far more likely that it was another gang trying to extend their territory."

"You're probably right," Chatpati said. "There's a criminal element at play in many businesses here. However, Avicenna and his ilk are small fish. Bangalore is a huge pond. Avicenna and colleagues are worried. Maybe they should be. Big Money buys Big Trouble."

The small boy was sitting on Nair's bike, playing at being a motorcycle policeman. A crowd of smaller children leapt about around him, begging to be given a go. One tried to climb on, but the boy pushed him off with glee. When the boy saw the policemen approaching, he leapt off and ran away, chased by his followers.

"A future Gas Gouda there," Chatpati said. "They start them young in Sultangunta."

"Where to now?" Nair asked, buckling on his helmet. "CNU?"

"Probably best to touch base," Chatpati replied. "Who knows who's been molesting whom today?"

He waited for Nair to start the bike, then climbed on.

"This thing is very noisy," Chatpati said. "Didn't you want something more modern? A Yamaha? Or a Honda? This feels like it's powered by steam."

"Steam, you say?" Nair replied. "Let's see."

Chatpati saw. And vowed never to mention steam again.

CHAPTER 16
MORE HEAT THAN LIGHT

B y the next morning, word of the Civil Nuisance Unit
was spreading. Raj entered Chatpati's office with a
clipboard list of the morning's reports. He read
from it.

"Fly-tipping in Ashok Nagar, outside the gates of the
office of the local MLA[1]. It was the MLA's secretary who
rang. A report of graffiti on the perimeter wall of the Gallery
of Modern Art. Public urination into the musical fountain
outside the Planetarium. Oh, and a flasher in the Parade
Ground."

"And how do you plan to deal with these reports?"
Chatpati asked.

"Well," Raj replied, looking apprehensive. "I wasn't
sure, so I was waiting for your direction."

"What do you think, Vasanth?" Chatpati said. Nair had
just walked in. Raj read the list out again.

"God!" Nair said. "Is this what we have to deal with?
The first two, fly-tipping and graffiti, are Municipal Corporation problems. Pass that onto them. Public urination and

public indecency are proper crimes. We should deal with those."

"Good," Chatpati said. "See to it. Except I would give the fly-tipping some personal attention. It pays to keep the MLA happy. Send one of the sensible constables to make enquiries. And the flasher is operating on Army grounds. We have no jurisdiction. Pass that on to the Military Police."

Raj wrote on the clipboard. "Which leaves the fountain urination."

"I'll deal with it," Nair said. "Give me the FIR. It'll give me a chance to look around the Planetarium, get to know the locals, practice some Kannada. I think I'm getting the hang of the language."

When Nair had left, Chatpati asked Raj to look into something.

"Coco2Go. The company selling packaged coconut water. Remember the TV advert? See what you can dig up on them. Start with the Registrar of Companies. I want to know when they were set up, corporate structure, directors and especially of any known association with organised crime."

When Raj had left, Chatpati picked up the phone. The ACP had left a message for Chatpati to call.

"Ah, Chatpati." The ACP seemed in an expansive mood. Probably demolished a large breakfast and about to take a nap on that sofa, Chatpati thought. "Just checking up to see how you're getting on with the launch of 'Bangalore's newest police innovation.' Not my words. The leader in the Mirror today. They mention you. In glowing terms. 'Courageous' it says. 'Forthright. A man of action.'"

"First I'm hearing of it," Chatpati replied, deadpan. "I don't read the newspapers."

The ACP clucked. "Naïve, Chatpati, naïve. Take it from me. It won't be long before they're baying for your blood. If I were you, I would use this opportunity to bank some capital with the media. There's a lot of heat about your Nonsense Unit. Use it before it burns you."

"No thanks. I plan to keep my pans out of the fire."

"I thought you'd say that," the ACP replied. "Which is why I've arranged an interview for you. With BTV. Nita Singh herself will do it. A brief slot for their daily news magazine programme. Her producer's terribly keen."

"No. Absolutely not."

"The Justice Minister agrees, Chatpati. I've spoken to him. You'll do it. That's an order. Not from me – I know you'll find some cunning way to disregard that – but from higher up. Just do it. OK?" The ACP did not expect an answer. "Great. The producer will be in touch to fix up a time in the next few days. His name is Derek Mendes. Make yourself available."

"Anything else I can do for you?"

The ACP could not have mistaken Chatpati's tone.

"Oh dear, you sound quite vexed," Srinivasan chuckled. "Too bad. Make the most of the opportunity. Or don't. I don't care. Just do it."

"Yes. Sir."

"Good, good. Well, delightful as it is to speak to you, I must be going. Oh, what's all this business about coconuts?"

Chatpati's eyes narrowed. He took a breath before he spoke. "What coconuts did you have in mind?"

"Don't play the fool. The German tourist. What's going on?"

"Nothing," Chatpati replied. "It's a dead end. Mr. Braun

thought coconut water had poisoned his wife. We looked into it. There's no evidence of anything of the sort. It's implausible."

"Glad to hear it," Srinivasan said. "Stop wasting your time on nonsense like that. You'll be a laughing stock if you're not careful. If you're going to be hanged, don't provide the rope."

"So grateful for your valuable insights, sir," Chatpati said. "First, the burning, then the hanging. Positively medieval."

"Listen to me, you insolent—"

Chatpati put the phone down. He considered what Srinivasan had said for a moment, then rose and went downstairs. He found Raj at his desk, scrolling through screens of text.

"Let's go, Raj," Chatpati said. "Lunch. On me."

They made their way down to the ground floor and headed out the rear entrance of the General Utilities Building onto Residency Road. There was an Andhra restaurant on the corner. They had to queue with the hungry office crowd on the stair leading up to the air-conditioned section on the first floor. It wasn't long, though, before they were shown to a booth by the head waiter in a bowtie. Raj wasn't a vegetarian, as it turned out, so, besides the traditional 'Andhra meals[2]', Chatpati ordered fried fish and the house speciality.

"How are you getting on?" Chatpati asked, sipping at his fresh lime soda[3] (sweet).

"OK, sir," Raj replied. "Fine." He seemed awed to be at lunch with the Inspector. "Thank you for the lunch."

It wasn't meant to be an interrogation, but Chatpati realised he knew very little about the young constable. Raj had grown up in Bangalore. His parents were immigrants from Tamil Nadu, his father a technician at the Water Treatment Plant in Marathahalli, some kilometres to the east. His mother was a housewife, but ran a small business from her kitchen, making fried snacks for sale in the local shops. Raj had a younger sister in college. He, too, was in the marriage market. Like Nair, he was not overly enthused about the prospect.

"Quite right, Raj," Chatpati said. "You're still young. Take some time to get to know what you want out of life first. Though I suspect your parents would rather see you hitched."

Their food arrived with a flourish. First, a freshly washed banana leaf was placed in front of each. Then, a line of junior waiters assembled at their table. The first heaped steaming white rice in the centre of the leaf and spun away. Another waiter whirled in with steel tumblers of sambar, rasam and dhal[4]. The third followed with a trio of steel buckets in one hand containing vepudu, crispy fried okra, pappu, lentils boiled with bottle gourd and pulusu, tomatoes stewed with tamarind. A dab of lime pickle heralded the rearguard, a youth bearing a pitcher of ghee which was ladled over the rice until the diners begged for mercy. Finally, the head waiter returned bearing steel plates of fried fish and the infamous Chicken Guntur, studded with dried red chillies.

Soon, their noses were running. Chatpati dabbed at his with a paper napkin.

"How are you finding Sub-Inspector Nair?" Chatpati asked. Raj went into a coughing fit. Chatpati assumed the dried chillies were not the cause.

"Fine, sir," Raj replied, between sips of fresh lime soda (salt).

"Really?" Chatpati said. "Honest opinion. In confidence."

Raj looked about as if Nair might be lurking in a nearby booth.

"I think he means well, sir. He's full of energy but-"

"But?"

Raj looked downcast. "But he thinks he's the Commissioner already, sir. He lords it over the men. They don't like it. The atmosphere changes when he comes in. He is always talking about his career, what he has done and how he wants to make it up 'the ladder', as he calls it." Raj paused. "I don't think he's planning on staying with us for long, sir. For him, the CNU is a – I don't know the right word, sir."

"Stepping stone?" Chatpati offered.

Raj nodded. "Yes, sir. But," he hurried on, "he is a very dedicated officer, sir. He is not corrupt. Very pure. Like Bhishma[5], sir. In the Mahabharata[6]."

Chatpati laughed. "I'm not sure I could manage the Sub-Inspector living forever. It would be very painful."

Raj grinned, visibly relaxing. "Yes, sir. He is a good man but also a troublesome man. Will he be staying long, sir?" This last tinged with hope.

Chatpati shook his head. "No. I agree with you. He is dedicated, but I think his biggest dedication is to himself. I don't fault him for it—we all need to make our way up in the world. Sub-Inspector Nair is destined for greater things than we can offer, I suspect. Let's try not to obstruct his progress."

Chatpati took another sip. "I need you to keep an eye on him for me, Raj. We've started off well and I don't want our progress to be impeded by Bhishma."

Neither wanted dessert; they felt fit to burst. They

waddled back to the CNU where another message awaited the Inspector.

"From BTV, sir," Seema said, her eyes large. "Derek Mendes. Producer of their news programme. They want to fix up a time for the interview."

They were quick off the bat, Chatpati thought. He found some slots in his calendar and instructed Seema to set it up.

"They have a choice of three dates," he said. "One hour maximum, Seema. And it will be here, at the CNU. I'm not going to their studio." The very thought of having to sit in a make-up chair having foundation applied did not appeal. "And if those dates don't suit, tell them we'll get back to them. And then conveniently forget to do this."

Some hours later, Raj knocked on his door. "I've got some information, sir." He held up a folder. "A preliminary search on the coconut company."

"Take a seat," Chatpati said. "Give me the highlights."

"Quite a young company, sir. Set up just over two years ago. Privately owned. Small board of directors. Offices in the MG Central building, sir, just down MG Road. In two years of trading, they've posted large losses, according to the annual returns."

"Any known criminals?"

"Nothing on the initial screen. The chairman is one K. M. Chandra. His first venture, apparently. He's quite young, only twenty-eight."

Chatpati explained what he and Nair had uncovered in Sultangunta. "An informant suggested it was a corporate operation to corner the tender coconut water market. First, wooing the vendors, then threats, then physical attacks. The man claimed Coco2Go was behind it."

"It seems a bit of a stretch," Raj said. "Perhaps it's a

coincidence. I mean, turf wars are not uncommon in Bangalore."

"I thought likewise," Chatpati said. He got to his feet. "Let's walk off that lunch of ours."

Raj leapt up. "Where to, sir?"

"Reconnaissance. Let's have a look at this coconut company."

CHAPTER 17

THE FUTURE IS BRIGHT, THE FUTURE IS COCONUT

The wrath of the noonday sun had mellowed into sultry sulkiness. Traffic was light and the air was breathable. They stuck to the shade cast by the high-rises along MG Road, skirting peanut sellers and shoe polishers.

The MG Central building was a glistening, steel-ribbed cylinder twenty storeys tall. The old Wesleyan Cathedral huddled in its shadow. A century ago, the British in their sola topis[1] had erected their legacy, the Cathedral, in red brick and Doric columns. Five generations later, the descendants of the brown-skinned natives who had built the Cathedral posted their retort in aluminium and glass. The helicopter landing pad added injury to insult. The Cathedral looked gloomily back to a past as pitted as its plaster, while MG Central stared the future down with a steely eye.

They were nearly in the giant's shadow when Raj asked a question that Chatpati had not quite expected. But should have, as it was only a matter of time before the question was asked. It was always asked.

"What was it like, sir? The Vidhana Soudha Incident?

Was it as made out?" Chatpati shot him a sharp look. Raj almost withered. "Sorry to ask, sir, I was just-"

"Bad," Chatpati replied. "As made out. Everyone asks."

"How did you know what to do? I mean, nothing like that had ever happened before. There was no training manual, no procedure-"

"For a drone attack by eco-terrorists using bio-engineered pesticide? No. There wasn't a manual to deal with that. The site commander was taken out in the first wave. We were without a leader. Someone had to do something. So we did."

Chatpati grimaced. "We should have gone for the children first. Rather than wasting time with the politicians. After all, politicians renew themselves every five years. It is my enduring regret."

"I was wrong to ask, sir," Raj said. "Sorry."

"That's OK," Chatpati said, his eyes fixed on their destination. "No apologies required for the asking of questions. It's our business, after all. Let's see what comes of a little asking in here."

Coco2Go occupied a suite of offices on the fifteenth floor. There was a uniformed guard whose sole job was to hold the glass door open. Chatpati thought that the company's failure to post a profit might be because of the sumptuousness of the office furnishings. The sheer breadth of panelled wood commemorated a genocide of forests. The receptionist's sari blouse was unnecessarily low cut, her attitude unnecessarily high-brow.

She looked them over with faint disdain. "Yes?"

"Police," Raj said, displaying his badge. "We'd like to speak to the Director, Mr. Chandra."

She raised an eyebrow. "Do you have an appointment?"

"No," Raj replied. "We'd like to speak to him all the same. We're investigating a crime."

A second eyebrow joined the first. "Please wait."

The oversized LED screen in the waiting area displayed a continuous loop of the advertisement they'd seen before. The grinning green coconut fled from the pursuing vendor before rendering him unconscious with a blow on the head.

"I hadn't paid much attention to this ad before," Chatpati said to Raj. "There's a bit of subliminal messaging going on here, don't you think?"

Raj nodded. "I see what you mean. The courageous coconut evading the dirty street seller. And the bacteria on the vendor's machete. Just marketing, though. Isn't it?"

"I'm not so sure. It's not just promoting a product, it's denigrating the competition. Though I suppose that's what marketing is all about."

"Good morning, gentlemen." An executive type approached, a slim man in a charcoal suit. The fabric was silk, the cut Italian, the tie pea green. "I'm Santosh Shetty, Director of Marketing. I understand you wished to speak to the Chairman. Perhaps I can be of help?"

Shetty was clean-shaven, his teeth polished a brilliant white. He wore his hair in a textured pompadour and trailed an expensive scent of bergamot and orange.

The policemen introduced themselves. "We'd like to speak to Mr. Chandra," Chatpati said.

"Regretfully, Mr. Chandra is not available," Shetty replied. "He's extremely busy and currently out on business. I'd be happy to assist, if I can. Or, if it's a personal matter, we could schedule an appointment. Mr. Chandra will probably be back in the office next month."

The policemen looked at each other. "Why not?" Chatpati said. "Lead the way."

Shetty led them through two sets of doors into a glass-walled conference room. A flat screen display hung on one wall. The receptionist appeared and set down a polished wooden tray bearing a cafetière and mugs. Each mug was emblazoned with the grinning coconut.

"There's tea, if you prefer," Shetty said. Chatpati shook his head. The receptionist poured and set a mug down before each, then sauntered out.

"We're looking into a matter that took place some months ago," Chatpati began. "I believe your firm approached several coconut vendors in Russell Market. Is that correct?"

Shetty's brow furrowed. "I seem to remember something of that sort," he replied. "It was before my time, you understand. I only joined the company recently. I believe my predecessor had hired a firm to recruit franchisees for our product. I can't remember if Russell Market was part of the strategic plan but I remember it being a city wide initiative. Why do you ask?"

"Several vendors alleged that they'd been threatened," Chatpati said. "By your representatives. When the vendors refused to take part."

Shetty shrugged. "The contract was terminated shortly after, as I recall. The company we'd hired to recruit vendors hadn't met their targets. We certainly did not know of any threats being made." He shook his head. "This company has a strong social ethos. Such actions would have been contrary to our Corporate Ethics Framework and our Social Responsibility Strategy. Totally unacceptable."

Chatpati nodded. "Are you saying that you had no knowledge of these threats?"

"Absolutely," Shetty replied. "No knowledge whatsoever."

"Some time after the threats were made, there were a couple of physical attacks on coconut vendors, again in that area. Know anything about that?"

Shetty looked horrified. "Attacks? You mean violence? Absolutely not! Again, that's not something this company would ever be involved in. Completely counter to the Fairness & Respect Charter. What would be the purpose?"

Chatpati studied the man. "Some vendors have said it was to eliminate the competition. Your competition."

Shetty flushed. He straightened his tie. "Really, Inspector, that's an outlandish suggestion. Forgive me, but you say this because you don't understand this company and our product. Street vendors are no competition."

"Oh?" Chatpati folded his hands. "They sell what you sell. For a much cheaper price. How are they not your competition?"

Shetty frowned, then got to his feet. "Let me explain what Coco2Go is all about."

Shetty moved to the end of the desk, facing the TV screen. He pressed a panel and a computer keyboard slid out. The TV screen on the wall lit up. A green coconut grinned at them.

"This presentation is for potential investors," Shetty said. "I won't bore you with all of it, but there are bits that might help you understand our Mission."

He pressed a button. The display changed to a map of India with a graph overlaid.

"The packaged tender coconut water market in India is worth about 20 million US dollars. Projected growth is 20 per cent in the next five years."

"The current market is divided almost equally between street vendors and the packaged product. Our projection is that, over the next five years, the packaged product will overtake the street by two to one."

The next slide was titled "Why?"

"You're going to ask why," Shetty said. Chatpati was not. Shetty continued.

"There are several reasons. Millennials have prefer lifestyle drinks that are both flavourful and healthy. Unsweetened natural beverages, such as our product, have been identified as a Key Mover in market surveys. Coconut water is a natural product. It works as a health drink and a sports drink. Today's young consumers are far more active than previous generations and far more conscious of what they consume, the ethics of production and the brand."

The next slide was called "Why choose Coco2Go?"

"We're the undisputed market leader," Shetty said, without a hint of irony. "We're true pioneers. We were one of the first to bring the packaged product to the market. Our product is pure and completely safe. It's pasteurised. The risk of contamination is zero. Our manufacturing facility has strict quality control, overseen by trained scientists."

The grinning green coconut appeared again, wearing shades and doing a jig. The luminous green was giving Chatpati a headache.

"We have a distinctive brand. This is our mascot, Coco The Coconut. Coco is cool. Coco is modern. Coco is fit. Coco is healthy. Coco represents the lifestyle aspirations of our customers. Coco has a presence on social media and is the figurehead of our advertising campaign."

The next slide displayed a branching tree depicting the company's corporate structure.

"Coco2Go is a relatively small but hugely dynamic private company. Our Chairman, K. M. Chandra, comes from a long line of successful entrepreneurs. He trained at Cornell University in America, a top Ivy League institution, before returning home to set up this venture. He's recruited a team of young and enthusiastic professionals. He provides strategic vision and tactical leadership. We're proud to work for such an inspiring individual."

Chatpati resisted the urge to roll his eyes.

The last slide was titled "The Future" and displayed a sunrise on a horizon framed by mountain peaks.

The single line read "The Future Is Bright. The Future is Coconut."

"You're right to wonder where we go once we've dominated the market," Shetty said. "Our horizon is unlimited. Our expansion strategy includes carbonated coconut water, flavoured coconut water and flavoured carbonated coconut water. You'll soon be ordering The Bangalore Sling and the CocoRita at five-star hotel bars across the city. We've lined up a celebrity chef to produce a range of coconut water inspired dishes. There will be a Coco2Go cookbook. We're looking at expanding into lifestyle apparel as well, in collaboration with market leaders in that sector."

Shetty returned to his mug of coffee before resuming his patter.

"I hope you can see now, Inspector, why street vendors are no competition. They're day labourers, piecemeal operators. Their product is boring. It's ordinary. Something you buy on a street corner. Their customers are passing trade. Saying they're a threat to us is like saying fishing boats are a threat to aircraft carriers."

Chatpati roused himself. "So how's that naval operation going? Making a profit, are you?"

Shetty smiled, entirely at ease. "You're not a businessman, Inspector. I can see that. No firm makes a profit straight away. It can take a few years. But we're moving in the right direction." Shetty looked as if he'd just thought of something. "Would you care to try some of our product? I'll ask Jayanti to get some." He reached for a buzzer.

Chatpati raised a hand. "No, thank you. I already have. From one of your promotional stalls. At a Metro station."

"Great!" Shetty said, the smile broader. "Great! So pleased to hear that. And what did you think? Be honest. We're always interested in feedback."

Chatpati did not smirk. "It tasted like coconut water."

"Exactly!" Shetty slapped the back of one hand into the other palm. "Exactly! The pure product. WITH all the natural goodness. WITHOUT the risks and bio-hazards of something sold on the street. Potable and portable. That's us. That's Coco2Go."

"What's your background, Mr. Shetty? You say you joined the company recently. What did you do before then?"

Shetty smoothed his tie flat. "Many things, Inspector. My background is finance. Venture capital. My passion is restructuring. Making struggling companies profitable."

"Like this struggling company?"

Shetty smiled. "It's true that Coco2Go's first year didn't go all that well. Which is why I was brought in. To help develop a new vision."

"So Mr. K. Chandra isn't that much of a visionary businessman, then? Despite the Cornell University degree."

"If you ask me, Inspector," Shetty replied, "real leadership skill is in recognising when things are going wrong and asking for help. Textbooks will help you learn about business, but being a successful businessman is a skill gained through apprenticeship. Mr. Chandra had a brilliant idea. He needed a little help to form that idea. That's where I came in."

"So you brought money into the business? Where from?"

"From abroad. I was part of a venture capital group based in Dubai. We fund companies all over the world. Mr. Chandra approached us and we liked the cut of his jib. So we got involved." Shetty leaned forward. "It's all legitimate, Inspector. Our accounts are independently audited and filed with the Registrar of Companies. We comply with all relevant government regulations, if that's your concern."

Shetty walked them out. At the reception, he handed Chatpati his business card.

"Do get in touch, gentlemen, if I can ever be of help in the future. We're a socially responsible organisation. If there is some local policing event that needs sponsorship, perhaps some charitable work that's close to your hearts, we would be proud to help."

Chatpati took the card by a corner and put it in his pocket. "You've been a great help, Mr. Shetty. Good bye."

"What did you think, Raj?" Chatpati asked, once they were back on the street.

"He talks a good game."

"I worry about a future that is coconut," Chatpati replied. "Do some more digging into Chandra and this Shetty fellow. Then, when Nair gets back, let's see if we can draw a line under this and put the coconut to bed."

CHAPTER 18
TENDER COCONUT TAMASHA

They found Nair in his annexed office. The Sub-Inspector was seated at the conference table, tapping away at a laptop.

"Ah, there you are," Nair said, folding the screen down. "I heard you'd gone out. Anything interesting?"

Chatpati let Raj explain first.

"A dead end," Chatpati said. "Coco2Go seems legitimate. I'm not convinced that the company is behind a global conspiracy to take over the coconut market. How did you get on with the case of the Planetarium fountain urination?"

"Oh, fine," Nair replied. He leaned back and put his legs on another chair. "I went to the planetarium. Spoke to the guard and the director. Made some suggestions. Though they seemed a bit alarmed to start with. Not sure why."

Chatpati could guess why. "What did you say? Exactly?"

"Exactly?" Nair's brow furrowed. "Something like 'I believest thou hast a public poop declaration made.' Why?"

Raj made a choking sound quickly and left the room. Chatpati kept a straight face. "Oh, nothing."

Nair shrugged. "I recommended CCTV installation. Also that they drain the fountain and take a sample at the next urination. For DNA. Oh, and I dropped by the MLA's office to look into the fly-tipping incident."

"Oh? I thought one of the constables was seeing to that."

"Well, you said to show interest. I thought a Sub-Inspector would make a more favourable impression than a constable."

Chatpati nodded. And ensure that your face is known to an important politician, he thought. Whose patronage might speed up your elevation.

"Any joy with that?" Chatpati asked.

"Got a licence plate from the CCTV. An auto-rickshaw, one of those cargo varieties, at 2am. I've asked Seema to track it down."

"Then?"

"Well, I thought I might arrest the driver and take him to the MLA to offer his apologies in person. And to clear up the rubbish he's dumped there. Followed by a large fine."

Chatpati had to admire Nair. It was a masterpiece in ingratiation. Well, he thought, if that expedited Nair's speedy exit from the CNU, Chatpati wouldn't interfere.

"Good plan," the Inspector said. "Perhaps you should video the arrest and put it on YouTube? A bit of publicity might warn the criminals off. You could front it."

Nair brightened. He sat up and smoothed his moustache. "Well, that's a great idea! Yes. We could have our own YouTube channel." He opened the laptop. "Miscreant fly-tipper gets his just desserts. Courtesy of Sub-Insp-, I mean, the Civil Nuisance Unit. I'll get straight onto it." He looked up. "We'll need a video camera. High-definition is best."

"Fine," Chatpati said, "Draw up a shortlist and I'll see what we can afford. Oh, and nothing goes online unless I've approved it. Clear?"

"Of course," Nair replied, sounding offended. "You're the boss."

"Yes," Chatpati replied. "I am."

Back in the restaurant, a pair of delivery men in orange overalls were unloading cartons from handcarts. Seema stood before them, writing on a clipboard. She handed the clipboard back to one man as Chatpati approached.

"What's all this?" Chatpati asked. "More office supplies?"

"No, sir," Seema said. "A gift. It came with a card." She read from it. "'To The Civil Nuisance Unit. From your friends at Coco2Go. The future is bright, the future is-'"

Chatpati raised a hand. "I know how it ends. Distribute it to the troops. And if any more arrives, send it back. Oh, and when you get a moment, see if you can find someone who runs Kannada language classes. For the Sub-Inspector. If he's going to be representing us, it's better that we don't come across as deranged."

Seema grinned. "Yes, sir!" She lowered her voice. "Though improving his language alone-"

"Quite," Chatpati said, suppressing a smile. "Quite."

Back in his office, he rang Colonel Rajvir Singh to update him on the conclusion of the park molestation case.

"A minor criminal, Colonel. Locked up. He won't be bothering your granddaughter again. Or anyone else."

"I am very pleased, Inspector," the Colonel said. "Very pleased. I hadn't expected such a swift resolution. I will tell anyone I know that if they have a problem, they should go to the Civil Nuisance."

"Unit," Chatpati said. "Civil Nuisance Unit, Colonel.

Pleased to be of service. Contact us again if we can be of help in the future."

Hemanth knocked at the door as Chatpati put the phone down.

"The Parade Ground Flasher has struck again!" he said. "We've sent up a Garuda."

Downstairs, everyone's attention was on the giant display. Even Nair had come out of his office to watch.

"Garuda Three is hovering above the Parade Ground, Inspector," Seema said. "The camera feed is on screen."

The screen showed a rectangle, divided into two halves. The eastern half was yellow sand, the parade ground proper, bounded by a perimeter wall and studded with tents. The western half was the green of the trees in the adjoining Cariappa Memorial Park. Just south of both was MG Road, traffic stuttering along.

"The park's been closed for months," Raj said. "There's supposed to be no public access. We think that's where the Flasher is. He struck ten minutes ago on MG Road. He pulled up his lungi and exposed himself to a solitary woman at the bus stop. When she raised a fuss, he leapt over the perimeter wall into the park. He's in there somewhere."

"Seema, switch to infra-red," Hemanth said.

The picture changed to grey-scale. The trees were dark grey now, the parade ground almost white from the heat reflecting off the sand.

A light grey blip appeared from under the trees, heading north, away from the scene of the crime

"That must be him," Raj said. "Oh, he's just disappeared again. Under a tree."

Seema spoke into her headset, then turned to them. "I've called it in to the Military Police," Seema said. "There are some soldiers training on the parade ground. They're being sent in. There they are. On screen now."

A cluster of five other grey blips moved from the parade ground into the park. They spread out into a line, beating west towards the suspect's last position. The suspect's blip suddenly reappeared and sped up. The five other blips also sped up in pursuit. All disappeared under the foliage. Ten seconds passed, then twenty, then thirty. There was no movement.

Seema looked up again. "They've got him."

The blips reappeared, five in a loose circle with one in the centre, all heading back to the parade ground. The central blip seemed to move with less enthusiasm than the others. All six blips stopped in a clearing just short of the tree-line.

"Zoom in," Hemanth said. "Get closer. And go back to daylight mode."

The display changed back to colour as the drone dipped down. They could now make out the five soldiers in their camouflage fatigues. The sun glinted off their helmets. The man in the middle of them was wearing a lungi and a vest. The soldiers ripped the vest off, followed by the lungi. The man in the middle was naked now, hands over his groin.

The soldiers closed in around the suspect. Arms rose and fell. Legs kicked out. The naked man fell to the earth and writhed beneath their blows like a landed eel.

"Presumably," Nair said, "it's Standard Operating Procedure for flashers not to wear underwear? I suppose it hinders speedy exposure of the goods."

Chatpati tutted and shook his head.

"All right. We've seen enough," he said. "Zoom out. Seema, ask the army to leave him in one piece. Send a couple of constables to pick him up from the parade ground. We'd like him clothed please. And contact the lady who made the report. She'll need to identify him. Or some part of him."

"Another one for the YouTube channel?" Nair asked as Chatpati passed.

"Why not?" Chatpati said. "Though censor the genitalia, will you? And the beating."

"What do you think, Inspector?" Hemanth said. "About the drones? You weren't in favour. But now?"

"Sign me up," Chatpati said. "I'm a convert. Good job."

"Sir," Seema called after him. "There's another call for you. It's not media. Claims to be from some charity."

"I'll take it upstairs."

An hour later, at 4 pm sharp, Raj knocked at Chatpati's office door, Nair at his shoulder. They stopped halfway through the doorway. Chatpati was at his desk, his head in his hands.

"Are you alright, sir?" Raj asked.

Chatpati mumbled into his palms, then looked up.

"Tamasha," Chatpati muttered. "It's a bloody tender coconut tamasha."

He waited for them to sit before describing the telephone call he had received earlier.

The voice on the line had been cultured and earnest. The accent suggested the caller was not a native Kannada speaker.

"My name is Shaji, sir," the caller had said. "Shaji Tharakan. I am one founder of StreetEatz. You may have heard of us?" Chatpati said that he hadn't. Shaji had laughed nervously. "Sorry. Please excuse me. I'm a little anxious talking to the police."

"Why?" Chatpati said. "Do you have something to be anxious about?"

Shaji laughed again. "No, sir. Not at all. In fact, I was calling to offer my two paisa[1] worth about a matter I hear you've been investigating." Chatpati heard the man swallow. "It's about the tender coconuts, sir."

Chatpati groaned inwardly. There was no escaping the bloody things. "Do carry on," he said, sincerely wishing he wouldn't.

"Well, sir, it might be better to speak in person. If that's alright? I can come to you?"

"What exactly is your interest in all this, Mr. Shaji?"

Shaji swallowed.

"Sir, I run a charity called StreetEatz. We work with street coconut vendors to improve their lot. Interest-free loans, advice about labour rights, basic training in marketing and so on. We are often the ones many of these simple folk come to when they are suffering hardship. I was in contact with a few of my clients in Russell Market, sir, and they mentioned you had been enquiring about the events of—well, you know which events. I thought I might help clear up this matter."

Chatpati was instantly suspicious. Was this another overture from the Sultangunta mafia?

"Are you, by any chance, a business associate of Mr. Avicenna Yousuf?" he asked.

"No, sir," Shaji replied. "I know the gentleman, of course. He owns a few produce stalls, but he is not one of our clients. He is a well-established businessman. Street-Eatz works with sole traders, sir."

Much as he wished otherwise, it was clear the tender coconuts were not about to release the Inspector from their hold. Chatpati agreed to meet the next day at the wholesale coconut market.

"It's at Silkboard, sir," Shaji had said. "Near the flyover.

Just ask anyone. I will be doing some training there in the afternoon. We can meet after."

Chatpati had barely finished his story when Nair rolled his eyes.

"Great. Another excursion into the wilds of coconut country. I thought we were done with this nonsense."

"Well, that's what we're here to decide," Chatpati said, turning to Raj. "What have you found out?"

Raj looked through his notes.

"First, the Director of Coco2Go, K. M. Chandra. As I mentioned before, only twenty-eight years old. He is the only son of K. G. Chandra, founder of Chandra Builders."

Raj looked at them expectantly. Both Nair's and Chatpati's faces remained blank. Raj continued.

"Chandra Builders, sir, is a very prestigious construction company. They have built shopping complexes, apartment blocks and office buildings all over Bangalore."

Chatpati nodded. "Only son. Rich business family. Lots of contacts. Lots of money. I can understand the only son going into business. But why coconut water? Why not just join Daddy?"

Raj nodded. "That's what I thought, sir. I looked into the social media profile of Chandra Junior. He's very active on Twitter and Facebook. Private education in Bangalore then went to the US for university. Cornell University. One of the top schools for business administration. But he appears to have left after only six months. He didn't complete the degree."

"So," Nair said. "Junior didn't do too well at university. What was it? Drugs? Drink? Girlfriend? I assume Daddy funded it."

"Probably," Raj said. "I looked at the cost of the Cornell degree, sir. It's two lakh US dollars. Ten million rupees."

Nair winced. "Oof. I bet Daddy Dearest wasn't pleased. Such an enormous amount of money spent with no particular gain. Anything else?"

Raj shook his head. "There's a social media black hole in his timeline for several months after his return to India. When he tweets again, it's all about his new start-up. That is Coco2Go."

"He's a man of expensive tastes. He drives an Audi coupé. Number plate CH4NDR4 JR. He's boasted on Twitter about buying a Lamborghini once his business takes off - there are selfies of him in the Lamborghini showroom. He's a member of the top private members' clubs, presumably on Daddy's tab. The Richmond Club, the Golf Club and the Turf Club. He has had three girlfriends in the last year, or at least, three women photographed by his side at various gala events. All three are fashion models. I've printed off the photos."

Raj paused. "Despite the playboy lifestyle, he still lives at home. With his parents."

"Good taste," Nair said, looking at the photos. "Cars, clubs and women."

"Expensive tastes," Raj replied pointedly. "Seems a vain man to me. Failed to make good in the US. Living off Daddy's wealth. I wonder if that's why Chandra Junior started Coco2Go. To prove to Daddy he could make it."

"Except he didn't," Chatpati said. "Or hasn't. Yet."

Raj nodded. "I also checked his social media feed. These three are his regular associates."

Raj held his phone out. It showed four men on a vast swathe of grass, all posing with golf clubs, their caddies assembled around them. "Chandra's the one on the left."

Chatpati studied the man in the green polo shirt. Chandra had clearly never gone hungry. His collar bulged.

His chin had a chin. The shirt was Ralph Lauren, the belt Louis Vuitton. His wristwatch was the size of a small terrapin. He had his mouth wide open, mid-laugh, one arm around the shoulders of the man on his left. Chandra was the only one wearing a baseball cap, that bearing an image of the grinning coconut.

"He always wears that baseball cap," Raj said. "It's in every photo."

"Who are these other clowns?" Nair asked.

"FINANCE! Magazine calls them 'The Young Turks'," Raj replied. "All self-made multi-millionaires. One runs Swifty, a delivery company for restaurants. The next guy makes garments for foreign designer labels. The last is 'an influencer', whatever that means."

"Self-made, wealthy, young men," Nair said. "Except Chandra, who's living off Daddy's money but no success of his own. Chandra Junior is out of his league. But pretending he's not."

"Anything on Shetty? The marketing director?" Chatpati asked.

"Not much," Raj replied. "Nothing obvious. Shetty keeps a low profile. I'll need a bit more time."

Nair yawned. "Scintillating. Really. Rich boys. Poor business. Good money spent on bad coconuts." He stretched in his chair. "So, where does that leave us with this case?"

"What do we have?" Chatpati said. "Allegations of poisoning by coconut water. Zero evidence. Allegations of threats by two Coco2Go salesmen. Hearsay. Allegations of violence against vendors. Possible, but this could be for multiple reasons. A failing coconut water business. Not a crime. A vain, young, moneyed man living beyond his means, funded by his family. Also not a crime."

Chatpati shut the folder and pushed it away.

"This case is officially closed," he said. He sat back heavily. "No more tender coconuts. If I see another packet of that stuff in this Unit, heads will roll."

"What about the meeting tomorrow?" Raj said. "With this Shaji fellow?"

Chatpati groaned. He rubbed his head. "Damn it. I forgot about that."

He sat up and took a deep breath. "OK. We'll go to the meeting. We'll hear what he has to say, try to wrap things up as quickly as we can and exit stage left. And that really will be the absolute end of it."

"Shall we go by motorbike?" Nair asked, as they got up to leave. "I've just had the Bullet tuned. You should see—"

"No," Chatpati said. "Absolutely not. We're all going. Three on a motorbike is bordering on molestation and, as you know, Sub-Inspector Nair, illegal. We're taking an auto."

"The Three Nuisanceers," Nair said brightly. "I like it!"

Chatpati did not.

CHAPTER 19

OF KINGS AND SAMARITANS

C harity worker Shaji's advice to "just ask anyone" worked reasonably well, once their auto-rick-shaw had toiled its way down Hosur Road the next morning. The air was thick with diesel fumes from the trucks rumbling back and forth between Hosur's factories and Bangalore's warehouses.

Nair had his handkerchief clapped to his face the whole way. Chatpati wore his face mask. Raj seemed entirely unaffected. Three Nuisanceers was a tight fit in the back of an auto and their sweat intermingled, despite much wrig-gling. The only relief came from the breeze when they were in motion, which wasn't often.

Traffic eased once they passed Madiwala, on the city's outskirts. The auto came to a stop outside the custard yellow facade of the Central Silk Board. The auto-driver, being an enterprising fellow, got out and asked a pavement soda water vendor the way to the coconut wholesale market.

"That way," the driver said on return, pointing to the other side of the fly-over, against the prevailing flow of traffic. It would take another fifteen minutes to find a break in the median to turn around and crawl back. Fifteen more minutes of sweat and fumes.

"Never mind," Chatpati said, paying the fare. "We'll walk."

The Municipal Corporation had dug up the pavements. Whether it was an attempt to improve the footpath or to reduce India's population burden was unclear. There were potholes and pitfalls everywhere, as deep as graves, glistening with brackish rainwater and speckled with mosquito larvae.

They had to step into the road, ironically, for safety. It was an entirely everyday occurrence that the simple act of getting somewhere might involve dicing with diesel-powered Death. They proceeded against the flow of traffic, relying heavily on the Indian motorist's well-founded fear of knocking policemen down. Chatpati set Nair as vanguard, a role he took to with elan. Sunglasses on, Nair parted traffic with scowls and imperious gestures. In short order, they had passed through the brief blessed shade of the fly-over and crossed to the other side.

Despite Nair's insistence on asking the way ("Fellow, wherefore be the tree fruit bazaar?" and "Human, dost thou knowledge of the cocoa not emporium?"), they found the wholesale market soon after. It was nothing but a bare acre of dust behind a row of medium-rise flats that cast a partial shadow over it. None of the policemen seen so many coconuts. Even Nair was impressed.

Coconuts lay on the ground in their thousands, in heaps, stacks and mounds. There were green ones, yellow ones, and even red ones. They formed hillocks and foothills. The valleys in between formed paths, populated by a swarm of sweating, sunburnt men heaving wheelbarrows and pushcarts. Coconuts were inspected, argued over and bargained for, the piles diminishing as each deal was struck, only to be renewed by a near-constant stream of lorries veering down the narrow approach road.

The presence of the police attracted much attention. There was the usual drawing away and fearful glances. Nair accosted a fellow with poor situational awareness who was fully engaged in counting a fat bundle of notes. The man started as Nair loomed in front of him. Nair's hat cast the Sub-Inspector's face in shadow, all dark except for the menacing glint of his Aviators.

"Fellow," Nair roared, grown ill-tempered by the heat, "wherefore inhabits the Shaji? Speak, verily, or, in sooth, thou presently my wrath will I unleashed."

The man leapt out of his skin. He erected a namaste as defence, back-pedalling all the while. Nair followed at close quarters. The man waved his namaste at a square breeze-block shed beneath a solitary tree in the corner.

"See Coconut King Kumar, sir," the man whimpered before fleeing.

Nair turned to Chatpati, puzzled. "Did I hear that right? Did he say Coconut King?"

"For once." Chatpati said. "For once, you got it right. He said Coconut King."

Coconut King Kumar was what Buddha would have looked like if his philosophy had been one of conspicuous excess instead of serene detachment. Everything about him approximated a sphere, from his bald head to his paunch. His eyes were round. He wore round framed spectacles. His short-sleeved shirt was a riot of polka dots. He sat cross-legged on a round stool. The only linear thing about him was his nose, a fine, pointed thing that swung towards the policemen as they appeared in the doorway.

The heat in the shed was stifling, but the Coconut King seemed unaffected. There was nary a drop of sweat on him. A solitary desk fan spun this way and that, rippling the stacks of paper on the solitary desk. A coconut acted as paperweight.

"Are you Coconut King Kumar?" Raj asked. "We're the police."

Kumar gritted his teeth. "Which idiot is it that's calling me the Coconut King? I have told those idiots! Any more of that and I'll kick them out. Was it a tall fellow? Or a fat one? And I can see you're the police. Why else would you be wearing uniforms? What do you want?" All delivered in a single breath.

"We're looking for Shaji. The StreetEatz charity." Raj replied.

"Oh, that fellow. Very good. Here to arrest him, are you? Thought it wouldn't be long before that happened." Kumar replied, turning his attention back to his papers. "You'll find him in the other building. The 'training centre', as he calls it. Ha!" He yelled towards the back of the building. "Raghava! Where are you, idiot?"

A teenager in shorts and a Metallica T-shirt appeared out of the darkness, carrying a ledger. "Yes, boss?"

"Take these policemen to that Shaji idiot. They're here to arrest him. Make sure he doesn't get away."

The boy led them between the glistening, green mountains. After a few turns, they found themselves at the far corner of the compound where a white-washed building stood hard against the perimeter wall. This was a far newer construction than the Coconut King's shed, built of brick with a tiled roof. The window glass was tinted. The door was sturdy and painted green. Someone had planted a small row of saplings that would, in a few years, provide shade, assuming they could suck some water out of the parched earth. There was even an air-conditioner. The boy pointed at the building and left, entirely uncaring whether Shaji got away or not.

Inside, it was cool and dark. There were three doors leading off the entrance, one open. Through it, they could see rows of sunburnt men squatting on their haunches on the bare floor, their backs to the policemen. Their attention was on a lean, bearded man wearing a homespun kurta and jeans. The man stood in front of a blackboard. There was writing on the board, the largest and only readable words being "Marketing" and "Brand" in English and Kannada.

The bearded man spotted the policemen through the open door and raised a hand. He said loudly, in English, "Please have a seat. In the next room. I will be finished shortly." He indicated a door to their right. The heads of his audience swivelled around then and, as quickly, turned away when they saw who the new arrivals were.

The office next door was cramped, barely wide enough for two men to stand shoulder to shoulder. It contained a desk, an office chair and a tall filing cabinet. The ceiling light was a naked bulb. There were two wicker chairs for visitors. Nair promptly occupied one. Raj gave Chatpati an exasperated look, then went outside. Chatpati took the remaining chair.

There was a stack of promotional brochures about StreetEatz on the desk. Chatpati picked one up and began leafing through it. Barely a minute later, they heard the murmur of conversation, followed by the sound of feet behind them. The class was over.

Shaji Tharakan inched his way around them, scraped through the gap between the end of the desk and a wall, and sat down below the single window. Close-up, he was older than he had first seemed, filaments of grey in his hair. The beard appeared patchy. Shaji's eyes flitted over them, then down to the papers in his hand.

"So glad you could come," he began in English. "Sorry. That ran on longer than I expected. They had many questions."

"Training, is it?" Nair was first to speak, his brow furrowed.

"Yes," Shaji replied, rearranging his papers. "Marketing and branding. It's a novel concept to these people."

"Rather pointless, isn't it?" Nair replied. "I mean, I can understand why it would work for Adidas and Pepsi, for example. But tender coconuts? Who buys their tender coconut based on 'the brand'? You just go to the nearest street corner."

Shaji smiled shyly, not quite meeting Nair's eyes. "A common misconception. But consider, if you had gone to two excellent restaurants, both offering the same fare, of the same quality, at the same price, but you got great service at one and poor service at the other, which would you visit again?"

Nair looked slightly put out and made no answer. Shaji continued, a bit more confident now.

"We're teaching these vendors to maximise their customer contact opportunities. Be friendly. Be attentive. Dress well. Use good hygiene. Wish people a good day. Deal with complaints. Do all these things and their chances of getting repeat custom increase. The brand," he said, "is not the coconut, it is the vendor."

Chatpati had had quite enough. "What did you want to speak to us about, Mr. Tharakan?"

"Please call me Shaji. Yes. I just wanted to make myself available to you in case you had any queries on the matter you are investigating? Is that correct? It is an investigation?"

"It's simply an enquiry," Chatpati said. "Do you know anything about the alleged threats to the vendors by the company Coco2Go?"

Shaji leaned back in his chair and folded his hands.

"To be frank, Inspector, I think people are reading too much into the situation. Several vendors asked for my advice when Coco2Go approached them with their franchise offer. The language used was intemperate, at best, and open to misinterpretation, especially by poor, uneducated people like the coconut vendors. I'm certain no threats were made."

"And what did you advise your clients to do?" Chatpati asked. "About the franchise offer?"

"I pointed out the advantages and disadvantages of joining such a firm, explained how franchises work, what targets were, contracts, that kind of thing. In the end, I said it was their decision."

"How many joined the franchise?" Nair asked.

Shaji studied him. "None. So far as I know." He leaned forward. "These are mostly illiterate people. They understand numbers and money, profit and loss – they have to because it's the difference between putting food on their tables or not – but most would have been fearful of tying themselves up to a big firm. Very few can even sign their own name. They use their thumbprints instead." He sat back. "Frankly, I'm surprised at Coco2Go's approach. If I was handling their franchise campaign, I would have told them not to waste their time."

"And what about the assaults?" Chatpati said. "Some vendors were attacked. By rowdies."

"I understand why you might see a connection," Shaji

replied "The one followed the other. But, again, when I met the two vendors who had been attacked, there was nothing to connect the attacks to any ulterior motive. Random violence against street vendors is, sadly, not uncommon. As I'm sure you know."

"There's information to suggest the rowdies were paid to attack the vendors," Chatpati said. "Who else might have an interest in frightening your clients?"

Shaji shrugged. "Some fall behind on rental payments on their carts. They borrow money from loan-sharks, against our advice. Others may owe protection money to local gangs. There are many plausible reasons. Anyway, the attacks soon stopped. There have been none since."

"Your name suggests you're from Kerala," Nair said. "You speak Malayalam[1]?"

"My parents are from Kerala," Shaji replied, looking down at his papers. "I grew up in the North, in Mumbai, then New Delhi. I've never lived in Kerala. We spoke English and Hindi at home. My Malayalam is non-existent, I'm afraid."

Nair said something to Shaji that Chatpati didn't understand.

Shaji started, then shook his head at Nair, smiling. "I'm sorry. I think you were speaking Malayalam there. I didn't understand what you said. Would you prefer to speak in Kannada? Or Hindi?"

"No," was all Nair said in reply. "English is fine."

"Tell us a bit more about StreetEatz." Chatpati said. "You said you're a charity."

"Yes, we are," Shaji said quickly. His eyes flicked back and forth between the policemen. "It's the first initiative of its kind in South India. We're an offshoot of another charity that started in New Delhi. We're funded by the Central

Government to a small degree, but most of our sponsors are Indian expatriates in the US who wish to contribute to the betterment of society. We're fully registered with the Charity Commission. We've been operating here in Bangalore for just over a year now. My background is in social work, which helps."

"You built this place?" Nair asked. "What do you do here?"

"Yes. This is our training centre," Shaji said. "It's small, but it serves well enough. We do a lot more." Shaji got to his feet. "Come, let me show you."

He led them back through the classroom and then another door. They found themselves outside at the rear of the building, in a bare patch of ground roofed with aluminium sheeting on wooden struts. There in front of them was a motorcycle with a wheeled trailer attached. The trailer was finished in aluminium and bore a licence plate. In it sat a machine, rather like an engine, with a fly-wheel and gears. Next to it, in a cradle, sat a toolbox and three jerry cans, one red, two white.

"This," Shaji said proudly, "is our mobile unit. We travel between our vendors regularly, making sure their equipment is in top condition. The machine is a petrol-driven knife sharpener. At every visit, we test their machete blades for wear, sharpness and condition. We check the condition of the carts, oil the axles, inflate or replace the tyres. We also dispense gloves and bio-degradable drinking straws. After every service, I fix a sticker bearing the StreetEatz logo to the cart displaying the date that it was last inspected."

Nair walked around the vehicle, examining it. "A 500cc Japanese engine. Good welding there. Brake-lights, indicators. Well made. What's in those containers? Petrol?"

"Yes, sir," Shaji replied. "Petrol for the knife-sharpener.

Food-safe lubricant to sharpen the vendors' knives and another kind of lubricant for the axles."

"Why is that jerry can red?" Nair asked.

"That's the non-food safe lubricant, sir. That goes on the axles, not the knives. The red can is to make sure we don't put it on knives by accident. It's part of our safety Standard Operating Procedure."

"It seems a lot of effort," Nair said. "For street vendors."

"It's future-proofing, sir," Shaji replied, sounding a little annoyed. "We're trying to improve the image of the street vendor being tarnished. I've seen the Coco2Go advertising campaign. It suggests street vendors are unhygienic. We need them to be seen as safe. This service is an essential part of that."

"You'll have heard of allegations of food poisoning from drinking coconut water," Chatpati said. "Several cases at various sites around the city. Know anything about that?"

"That is pure speculation," Shaji replied. "Tender coconut water is perfectly safe to drink. There's plenty of science to back that up. You're far more likely to die from a bad samosa than from tender coconut water."

Nair gave Chatpati a superior look.

Chatpati ignored it. "Well, I think we've seen quite enough," he said. "We'll take our leave."

Shaji walked them back through the building to the front door and out into the sun.

"How is your investigation progressing?" Shaji asked conversationally as they stepped through the door. "If you don't mind my asking? Only my clients are quite anxious. They're poor, illiterate people-"

"Yes," Chatpati replied. "You said that already. I wouldn't worry. I can't see anything in this matter that speaks of criminal activity. Good luck with your social enterprise."

He turned to go when Nair spoke. "You don't have a brochure handy, do you? In case we need to get in touch. Or if we identify a vendor who might benefit from your input? You work for free, correct?"

Shaji looked surprised. "Why, yes. There is no charge. That is thoughtful of you. I'll just go get one."

Shaji disappeared through the door.

"What's going on, Vasanth?" Chatpati growled. "What are you up to?"

"A hunch," Nair said. Shaji reappeared shortly with a brochure. Nair took it and they left.

"Want to tell me what this hunch is?" Chatpati said, once Shaji had disappeared from view behind the coconut mountains.

"That fellow is lying. He speaks Malayalam," Nair said. "I called him something vulgar in that language to test his understanding. Did you see him jump?"

"I've seen lots of people jump," Chatpati said. "Most recently, every time you speak Kannada to them. So what if he speaks Malayalam? Maybe he doesn't speak it well and didn't want to be embarrassed in front of the fierce Sub-Inspector. He looked nervous just being in the same room with us."

"Perhaps," Nair said, frowning. "Something about this feels less than satisfactory."

"What's satisfactory," Chatpati said, "is that this is the absolute end of the coconut matter. Let's get out of this place. I don't ever, ever want to see another one of the cursed things."

"Amen to that," Nair replied.

They found Raj at the Coconut King's shed, sipping

from a tender coconut through a straw. The Inspector pointed a finger at it. "Toss that bloody thing! We're leaving."

"I've requested a Hoysala," Raj said. "It'll be here in five minutes. Unless you want to take an auto?"

Chatpati looked over to the scrum under the flyover that, when in motion, might pass for traffic.

"Absolutely not," said Chatpati.

"Amen to that," said Nair, with feeling.

CHAPTER 20

MORE THINGS IN HEAVEN AND EARTH

They were in luck. The Hoysala was air-conditioned. It made the lack of swift progress through traffic bearable.

"What did His Majesty, the Coconut King, have to say?" Chatpati asked Raj. "I assumed you well used your time while we were with Shaji." Nair had been staring out the window but turned as Raj spoke.

"The Coconut King is not one of Shaji's fans," Raj said. "StreetEatz arrived about four months ago. Shaji pays rent to the landowner to use that corner. He erected his building in double-quick time and started working with the vendors. I got the sense the King resents Shaji, that he thinks Shaji is up to no good. Is he?"

Chatpati looked at Nair. "The Sub-Inspector seems to think so."

Nair shook his head. "I have the feeling I know him from somewhere. I can't remember where, though. Notice anything about him?"

"He has a scar on his cheek," Chatpati said. "Under that

patchy beard. And a very slight limp. Bike accident, perhaps?"

"Maybe," Nair said. "The whole meeting was odd. He had nothing useful to say and seemed very keen to reassure us that all was well. And he seemed equally eager to find out what we were thinking."

"What're you saying?" Raj said.

Nair shook his head and looked back out the window. "I'm not sure. Yet."

Chatpati's phone buzzed. It was Seema. "Sir. The TV crew are here, sir. For the interview."

"Bullocks," Chatpati said. "I forgot." He looked at his watch. "We'll probably be just on time. Let them know."

"OK, sir," she replied. "They want to set up their equipment. There are lights and things."

"Fine," Chatpati said. "Whatever. Let them sort themselves out."

By the time they arrived back at the CNU, the former nightclub had been transformed into a television studio. Two chairs faced each other on the dance floor, surrounded by three enormous lights on stands. A single camera stood behind one chair, lens pointed at the other. A man wearing headphones was walking around the floor with a boom mike.

The producer, a rather prosperously proportioned chap in skinny jeans that were too young for him, accosted the policemen as they entered.

"Ah. The star of the show! Such a pleasure to meet you! I'm Derek Mendes, producer. Nita is just having some light make-up done, then Joy will be ready for you, Inspector. She's a marvel with the brushes, you know. You'll look GREAT! This way, please."

Although it was nearing home time, none of the Unit's

police officers seemed in a hurry to leave. They clustered around their desks in small groups, chatting. Everyone wanted to watch Inspector Chatpati being interviewed by award-winning journalist and broadcaster, Nita Singh.

Some minutes later, imperfections smoothed away with foundation, Chatpati was in the chair facing the lens. The camera's red light was on.

"Just setting exposure, sir," the cameraman said. "You can relax."

"We thought this would be a great backdrop," Mendes said, at Chatpati's side. The producer framed said backdrop with his hands. "You know, the computer console, the screen, the drones. A great example of modern hi-tech policing! And the disco ball adds SUCH a quirky touch." There was a twinkle in his smile. He leaned in close. "I'm SUCH a fan of your work! Oh, here's Nita."

In real life, Nita Singh was short. She wore power heels. She sported a curly bob, just the right side of neat. Her eyes were wide and outlined with kohl, the nose a smidgeon too broad to be considered conventionally beautiful.

"So pleased to meet you, Inspector," she said, extending a hand. Her grip was firm, her gaze direct.

She took the chair opposite. Mendes handed her a clip-board. The sound man materialised at Chatpati's side and fiddled with the placket of his uniform shirt.

"Just a lapel microphone," Mendes said. "Now, just relax. We'll start with some general chit-chat, just to get you into the flow, then Nita will start with the questions. It'll only be about thirty minutes. We won't use all of it for the package, but it makes sense to film more than we'll need. Ready, Inspector?"

Mendes didn't wait for an answer. He spun around to face the audience and raised his arms.

"OK, silence everyone! No noise please while we're filming! Sit, stand, whatever. If you're sitting, stay sitting. If you're standing, stay standing! Dance floors can be very noisy!"

Beyond the glare of the lights, Chatpati made out people rushing for vantage points. Raj and Seema were on his left. Raj gave him a thumbs-up. Hemanth and three other constables sat at a table directly behind Nita Singh. Nair was in the back, leaning against a billiard table. Chatpati felt like a cabaret act.

"Inspector Chatpati," Nita began, "thank you for speaking to us today."

"My pleasure," Chatpati replied. His throat felt tight, his voice small.

"Don't worry," Mendes sang from beyond the lights. "It's normal to be nervous. Just focus on Nita. Pretend you're just having a chat."

Easier said than done, Chatpati said. He tugged at his collar and sat up.

Nita continued. "Of course, your face, and your name, is well known to the people of Bangalore. In fact, one could go so far as to say all over India and, perhaps, the world. How does it feel to be so famous?"

"I'm not sure that's the case," Chatpati replied, his voice stronger.

"Really?" If the surprise in Nita's voice was affected, it was well done. "You go from being a humble Sub-Inspector, working the streets, to being appointed the head of Bangalore's newest crime initiative, all in the space of a few months, and you don't think about it?"

"Actually, I was promoted to Inspector before they put me in charge of the Civil Nuisance Unit. The two events were not synchronous."

"Nevertheless, you have become very prominent in the public eye for a police officer of your rank. Surely, that's had its advantages. And drawbacks?"

Chatpati folded his hands. "It's not something I think about. I just focus on the job at hand."

"Commendable," Nita said without a trace of irony. "And what about the incident that brought you to prominence? The attack on the Vidhana Soudha. An attack in which many people died and countless others were hospitalised. In which you were personally involved! Surely, that must have had some impact on you? Personally? Professionally?"

Chatpati blinked. "No. It's in the past. Everything you need to know about it is in the Independent Commission's report on the matter. It's not something I intend to talk about."

"Surely, Inspector-"

"I said I'm not about to discuss it. Let's move on."

She did. Neatly. "Clearly, such an event cannot help but leave its mark. Let's talk about the Civil Nuisance Unit. Who came up with the idea?"

The rest was easier. For a while. Chatpati took her through the concept, the mission and the challenges. Nita listened with apparent interest, letting him speak, allowing him to gain confidence before she changed tack.

"Thank you, Inspector. I'm sure it will hearten the citizens of Bangalore to know you're working so hard on their behalf. To keep them safe."

She paused for a moment before she asked the next question.

"Perhaps you can tell us what you're doing to keep the public safe from the dangers of adulterated coconut water?"

The question hung in the air. Somewhere beyond the lights, someone gasped.

Chatpati felt something heavy in the pit of his stomach. It had the consistency of lead. He was suddenly aware of the thud of his pulse against the strap of his watch.

"I'm not sure what you mean," he replied.

"We've had information that you are investigating cases of poisoning from the consumption of street tender coconut water." She looked at her papers. "Nine cases in all, over the last three weeks." She looked up at him. "And three deaths. What can you tell us about that?"

"I'm not at liberty to discuss details of any police investigations," he replied.

"So you are investigating?" she said, a note of triumph in her reply. "If there is sufficient cause to investigate, surely there must be a risk to the public? Correct?"

Chatpati said nothing, jaw clenching.

"Surely," she went on, the tone now that of astonished admonishment, "surely, if there is a risk to the public from the adulteration of foodstuffs, criminal adulteration, you have a duty to warn? Have you done so? If so, when? If not, why?"

"There is no evidence of any criminal activity," Chatpati replied through gritted teeth.

"So. You're saying that you investigated, and that you found no evidence. So far," Nita said. "Tell us what you've found, then. Let the people decide. Let the grieving families of those three dead people decide whether what you're doing to 'keep them safe' is sufficient."

"Those were your words," Chatpati said, "not mine."

"Oh? Are you saying your job doesn't involve keeping the public safe?" She sounded incredulous. "What's all this for, then? All this expense? Manpower? Effort? Just stage dressing for the Justice Minister's promises?"

Chatpati suppressed a sigh. "Our job is to investigate crime. That is how we go about keeping people safe. We-"

She interrupted him. "Oh, so now keeping people safe is a part of your job? Not what you said earlier!"

"As I was saying," Chatpati said, each word deliberate, "we investigate crime. We have found no evidence of criminal activity relating to alleged adulteration of tender coconut water. We have found no evidence of an enduring risk to public safety."

"Then how do you explain these cases?" She held up a photo. "Jayalakshmi. A humble street sweeper employed by the Municipal Corporation. Dead." Another photo. "Ahmed Ali. He pushed a handcart in Russell Market. Dead." A third, this one familiar. "Mohan Rao. A young banker. Dead."

Nita shook her head. "Three deaths. All after consumption of coconut water. From street vendors. You have nothing to say about that?"

Chatpati began to speak, but she spoke over him.

"Inspector Hari Chatpati, thank you for your time."

The lights dimmed, and it was over. Chatpati blinked. The world was suddenly dark.

Nita Singh rose and headed for the exit without a word. Mendes followed. Chatpati was vaguely aware of the sound man unclipping the mic from Chatpati's shirt. He supposed he should get up and, after a minute, he did so.

Inspector Chatpati stood in the middle of the dance floor, unsure about what had just happened. He wondered what to do next. He looked around at his team. None met his gaze except Nair, still leaning against the billiard table in the back. There seemed to be something beyond pity in Nair's face, but Chatpati couldn't quite make out what.

The sound of low and dangerous voices brought Chatpati out of his dazed state. By the saloon doors, Raj had the producer by the collar. A pair of constables had joined him. Mendes was surrounded. The producer looked like a rabbit caught in the headlights.

Chatpati walked over and unfastened Raj's grip. The producer shrank back, his eyes full of fear.

"Better get going, Mr. Mendes," Chatpati said. "You have ten minutes to remove your equipment. Or we will deliver it to the ground floor. By gravity. Via the balcony."

Mendes fled.

Later, much later, when the lights in the restaurant had dimmed and the sound of feet and chatter had faded away, Raj knocked at Chatpati's office door.

"Are you alright, sir?" Raj's face was full of concern. "Everyone's gone home, sir. You should too. Madam will be worried."

Chatpati wasn't aware of how much time had passed. He had been watching the pendulum on the grandfather clock swing back and forth. He had discovered that the pendulum's oscillation had a distinct bias to the left. The clock was also twelve minutes slow. He'd reset it twice.

"Nirmala is used to policemen's hours," Chatpati replied. It surprised him how normal his voice sounded.

"The interview was a trap, sir," Raj said, suddenly angry. "They set us up."

"Yes," Chatpati replied. "It was." He got to his feet. "Come. Give me a hand."

Together, they tilted the clock to one side while Chatpati placed a scrap of folded cardboard under it. They set it down again. Chatpati examined it for a minute, Raj fidgeting by his side.

"That's better," the Inspector said. "It's more even now."

"What, sir?" Raj said, concerned again. "The clock?"

"The clock," Chatpati said. "And other things." He turned to Raj. "Let's head out. I've got something for you to do tomorrow. I'll explain on the way down."

CHAPTER 21
#BADCOCONUT

Nirmala was still awake when Chatpati got home. Her favourite late-night family drama serial was on TV. On screen, the richly clad matriarch was laying into her newly arrived daughter-in-law. The bridegroom stood helplessly to the side. Chatpati could empathise with the man.

Nirmala switched the TV off before she went into the kitchen to warm his dinner. Once Chatpati had changed out of his uniform, they ate together in a companionable silence at the tiny kitchen table.

"How did your interview go?" she asked after a while. "The trailer is all over BTV. 'Special feature with Inspector Chatpati, hero of the Vidhana Soudha'. It's on tomorrow." She read his expression. "Not well then."

"Not one of my finer moments," he replied. "I don't think you'll

want

to watch it."

"I'm going to watch it, Hari. It's probably not as bad as you think it was."

By the time he came out of the bedroom the next morning, she had changed her mind. She had been watching the interview on the living room TV. When she heard him, she turned it off.

"That bad?" he asked.

"I'll get your breakfast," she replied, rising. "You'll have a busy day ahead of you. I'm making dosa. With extra masala. For endurance."

He turned the TV back on.

"And now," Nita Singh announced, "in case you missed it, our special investigative feature on the outbreak of food poisoning linked to street coconut water in Bangalore. Plus, what the police are doing, or failing to do, to protect the public. You be the judge."

It started with a montage of shots of tender coconut vendors at various points across the city. Chatpati recognised Senthil, the Cubbon Park vendor.

"Tender coconut water," the voice-over said. "Widely recognised for its health benefits. It's a popular drink amongst residents of Bangalore and all over India and the world. Full of nutrients and electrolytes, cheap and safe, it's the go-to drink for those on the move and in need of quick refreshment."

A collage of three photos faded in on the screen, the portraits of the dead people Nita Singh had shown Chatpati the evening before.

"But for these unfortunate residents, tender coconut water was the last thing they consumed. Before they died."

There followed a slow fade to the pathologist, Dr. Saleem, on a stool, swamped by his white lab coat. Behind him stood a row of glistening steel autopsy tables.

"Dr. Saleem Mammoo is Chief Pathologist at Lord Curzon hospital. He performed the autopsies on the unfortunate victims and was the first to suspect that something was wrong."

"It wasn't right," Dr. Saleem said. "The cases were assumed to be food poisoning. But their stomachs were empty. Except for remnants of some liquid."

"Which might have been tender coconut water?" the interviewer said, off-camera.

Dr. Saleem nodded. "It's possible. Yes."

"And there were more cases?"

"Yes. Sadly. Though none of the others died. Obviously, I couldn't perform autopsies on them for that reason."

"But you still believe those other cases resulted from poisoning?"

Dr. Saleem nodded. "The symptoms were identical, though less severe. I'm sure the cause was the same."

"What did you do?"

"I informed the Public Health authorities. And the police."

Cut to an exterior shot of the Public Health Institute, a modest grey villa on a side-street, the gates closed.

"No one from the Public Health authorities was available to comment. A written statement said they were 'looking into the matter.' However, the police confirmed they were investigating."

The next shot was a close-up of Chatpati from the interview the evening before. Chatpati thought that the on-screen Chatpati looked distinctly unphotogenic: nose too large, brows too thunderous. He looked annoyed. The Chatpati on-screen was speaking but silently. The voice-over spoke for him.

"Inspector Hari Chatpati is well-known. Just a few months ago, he was in the storm's eye. His personal bravery in the Vidhana Soudha attack received national acclaim."

A fuzzy still photo appeared, the one that had made the front pages for weeks afterwards, taken by a news photographer in Cubbon Park shooting through the gates of the Vidhana Soudha using a powerful telephoto lens. Inspector Chatpati, hatless, uniform damp, was leaning over the balustrade on the ground floor of the parliament building, handing down the limp body of a schoolchild into the waiting arms of a fireman.

"The Government richly rewarded the Inspector for his bravery. He was appointed to command Bangalore's first Civil Nuisance Unit. But is a hero the right person to lead a so-called 'elite unit', especially when he has only recently been promoted from the relatively junior rank of Sub-Inspector? Was the promotion deserved? However brave the single act that brought the Inspector to prominence, does he really have the judgement and ability one needs for the senior position he holds?"

Chatpati was on-screen again. The clip had been edited to exclude the earlier banal questions. Nita Singh's question rang out.

"I'm sure it will hearten the citizens of Bangalore to know you're working so hard on their behalf. To keep them safe. Perhaps you can tell us what you're doing to keep the public safe from the dangers of adulterated coconut water?"

THE REST WAS as he remembered, but somehow worse for being a spectator.

The camera zoomed in on Chatpati's face for his last words.

"As I was saying, we investigate crime. We have found no

evidence of criminal activity relating to alleged adulteration of tender coconut water. We have found no evidence of an enduring risk to public safety."

The picture changed to a view from the gilded rooftop of a Gothic cathedral, looking out onto a European city, a panorama of domes, skyscrapers and cranes set against a distant rim of mountains under a brilliant sky. The voice-over continued.

"No enduring risk to public safety. Those were the words of Inspector Chatpati. Mr. Günther Braun, recently a tourist to Bangalore, thinks otherwise. Mr. Braun's wife fell seriously ill after drinking tender coconut water. She was lucky to survive. We spoke to Mr. Braun from his home in Vienna by video-link."

Mr. Braun was at his dining table. He wore a jumper.

"I am sure it was coconut, ja? Klar. Clear. I tell the police, the Inspector. I tell the doctor. I tell the Konsulat."

"And what did they do?" Nita Singh's voice asked.

"Nothing! They do nothing! People are danger, I say. Big danger. But nothing is done. Inspector is good, ja? Good man. But he not take this serious. No one take it serious."

Next, a shot of the MG Central building, followed by an interior view of Coco2Go's offices. Santosh Shetty was in the glass-walled meeting room. The voice-over continued.

"Mr. Santosh Shetty is the Marketing Director of Coco2Go, a company that makes packaged coconut water. He told us what led his company to enter the coconut water market."

Shetty's grooming was immaculate, his delivery slick.

"We've always worried about the hazards of the street product. We pasteurise our product for safety. It's all about hygiene. That's our raison d'être. To bring all the benefits of *tender coconut water to the market in as safe a way as possible."*

"Are you saying," Nita Singh asked, off-camera, "that the street product is unsafe?"

Shetty's smile was knowing.

"I'm just asking the consumer to consider what the difference might be between our product, manufactured under ISO-certified processes with strict quality control, and a raw, unwashed fruit of uncertain provenance bought off a random street corner. Which would you want your family to drink? Of course, consumers will make their own choice."

The picture changed to a familiar walled compound filled with heaps of tender coconuts. A man on a motorcycle hitched to a trailer rode into view and dismounted before walking towards the camera. The voice-over continued.

"Mr. Shaji is director of StreetEatz, a charity that works with street tender coconut vendors. He spoke to Nita Singh."

Nita Singh's voice again, off-camera.

"What do you make of allegations of adulteration of tender coconut water?"

Shaji was wearing sunglasses. The backdrop was a solid wall of tender coconuts. Shaji shook his head as he answered.

"There is no evidence that the street product is unsafe. It's all hearsay."

"But nine cases? Three deaths? All after consuming tender coconut water from street vendors? Surely that's more than a coincidence."

"It must have been something else. There's no evidence of a causal link."

"But the police have been investigating."

Shaji nodded.

"Yes. Inspector Chatpati. I was honoured to receive the

attention of such a renowned officer. They came and asked some questions and interviewed the vendors."

"But you seem to think they didn't do enough, correct?"

Shaji shook his head.

"It's not my place to say, but it might have reassured the public if the police had taken samples of the coconuts for testing. I mean, questioning vendors is fine, but the vendors are merely sellers. They're not scientific experts, they're not educated. They trust that what they buy from the wholesale market is safe. They're not in a position to know if it's not."

Nita Singh went straight in for the kill. "So you say that tender coconuts might be unsafe?"

Shaji shook his head again.

"Not at all. Tender coconuts are absolutely safe, but to prove the case to the public, it might have been better if the police had taken samples and had them tested. The results would have come back as clean, of course, but that would have helped settle the question once and for all."

The picture changed to the General Utilities Building, followed by a close-up of the drones, rotors spinning. A panning shot took in the interior of the CNU. Seema was at her desk, her back to the camera. Constables crossed the dance floor, self-conscious. The disco ball glittered above.

"So there we have it. An elite police unit, created at enormous expense, equipped with the latest technology, headed by a hero, a man of supposed integrity. In its first public outing, dealing with a serious question of a potential threat to public safety, how has the Civil Nuisance Unit fared? You be the judge. We'll be hosting a panel discussion after the lunchtime news. Until then, join the discussion on our Facebook and Twitter pages, using #GoodCoconut and #BadCoconut to tell us what you, the consumers, think."

"And now, in other news—"

NIRMALA KNEW all was not well when she had to call her husband to breakfast a second time. Chatpati was not one for lingering. He was not in the living room where she had left him. She found him in the small glassed-in balcony off the living room, looking out.

The city lay in the distance, the view segmented by the silvered glass facades of the four other skyscrapers that made up Five Star Layout. Chatpati had his face to the glass, looking down at the shantytown that had sprung up around the bases of the buildings soon after he and Nirmala had moved in. That was where the drivers, the cooks and maids lived, those who served the affluent residents of this premium residential development.

"Hari? Are you alright?" Nirmala said, laying a hand on his shoulder. "What are you looking at?"

"Down there," he replied, face still turned away from her. "The dusty scratchings of the poor." He paused. "Did you watch it?"

"Yes," she replied. "In the big scheme of things, what does it matter? You know what the media is like. It's called a circus for a reason. It means nothing."

He turned back to her, his face thoughtful. "I think it matters. In all the fuss about coconuts, I'd lost track of how this started. Three people dead. Being confronted about it like that was embarrassing. But perhaps I needed that."

"So now you remember," she replied, fondly rubbing his ear. "So go on and do what you do. I know you, Inspector Chatpati. You're at your best when you're irritated. Get irritated. But first," she said, turning away, "eat your breakfast. Before it gets cold."

By the time he'd got to work, Chatpati's irritation at being made a fool of had pupated into something altogether more prickly, its wings unfurling, aflutter with nascent rage. That, it turned out, was also the mood of the population of Bangalore, at least those who owned a smartphone they could type into with both thumbs.

"Twitter's gone crazy," Raj said from his computer screen as the Inspector walked in. "As has Instagram. And Facebook. #BadCoconut is trending across Bangalore!"

"What does that mean?" Chatpati asked. "Is that good? Or bad?"

"Both," Raj replied. "It's good for someone. And bad for someone else."

"And how is it for Inspector Chatpati?"

Raj looked furtive. "Maybe you should see for yourself, boss."

Chatpati was a social media virgin. He'd never seen the appeal of interminable dialogue with an infinite assembly of idiots on inanities. He could get that from the ACP by picking up a phone. His professional experience suggested that most of humanity had nothing particularly interesting to say. A significant proportion was just plain stupid.

Raj showed him how to scroll through the feeds on Twitter that morning. It only reinforced Chatpati's views on social media.

#BadCoconut was a hotbed of speculation about the demerits of tender coconuts.

#GoodCoconut was the opposition.

The ether resounded with the ping-ping-ping of furious electrons colliding.

@SingleSexyGal: Sooo dangerous! I mean, wld u put something to yr mouth that some unknown guy just handled! Might as well lick his fingers! Yuck! #BadCoconut 🤮

@Coco2Go: Safe packaged pasteurised tender coconut water! Available at all good retailers! Forget dubious hygiene! Stay alive! The Future is Bright! The Future is Coconut! #GoodCoconut #CocoLovesCoconuts

@KalNayak234: @SingleSexyGal Right on, bro. What's so tender about coconut anyway? I prefer kiwi fruit #BadCoconut #GoodKiwiFruit

@Coco2Go: @KalNayak234 Kiwi fruit flavour coming soon! Also raspberry! And mango! 🖤🖤 🖤#GoodCoconut

@KalNayak234: @Coco2Go You rock! 👍
🖤

@KurlMarx99: @Coco2Go U r corporate oppression of the masses. Harvested by children! Children! Sent up trees. Modern day chimney sweeps of India! Shame! #BadCoconut

@Coco2Go: @KurlMarx99 Our product is organic. Our suppliers NEVER use child labour. Children should be at school, not up coconut trees! #GoodCoconut #Coco2Go

@J23Singh: I always drink tinder cocnut water nver hd problem continue to drink. Safe safe safe! OK!

@SingleSexyGal: @J23Singh So old fashioned, uncle. Its like sold ON THE STREETS! #bacteria #foodpoisoning #3dead #BadCoconut

@J23Singh: @SingleSexyGal nevr hd any problem. I will buy street only. Support coconut sellers. Jai Hind! #GoodCoconut

@KalNayak234: @J23Singh Get real, old man. How u xplain 3 deaths? Corrupt! Police corrupt! Coconuts sold by corporations! Corporations pay police! Police ignore deaths! #BadCoconut #BadPolice

@MrsJyothi: shameful behaviour @KalNayak234 police keep people safe without them where is india crime is rampant we need good police like Chapati inspector #GoodPolice #GoodChapati does yr mother know what ur tweeting

@KalNayak234: @MrsJyothi up yours auntie #BadAuntie #BadCoconut #BadPolice Chapati is corrupt #CorruptChapati

@J23Singh: @KalNayak234 @MrsJyothi your language unnecessary police is doing best with minimum #ShowRespect

@Coco2Go: Respect police. Police sometimes get it wrong but they try hard! Coco 🖤 police.

@BangPoliceOff: No evidence of coconut adulteration. Don't spread rumours. Dangerous for public safety #SafeCoconut

@Coco2Go: @BangPoliceOff Safest coconut is Coco2Go. #GoodCoconut

@KurlMarx99: People rise up against oppression! Boycott tender coconut! #BadCoconut #CapitalismCronies #CorruptPolice

@Coco2Go: @KurlMarx99 Boycott is not the way to go-go. Coco2Go is the way to go-go 😃 #GoodCoconut

> @KurlMarx99: @Coco2Go Bugger off, you child slave driver! Burn all coconuts! #BadCoconut #MarxHatesCoconuts

> @BangPoliceOff: @KurlMarx99 Incitement is a crime under Indian Penile Code. Moderate yr language. Or face consequences #BeCool #BeKind

> @KurlMarx99: @BangPoliceOff Go moderate your mother 👍 #BadPolice #BadCoconut

> @BangPoliceOff: @KurlMarx99 You will be arrested soon. #Criminal

> @KalNayak234: @BangPoliceOff @KurlMarx99 Police brutality in action. Incompetence breeds brutality 👍 👍 to the police #BadPolice #BadCoconut

"WHAT DID I SAY, BOSS?" Raj said. "It's crazy."

Chatpati shook his head. "It's gone from licking someone's fingers to moderating mothers to a digital arrest in three screens. Who is this @KurlMarx99, anyway?"

"Some angry guy," Raj said. "There're loads of them on the Internet."

Chatpati scrolled through the feed. "@Coco2Go seems to be getting in on the action. Never losing an opportunity to promote their product. This must be good for them. Oh, and why am I appearing as Chapati? Not that I mind a bread taking the heat."

"Auto-correct," Raj said. "Chapati is more popular than Chatpati."

"Well, that's certainly true. I appear to be persona non

grata amongst the #GoodCoconut crowd. They're blaming me for saying tender coconuts are dangerous. But I didn't. You were there."

"That's social media, boss," Raj said. "Half-truths and outright lies. Take your pick."

Facebook and Instagram were the same. An endless spiralling debate about coconuts. Chatpati soon tired of it, but the thing, it seemed, was inescapable.

The midday news was full of it. The sale of tender coconuts on the street had taken a serious blow. There was a special report.

"I'm talking to you from the coconut wholesale market just outside Madiwala," the reporter said to the camera.

The scrolling banner at the foot of the screen said "Ravi Desai, Reporter, Silkboard Coconut Market.' Behind Ravi lay the expanse of Coconut King Kumar's kingdom. The only difference was that the mountains seemed to have grown skywards. A line of trucks was stalled on the approach road.

"Demand for street tender coconuts has fallen dramatically," Ravi said. "As a result, the movement of the product out of this wholesale market behind me has come to a standstill." He turned and pointed at the trucks. "Those lorries are carrying product in to the market from Karnataka and neighbouring states. Because the coconuts aren't moving out of the wholesale market, there's no space to place the product coming in. We spoke to a few vendors around the city."

The scene changed to Russell Market. Reporter Ravi was standing next to Avicenna Yousuf. Behind them were three pushcarts full of coconuts.

"Mr. Avicenna here owns a tender coconut business in Russell Market, the largest of Bangalore's fresh produce

markets. Mr. Avicenna, you own three stalls here. What's been happening to your business?"

Avicenna shook his head. "It's very slow. I would say business has fallen by over eighty per cent."

"Really?" Ravi did a good job of sounding shocked. "Eighty per cent? That means-"

"Yes," Avicenna nodded. "Out of one hundred coconuts, we have only sold twenty."

"Quite," Ravi said, looking mildly annoyed. "That is what eighty per cent means. And why is this happening?"

"Many customers are avoiding the tender coconut stalls. Previously, we had excellent business. Now, even our regular customers have said they don't want to drink it. They say they are worried about illness, about poisoning. That, I think, is the main reason."

"And is there a risk?" Ravi asked.

Avicenna shook his head so hard it looked like it might fall off. "No, no, no, no, no! There is no risk. Yesterday, tender coconuts were safe. Today, they are still safe."

The scene shifted back to Ravi at the wholesale market.

"The problem is, because the public aren't buying, supply is exceeding demand. The price of tender coconuts has crashed. Producers across the state are rushing to move their product as fast as they can, to cut their losses. As more coconuts flood the market, the price spirals down further."

Ravi looked straight at the camera. "It looks like the tender coconut business might be in free-fall. Back to you, Nita, in the studio."

Nita appeared on the screen. She looked at the camera.

"A temporary setback? Or death knell? That's the question we're asking."

She straightened up and shuffled her papers.

"To help us map the possibly terminal decline of this much-loved drink, we have two experts in the studio."

Shaji Tharakan appeared on screen. He wore a well-pressed long-sleeve shirt. Horn-rimmed spectacles had replaced the sunglasses.

"Mr. Shaji Tharakan is a proponent of the tender coconut lobby," Nita said. "He has a long association with Bangalore's coconuts."

The next face on the screen was also familiar. He had a round face with hamster cheeks. He wore an emerald green silk shirt under an open three-buttoned suit jacket. The baseball cap on his head bore the logo of a grinning green coconut.

"K. Chandra is CEO and founder of Coco2Go, a company that markets packaged tender coconut water in Bangalore. Thank you both for your time."

The two guests had barely nodded a greeting before Nita launched forward in her trademark style.

"Mr. Shaji, the street tender coconut market is dead. Isn't it?"

Shaji looked taken aback. He blinked rapidly, then recovered.

"Not at all!" Shaji replied. "It's alive. And kicking. And what keeps it alive are the people that sell tender coconut water. People are at the very heart of the business. Ordinary people. The ones who harvest it, who transport it, who push their carts through heat and dust and traffic, who cut the coconut, who serve it. All to make a living. Just like you and me."

Nita nodded, studying her notes before she skewered Shaji with her gaze.

"But, surely, you cannot compete with companies like Mr. Chandra's here. Especially considering these concerns about

the safety of street coconut water. Why not admit that the packaged product is safer."

"Not at all," Shaji said. "There's no scientific evidence that street coconut water is unsafe. Not a shred."

"Well," Nita replied, sceptical, "what about the three deaths we reported on not two days ago? Did you see that report?"

Shaji nodded. "I did, Nita, and I also saw the police saying that they investigated it and that there was no evidence."

Chandra broke in."No evidence of anything criminal. Excuse me for interrupting, Nita, but I think we need to be precise. If you're talking about your special interview with the police? Am I correct?"

Nita nodded. Chandra continued.

*"Extremely well made, may I say? Top-notch investigative journalism. As I was saying, Inspector Chatpati said there was no evidence of anything **criminal**. He didn't say there was no evidence of anything **dangerous**. We need to be clear about exactly what was said. And what was not."*

"Oh?" Nita's eyebrows rose. "Are you saying the street product is dangerous?"

Chandra smiled and gave a small shrug. "I'm not an expert in the street product. What I am, though, is someone who buys tonnes and tonnes of tender coconuts. For our product." He pointed at his hat. "Coco2Go."

"Yes, yes," Nita replied, a note of irritation in her voice. "We know your product. What are you trying to say?"

"We pasteurise tender coconut water," Chandra said. "Because it is a raw product. Any raw foodstuff is susceptible to contamination. Our labs go to great lengths to ensure its sterility. Our ISO-certified labs, by the way. Run by highly trained scientists."

Chandra raised his hands in an apparently placatory gesture.

"Now, I'm not saying the street product is dangerous, but ask yourself which product is most likely, of the two, to be a serious hazard to your health? The one that's processed and packaged in laboratory conditions, to strict international standards? Or a random coconut of uncertain provenance, brought from somewhere by someone, passing through countless unwashed hands to be handed to you by another pair of unwashed hands, cut open with a rusty blade and served to you on a dusty street where someone may have urinated not five minutes earlier?"

"I object," Shaji said, raising an arm. "I object."

Nita ignored him and turned to the camera. "I'm afraid that's all we have time for. Let the court of public opinion decide. Join the debate on our social media feeds, using hashtags #GoodCoconut and #BadCoconut."

She looked down at her notes again. "And I have to say that, so far, #BadCoconut seems to be winning."

She looked back up at the camera. "That's it for the lunchtime news. Here's Aarti with the weather."

CHAPTER 22
HEROES AND ZEROES

"Quite ridiculous," Nair said, as the news ended. They'd all ended up watching it on the central display. "It's a storm in a coconut shell. It'll blow over soon."

Chatpati shook his head. "I'm not so sure. If anything, it looks like it's going from gale force to typhoon. What it has reminded me of, though, is that there are still three unexplained deaths. I think I was too quick to dismiss them. Because the only common factor we could find was coconuts."

He pushed his chair back and stood up. "Implausible does not mean impossible."

"What do you propose, boss?" Raj said.

Chatpati ran a hand through his hair. "I hope I will not regret this. Meet me up in the office in ten minutes. Bring all your files. We're going to go over this coconut caper with a fine-tooth comb. Starting at the very beginning."

When Chatpati's office door opened again ten minutes later, it wasn't Raj. Or Nair. It was Hemanth. He was panting from his run up the stairs. Through the open door, the faint sound of shouting filtered through. Many voices. In unison.

"Inspector," Hemanth said, "you should see this."

The rest of the team were already out on the decking of the open-air lounge, crowding the railings. Some were pointing down to the street twenty-four storeys below. Chatpati pushed his way through to Nair's side.

"Down there," Nair said. "At the entrance. It's a demonstration."

There was an untidy knot of people assembled just inside the gates that led to the front entrance of the Utilities Building. Chatpati counted about fifty heads. The crowd faced a man who stood a few paces in front of them, his back to the entrance of the cinema on the ground floor. The man had a megaphone in his hand. He raised it at the crowd. His voice carried up to the watching policemen. The voice was familiar.

"Tender coconut vendors of Bangalore!" the man shouted into his megaphone. "We are here today to demand justice!"

"Yes!" the crowd roared.

"Your good reputation has been despoiled! Your earnings have been lost! Your livelihoods are in jeopardy!"

"Yes! Yes!" returned the crowd.

"Who is responsible for this outrage?"

"Chatpati!" came the howls. "Chatpati!"

"Who do you want?"

"Chatpati! Down with Chatpati!"

The CNU team watched with growing disbelief as four carts of tender coconuts appeared around a far corner and down MG Road. Traffic slowed behind them, horns blaring. Disbelief turned to alarm as the carts turned in through the gates. And were upturned.

Coconuts bounced off the tarmac. Coconuts bounced into the road. Traffic came to a halt. More horns joined the chorus. In a minute, the main entrance to the Utilities Building was a sea of rolling green.

Banners rose above the heads of the demonstrators, too far away to read. The banners jigged as the shouting grew in pitch and volume. A minute later, a white van bearing the BTV logo screeched to a halt on the opposite side of the road. A reporter leapt out, followed by a cameraman and a third man bearing a boom mic. They crossed the median, picked their way through standing traffic and kicked coconuts out of the way to clear a space on the near pavement, just in front of the gates. The reporter faced the camera, gesturing to the protest behind him.

The clamour of horns now echoed into the distance. The queue of traffic tailed back east almost all the way to Trinity Circle half a mile in the distance. Chatpati could see faces pressed up against the window glass of the office buildings across the road. People were spilling out onto the streets for a look. The spectators numbered in their hundreds, all streaming down MG Road, vying for a vantage point.

Seema had her hand over her mouth. "My. God." she said. "What's wrong with them?"

"I think the typhoon just became a hurricane," said Chatpati to no one in particular, his face inscrutable.

"Inspector," Hemanth said at his shoulder, "shall I deploy a drone? Get a closer look at the protestors?"

Chatpati grimaced. "Not sure I want to see what's on those banners, Hemanth, but go ahead. Just stay high. Don't give them any reason to get any more vexed."

Chatpati wasn't sure how high a flung coconut could

travel but a drone crashing down on heads would not help calm the situation any.

Hemanth tapped Seema on the shoulder. "Let's get Garuda One spinning up."

Chatpati followed them back inside, closing the glass door behind him.

The giant display came to life as the drone took to the air. Tens of heads, seen from above, spun gently around the screen as the drone flew a lazy circle. Most were bare-headed, some bald, some wearing head-cloths against the sun.

The writing on the banners was now clear. One said "CHATPATI NO HERO! JUST ZERO!" Another depicted the Inspector's face with horns and a forked tongue. A third demanded "JUSTICE FOR COCONUT MEN!"

As the drone dipped down, the frontage of the cinema came into view. The cinema manager had half-lowered the shutters. He stood just in front of them, speaking quickly into a mobile phone. A pair of porters flanked him, wielding brooms. All three looked ready to retreat at the first sign of trouble.

The leader of the demonstrators waved his megaphone in the air, the other arm raised in a fist. A hundred other fists joined his.

"Chatpati! Chatpati! We want Chatpati!" The fists pumped the air.

The drone's camera zoomed in on the leader. He had a full beard and a slight limp as he ranged across the courtyard.

"Shaji," Chatpati said. "Bloody Shaji!"

They switched to the news channel. BTV were already streaming live from the roadside.

The reporter was Ravi again, his plosives positively

explosive with excitement. He stood on the kerb, behind him the background formed by three lanes of immobile traffic, drivers standing by their open doors. Beyond, the coconut vendors were leaping about and screaming slogans. The banners bounced back and forth. There were coconuts everywhere.

"It's mayhem here on MG Road, the very heart of central Bangalore. We're just outside the Utilities Building, head-quarters of the elite Civil Nuisance Unit. Why is that relevant, you ask? Because these people, coconut vendors from all across the city, are calling for the head of the head of the CNU, Inspector Hari Chatpati."

"Traffic has stalled. The vendors have filled Bangalore's principal thoroughfare with coconuts. And there are more coming! Coconuts, that is."

Nita Singh's voice spoke next. "Thanks, Ravi. What do the vendors want?"

Ravi nodded, clutching at his earpiece.

"Well, that's an excellent question, Nita. We haven't yet been able to make it in to speak to the leader of the demon-strators. We do know that the demonstrators are calling for Inspector Chatpati's resignation. Because they feel the Inspector has damaged their reputation. By feeding the now widespread belief that street coconut water is dangerous! I believe it was you, Nita, who broke that story, just a few days ago! On this very channel!"

Nita's voice was warm. "Thanks, Ravi. Indeed. I remember it well. As I recall, the police said there was no evidence of any harm from tender coconut water. Why are these vendors so riled up?"

Ravi shook his head. "The very suggestion of such a thing,

205

coming from a prominent figure, has turned public opinion. I spoke to one vendor just before we went live. He said his takings have fallen off dramatically after that broadcast. The public just aren't buying tender coconuts any more. It's fear. And that's a dangerous thing."

Ravi disappeared to be replaced by Nita Singh in the studio. "Indeed, it is. And now, it's time for a break. When we come back, we'll have the latest on the trial of Govind Prabhu."

THE AD BREAK began with a dancing green coconut. Chatpati punched a button, and the screen went blank.

"But that's just wrong," Seema said. "You said there was no link. It was the journalists who said there was!"

Chatpati shook his head. "The demonstrators are being led. They don't watch the BTV English news. All they know is what they've been told. And we know who's been telling them."

Nair stuck his head in through the lounge door. "As if it couldn't get any worse. Traffic Division has arrived."

Two Hoysalas had pulled up around the corner. Chatpati watched the Traffic policemen saunter down the pavement, shoving spectators to one side. They tried to push their way through the demonstrators and were rudely rebuffed. The Traffic policeman ran, dodging a hail of flying coconuts. Spectators scattered. Drivers leapt about like goalkeepers, trying to protect paintwork. Some succeeded.

The Hoysalas reversed at speed, back the way they had come and disappeared. A cheer went up from the demonstrators. The banners bounced with the vigour of victory.

Some minutes later, the Hoysalas reappeared at a safe

distance further up the road, at the junction where MG Road meet Brigade Road. The Traffic policemen deactivated the traffic lights and began diverting standing traffic with ill-tempered whistles and threatening gestures. The stalled vehicles on MG Road started moving again, the growl of engines punctuated by the snap, crackle and pop of coconuts exploding under wheels.

"What a bloody disaster!" Nair said. "That Shaji idiot. I knew there was something not right about him." They had convened inside, doors closed against the din. "I say let's deploy the Riot Squad. Disperse those idiots with a few tear-gas canisters and snag that Shaji. A bit of softening up and his coconuts will never be the same."

"Bad idea," Chatpati said. "That lot down there are already agitated. The slightest provocation and this might turn into a full-scale riot. They might set the cinema alight. And with it, this building. Let's just sit tight for the moment. Maybe they'll go away once they've made their point."

There was little chance of that. As the morning wore on, the demonstrators erected a makeshift tarpaulin canopy in the cinema courtyard. They settled in its shade. At lunchtime, more pushcarts arrived with packets of food and water. The demonstrators ate. A few napped.

The cinema had closed, its shutters now fully down. A few of the other businesses inside the Utilities Building had also closed. No customers wished to brave the sea of coconuts. A few of the business owners rang, some to express their regrets, most to express their anger. The Civil Nuisance Unit had itself become a civil nuisance.

Raj watched the day unfold on social media, reporting back to the team at intervals. There was much outrage. It didn't help matters.

#GoodCoconut had allied itself to #BadChapati and #CorruptPolice. The street vendors were portrayed as victims, the Inspector as villain. Conspiracy theories bloomed, cross-pollinated and set seed, spawning alternative stories that spread like Ebola. Unrelated video clips of police brutality and bribe-taking circulated in short order.

#BadCoconut, the opposing faction, had joined forces with #FilthyVendors. These clips showed street vendors indulging in dubious practice. The one gaining greatest traction was that of a vendor peeing into a ditch before cutting up a coconut. Without washing his hands. Vulgar jokes about flavoured coconut water followed. Epidemiologists wailed. Microbiologists warned.

Bangalore churned itself up into an electronic froth. Inevitably, reality followed suit.

By mid-afternoon, news came in of demonstrations elsewhere in the city. Coconut vendors in their dozens had blockaded police stations in Cottonpet, Bharthinagar, Seshadripuram and Malleswaram. There was even a gathering outside the Commissioner's office. BTV News screened breathless reports every half-hour. Every report carried pictures of banners calling for the downfall of Inspector Chatpati.

At four o'clock, there was a rousing cheer from the demonstrators below. The CNU team rushed to the balcony to see. Three Hoysalas were parked on the street outside the gates. There was a police officer facing the demonstrators now, Shaji at his side. Shaji raised both arms for silence before the policeman began speaking through the megaphone. The voice was familiar. And unwelcome.

"I promise you," yelled ACP Srinivasan, "the Commissioner has heard your concerns! There will be a full investigation! And anyone who has been guilty of raising false rumours will be disciplined! Whoever he is! Even if he is a hero! No one is above the law!"

The ACP ended with a finger pointed skywards. Aimed squarely at the CNU twenty-four stories above. There was another swell of wild applause from the crowd.

Chatpati turned to his team.

"Back to your stations," he said. "The Emperor arrives shortly."

Chatpati waited for the ACP in the middle of the dance floor. Srinivasan crashed through the saloon doors like a horny bull, a junior officer in tow. Srinivasan's face was flushed. There was sweat on his brow. Chatpati had never seen the ACP sweat.

Srinivasan slowed to a canter. He applauded as he approached.

"Congratulations!" he cried. "Congratulations, Inspector Chatpati. Your Common Nonsense Unit is not even officially open and you've brought the entire city to a standstill!"

Chatpati stood unmoving, legs apart, arms crossed.

Srinivasan's approach turned into a promenade. The ACP wandered between the tables and out into the open-air lounge. He kicked at a drone. He scuffed the parquet. He glared at the disco ball. Finally, he came to a stop a foot away. Chatpati had not moved a muscle.

"Nice," the ACP said. "Really nice. Love what you've done with the place. It's so you. Just the right blend of ridiculous and useless."

"Well," Chatpati replied, "you should know. Sir. Being an expert."

"Oh, bravo," the ACP replied, applauding again. "A pity your skill for rhetoric was sorely lacking the other day. Great interview, by the way. I've recorded it. We're going to use it for our Media Skills training course. As an example of how not to do it."

Srinivasan waited for a counter, his eyes slits. Chatpati said nothing.

"Oh, well," Srinivasan said, disappointed, "back to business, I suppose. I've come to tell you that I'm placing you on administrative leave. Pending an internal review. By me. Of this whole sorry, ill-conceived set-up and the furore you've raised."

Chatpati shook his head. "So sorry to inform you, sir, but you don't have the authority. Only the Commissioner can do that. Or the Justice Minister."

Srinivasan's eyes narrowed. "The Commissioner agrees."

"Very well," Chatpati said, unperturbed. "You have it in writing, then." He held out a hand. "I'd like to see the order. Sir."

Srinivasan stood stock still. "You'll have it," he growled. "Rest assured. Before the day is out! You will. I'll see to that."

Chatpati crossed his arms again. "Oh well, in that case, I'll stay. Until I have it in writing."

Someone tittered in the background. The ACP swung around. He scanned the policemen arrayed around the dance floor. Their faces were inscrutable. He turned back to Chatpati.

"Suit yourself," Srinivasan said. "Until then, I am withdrawing all Central Division volunteers back to their home units. Effective immediately. That is entirely within my authority, since I'm paying their salaries. The officer there has a list. See that it's implemented. Within the hour."

Srinivasan turned back to the watching policemen. Some faces now registered dismay.

"Yes," Srinivasan said, nodding, "this is the problem. When officers create personality cults. When it becomes about the man, not the job. This is what we have to guard against, this subtle corruption of purpose." He turned back to Chatpati again. "Well, that cult ends today. Any police officer who does not comply with this order will face disciplinary action. Remember what that will involve. And choose wisely."

The ACP gave Chatpati a parting grin. "Let's see you run your precious Unit with no officers."

Chatpati watched him go in silence. Thunderbolts, he had to admit, had a way of landing where they chose.

CHAPTER 23

An Absolution for Sins

Chatpati resisted the urge to retreat to the sanctuary of his office; he knew he should remain with his team. He waited while Raj looked through the list.

"Ten," Raj called out. "We're losing ten. Leaving us with zero constables."

"Ah," Chatpati said. That was bad. "The ACP has holed us below the waterline."

Raj nodded. He looked grim. "I'm on the list," Raj said.

Chatpati nodded back. Worse again.

"I don't feel so well, though," Raj said. "I might have to take some sick leave. For a week, maybe. Which I believe you've already authorised, Inspector."

It took Chatpati a moment to catch on. "Of course," he replied. "How could I have forgotten?"

"I'll let the ACP's office know. And submit the required paperwork," Raj said. He almost winked.

"Ah, yes. The paperwork. It's in my office?" Chatpati said. "Isn't it? And I signed it?"

"Yesterday," Raj said, nodding. "It was yesterday. I'm sure of it."

"I'm staying, sir," Seema piped up. "I came from Traffic, not Central, so you've still got me."

"I'm in too," Hemanth said. "I'm private. And still on contract. To the Unit. Count me in."

It wasn't much, but it would have to do. Chatpati made his way around the constables who had been recalled. They all seemed genuinely sad at having to leave. Constable Krishna was almost in tears.

"It's very unfair, sir," Krishna stuttered. "Very unfair." Chatpati clapped him on the shoulder and wished him well.

When he had done his rounds, he caught Raj's eye. "Did you manage it?" he asked. "What we spoke about yesterday?"

Raj nodded. "As you thought. It's him."

Chatpati was suddenly furious. Suspicion was one thing but confirmation another entirely.

"Where's the Sub-Inspector?" he said, looking round for Nair.

Raj cocked his head. "In his office. He seemed quite upset at it all."

Chatpati frowned. "I wonder why. Bring him up with you. In ten minutes."

Chatpati made the call he had meant to make earlier, before Srinivasan fired his latest broadside. Dr. Saleem, the pathologist, answered straight away. He sounded even more jumpy than usual, but seemed to relax when Chatpati made it clear he bore Dr. Saleem no ill will.

"I'm very sorry, Inspector," Saleem said. "I didn't mean to land you in it. They edited the interview with me, you see. I said you were the only people to take my concerns seriously, but they left that out. I'm very sorry." He sounded devastated.

"Never mind," Chatpati said. "It's done now. If anything, we're both victims of conspiracy. However, I think I can see a way out. One that helps us both, but I need your help."

Saleem's reply came in a rush. "Anything, Inspector. Whatever you need. Anything."

Chatpati asked. And received.

Raj entered some minutes later, Nair at his shoulder. Nair lacked his usual vim. He took his seat without saying a word, gaze on the floor between his feet. Raj took the seat next to him.

"Why so downcast, Vasanth?" Chatpati said.

Nair looked up, as if waking from a dream. He shook his head.

"It's just so vindictive," Nair said. "What happened in there. I'm appalled. Isn't there anything you can do, boss?"

Chatpati scratched his chin. "Not sure. Maybe. The Justice Minister might intervene, but, to be honest, I'm not sure it's worth it anymore."

Nair's jaw dropped. "But you can't give up now! I mean, we've barely just begun. We've already snared a dangerous criminal, that drunkard Chikka Rajan. And there's still this coconut thing. There's clearly more to it than we first thought. Someone's got enough of an interest to land you in it! The news report and now the demonstrations. That's not coincidence!"

Chatpati nodded. "I know. I agree. However, an engine can't run if one of its pistons is misfiring. You understand the analogy, Vasanth?"

Nair looked blank. "Misfiring? Yes, but what's that got to do with anything?"

Chatpati got to his feet and walked over to the grandfather clock. It was running slow, as expected. Chatpati opened the case and set the correct time before turning back to them.

"I should explain," Chatpati said. "The last time I spoke to the ACP, before today, that is, was on the phone a few days ago. When he rang to tell me he'd set up the TV interview. Set-up is the right word. Because that's what it was. A set-up."

Nair frowned and nodded. "And?"

"Something the ACP said just before he rang off struck me as odd. His exact words were 'what's all this about coconuts?'"

Nair looked away. His knuckles were white on the armrest.

Chatpati walked back to his chair and sat down, looking Nair in the eye.

"Which got me thinking," Chatpati said. "How did the ACP know anything about coconuts? At the time, there were only three people who knew about this tender coconut tamasha. All three are in this room. I didn't tell him."

"Nor me," said Raj, turning in his chair to face Nair.

"Which leaves," Chatpati said, "you."

Nair was rigid in his chair, but his gaze flitted around the room like a captive sparrow. There was a light sheen of sweat on his brow. He was breathing quickly, Chatpati noted, the nostrils flaring with each breath. Nair made to speak, but Chatpati raised a hand.

"You're wondering what to say. Let me make it easier for you," he said. "I had Raj look at the call log on your phone." Raj placed a sheet of paper on the desk in front of Nair. "Three calls to the ACP's office. His direct line. The

215

first the day you joined the Bangalore Police Force. Another the day before the ACP called me. And a third just after that disastrous TV interview. The first is perfectly understandable, the last two less so. Care to explain?"

Nair was in the throes of some deep emotion he was struggling to control. Suddenly, the tension slid out of him in a sigh. He slumped in his chair, head in his hands. When he looked up again, his eyes were wet.

"I'm sorry," Nair said. "I let you down. I'm sorry."

"I knew it!" Raj leapt to his feet, chair skidding back. "You're a bloody traitor!"

Chatpati stopped him. "Raj. Let's give the Sub-Inspector a bit of space. Go get him a glass of water."

When Raj had stamped out, Chatpati studied Nair.

"It's alright, Vasanth. I understand. At first, I was furious, of course. I wanted to throttle you, but then I put myself in your position. What would I do if I had arrived as a young Sub-Inspector in a brand new city, into a new police force, and was then asked by a very senior officer, the Assistant Commissioner of Police, no less, to spy on another officer? Bearing in mind that the ACP's goodwill is essential to my future career prospects. With so much at stake, I would do as I was asked. That's how it was. Wasn't it?"

Nair studied his hands. He kept turning them over, looking for something he didn't find. The only sound was the tick-tick-tick of the pendulum. Nair did not reply until Raj returned and slammed a glass of water on the desk. Nair dabbed at the spillage with the tissue he had been wringing in his hands.

"You're right," Nair said, softly. "The ACP said you were unstable. A liability. A wild card. Someone who didn't respect the rule of law. He called you corrupt. He ordered me to keep him informed."

Raj sat in judgement, arms crossed. His voice was scathing. "How could you? Are you blind? Wasn't it obvious that the ACP was lying?"

"Yes," Nair said, nodding "But only later. After we'd snared that villain, Chikka Rajan. And been to Cubbon Park. And Russell Market."

Nair was pleading now. "I said to the ACP that his fears were unfounded. That you were a good policeman. That this Unit was doing good work. Which is why I rang him after that interview. I was horrified. I knew that Nita Singh had used the information I gave the ACP to ambush you with." Nair shook his head. "Srinivasan just cackled. And put the phone down. I see now that the ACP has other motives."

He looked Chatpati in the eye again. "I'm very sorry. I don't know what I can do to put this right."

"What else did you tell him about the coconut case?" Chatpati said. "Names? Dates? Places?"

"No," Nair said, "none of that. I just said we were investigating poisoning from tender coconuts but that there wasn't any evidence of a crime being committed. The ACP didn't ask for details. Nor did I give him any."

"Which is why I never tell the ACP anything," Chatpati replied. "He has no head for details. Or discretion."

Chatpati folded his hands. "I appreciate your confession, Vasanth. It was well done. The product of your Catholic education, no doubt. What's the appropriate reply? You are forgiven your sins, my son. Say ten Hail Marys and feed the poor as penance."

Nair blinked at him. "Are you serious?"

"Oh, yes," Chatpati said. "I don't bear grudges. And, if it's any consolation, I don't think the information you gave the ACP made its way to Nita Singh and her team. He didn't tell her because, like us, he wasn't aware of the significance."

Nair sat up straighter. "How? What do you mean? The ACP—"

"Mentioned coconuts to me, but nothing else. He didn't know any details about the individual cases. If he had known, he would have battered me over the head with them. Nita Singh did, though. Who gave her those details? It wasn't Srinivasan. It wasn't us. She got that from someone else.

"It must be the pathologist then," Raj replied. "Obviously. He's the only other person who knew of the three deaths. He must have informed Nita Singh."

"Possible," Chatpati allowed, "except he didn't. I just rang him. When Nita Singh interviewed Dr. Saleem, she already had the names of the three deceased. The pathologist did not give Nita the names. He merely confirmed, when confronted, what she already knew."

Nair uncoiled, brow set. "Which means there's someone else. Someone else who knew, someone who set us up."

Chatpati nodded. "Yes. One other person. Or persons. The ones responsible for the deaths. The murderers. Because that's what I think this is now. It's murder. With coconuts."

The clock's pendulum completed twenty oscillations before anyone spoke. Raj was first.

"I see now," he said. "The murderers tipped the media off, hoping to land you in it. But that was a mistake. They showed their hand."

"Exactly," Chatpati replied. "We now know that someone else knows. And how could they, unless they were behind the murders? It was a terrible mistake on their part.

If they had let it lie, we would have forgotten all about the coconut poisonings. We'd already closed the case. And they would have got away with it. "

"So, what do we do now?" Raj asked.

Chatpati pointed at the door. "Head downstairs, both of you. I have a call to make, then I'll join you. I need someone to run interference, so that the ACP doesn't sink us completely while we reopen the coconut investigation. The Commissioner must not make a written order. I can't refuse that."

They headed for the door. "One last thing," Chatpati said to their retreating backs. They stopped and turned.

Chatpati pointed at Nair.

"If you ever betray me or this Unit ever again, you're finished. No third chances. From now on, if there's something I need to know, you tell me. Are we clear?"

Nair swallowed, then nodded. "Clear. I won't let you down again. Thank you, Inspector."

Raj sneered at Nair, his tone caustic. "And while you're at it, stop acting like such an entitled ass."

Nair swelled. "Listen!" he began, "I am still your superior officer-"

"Humph," Raj sniffed, walking out the door, "superior in rank, but nothing else. Shut up for a while, why don't you?"

When the door had closed on their bickering, Chatpati made another call. The Justice Minister was unavailable, the PA said, but she would pass on the message.

"It's a matter of some urgency," Chatpati said.

"It usually is," was her reply, "but I'll mention it especially, Inspector."

It was a much diminished team that awaited Chatpati on the dance floor. Hemanth, Seema and two others, constables, Aramada and Jaswant Singh. With Nair and Raj, that made six.

Jaswant Singh saluted. "I told the ACP I'm not going back to Central, sir. I told him I work for seva[1], not salary. He can fire me if he wants. God will find me another job."

Aramada was next to salute. He was the tallest man in the room, six foot four, of the warrior Kodava[2] clan that hunt wild boar with long knives. "We Coorgis fear no man. I, too, am staying."

Seema was despondent. "Sir, they've cancelled the helpline number. We won't be able to take any calls. And Traffic has said they're withdrawing the Hoysala service. They've heard the CNU has been shut down and that they are under no obligation. The news is all over the police force."

"We still have access to PoliceNet, though," Hemanth said. "And the drones are entirely ours."

"Well," Chatpati said, leaning on the console, "it's not all bad. With the helpline closed, we will not be deluged with calls about civil nuisances. We can focus all our efforts on the plan. I'm calling it Operation Thunderbolt. Our first action is to find out who tipped BTV off about the deaths."

"And how do we do that?" Nair asked.

Chatpati looked at them all. He raised his index finger and wiggled it.

"Sort of like a rectal examination," he said. "Probe for a point of entry, then apply judicious pressure. Listen."

CHAPTER 24
CRUISING UNDER THE STARS

I t took three days for the Civil Nuisance Unit to get their first break. The team camped out in the former nightclub, families fore-warned. Nirmala, well used to her husband's extended professional absences, decided to visit her sister in Madras. Chatpati saw her off on the early morning Shatabdi Express from Bangalore Central.

"Be careful, Hari," she said to him through the carriage window. "Look after yourself." He nodded to her from the platform. "I know you won't," she continued, "but at least look after your people, who will look after you. Call me anytime. Remember, I'm only a few hours away."

She blew him a kiss as the train moved off. He waited till the last carriage had disappeared from view.

Chatpati arranged for meals to be ferried up three times a day from the vegetarian eatery on the ground floor. Raj set up makeshift cots in Cloud24's private meeting rooms. It was just as well, because there was plenty to do without having to think about food and sleep.

Anchorwoman Nita Singh was their first target, but she proved a hard nut to crack. Her life had no visible seams.

Her driver ferried her from her villa in the affluent suburb of Koramangala to the BTV studio at 5 am on weekdays and drove her back at 6pm. She had a live-in maid, a cook, and a security guard. Nita Singh had no children and no active romantic interests. She went nowhere else apart from trips to her hairdresser and to her local gym.

BTV News producer Derek Mendes turned out to be riper fruit. Not only did Mendes have tastes in designer clothing that generated large credit card bills, but he was also a frequent visitor to his private members' club, the Centennial off St. Mark's Road. The Centennial Club occupied a large villa set in landscaped grounds that the British had built for their senior civil servants. The building had been refurbished thrice since. Now, The Centennial offered billiards, tennis, badminton, squash, a beauty salon and a swimming pool, but it was the bar that Mendes frequented the most. The first night, Mendes emerged, barely able to stand, held up by a pair of concierges, who unfolded him into the back of a taxi. The surveillance team had expected the same routine the second night, but it was not to be.

"He's moving," Constable Aramada whispered. He was in the driver's seat of a battered van Raj had borrowed from an uncle who ran a vegetable wholesale business. The thing was haunted by the Ghost of Cabbages Past.

"There is no need to whisper," Chatpati said from the passenger seat. They were both in plain clothes. "He can't hear us."

They'd parked the van directly opposite the club entrance off St. Mark's Road. It was 9 pm. There was no shortage of noise and traffic.

"Sorry," Aramada said, lowering his binoculars. "He's just coming out of the gate. Looks well oiled and very unsteady on his feet. Maybe he's going to catch an auto."

He didn't. Mendes staggered out of the gate and tottered up onto the pavement. They watched him cross the road, stumbling through traffic before turning the corner onto Lavelle Road. Mendes disappeared into the shadow of St. Mark's Cathedral. Lavelle Road was a one-way. They could not follow in the van without attracting attention.

Chatpati leapt out. "You go around," he said to Aramada. "I'll follow on foot. Keep your radio on."

Chatpati caught up with Mendes as the producer weaved his way along the pavement, bumping into the odd pedestrian. At the next junction, Mendes waited for the traffic lights to turn red, swaying gently in place, a hand out against the railings to steady himself. He teetered across the intersection, then clambered over the railings into Cubbon Park, nearly ending up on his face. Chatpati ran on in pursuit, making it across just as the lights changed back. He made a more studied traversal of the railings, then called Hemanth at the CNU.

"Yes, Inspector?"

"Mendes has gone into Cubbon Park. I'm following on foot but it's dark. I might lose him. Can you deploy a drone? Take a fix on my position. He's about thirty yards in front, just passing Queen Victoria's statue, heading north-east."

A minute later, there was a hum overhead. A dark shape flitted across the stars.

"Garuda Four just passed you, Inspector. I think I have him. He's crossing the footpath. Zigzagging about all over the place. That him?"

"Yes," Chatpati replied. "Had a few too many whisky sours, I suspect. I'm going to hang back. Let me know when he stops."

He followed Mendes, staying in the shadows cast by the lampposts on the path. There were figures in the darkness, he realised, under the trees flanking the path. The base of each tree trunk had a body draped across it.

For a moment, Chatpati thought he had wandered into some ancient grove guarded by spirit beings, the yakshinis[1] of folklore. He drew closer, only to realise that these were no ghosts, just men. Dressed as women. It was a netherworld of sorts, but there was nothing celestial about it; the treasures they offered were all too earthly.

One stepped away from his/her trunk and called to the Inspector, fingers beckoning. He/she wore a tatty sweater over his/her churidhar. The face was pocked with chickenpox scars, the wig askance, the lips painted scarlet.

"Hey, sweetheart," the transvestite called in a gravelly voice. "Looking for some quick fun? In here. I'll make you happy. Whatever you like."

Chapati turned away and sped up. "What's the matter?" he/she called after him. "Too young for you? You're no prize either, babe."

Mendes had disappeared from view. He was no longer on the path. Chatpati stopped in the shadow of an untenanted chestnut and waited. A few minutes later, his radio buzzed.

"He's stopped," Hemanth said. "There's a pond about a hundred yards west of the path. There's a bench on the northern rim of the pond. Mendes is in the middle of a thicket just north of the bench. I can talk you in. You should know, sir—he's with someone. Shall I send backup?"

"Aramada's somewhere in the vicinity. Guide him in to that location."

Chatpati had to decline two more invitations before he found the pond and the bench. He crept into the shrubbery, feeling his way along the tree trunks, careful to place his feet between the tree roots. He advanced towards the sounds of human passion emanating from a small clearing just beyond. He paused a moment to activate the flashlight on his phone and stepped out.

Mendes was up against a tree trunk, his back to the bark, legs apart. His trousers were undone and had slid down to his knees. Another man, a muscular fellow, naked above the waist, stood between Mendes' legs, his arms wrapped around Mendes' torso, his lips planted on Mendes' own. Mendes' eyes were half-closed, the expression one of bliss.

As the light caught them, the muscular man turned his head towards Chatpati, his face registering alarm. The man coiled away, one hand flying up to conceal his face. Chatpati's last sight of him was a pair of bare shoulders disappearing into shrubbery. Mendes only opened his eyes when Chatpati grabbed him by the collar and pulled him upright.

"Police," Chatpati said. "Derek Mendes. You're under arrest. Pull your trousers up. Idiot."

A minute later, Aramada thundered into the clearing in a flurry of branches, baton flailing. There was no need. Whisky had rendered Mendes incapable; his resistance deflated as swiftly as his libido. The policemen dragged him away, their passage back through the groves of passion marked by the sound of fleeing feet and dissipating lust.

They bundled Mendes into the back of the cabbage van. Aramada closed the doors and chuckled. "Well, that's tonight's business in Cubbon Park interrupted, Inspector."

Chatpati shook his head and made no reply.

En route to the Utilities Building, Chatpati summoned Raj and Nair back from their vigil outside Nita Singh's residence. The pair walked into the CNU just in time to see Aramada dragging Mendes out through the kitchen doors by his collar. Mendes' shirt was soaking wet, his thinning hair plastered to his forehead.

"I dunked him in the large sink a few times," Aramada announced proudly. "He's awake and ready to talk now."

Mendes looked up at Aramada, gave him a lop-sided grin, then bent forward and vomited on the floor.

"Idiot!" Aramada shouted, leaping out of the way. "You're mopping that up now! It's parquet!"

Mendes was in no fit state to handle a mop. He could barely stay in the chair he was placed in. He slumped one way, then the other, until Aramada propped him upright with a chair on either side. So enclosed, the producer made a sorry figure. Bark chips studded his linen shirt. There were stains on his trousers. His zip was half open, his belt unbuckled.

Mendes squinted at the police officers arrayed around him.

"Looks like you got your revenge," he mumbled. "Should've known you would. Police hate gays. Always have."

"I couldn't care less about your sexual preferences," Chatpati replied. "That's your business. Unless it's in a public place. When it becomes mine."

Mendes heaved. Nothing came up. He wiped his lips with the back of his hand, examined it, then wiped it on his trousers.

"What do you want?" he said.

"It's very simple," Chatpati replied. "You tell us how you came to know about the poisoning cases. Who told you?"

Mendes looked confused for a moment, then said "Anonymous. Tip-off."

"How?"

"Phone call. Text message."

Chatpati nodded. "You'll get me that number. Tomorrow. By 10 am."

Mendes tilted his head back. His eyes rolled in his head. He barely managed the next word.

"Or?"

"Or you're charged. Public indecency. You'll go to trial." Chatpati waved his phone at Mendes. "And we file this as evidence. It's a pretty good recording. Your face is very clear. As are the other less salubrious bits."

Mendes' head sagged. A rumbling sound filled the room.

"He's snoring!" Nair said, incredulous. "The bloody idiot's asleep!"

"Can't blame him," Chatpati said. "He's had a long night. He'll be more receptive in the morning."

He turned to Aramada. "Lock him up in the cell. Then head home. All of you. It's been days since any of us have seen the inside of our own bedrooms. Good job tonight. We've got our first actual break."

"Someone should stay with the prisoner," Raj said. "I'll do it."

"No, you don't," Chatpati replied. "I'm staying. Nirmala's away, and I have some work to do. See you in the morning."

When the last of them had trooped out and the doors locked, Chatpati went to check on Mendes. The producer was fast asleep on his side, snorting into his pillow, sans belt and shoelaces. Chatpati didn't think that Mendes would sober up and hang himself in the middle of the night, but he didn't intend to take any chances. He padlocked the door, then, instead of heading up to his office, went out into the open-air lounge.

The night was chilly, the wind quick. The decking squeaked underfoot. There were flashes of lightning in the far distance, a harbinger of storms to come. Leaning over the railing, Chatpati could just see the brake lights of a taxi pulling up the loading ramp below. The headlights lit up the figures of his team on the tarmac. Their laughter floated up to him, the words indistinct.

That was good, he thought. Where there was laughter, there was hope.

He looked out over the dark city. The booming bass-line of electronic dance music carried from the nightclubs on Brigade Road nearby. A DJ was shouting something indiscernible, followed by whoops of delight from his audience. Twin rivers of light, silver and red, flowed down MG Road, the traffic still relentless. He followed the glowing traces west to the vast blackness of Cubbon Park, ringed by ranks of glittering spires. Beyond the park, he could just make out the pillars and dome of the Vidhana Soudha, bathed in the golden glow of floodlights.

A sudden gust set the rotors of the drones spinning. The machines hissed at him like a nest of snakes.

That was all it took to take him back there. To another distant hiss against a cloud-spattered sky. The beginning of it all. And the end.

CHAPTER 25

ENDINGS AND BEGINNINGS

I t had all started on that morning, four months ago, in the basement briefing room underneath Central Division HQ. The walls were charcoal grey, the floor black, the unforgiving duality seeming to suck up the blue-grey light from the fluorescent tubes in the ceiling. There were only enough chairs for forty people. Chatpati had arrived early and snared a seat in the front row. The late-comers slotted themselves in against the walls and spilled out into the corridor.

Alok Sharma, Superintendent of Police, walked in at 6 am sharp. The babble died down as Sharma laid his papers on the lectern. Sharma was the prototype IPS[1] officer: well above the minimum 165cm in height and 84cm chest girth, with perfect near and far vision. His uniform was crisp, the creases ironed to a knife-edge. The trousers were tailored to fit the muscular thighs of a runner. He had a reputation for fierceness and fairness, an unusual combination in the police force. He took off his Aviators and began.

"Good morning," he said, his unamplified voice carrying to every corner. "It's going to be a busy day. Many of you will have done this before. Some will have not. Regardless, you'll have the details of your individual assignments in your briefing notes. I'll assume you've already gone over them. What's not included is the latest threat update. For obvious reasons, that's not been printed out. So here it is. Pay attention. Oh, and if you have questions, ask them as they occur to you."

"Today is the official opening of Parliament. You know that. What you don't know is that both central and state intelligence services have independently raised the terror threat level. There is a high likelihood of an attack. Possibly on the Parliament. Possibly today."

There was a brief murmur from the assembled policemen.

Sharma nodded. "We don't know who or how, just that it's likely. So, besides the usual security precautions, all roads leading to and from the Vidhana Soudha will be closed off."

A map of the area appeared on the screen behind him. The Vidhana Soudha sat in the centre of the screen, Cubbon Park to the east, the Racecourse to the west.

"Palace Road, Sheshadri Road, Ambedkar Road and Raj Bhavan Road, the four roads surrounding Parliament will be closed to vehicular traffic. Hoysalas and Traffic officers will man the intersections. Pedestrians will are to be confined to the far pavement. A no-fly zone is in place for a radius of five kilometres. That means nothing is in the air. No aircraft. No helicopters. Not even kites."

An officer raised a hand. "Metro, sir?"

Sharma nodded. "I was coming to that. The Vidhana Soudha metro station is closed. All metro trains will pass through without stopping."

Chatpati was next. "What about Cubbon Park, sir?"

"Open," Sharma said. There was another murmur from the audience. "I know. At the briefing yesterday, I suggested we should lock it down, but the Mayor and the Chief Minister said it would be too much of an imposition. Apparently, the common man gets something out of watching dignitaries arrive. And the dignitaries like to be seen. So that's where Common Man will be. In Cubbon Park. There'll be a police presence in the park, though. Uniform, mounted and plain-clothes."

"The command post for Cubbon Park will be based in the parking lot of the High Court building, just across the road from the Vidhana Soudha gates. The commander is designated callsign Green One. Easy to remember. Green for park. Green One will be second in command in case I get taken out." Sharma smiled. "Let's hope it doesn't come to that. I have a tennis match tomorrow."

Laughter lightened the mood. Sharma continued, serious again.

"I'm going to run through the call-signs for the Vidhana Soudha itself. I will be Gold One and based on the portico at the main entrance. Bronzes will be Inspectors on the grounds of the Vidhana Soudha. When I call your sign, stand up so your subordinates know who you are."

Chatpati was Bronze One. His task was to man the main gates at the eastern end of the perimeter, directly opposite the park. His team comprised a Sub-Inspector and ten constables. Bronzes Two to Four would patrol the remaining perimeters at the remaining points of the compass.

"There will also be a detachment of CRPF[2] officers based in the building itself. They are armed and ready to respond in case of an attack. The commander will be

Phoenix One. Phoenix One will only deploy under order from me or Green One. Is that clear?"

As clear as it could be, Chatpati thought. It was a lot to take in.

"Just familiarise yourself with your individual role," Sharma said. "Don't get too overwhelmed by the all the details. Memorise the key bits and keep your copy of the briefing at hand. We'll check radios at 7 am once we're on site. Questions?"

Chatpati raised a hand. "Sir, Bronze One. I'm in charge of the gates. What do we do if a dignitary arrives without credentials?" Laughter broke out. Chatpati felt himself flushing. He rushed on. "Sorry to ask, sir. Stupid question."

"Quieten down," Sharma said. "It's a fair question. It's happened. The priority is security. Check all ID. Your briefing notes contain photographs of all the dignitaries and their assistants. If the face fits, let them in. If there's any doubt, escort the vehicle to the main entrance and let me know. We'll screen them there. We want to keep it safe but we don't want to annoy our political masters. Any more than absolutely necessary."

It had all gone well. All the politicians had arrived in reasonable order. There were no bombs in their cars. Credentials passed muster without exception. The radio chatter had been brief and focused. By 10 am, the message came Parliament was in session.

"Stand down but stay alert," Sharma reminded them. "It's not over yet."

The other officers in Chatpati's detail had been chatting amongst themselves when it began. Animated discussion about cricket had rendered them deaf to everything else. Chatpati had been standing by the gates a distance away, looking out across Ambedkar Road to the park. There were crowds of onlookers thick against the park railings. A couple of news reporters had installed themselves on the far pavement, facing their cameras, backs to the Parliament. With traffic suspended, it was quiet enough that Chatpati could almost make out what they were saying. It was a fair day, the heat of the sun tempered by a smattering of cloud.

Chatpati was the first to hear the buzz. He scanned the road, looking for an errant moped. Nothing. The traffic barriers at either end were intact, guarded by paired Hoysalas. He looked through the crowd across the road. Nothing again. It was only as the sound grew louder that he looked up and saw something flit across the sky.

"Gold One, Bronze One," Chatpati said into his radio.

"Gold One," came Sharma's reply. "What is it?"

"A drone, sir. Heading in from the park, towards the gates. About a hundred yards away."

Sharma cursed. "Bloody news drones. There's a complete ban on air traffic. They should know better. Hold."

"Orders, sir?" Chatpati asked. The drone was approaching swiftly. It was white, almost invisible against the clouds. "It's coming in fast."

"Hold, I said."

Seconds later, the machine passed directly overhead, barely ten feet above the gates. Something glinted under its belly. The other policemen in Chatpati's detail saw it as well. One pointed. Heads turned to follow. Chatpati felt the clutch of a nameless dread.

"All units," Chatpati said. "Be alert! Unidentified aerial vehicle heading in towards the main entrance!"

"Maintain radio silence," Sharma replied. "Await orders. Phoenix One, come in."

They watched, paralysed, as the drone dipped, losing height until it was just a few feet above the manicured lawns that sloped up to the Vidhana Soudha's portico. The machine jinked left, then right as it sped on. Chatpati could see Sharma's command detail under the portico, the uniforms a distant khaki blur against the foot of the marble columns. He saw an officer point. There was a glint of binoculars.

That was all there was time for before the drone darted up into the air. And smashed into a column. The tinkle of its demise took a second to arrive.

"It's crashed," Sharma said. "All units, to your stations! Phoenix One, come in, please. We have—"

The radio cut out.

"Close the gates!" Chatpati shouted at his men. "Get a bloody move on! Close the gates! No one gets in or out!"

Operating on gut instinct, Chatpati sprinted towards the building. He took the lawn railings at a run, landed awkwardly on the grass and almost fell. He picked himself up. The Vidhana Soudha loomed above him. The slope of the lawn hid the base of the great white columns from view. He could not see Sharma's detail.

"Gold One, come in," he shouted into his radio as he ran. "Gold One, come in."

He took the marble steps in twos. He was halfway to the top when the smell hit him. A smell he recognised straight away.

"Organophosphate." This from the doctor in the Casualty Department in Hosur during Chatpati's first posting as a Sub-Inspector a year prior. The doctor had motioned to the victim, laid out on a cot. The young farmer had been naked except for a thin pair of shorts. There was a breathing tube in the farmer's throat. It was connected to a ventilator cycling back and forth like a water pump. The farmer's ribs flared as the machine pushed air into his lungs.

The smell had been overpowering. Chatpati had had to cover his face with a handkerchief.

The doctor had laughed. "You'll soon get used to it," he'd said. "It's lethal stuff if you swallow it, almost as bad if it gets on your skin. These farmers use it to kill pests, but it works equally well on humans. It paralyses the nervous system. The breathing stops. Suffocation, then death. If I were a farmer, though, I'd pick a less terrible method to commit suicide."

It was that same smell, a throat-closing chemical stench. Chatpati clapped his handkerchief to his face and ran on. As he neared the top of the steps, he saw the five khaki-clad bodies prostrate on the floor. The uniforms were damp. There was a glossy sheen to the marble under their bodies.

"Gold One is down!" Chatpati said into his radio. "Repeat, Gold One is down!" He ran upwind, eyes still on the fallen. Some bodies were still moving, he saw. Sharma was among them. The Aviators were on the ground beside him.

Chatpati's mind raced. What to do? What the hell to do?

He thumbed his radio, his voice high. "Green One! Come in! We have a chemical attack. Gold One is down!"

The radio began squawking back at him, the voices indiscernible, panic the only discernible commonality. He turned back to the gates and looked around the grounds. From his vantage point high above the grounds, he could see policemen converging on the Vidhana Soudha from all directions.

"Green One! Come in!" he tried again. "Gold One is

down. Green One, you need to take command! We need orders!"

Green One made no response. Orders there were none.

He felt his heart racing. Something, from somewhere deep within him, reached out and plucked one thought from the jumble that tumbled, end over end, through his mind.

He thumbed the radio again.

"Attention, all units! Radio silence. This is Inspector Chatpati. I am Bronze One. Gold and Green are down. I am taking command. Listen carefully to my orders."

"All units are to stay clear of the Parliament entrance. Bronze Two, contact fire and rescue. We need ambulances and fire engines. This is a chemical attack. Likely organophosphate poison. Five officers are down. We need protective gear. Retrieve the casualties and wash the area down. Acknowledge!"

"Bronze Two, received," came the reply.

"Bronze Three and Four, secure the Vidhana Soudha. Secure all entrances and doors."

"Bronze Three. Received."

"Bronze Four. Received."

Chatpati took the remaining steps at a run. He gave the bodies a wide berth and ran in through the entrance. Twelve CRPF officers in camouflage fatigues raced up the stairs from the basement, rifles at the ready. The officer leading them was a Sikh.

"Phoenix One?" Chatpati asked.

The officer nodded. "Captain Deepak Singh. What's going on?"

Chatpati explained as quickly as he could. "How many men do you have?"

"Forty," Singh replied. "What are your orders?"

"Ten with me," Chatpati said. "You take the others. Secure the perimeter. There may be more drones inbound. If you see any, shoot them down."

The Captain spoke into his radio. More armed men appeared. Quickly and calmly, the Captain divided them into two groups. The Captain turned to Chatpati.

"Corporal Madhav is in charge of your lot, sir," he said. "He'll take your orders."

Madhav stepped forward and saluted. He was Nepalese, of that sturdy stock who roam the crests of the Himalayas for a living.

"Good luck, Gold One," the Captain said.

"I'm Bronze One," Chatpati replied. "Gold One is down."

"Consider yourself promoted. You're Gold One now." Singh replied, matter of fact. He saluted, then turned and ran off, followed by his group.

Madhav looked at Chatpati. "Your orders, sir?"

"Follow me," he said. They raced down the corridor.

Four police constables guarded the great doors into the Chamber, rifles across their chests. They leapt to one side as Chatpati shouldered the doors.

The great doors crashed open, the thud echoing back as the soldiers ran in. The Parliamentary Chamber was huge, the size of a cinema, the roof at least fifty feet above, finished in teak and glowing with shimmering chandeliers. An arcade of galleries spanned three of the walls above them, all facing the Speaker's dais on the far wall. Distant faces stared at them from on high, like surprised angels. He could see the 'O's of open mouths and the whites of widening eyes.

The way ahead was down a central aisle floored with luxuriant green carpeting. To either side of the aisle, discontinuous arcs of solid wooden desks and chairs faced forward. There were many open mouths there too, these the parliamentarians. A number were already on their feet.

The Speaker was among them. He pointed down at Chatpati from his dais on high. There was fire and brimstone in his voice as he shouted into the microphone.

"What is this? How dare you! This House is in session!" It sounded like the voice of Jehovah. It thundered off the walls, drowning the gasps.

Chatpati ran up the steps to the dais, his feet clattering on the wood. Behind him, he could hear Madhav shouting to his men.

"Spread out! Secure the doors!"

The Speaker turned to face the Inspector. The Speaker's chin quivered with rage.

"Such impertinence—" began the Speaker.

"Quiet," Chatpati said. More parliamentarians were on their feet now, disbelief on some faces, anger on others. Chatpati grabbed the Speaker's microphone.

"This is an emergency!" he said. "We're evacuating the Chamber. For your safety. You will follow my orders."

The Speaker gave Chatpati a shove. Chatpati lost his footing but saved himself by grabbing the balustrade before he went tumbling down the dais steps.

"How dare you!" the Speaker began again. "This is Parliament! I am in charge here!"

Chatpati unholstered his revolver and pointed it at the Speaker. The man quailed and stepped back, hands up.

"Listen to me," Chatpati said. "This is not a debate! We are going to evacuate the Chamber now, starting with those down here! Spectators in the galleries, remain in your seats. You are safest where you are. Corporal Madhav, escort the MLA's out please. Shoot anyone who refuses!"

Madhav's voice carried. "Affix bayonets!"

Under Madhav's instructions, the CRPF officers split themselves into pairs and herded the Parliamentarians out. A few of the politicians made to argue but soon realised that the point of a bayonet does not do discussion.

"Where to, sir?" Madhav called up. "Where shall we take them?"

"Where you were stationed." Chatpati shouted back. "Take them underground. To the basement. Lock them in. Leave a few man to guard them then come back with the rest. We need to clear the galleries."

Chatpati found his way back out of the Chamber then up the stairs to the spectators' gallery. Many of the civilians were already on their feet, milling in place, torn by uncertainty. A few were heading for the doors.

"Stay where you are!" Chatpati shouted. "It's not safe out there. You're safer in here. Wait. We will escort you out. Get back in your seats."

He roamed the aisles, revolver out. People filtered back to their seats in haste.

The gallery doors opened. Madhav and his men appeared.

"Start clearing these sections," Chatpati said. "You lot take the left, Madhav the middle. You two, come with me. We'll take the right. We'll evacuate in that same order. One section first, followed by the next, then the last. Take them downstairs as well, to the basement."

Chatpati's section was full of schoolchildren, none older than eight, chaperoned by four nuns in grey habits. The nuns moved amongst the children, voices low, radiating calm. The children looked excited but not frightened. To them, this was just another adventure.

One nun turned to him as he approached.

"I'm Sister Margaret," she said. "We're from Saint Theresa's Primary School. Perhaps not the best day for a school trip. Inspector, is it?"

"Yes," Chatpati replied. "Can you gather up the children? We'll leave shortly."

"Yes," Sister Margaret replied, "and we'll be ready." She called to the others. "Jacintha! Anne! Mary! Gather the children. Quickly, now!"

The soldiers had just evacuated the first section when the second drone arrived. Chatpati heard the buzzing from the Chamber below. Dread's icy grip clutched at him again.

He rushed to the railing and looked down on the empty Chamber below. The drone floated in through the open doors that Chatpati's team had rushed through just minutes earlier. It had eight black limbs radiating out from a black body. It spun gently about its axis as it advanced down the central aisle. From above, it looked like the Sudarshana Chakra, the legendary discus of the Hindu God Vishnu, deadly and unstoppable.

"Madhav!" Chatpati shouted. "Quickly! Get them out!"

Panic bloomed like wildfire. Civilians rushed for the single exit. They shoved at each other with elbows. They used their hands as claws. They fell on the steps and were trampled. They grappled in the doorway and were crushed.

Chatpati watched all this with horror, suddenly powerless. He glanced over the railing again. The drone was doing a leisurely circuit of the Chamber below, flitting from empty desk to empty desk. He imagined it looked quizzical. The machine had a camera on either flank, both pointed downwards, swivelling this way and that. The machine was unaware of them, he realised. He knew that would not last.

He looked back at the doors again. The scrum was worse. The soldiers were now deploying rifle butts to heave people through the crush. Screams and groans rent the air. He heard the first skitter of alarm from the children behind him. He spun around. The children were huddled around the knees of the four nuns. The nuns waited patiently, serene in their expectation of deliverance. The only serenity in the whole place, he imagined.

He knew, without being told, what would happen soon. They were trapped. The machine would soon rise. It would see them. When it deployed its payload, as he knew it would, they would all die, singly and severally. Choking and gasping. Ribs flaring to stillness.

There was no escape. No time for escape.

He looked around, and up, and that same something from deep inside spoke to him again.

"Madhav!" he shouted. The corporal released the woman he was manhandling towards the exit and turned. "The sprinklers! Can you see them? Shoot! Shoot at them!"

Madhav's face betrayed a brief bewilderment but, trained soldier that he was, he did not let that impede an order. Madhav barked at two of his men. They raised their rifles.

Three shots rang out, the boom echoing around the chamber. The children screamed and clutched at the nuns' skirts. The nuns dropped to their knees, pulling their children to them.

There was a fine hiss in the air and then all was drowned out by the ringing of alarm bells.

The sprinklers turned on just as the drone floated up to the galleries. It hovered in the middle of the Chamber's expanse, above their heads now. It yawed gently, one way, then another, the spray from the sprinklers churned into mist by its rotors. The drone had a cylinder strapped to its underbelly, a long, silver thing held in place by clasps.

The machine's camera eyes swivelled. One looked Chatpati in the eye, the lens cycling. A single moment passed, the space of a heartbeat, while the hunter studied the hunted. Then, it shot up to the ceiling, hovering for an instant before it dived.

Another flurry of shots rang out. Two hit home. Two rotors splintered into fragments. The machine's earthward swoop turned into a lateral jink. The wounded drone tumbled end over end through the air and ricocheted off the panelling at the end of the gallery. There was an audible ping and then that smell again.

The rest he could only recall in flashes. A nun throwing herself over her children. Small bodies tumbling forward in panic. Wails. Cries. Madhav's face as he rushed up. The Corporal's groan as he heaved a prostrate nun over his shoulder. The very slight weight of the child in Chatpati's arms. The twitching of that slight body as the seizures took hold. The fine froth at the nostrils. The limp limbs batting against his chest in time with the thud of his feet on the stairs as he ran down to the ground floor. The fireman's drawn face on the earth below the balustrade. The arms reaching up for the child. The cascade of water from the hoses drenching him.

The final image was of the final drone dipping towards them from the sky. A fusillade of shots, like thunderclaps. The machine tumbled to earth, scattering policemen as they ran for their lives.

Later, they would learn that the Farmer's War Party had done their homework with exquisite care. The pesticide had been bio-engineered in a converted cowshed to enhance its lethality. An operative, hired as a cleaner months before, had drawn up detailed plans of the Vidhana Soudha. They had plotted alternate routes into the Chamber, through the colonnades on the upper floor and down stairwells. Certain doors and windows had been left open on the day. The simultaneous attacks on the Vidhana Soudha and the High Court had decapitated the command structure with one stroke.

The Commission of Inquiry had found that Chatpati's quick thinking in setting off the sprinklers had damped down the spread of the poison in the Chamber. Many more might have died otherwise, but that was of no comfort to the Inspector.

Superintendent Sharma survived but was medically retired from the police force. Chatpati had been at the ceremony where Sharma had received his commendation. Sharma had insisted on standing, rising unaided from his wheelchair to salute. Alongside Captain Singh and Corporal Madhav.

Sister Margaret had been there as well, her response to Chatpati's outstretched hand a bear-hug. Chatpati's vision swam as he mounted the dais and took the Justice Minister's hand. The medal lay heavy against his chest, like the weight of that child's small, limp body. He'd put it away when he got home and never taken it out again.

Another series of bangs brought him back to the present, back to the open-air twenty-four floors up. Someone was letting fireworks off on the parade ground. He could see the flashes in the distance. The drones whined at him from the decking, the wind quicker now.

He rubbed his eyes, closed the door, and went back into the quiet darkness.

CHAPTER 26
BLOODY SHAJI

Justice Minister Urs rang at 6 am. Chatpati jolted out of a dreamless sleep. His back ached. Restaurant chairs weren't designed for reclining. The Minister sounded as fresh as a daisy.

"Hari, I would apologise for ringing so early, but I suspect you're already up. Quite difficult to sleep, I imagine, with a demonstration on your doorstep."

"Yes, sir," Chatpati replied. "No peace for the wicked. Hence, no rest for the police."

"I got your message. Tell me what's happening."

Chatpati explained as quickly as he could. "We're hamstrung, sir. The CNU is dead in the water. Srinivasan wants to shut us down."

The Minister sighed. "This is quite tedious. Srinivasan has been on my radar for some time. It's said he has some political leanings. My sources tell me he's allied himself with the Opposition. Covertly, of course. It might help his future political career if he helps discredit the Government. By disbanding one of its flagship initiatives."

The Minister was silent for a while. Chatpati waited.

"Let me see what I can do," the Minister said. "The Unit still stands, as does your appointment. You may ignore any order removing you from service unless it has my signature. The issue of resources is a bit more complicated. The agreement was that manpower come from existing police resource until the Unit was up and running. That was a gentleman's agreement between the Commissioner and me. I'll speak to the Commissioner. Discreetly, however, since it wouldn't do for a politician to be seen to pressure the police. It may take some time. Meanwhile, continue to do what you can."

"Thank you, sir," Chatpati replied. "I'm sorry if the BTV interview and the demonstrations have put you in a difficult position. Some of it looks like a set-up. We'll get to the bottom of it."

The Minister's laugh was a short bark. "Difficult? Welcome to the world of politics, Inspector. You haven't earned your stripes until you've had your first ambush. And had your portrait rendered as a demon on a banner or two. Consider yourself blooded. The howling will sound until the next misadventure comes along, then the howling will move on to chase that. Pay it no heed. Carry on."

Chatpati ordered some black coffee and a bottle of mineral water from the eatery on the ground floor and, when it arrived, took it to Mendes. The producer was sitting up on the cot, staring at the cuffs tethering his ankle. Chatpati set the drinks down before him.

"Coffee," Chatpati said. "And water. Drink up. You'll feel better for it."

Mendes did so in silence, his eyes on the Inspector. "What now?" he said.

"Your choice," Chatpati replied. "You remember what

the both of us spoke about last night? Or do I need to refresh your memory?"

Mendes looked away. "No. I get it. Have it your way."

Chatpati watched from the balcony as Mendes hailed an auto. The producer had looked up before he got in. Their eyes met briefly. Despite the distance, there could be no mistaking the meaning behind the Inspector's firm nod.

Nair thundered up the ramp on his Bullet just as the auto pulled away. Nair gave the auto such a glare that the driver nearly crashed into a stack of cartons. Chatpati ducked back in before Nair looked up.

"Good night's sleep?" Nair asked as he strode in. "You look like hell."

"Fair to middling," Chatpati replied. "I need a shower. And a change of clothes."

"Why don't you head home?" Nair said. "Freshen up. Take a nap. I'll call you when something develops. Something will, I assume?"

Chatpati nodded. "Yes. Mendes has till 10 o'clock. It's just gone eight. He knows the consequences of failure. Fine. I'll be back in the afternoon. You know what to do when Mendes rings?"

"Easy. Straightforward police work. Leave it to me."

Chatpati did not move. Neither did Nair.

"You can trust me," Nair said, finally. "Promise."

The flat seemed oddly desolate without the background music of Nirmala's daytime soaps. She'd left food for him in the freezer. He called her while it defrosted in the microwave.

"How are you holding up?" she asked. Piano music tinkled in the background.

"Fine," he said, "though not as well as you, by the sounds of it."

"We're at the Madras Club," she replied. "Kalpana's husband has a corporate membership. It's very nice. You'd hate it."

"Let me guess," he said. "Live music. Waiters in tuxedos. Cocktails by the pool."

"Pretty good deduction, Inspector. Except the waiters are in Nehru jackets. Tuxedos are so colonial, don't you know? This is a modern Indian club now. And the cocktails are excellent."

"Glad to hear it."

"How's it going? Is restitution on the horizon? Should I be ordering a new kitchen? Or should I be looking at what I can get for the existing furniture?"

He grinned. "Hmm, I'm not sure. Order nothing just yet. Except for cocktails. All will be clear soon, I hope."

"Glad to hear it," she said, laughing. "Two Bellinis in and things are looking blurry at this end."

He ate quickly and showered. He packed a couple of spare sets of clothes, a toothbrush and a razor. By the time he made it back to the Unit, it was mid-afternoon.

Seema and Hemanth were playing cards with Aramada and Singh. The pot was soda bottle tops. Raj was at his desk, tapping at the keyboard. They rose as Chatpati entered, but he waved them back down.

"I officially ban all salutes and standing to attention. For now," Chatpati said. "What's the game?"

"Poker," Seema said, excited. "Aramada's teaching us. I'm winning."

"Beginner's luck," Aramada said, dealing. "Care to join us, boss?"

Chatpati shook his head. "Carry on." He went over to Raj's desk. "Where's the Sub-Inspector?"

"Benedict Arnold is out on the prowl," Raj said. "He's chasing down the producer's lead."

Mendes had come through. The producer had forwarded the telephone number of the caller who had given Mendes the tip-off about the deaths.

"It's a burner phone," Raj said. "It's not been active for days, probably discarded now."

"Smart," Chatpati replied. He did not sound crushed, but he was. "I'd hoped the criminal in question would have been less savvy."

"He's not as clever as he thinks," Raj said. "We know where he bought the SIM card. And when. Nair's there now. It's a mobile phone outlet in Indira Nagar. I'm waiting for his call."

They didn't have long to wait until Raj's phone rang. It was Nair.

"Put it on speaker," Chatpati said.

Nair's voice came through loud and clear. There was traffic in the background.

"I've sent it through," Nair said. "You should have it now."

"Got it," Raj said, tapping at the keyboard. "I'm opening it now. The Inspector's here."

"Good afternoon, boss," Nair said. "It's a small place, just off 100 Feet Road. Mom-and-pop kind of business, but they're an authorised re-seller. Handsets and SIM cards. I guess the villain picked this place because it looked out of the way. The time stamp on the receipt says 11.43 am. Paid for in cash."

"What about ID?" Raj asked. Indian law required three forms of identification for the purchase of SIM cards.

"The proof of address was faked," Nair said. "It was a driving licence. The vendor took a photocopy, as required by law. It's bogus. It belongs to the deceased victim of a hit-and-run accident in Malleswaram a week ago. The buyer also provided two passport photos, but I'll bet the buyer is some small-time criminal paid to do the deed by the real masterminds. He'll have disappeared back to wherever they found him, richer than he was before. We'll never find him."

It was a dead end. Chatpati felt deflated. "That's bad news," he said.

"It's not all bad," Nair said. "There's a pub a few doors down. They've had some issues with the neighbours. Residents are apparently not keen on a drinking den next door. The pub's been the subject of some vandalism. So the pub owner installed CCTV."

"And?" Chatpati said.

Nair chuckled. "Look at the CCTV footage. I got the pub manager to email it to Raj. Tell me what you see. At 11.45 am."

The footage was in black and white. It showed a busy residential street with shoppers coming and going. There were rows of motorbikes parked on the pavement. Traffic was light. A man stepped into the frame from the left, the door swinging shut behind him. The man had a plastic sleeve in one hand. The lettering on the door said, "Vinayak Mobile Services. SIM Cards. Phones. Latest models. Good prices."

"The guy wearing a checked shirt and jeans," Nair said. "See him?"

"Yes, but so what?" Raj replied. "We know what he looks like – you already have the passport photo. You said there's probably no way to trace him."

"Wait," Nair said, "keep watching."

The man crossed the road, heading towards another

man waiting on a motorcycle. The first man handed the plastic sleeve over to the motorcycle rider, who handed back what appeared to be a wad of money. The rider's back was to the camera. There was nothing distinctive about the rider's back. There was nothing distinctive about the motorcycle either, except for the fact that it was attached to a trailer. A custom-built trailer bearing a custom-built knife sharpening machine.

The two men parted ways. They caught a brief glimpse of the rider's bearded face as he rose from his seat to kick the motorcycle into life.

"Bloody hell!" Chatpati said. "It's bloody Shaji!"

"Yes," Nair replied. "The man who bought the SIM card hands it over to Bloody Shaji, the unsung hero of the tender coconut fraternity."

CHAPTER 27

SPLINTERS AND THUNDERBOLTS

N ews of the first attack broke while they waited for Nair to return. It started with a ping on PoliceNet.

"Priority One" the display said in a cut-glass English accent. "Priority One Alert."

Seema rushed over to the console, Chatpati and Raj following close behind. There was a single glowing red marker on the map.

"It's a major civil disturbance, sir," she said, listening to the chatter on her headset. "On the outskirts of town. Hosa Market, just inside the southern ring road."

Two more Priority One alerts appeared on the map within four minutes.

"More of the same," Seema said. "Rioting. Destruction of property. Assaults." She looked up at them. "All three sites are produce markets. All south of the city centre."

They listened to radio chatter on the nightclub sound system. The police stations at JP Nagar and Bellandur, within whose jurisdictions the sites of the attacks fell, were small local stations. They had insufficient manpower to attend to all four incidents at once. They called for urgent assistance. Central Division was despatching available forces south to support them. Hoysalas were being diverted from Traffic duties. Fire engines were en route.

They switched to BTV just as "Breaking News!" appeared on screen.

Nita Singh spoke to the camera, her face grave.

"We're hearing about episodes of public disorder taking place around Bangalore this morning. Details are still sketchy, but there have been at least three reports of violence on the streets in the last three hours. We're going live to our reporter, Ravi, who's on the scene at the Hosa Road Market, near the HSR Layout."

Roving reporter Ravi appeared on screen, wearing a motorcycle helmet, its visor down, and holding a microphone. Behind him were rows of shopfronts set into a concrete facade. Most of the shopfronts had their shutters down. A couple were in flames. The remnants of upturned pushcarts smoked in the background. There was produce all over the pavement. Firemen dragged hoses through milling crowds. A solitary policeman tried to disperse the onlookers, waving his lathi[1] with little effect. The hubbub of panic filled the air.

"Thanks, Nita. Yes, it started just an hour ago at this produce market in the city's south, on what should have been a routine day of trading here. The market was full of shoppers when a gang of rowdies arrived on two-wheelers and began attacking the vendors. The rowdies were reported to be wearing face coverings and carrying hockey sticks."

"They destroyed stalls. When the stall-holders tried to intervene, they were beaten. A number have been taken to hospital. The attackers set fire to the stalls with petrol bombs, then escaped. We have some footage from a bystander's phone, which we're going to show you now."

The view changed to the same row of shops, taken from another angle. The picture wobbled badly. People fled in disarray. In the distance, a gang of masked men wielding hockey sticks and crowbars were demolishing a wooden cart, the blows splintering the wood. The cart sagged, then collapsed. Tender coconuts tumbled to the ground. The men turned towards the crowd and ran at them, weapons raised. The intrepid citizen journalist lost his nerve and ran.

Ravi appeared back on the screen. By his side was a wizened man with great grey moustaches clutching a blood-stained cloth to his head. Ravi spoke to camera.

"This is Thimappa. He is the owner of the stall that was destroyed on that clip. He was struck on the head while trying to defend his property. Thimappa, tell us what happened."

The old man shook his head, looking dazed.

"They smashed it, sir. They broke my cart to pieces. And they hit me. I fell down. They kicked me till someone dragged me away. I am bleeding, sir. I have to go to the hospital."

Ravi nodded.

"But you said the rowdies said something to you? Before the attack began?"

Thimappa nodded.

"Yes, sir. Before they started attacking me, one asked if I sold tender coconuts. Yes, I replied, you can see they are tender coconuts. Good quality, I said. Please try one, sir. Then the man called me some very bad words. You're trying to poison me, he said. You coconut sellers are all just scum, trying to kill the public, he said. We won't take it anymore, he said. Then they began beating me, sir. That is all."

Ravi nodded again. "Thanks, Thimappa. You'd better get to the hospital now."

Ravi turned to the camera.

"As you heard, Nita, this appears to be a targeted attack on coconut vendors. It looks like a violent backlash against tender coconuts has begun."

Nita appeared back on the screen, nodding.

"Thanks, Ravi. We've heard of two more attacks at Hulimavu and Anjanapura, just a few kilometres to the west. Again, the first reports suggest that coconut vendors have been the targets. The latest disturbing development in what has been a disturbing story."

Nita looked up at the screen as the phone footage of the attack looped on the screen behind her.

"We're trying to get someone from the police to tell us what they're doing to restore order in the city. Yet again, it looks like Bangalore Police have been caught napping. We'll bring you live updates throughout the day as this develops. In the meantime, on a day of violence in the city, stay safe."

NAIR STRODE THROUGH THE DOORS, helmet in hand.

"What's going on?" he called. "I've been overtaken by a Hoysala and two ambulances screaming down the road with sirens and lights."

Raj filled him in. "Looks like the public backlash has begun. #BadCoconut seems to gain traction."

"Doesn't make sense," Nair said, once they'd watched the news footage again. "It looks organised to me. All three attacks started within minutes of each other. That's not the way genuine public disorder starts. I've policed quite a few student demonstrations back in my old job in Cochin. It starts with speech-making and banners and shouting. The police show up. The protesters throw things. The riot police arrive. Then the protestors overturn a car or two. Then the police charge. The protestors retreat, then they set something on fire. The police respond with water cannon and tear-gas. Answered with petrol bombs. Then another charge. It takes hours to evolve."

"I agree with you," Chatpati replied. "The locations are all peripheral, served by relatively small police stations some distance away. The attackers arrived, struck, and disappeared before the police could respond. It's like guerrilla warfare."

"There's a whiff of something criminal about this." Nair said. "But to what end?"

Chatpati shook his head. "Unclear. Anyway, there's precious little we can do about it. It's far beyond a Civil Nuisance. Let's focus on the task at hand."

"Bloody Shaji," Nair said. "I say again we should snare the villain. We know where he's going to be. At the Silkboard coconut kingdom."

Chatpati got to his feet and studied the glowing blips on the screen.

"Let's think about this a bit," the Inspector said. "Shaji's supposed to be working for the vendors. So why slip details of the deaths to the media? That's not to the vendors' advantage. All it's done is destroy the vendors' reputation. It's as if Shaji's trying to sabotage his own interests."

"What've we got to charge him with, anyway?" Raj asked Nair. "So far, all he's guilty of is getting someone else to buy a SIM card for him. Hardly a major crime."

Nair considered this, then nodded. "I suppose you're right. So what then?"

"Well, Sub-Inspector Nair," Chatpati said, placing an

arm around Nair's shoulders. "I have another task for you. I need you to take something to someone. We need help. Time is short. Events are overtaking us. We don't have the bodies we need to chase this down alone."

"No problem," Nair said. "Where am I going?"

"Think of it as taking a cruise. Not a 'midnight in Cubbon Park' cruise, more an ocean cruise. To the Maldives."

Dr. Saleem, the pathologist, called soon after Nair had left on his mission. Saleem's voice trembled with anxiety. "Three more cases, Inspector! Three more! Just this morning! I've just received the notifications."

"All alive?" Chatpati asked. "Any deaths?"

"No deaths. So far. But it's the same pattern. All between 8am and 10am this morning."

"Send me the case details," Chatpati said. "As soon as. And whatever you do, don't speak to the media. Even if they arrive with a TV camera and stick it in your face. Things are heating up. The last thing we need is more media speculation. Ring me directly if there are any more cases."

"Surely, not for another two weeks, Inspector?" the pathologist said. "That's the pattern, isn't it?"

"I have a feeling the pattern is about to change, Dr. Saleem. Don't ask me why. Just be vigilant."

#BadCoconut and #GoodCoconut were still at odds on social media. #BadCoconut was winning, if judged by the number of retweets, the ferocity of attacks on #GoodCoconut and the volume of threats against tender coconut vendors.

"Is it just me?" Chatpati asked Raj, looking over Raj's shoulder at the screen. "Or has someone just upped the ante?"

"Not just you, boss. Good thing you asked your travel agent for help."

"Ah. Yes," Chatpati said, looking out the windows. "I wonder how the Sub-Inspector is getting on."

CHAPTER 28
-SAVES NINE

Vasanth Nair parked his Bullet outside the fish stall at Johnson Market. He looked around for potential threats. The fish looked old but apart from that, there were no petrol bombs or hockey-sticks. The solitary tender coconut vendor outside the mosque seemed unharmed but unprosperous; the mound of unsold coconuts on his cart was huge. Nair bought a coconut out of pity and the man handed it over with excessive delight. Business was slow, the vendor agreed, no one was buying.

Nair walked the remaining few hundred yards to Myrtle Lane. His shirt was too tight, the trousers too loose but the Inspector had insisted on plain clothes and the only boutique in the Utilities Building that was open didn't cater to Nair's demographic. Hawaiian shirts were not his thing, nor were chinos, but at least the socks and shoes were his own.

The gate-guard at Falcon Travels was new. He nodded as Nair approached and opened the gate.

"Sub-Inspector, welcome," he said. "Please follow the path to the left. As earlier."

Miss Asha was waiting for him at the reception desk. She smiled.

"So glad to see you again, Sub-Inspector. Please. Follow me."

Mary D'Souza was waiting for him in the conference room.

"So pleased to make your acquaintance," she said. Her grip was pleasantly cool. The green of her irises seemed to swallow him up. "We didn't quite meet the first time you called with the Inspector. Please take a seat."

Nair tried to speak, but his tongue wasn't cooperating. He tried again.

"Glass of water?" she asked, placing a crystal tumbler before him. He took a drink and had another go.

"The Inspector called?" he ventured. Nair's ears confirmed that what he said was what he had intended to say.

She nodded. "Indeed. He said you had something for me?"

Nair gulped. He managed a "Yes."

She took the folder from him and set it aside. She smiled at him.

"We'll look into it directly. I have allocated one of our agents to the task." She placed her forearms on the table and leaned forward. "Anything else, Sub-Inspector? Do you require a lift back to the Utilities Building? Something a bit more discreet than your Bullet, perhaps?"

Nair blinked. Twice. He thought of several replies he could make. His tongue seemed to have permanently broken off relations with his brain. "No," was all that squeaked out.

"Of course," she smiled, rising. "We'll be in touch as

soon as we can. Asha will show you out. So pleased to meet you. Do come again."

He made it down the path and through the gate without embarrassing himself further. By the time he'd rocked the Bullet off its stand, his brain got back in touch. He remembered what he had to do, something he hadn't mentioned to the Inspector.

He wasn't disobeying the Inspector's orders, he told himself. Really, he wasn't.

Jimmy Koshy answered straight away. Koshy had been Nair's contemporary in training and was now notionally second-in-command of the Cochin Vice Squad. Koshy's voice was the same deep, belly-born rumbling Nair remembered. It rattled windows.

"Well, well, Vasanth Nair. There's a name that hasn't flashed up on my phone for a while. How are you, you yogic athlete? Still unadulterated by wine, women and hard drugs?"

There was music in the background and a tinkle of glassware.

"Where are you, Koshy?" Nair asked. "It sounds like a nightclub. It's early afternoon, for heaven's sake."

"Hey! What do you think, Nair? I'm a respectable Sub-Inspector of Vice. This is strictly work." Koshy lowered his voice. "Actually, it's a bar. But it's strictly work. What can I do for you?"

Nair explained what he needed. "Can you do it? I've processed it. I just need you to run it."

"Anything for you, Nair, you good Brahmin, you. Send it over. You still have my contact details, right? Oh, that's my target on the move. Must run. Literally. Look me up when you're in town next. We can go out for beers. Or some fish curry, if you prefer."

Nair hit 'SEND' on his phone screen and the electronic file flew off with a whoosh. It wasn't a betrayal, he told himself again, more making amends. And it was now time for more of the same.

Nair rode back to MG Road, passed at speed by a Hoysala with sirens howling. He took care to park a distance away from the Utilities Building. He threaded his way through spectators, staying on the pavement across the road from the building until he was directly opposite the entrance gates.

The demonstration was still ongoing, though the enthusiasm had waned with the heat. It had turned into a sit-in. They had posted sentries, Nair noted. There was a vendor on every street corner holding a phone. The news of the morning's attacks must have reached them.

Nair rang the CNU. "I'm in position," he said. "Target still there?"

"Yes," Seema replied. "He's giving an interview to BTV, just inside the courtyard. Garuda One and Two are ready to go. I'll let you know when he moves."

It wasn't long before Bloody Shaji emerged. He shook hands with a couple of vendors at the gates, accepted their congratulations with a nod of the head, and walked out onto the road. He hailed an auto and got in.

"He's got into an auto," Nair said. "I'm just heading back to the bike."

"Don't hurry," Seema replied. "We have a visual fix on the auto. I'll talk you in. And don't forget the respirator mask. The Inspector said to remind you. Shaji must not recognise you."

Nair slipped it on. As if, he thought to himself. Shadowing smugglers on foot through the alleyways of Fort Cochin at midnight was a much tougher challenge. Nevertheless, he was grateful for the drones. What with the vagaries of traffic and traffic lights, he lost the auto twice.

He caught up with it just as the auto discharged Shaji at the access road leading to the Coconut King's compound. He watched Shaji edge past the lorries parked grille to tail-gate, their flat-beds full of tender coconuts ageing in the sun. There was hardly a soul to be seen within the compound itself; the comings and goings of pushcart vendors seemed to have ceased entirely.

Nair retreated to the Silkboard fly-over and waited under a concrete pillar. Ten minutes later, Seema came over the radio.

"He's on the move again," she said. "Heading back north, back the way he came. He's on his bike. With the trailer. You can't miss it."

It looked like Shaji was heading back into town but a kilometre on, just after the police station at Adugodi, he made an illegal right turn through a break in the concrete median. Nair caught sight of the trailer's brake-lights disappearing down an alleyway between two tall apart-ment blocks. Nair resisted the urge to follow directly, biding his time until he reached the next junction. He made a rapid U-turn and doubled back. The painful personal failings of the last few days had damped down Nair's innate instinct to action. Chatpati's last instructions rang in Nair's ears.

"Keep your enthusiasm in your pants, Vasanth," Chat-pati had said. "There's a lot riding on this. Not just your future, but all of ours. If Bloody Shaji knows we're on to him, we're done for. It's back to Cochin for you, Traffic for Seema, foot patrols for Raj and the meat market for me. We're counting on you. Don't let us down."

Nair parked the bike in the parking lot of an apartment block and trotted down the alleyway on foot. He emerged onto a dirt track that descended into an open square of shrubby waste-ground, about half an acre wide, bordered by trees on three sides. There was a roofless, half-built brick building on his right. To the left, a dusty path lead through a gap in a low brick wall under a stand of trees. The trailer tracks headed left.

"I've lost visual contact," Nair reported, "but I think I know where he is."

"To your left," Seema replied. "There's a bungalow just beyond that clump of trees. He's gone inside, so you should be safe to approach. Once you're near, I'll withdraw the drones. They'll be idling on the roof of that apartment building. Call if you need them."

Nair ducked into the tree-line and crab-walked along the wall, leaping over it through a natural gap in the shrubbery. The bungalow was in a poor state of repair. The roof tiles were askew. The windows were barred, the paint on the shutters peeling. The grounds were over-grown and unkempt, weeds sprouting in clumps through patchy gravel. A creeper had laid claim to one half of the porch, the flush of its heart-shaped leaves almost concealing the motorbike and trailer. There was a second motorcycle parked there, this one an expensive Yamaha road bike with a blue racing cowling.

Nair stayed still and watched for several minutes. The interior of the house was dark and impenetrable. There was no sign of movement or any sound. He was about to make a dash for it when he remembered his phone was not on silent. Nair fished it out just as it rang, sounding the first few bars of "Nineteen", Paul Hardcastle's seminal 1980s hit. He stabbed at it, and Paul Hardcastle was silenced.

He edged back until his back pressed against the wall. If Shaji came out, Nair decided he would leg it back over the wall. He hadn't worn the right shoes for escape, but he would have to make the best of it.

He switched the phone to silent, glancing up all the while for any sign that he had been detected. After several minutes of stillness, he was about to creep forward again, when his phone vibrated.

"Yes?" he whispered. "What is it, Seema?"

"The Inspector said to remember to put your phone on silent," she whispered back.

"You don't have to whisper," Nair hissed back, "and, yes, I've put it on bloody silent!"

The nearest corner of the house seemed the best bet, the least overlooked. Nair scuttled across the gravel and ducked down, his back to the warm brick. He heard a door open around the next corner. He tiptoed to the corner, turned his phone to camera and stuck it out, watching the screen.

There was a good reason Shaji hadn't heard Paul Hardcastle. Shaji was wearing a white plastic boiler suit. He had a plastic visor strapped to his forehead and a mask over his face. He was bent over a kerosene stove set on the concrete floor outside the back door. Shaji pumped the stove's handle a few times, then set a match to it. The flame caught and flared. He adjusted the stove till the flame was steady, then went back inside.

A minute later, he emerged bearing a huge aluminium pot, the kind used by Muslim caterers to cook biryani for wedding guests. This one was large enough to feed a hundred. He placed the pot on the stove then returned with a jerry can. He emptied the jerry can into the pot, then went in again. When he next came out, he carried a sack. He upended the sack into the pot. That done, he cast the sack to one side and went back inside.

Nair waited a minute. He heard Shaji clattering about deeper in the house, nearer the front. Nair weighed the odds. The presence of a second motorcycle suggested someone else was in the house. Shaji or that other person might be keeping a watch from the single window out the back. They might come out with another sack. They might be armed. He remembered the Inspector's words. "We're counting on you."

Nair, however, was a man of action. And it was his gut that decided it for him, just when his brain was bellowing at him to make himself scarce. He slipped around the corner and crawled under the open window. An acrid chemical smell wafted out. The back door was ajar. He reached under it and gently drew it shut. He scooped up the sack and retreated backwards on all fours.

When he reached the shrubbery, he heard the door open again. He didn't wait to find out if Shaji was alone or armed. He leapt the wall and ran.

Sprinting across the clearing towards the cover of the alley, the inadequacy of his footwear became apparent. One loafer slipped off. Nair skidded to a halt, retrieved that one, and threw it in the sack. He was taking the other off when a buzz told him the drones were overhead. He waved the drones away with the other shoe, chucked that in the sack, then took to his heels in socks.

He ducked into the alley and skidded to a stop. His socks, a fetching pair of grey mercerised cotton spandex, were intact, though he feared they would never be the same. He peeked around the corner, retrieving his loafers by feel from the sack. Shaji did not appear at the bungalow gate. Nair slid his loafers back on and returned to his bike.

His phone leapt around in his pocket. He stowed the sack under the bike seat before he answered.

"Are you alright?" It was Chatpati. Nair was pleased to hear the strain in the Inspector's voice. "We saw you running! I've got the Adugodi police station on hold. Do you need help?"

Nair leaned on the Bullet. "I'm fine," he panted. "Just a bit winded. I think I got away clean. Any sign of Shaji?"

"No one's followed you, if that's what you mean," Chatpati said. "Was it necessary to go all Special Operations into the scrub?"

"All in a day's work, boss," Nair replied. He felt tingly and alive. "I wanted to see what he was up to. Shaji's in there with someone else, I think. There's a second motorbike. I'm going to wait here for him or his comrade. There's only one way out and I'm right next to it."

"We're in the van headed out to you," Chatpati said. "We'll be there in half an hour. Stay out of sight until we get there."

CHAPTER 29

BREAKING AND ENTERING

T here was a tea shop directly across the road from the alley. It sat between a furniture store and the yard of a demolition firm. Nair imagined it must have been a vacant lot until the proprietor decided to roof it over with aluminium sheeting. The sign was hand painted, plain white on a rectangle of plywood. "Manickam Tea & Snacks Shoppe" it said.

Nair chanced a crossing of Hosur Road without the benefit of uniformed invulnerability. He clambered over the median with haste and little grace. His shoes stayed on. No vehicle knocked him down, though a lorry gave it a decent go.

Nair took a seat on a bench facing out. He had a perfect view of the alley. He opened up the BTV News feed on his phone while he waited for the Inspector to arrive.

Shaji was on, being interviewed by Eager Ravi, the clip clearly part of the interview Shaji had been giving earlier, before he left the Utilities Building. They were standing in the cinema courtyard, their trouser cuffs awash in a sea of coconuts.

"It's a tragedy," Shaji said. "These are poor, illiterate people. They are the victims. Of falsehoods, of rumours, of the media. They have no means to fight back except through protest. And that's what they are doing. It's a righteous expression of their anger. And the Government must listen."

Ravi nodded absently. He clutched at his earpiece. "I'm just hearing news of another three suspected cases of coconut water poisoning. What do you have to say to that?" He thrust the microphone at Shaji. "Just when you say tender coconut water is safe to drink."

Shaji shook his head. "It cannot be. Tender coconut water is safe to drink. It must be something else. It's all part of this grand conspiracy to disempower the poor."

Eager Ravi nodded again. "Thank you, Mr. Tharakan. We're going back to the newsroom for the latest on this most recent outbreak!"

NAIR SWITCHED it off as his tea arrived. He saw the cabbage van pull up outside the apartment block. He waved to them from the shop entrance, blew thrice on his tea to cool it and downed it, burning his tongue in the process. Hissing like a dragon, he threw some money at the owner and ran back across the road.

He retrieved the sack, then slid in next to Chatpati. Aramada was in the driver's seat.

"Good to see you, Vasanth," Chatpati said. "You had us worried there. What's in the sack?"

"Haven't looked," Nair replied. He explained what he

had seen at the bungalow. "I was hoping some of what he dumped in the pot might be in the sack." He plunged his hand in. "Ah, it's empty. Oh, no, there's something here."

He opened his fist. Lying in his palm was a broken twig, bearing a single leaf and a cluster of crimson berries, the fruit the size and shape of pearls. "Odd," he said. "It's foliage." He turned the sack inside out and shook it. There was nothing else in it.

"What is it?" Chatpati asked. "You're the botanist, right?"

Nair shook his head. "My interest is trees. This is some kind of creeper. I'm not too hot on those. This was growing over the porch of Shaji's squat."

"Why would he be boiling it?" Chatpati asked. "Does it have some kind of nutritional value?"

"I'll need to find out what it is first," Nair said. "When we get back to base. Did you know there have been another three cases of poisoning?"

"Ah." Chatpati said. "So it's out already, is it? Yes, the pathologist rang me. All three victims are alive, it seems. Same pattern, though. I told Dr. Saleem to keep a lid on it."

"A handful of notes will loosen most lids, er, sir," Aramada said. "If not the doctor, there will be onlookers, bystanders, ambulance drivers, hospital porters, orderlies—"

"OK, OK, Aramada, I get the idea," Chatpati replied. "There are lots of people who might sell the news."

"It's high profile now," Nair said. "Any pensioner who has a heart attack near a coconut will be labelled a poisoning victim."

Aramada's radio squawked. He listened, then turned to them. "HQ, sir. The drones are running low on charge. They need to return to base. Hemanth can send the other two out."

Chatpati shook his head. "No need. What we need to do next calls for men, not machines."

They waited. And waited. The cabbage smell in the van became overpowering, so they decamped to the tea shop. And waited. And waited. The tea shop closed, and they had to return to the van. The sun went down. Rush hour came and went. The street lights flickered on. Aramada was just about to get out to hunt for a place to piss when they heard an engine roaring up the alleyway.

They ducked down as the blue Yamaha zipped out of the alley and turned down the road. Nair was out of the van and onto his motorbike in a flash. He heaved the Bullet off its stand and let it roll back under its own weight, starting it as it did so. He nodded back at them, then took off in pursuit. They watched him in the wing mirrors as he raced down the road, gliding in and out of traffic. Nair was putting his helmet on with both hands while steering with his knees.

Aramada shook his head in admiration. "He is a real stunt man, our Sub-Inspector."

"One day, he'll be a dead stunt man," Chatpati said. "Let's pray it's not today. After we wrap up this case would be preferable."

Chatpati and Aramada made their way to the bungalow under cover of darkness. There were lights in the over-looking windows of the apartment buildings behind them but no silhouettes of watchers. They climbed over the gate and approached the bungalow.

Shaji's trailer bike was still on the porch. The bungalow lay in darkness. They circled the perimeter, sticking to the walls and ducking under windows. They listened for signs of life and heard none. There was a padlock on the front door and another on the rear. Unless Shaji had locked someone in, the bungalow was empty.

"Any good at picking locks?" Chatpati asked Aramada, half in hope.

"Yes," the constable replied. "With a crowbar."

Chatpati thought about it. "Can you do it in one go?"

"Easy."

It was. Though it took three. Aramada blamed it on the absence of the right tools. He'd had to use a wrench instead of a crowbar. A wrench was all they could find in the cabbage van.

Chatpati slipped the broken padlock into a plastic sleeve and pocketed it. "Maybe that villain will think he forgot to lock it," Chatpati said. "Better than leaving it behind."

They went in through the rear door. Though the shutters on the windows were open and an evening breeze flowed through the house, there was still a strong chemical smell in the room. Aramada flicked a switch and a fluorescent tube flickered on in the ceiling. It was a kitchen in name and a laboratory in nature.

There was no refrigerator, microwave or oven, just a newish kerosene stove, still warm. The granite counter bore several jerry cans. Aramada read the labels. "Hydrochloric acid. Chloroform. Ether. It's like school chemistry class, Inspector."

The dilapidated kitchen cupboards contained various chemistry apparatus: spirit burners, a selection of funnels and sieves, glass pipettes and conical flasks. Another cupboard contained stacks of plastic boiler suits, disposable face-masks and boxes of blue nitrile gloves. There was a stack of aluminium pots under the counter, next to a rubbish bag full of soiled gloves and disposable wet wipes.

"Put some gloves on," Chatpati said, fishing a pair out of a box. "Whatever he was cooking might be hazardous. Let's look over the rest of the house."

There was an ancient wicker sofa in the living room, the dust on it almost thick enough to serve as upholstery. The ramshackle bed in one bedroom looked like it might collapse with the next gust of wind. The bathroom was only worth pissing in, Aramada taking advantage. A rat scurried away from under the toilet into the open drain in the shower. Aramada kicked at it as it scurried past, upsetting his aim.

The last bedroom contained more jerry cans, these unlabelled. Some of the jerry cans, Chatpati noticed, were red.

"What now, boss?" Aramada asked. "Seen enough?"

Chatpati pointed. "Let's take one of these each. You take a white one, I'll take a red. Make sure the cap is on tight, Aramada. And don't let it touch any bare skin. Let's go slowly. Take your time. Watch your feet. Now is not the time for spillages."

Chatpati rang Nair once they'd safely regained the van. Nair answered straight away.

"Where are you? All well?" Chatpati asked.

"Fine. I'm outside a sweet little villa in Cox Town, just north of Ulsoor Lake. It's where Bloody Shaji lives, I think. He made pretty good progress on that bike. It's a beast. 900cc engine, at the very least. I'd have lost him if it weren't for a bus accident on the way. Nice place, this villa. It's on a prosperous residential street. Walled garden, a driveway. The residents look as pedigree as their dogs. The entire set-up seems out of his price range. Unless he's defrauding his charitable American sponsors. Which is possible. Find anything interesting in the bungalow?"

"Possibly," Chatpati said. "We're going to drop these items off at the CNU, then call it a day. Head home. We start early tomorrow. Plain clothes, but bring your ID."

"Great," Nair said. "I'll see you bright and early."

CHAPTER 30
EVERY COCONUT HAS A SILVER LINING

At 6am the next morning, Chatpati, Aramada and Raj were installed in Manickam Tea & Snacks Shoppe, the van parked on the verge. They were the first customers in. Nair arrived just as they finished their breakfast of idlis and coconut chutney The policemen were all in plain clothes as agreed.

Aramada's idea of plain clothes was a track suit and running shoes. "It's how I go to the gym," he explained. "Don't worry. I've had a shower."

They convened around the back of the van.

"What's the plan?" Nair said.

"We're going to follow Shaji," Chatpati said. "Let's see where it leads us. The drones are charged up. Garuda One is sitting on the roof of that apartment building. Garuda Two is hovering above Shaji's address in Cox Town, the villa you followed him to yesterday."

They squashed themselves into the front of the van, windows down and rear doors open to disperse the cabbage smell.

Chatpati handed the walkie-talkies out. "We'll use

radios instead of our mobiles. I've set the channels. Use the Bluetooth headsets. Looks less suspicious."

"Super," Nair said. He tucked the radio into a trouser pocket. "We should have call-signs. Can I be Bullet One? You can be Cabbage One."

No," Chatpati said flatly. "You will be Nair. Irretrievably, I'm afraid."

Nair pouted. Chatpati ignored him and streamed the BTV News on his phone.

The protests outside the Utilities Building continued.

"It's turned into a sit-in," Eager Ravi said. He was wearing the same shirt from the day before. "About thirty tender coconut vendors spent the night here and more are due to turn up today. This is the fourth day of agitation against the elite Civil Nuisance Unit. The vendors allege it is the words of Inspector Hari Chatpati, hero of the Vidhana Soudha attack, that have lead to a sharp decline in their sales."

Ravi looked down at a sheet of paper in his hand. "Yester-day, BTV received news of more cases of poisonings from drinking tender coconut water." He looked at the camera. "It may be that there is more to this than meets the eye. Could it actually be the case that Inspector Chatpati was right? Is tender coconut water a hazard to human health? Back to Prashanth in the studio."

"They're still saying you made the allegations," Raj said, incredulous. "Nita Singh made that allegation. You denied it. We were all there. We saw it!"

Chatpati shook his head. "Doesn't matter. What's

broadcast becomes the truth. Inspector Chatpati is officially bad news."

The BTV anchor that morning was a man who was clearly finishing the night shift. His suit was creased. His bald patch glistened under the studio lights. He looked at his notes as he spoke.

"Intriguing, Ravi. Thanks for that report. And on a related matter, we have some interesting financial news. We go to our Financial Reporter, Manohar. Manohar, what have you got for us?"

The screen split in half, Manohar appearing on the left. Manohar looked as business as Wall Street. He had hair that was spiky with gel. The suit jacket he wore was black, with dagger-point lapels. His cufflinks glittered as he shuffled his papers. A grinning green coconut appeared on the screen behind him, dancing a jig.

"Thanks, Prashanth. Yes, interesting indeed. It's a day for dancing, if you happen to be in the packaged tender coconut water business, that is."

"We've just learned that Coco2Go, the company whose mascot you see on screen behind me, is planning an IPO, an Initial Public Offering on the Stock Exchange. Coco2Go is going public. They'll be selling shares on the stock market. And traders say the expected offer price is going to be eye-watering!"

"What's so special about that?" the anchorman asked.

"Well, you might ask." Manohar replied, grinning. "So far, Coco2Go has yet to turn a profit. It's posted losses every year since it started trading. It's practically unheard of for a private company that's yet to make any money to list on the stock exchange. That they're even thinking of doing so reflects

*the financial market's expectation that the company is
perfectly poised to exploit the current turmoil in the tender
coconut market. As Ravi mentioned in his piece."*

*Prashanth smiled. "Well, I suppose every coconut has a
silver lining!"*

*Manohar guffawed. "Indeed. It's an ill wind that blows
nobody any coconuts!"*

*Prashanth looked nonplussed. "Um, yes, whatever. Thank
you, Manohar."*

*Manohar looked slightly crestfallen as he disappeared
from the screen.*

"Interesting," Raj said. "Chandra is going big time. He's
seizing the opportunity."

"What did you think of that branch in the sack,
Vasanth?" Chatpati said. "Did you look it up?"

"No time," Nair replied. "I got home fairly late. The
landlady turns the Wi-Fi off at 6pm. All her tenants are
bachelors. She's a strict Catholic. She says late-night Wi-Fi
encourages immoral thoughts. I sent a photo to my university professor this morning though. He'll be able to identify
it."

"You're sure that plant was what Shaji was boiling
yesterday?"

"Well, I didn't look in the pot," Nair said. "There wasn't
time. That twig was all that was left in the sack. I suppose it
could just have been a random remnant. Did you find
anything like that in the bungalow during your recce?"

"No," Chatpati replied. "Though we were looking
around by flash-light, mostly. He might have buried whatever it was. Or taken it away with him."

The radio buzzed. "He's just passing Madiwala, Inspector." came Seema's voice.

They hunkered down in the van as Shaji appeared in the distance. The blue Yamaha disappeared down the alley.

"Action stations," Chatpati said. "Raj, go with Nair. We'll follow."

"Roger that, Cabbage One," Nair shouted as he leapt out. "Get a move on, Raj!"

Fifteen minutes later, Shaji emerged on the trailer bike. He made an illegal right turn, rode against the flow of scant traffic for a hundred yards, then slipped through a gap in the median to gain the other lane. Nair gave him a head start, then followed in his tracks, dodging an oncoming bus that commemorated Nair's passing with a blare of its horns and a fist out the driver's window.

Aramada started the van and followed Nair. Chatpati looked up through the windscreen. Both drones were also in pursuit, a hundred feet above and half a kilometre ahead.

As Chatpati had expected, Shaji's first stop was outside St. Gregory's Hospital. Aramada parked the van just short of the hospital entrance. There was a coconut vendor set up on the opposite pavement a hundred yards further on, under the shade of a neem tree. They saw Shaji's bike parked alongside the vendor's stall. Shaji and the vendor were talking. Chatpati couldn't see the Bullet. He raised Nair on the radio.

"We're in the hospital parking lot," Nair said. "I've told the guard Raj has piles. We're going to dismount and see if we can get a better view. Raj, walk as if your rear end is hurting."

"No, I bloody won't!" Raj hissed back. "Couldn't you have picked some other condition—"

"Enough," Chatpati replied. "Keep it professional.

We're a hundred yards away. We need to get closer without arousing suspicion. I want to see what Bloody Shaji's up to."

"We could limp over," Nair replied. "Tender coconut is supposed to be good for all kinds of illnesses. Maybe even piles. Oh-oh, the guard is coming over. Limp, Raj. Limp, dammit! Clutch a buttock or something!"

Aramada spoke up. "Those two are no use, Inspector. He knows their faces. I'll go. He doesn't know me."

Chatpati fished out the binoculars and watched. Aramada crossed the road and ambled along towards the neem tree, as if he were out for his morning exercise. Aramada made his way along the pavement towards the vendor in a series of squat lunges, ending with a final flurry of jumping jacks under the tree. If Chatpati could have screamed, he would have, full-throated, out the window. He would have thrown stones at Aramada.

Shaji and the vendor grinned at Aramada. Aramada pointed at the coconuts. The vendor picked one and offered it to him. The constable examined it, shook it, then tapped it. He shook his head and handed it back, pointing to another. This happened thrice.

In the meantime, Shaji pulled the starter of the knife-sharpening machine. The thing rattled into life. Through the hospital gates, Chatpati could now see Nair, helmet still on, deep in conversation with the gate guard. The guard gestured towards the Casualty department. Raj, helmet also on, was bent over, one hand on his buttocks.

Chatpati looked back at the vendor. Shaji had a machete in his hand, the traditional tool of the coconut vendor. Shaji placed the blade to the spinning grindstone. Sparks flew. The pitch of the motor turned into a whine.

Aramada leapt back in mock-horror then laughed. The

vendor laughed. Shaji laughed. Aramada took his time draining the coconut, then handed the shell back. Aramada pointed to another coconut.

By the time Shaji had finished sharpening all the vendor's knives, Aramada had downed three tender coconuts and made two jokes, all of which seemed to have gone down a treat. All three chatted for a minute before Shaji raised a hand, got on his bike and rode off.

Chatpati looked left. Nair was now arguing with the guard, arm upraised like some enraged Statue of Liberty. Raj was on his knees. The guard ran off towards the Casualty entrance.

"Come in, Idiot One," Chatpati hissed. "That's you, Vasanth! Shaji's on the move! Get after him!"

Nair turned to Raj, who jumped to his feet. They leapt on the Bullet just as the guard reappeared at a run, pushing a wheelchair. The roar of the engine drowned the guard's shout as the Bullet surged out onto the road. Going the wrong way.

"Left!" Chatpati shouted, head and shoulders out of the driver's window. "Left! Not right!"

Nair set the bike into a skidding turn. Raj almost fell off before Nair righted it. Raj clutched at Nair as the Sub-Inspector gunned the throttle. The Bullet thundered past the van, picking up speed. Raj seemed to have all four limbs wrapped around the Sub-Inspector.

Aramada was making his way back across the road in a series of jump squats. Chatpati waved him on. "Hurry up!" he shouted. Aramada cast a glance over his shoulder at the vendor, then trotted back. He leaned down at Chatpati's window, panting slightly.

"What happened?" Chatpati asked.

"Nothing much," Aramada replied. "We had a chat. A

few jokes. I drank three tender coconuts. The Mandya one was the best. The villain sharpened the machetes, then he left."

"That's it? He just sharpened the machetes?"

"Well, yes," Aramada replied. "Though he had a slightly odd way of doing it. I know about knife sharpening, you see. We hunt with knives in Coorg. It's normal to wet the stone with water before you sharpen it. Gives it a better edge. But he wetted the blade, not the grindstone."

Something flickered in Chatpati's mind, the sensation akin to the end of a movie when the reel flaps free.

"Tell me again," Chatpati said, suddenly breathless. "Exactly."

Shaji had wet the machete with a solution from a white jerry can. He had sharpened the blade on the grindstone, then set the blade down before donning a pair of gloves. He had retrieved a rag from a plastic sleeve.

"He poured some fluid from the red jerry can onto the rag, then gave the whole blade a coating. I asked him about that," Aramada continued breezily. "Told him about my knife sharpening technique. He said my way of doing it was fine for hunting but that the stuff from the red can was to sterilise the blade, you know, keep bacteria and things from growing on it." Aramada shrugged. "New to me. We use our knives to hunt. Killing boars doesn't need a sterile knife." He started at the look on Chatpati's face. "What's wrong?"

"That bloody swine," Chatpati hissed. "The red can! The red can! That bloody swine said the red can contains the dangerous stuff! The stuff you were NOT supposed to consume!" He stared at Aramada. "It's poison! He's coated the blade in poison! Quick! Confiscate those coconuts!"

Aramada was already in full sprint by the time Chatpati had clambered out of the van. Another client stood under the neem tree, a pensioner in shirtsleeves and flip-flops carrying a nylon shopping bag. There was a loaf of bread sticking out of the bag. An instant later, the loaf was airborne as Aramada punched the upraised coconut out of the pensioner's hand. The coconut went the way of the loaf, followed by the pensioner. All three landed in the pile of coconuts.

The production of police ID soothed tempers instantly. Aramada helped the old man up. Chatpati apologised to the pensioner as the old man retrieved his dented loaf.

"It's no problem," the pensioner replied, righting his spectacles. "Anything to help the police."

Chatpati paid the pensioner for the lost coconut and the deformed loaf, then turned to the vendor.

"You're closed for business. We're confiscating your knives. All of them."

The man began wailing. "But, sir! My family! My children will starve, my wife—"

"Yes, yes," the Inspector replied, raising a hand. "I know the patter. Save your breath. Aramada, take a coconut count and this man's details. The CNU will reimburse his day's loss. When you're done, take an auto-rickshaw and join Raj."

Aramada saluted. "Where, sir?"

"That villain's next stop. Cubbon Park."

Chatpati wrapped the knives in a piece of old sackcloth, secured it with twine and ran back with the package to the van.

"Vasanth, where are you?" he called as he started the van up.

"Raj here, sir," came the reply. "The Sub-Inspector is driving. Best to let him concentrate. We're nearing Cubbon Park. What are your orders?"

Chatpati told him as quickly as possible. "Once Bloody Shaji's done at the park, send Nair after him. I'm sure Shaji will be headed to Russell Market next. I'm headed directly there now. You confiscate any knives Shaji sharpens, but only after he has left. Do not let Shaji see you. Do not let anyone drink from any coconuts cut open with those knives! Are you clear?"

"Yes, sir," Raj replied, his voice thin. "Take the knives. No drinking from—oh, God!" There was a blare of horns and a squeal of brakes before Raj's voice cut out.

Chatpati put the van in gear. He hoped Raj was still alive. If Nair was, that would be a bonus.

CHAPTER 31
VILLAINOUS CALUMNY

Chatpati checked in with the CNU en route. Seema confirmed that both Bullet One and Bullet Two were still alive. Shaji had just left Cubbon Park, Nair in pursuit. Raj was confiscating knives.

Chatpati's route to Russell Market was more direct. It avoided running the gauntlet of Central Bangalore's nefarious one-way system. He arrived well ahead of their quarry. He parked the van under the tree next to the tea stall they had been at earlier.

Chatpati got out of the van and thumbed the radio. "Vasanth, where are you?"

"Stuck," Nair replied. "In traffic. Just outside the stadium. There's a cricket match on. The entire area's heaving. The villain is stuck as well. I've got him in my sights. It'll be half an hour at least. I'll call in. Bullet One, out!"

Chatpati ordered a tea from the stall. The owner was just pouring it out from the steaming kettle when Chatpati felt a tug at his waistband. He looked down. It was the small boy. Chatpati held out a hand. The boy placed a phone in it and run away.

"Mr. Avicenna," Chatpati said, "is your boy on permanent lookout? What is he, the Russell Market reconnaissance unit?"

"Ha, ha, ha," Avicenna chuckled. "You know how it is, Inspector. It pays to be watchful." His tone changed, suddenly serious. "We have heard rumours, Inspector. Nasty rumours."

"If it's about the coconuts, don't worry yourself. We're on the case."

Avicenna sounded surprised. "Oh? That is very good. I have seen no riot police in the area, but maybe they are stationed somewhere else?"

"Riot police? What do you mean, riot police? I'm talking about the coconut water poisonings."

Avicenna sighed. "I see. I thought it was too good to be true. Listen."

Avicenna's network of informants had warned of an attack on the market.

"Not just Russell Market," Avicenna said, "all over the city. Organised. There's a lot of cash and Bitcoin changing hands. Hosur Reddy's gang from Raja Market is involved. Also, Lorry Rai's crew. And Cooker Gouda."

"Cooker Gouda?" Chatpati asked. "Not-"

"Yes, Gas Gouda's son. Some rowdies have been called in from the outlying districts. Nelamangala. Tumkur, even Hosur. It's going to kick off, Inspector. Do something."

"Does this have anything to do with the attacks on markets yesterday? You saw the news reports?"

"I fear so, Inspector," Avicenna said. "That was a practice run, I think. To see how the police respond. The real tamasha will happen in the next few days."

"And did the police response pass the test, do you think?"

Avicenna was silent for a moment. "No. The police ran to the crime scene while the criminals ran away. Do something, Inspector. These people are serious. Lives are at stake."

The small boy reappeared after Chatpati ended the call. The Inspector shook his head.

"I'm keeping it," he said. "Here. Have a tea instead."

Nair called in shortly after. "I'm on Sultanji Street. Halfway up from the main market square. Just round the corner from that hellhole of a meat market. I've got Shaji in my sights. Shall I nab him?"

"Don't," Chatpati said, getting back into the van. "Let him do his thing, then confiscate the knives from the vendor after he's left. Let the drones follow him. I'm coming to you. You stay put."

Chatpati found Nair easily. Nair was in the middle of a commotion. There was a small crowd around the coconut vendor, this one a fierce young woman in a blue sari with a matching pushcart. Nair's head was clearly visible above all the others.

"Who the hell are you, bloody hyena!" the woman screamed at Nair. "Help! Help! He's trying to steal my coconuts!" Nair's head bobbed back and forth as the crowd jostled him.

"Halt!" Nair shouted at the top of his voice. "I am an officer of the justiciary! Coconut apprehension is my goal! Thou interferest at thine peril! Mine arm is poised like a tension bow! Don't make me firing!"

The crowd paid Nair no heed. It was getting ugly. Hands pulled at Nair's shirt. He batted them away. Someone swung a punch, which Nair barely dodged.

Chatpati blew the van's horn and drove into the crowd.

They leapt out of the way. Chatpati got out of the van, revolver in hand.

"Bloody bastards!" he shouted. He pointed the gun at the angry faces, turning slowly in place like a lethal lighthouse. "Want a bullet in the face? Do you? Mess with the police, will you? I'll finish you all! Bugger off!"

"Verily!" Nair shouted from behind. "Dissipate, calumny! Ere I withdraw mine own armament and discharge in thine heinous visages! Darest thou cast thine villainous hands on the righteous officers of the justiciary? Dissipate, I say!"

The crowd dissipated as if by command. An instant later, it was just the two policemen and the woman. She began her litany on cue. "Oh God! My children—"

Nair spun on her. "Tranquillity, thou harpy!" The harpy found tranquillity instantly.

Once the formalities had been dealt with, Chatpati called the CNU. They were stretched perilously thin. Raj and Aramada were a good half hour away. If Shaji planned more stops, they might have no time to prevent another poisoning.

"Looks like he's called it a day," Hemanth replied. "He's made no more stops. Heading north-east, out of the city, National Highway 75. Oh, he's taken a right, just past the Jalahalli Metro. He's heading into Peenya. The industrial estate."

"Stay on him," Chatpati said. "Tell the others to return to base. See you shortly."

"Thanks," Nair said, tucking his Hawaiian shirt back into his trousers. "That was getting ugly. Perhaps I should have a firearm too?"

"If you keep speaking Kannada like that," Chatpati

replied, "you may well have justifiable cause to defend yourself with lethal force. We'll discuss it later."

Chatpati held out his hand. "Well done, by the way, Vasanth. I'm proud of you."

Nair started then, hesitantly, took it. He smiled back at the Inspector. He looked like a small boy who'd won the day for his school cricket team.

"Why, thank you, boss," Nair said. "Thank you."

Nair thundered off shortly after. Chatpati waited for Raj and Aramada, who arrived in an auto-rickshaw.

"You drive," Chatpati said to Aramada. "Back to the CNU. Good job, boys. Very well done."

Chatpati rang the ACP's office on the way back. Mina, the PA, sounded surprised to hear his voice.

"Inspector! What can I do for you?"

"I need to speak to the ACP," Chatpati said. "It's urgent."

"Please hold." She came back on the line a minute later. "The ACP said to say he's busy dealing with 'more important things'. I'm sorry, Inspector, those were his exact words, not mine. He ordered me to say just that. Sorry."

Chatpati gritted his teeth. "Tell him I have information that more rioting is going to break out in the city. Tell him to call me if he doesn't want a bloodbath."

Raj cast him an anxious look. "All OK, boss?"

Chatpati shook his head. "No. All is very much not OK."

He tried the Commissioner's office next. The Commissioner was in a meeting with Division Heads and couldn't be disturbed. Chatpati left the same message, then rang the Justice Minister.

"Minister Urs is in New Delhi, Inspector," the PA said. "I will pass your message along directly once he gets out of his meeting with the Home Secretary."

"When will that be?" Chatpati said. "This is extremely urgent."

"This afternoon, I should think. Rest assured, I will make sure your message gets to him."

They were approaching the Utilities Building. The demonstration was still going on. They made their way up the loading ramp without event. Being in a cabbage van helped. No one gave them a second glance.

Chatpati despatched Raj and Aramada upstairs with the confiscated knives. Once they had disappeared into the freight elevator, he fished the business card out of his wallet and made the call.

"Inspector," Mary D'Souza said. She'd answered on the first ring. "So pleased to hear from you. I have the information you requested. I think you'll be pleased."

"Great," Chatpati said sharply. "I mean, thank you. Please send that over to the CNU if you can. I'm ringing about another matter. Sorry if I sound short."

D'Souza said nothing while Chatpati explained.

"Leave it with me," she said after he'd finished. "I'll try to get your message through to the Minister directly."

"Thanks," he replied. "I appreciate it."

"Common purpose, Inspector, whatever your earlier misgivings. We work together and help each other out. Oh," she paused, "I just realised your phone is unencrypted. We'll need to figure out a more secure way of communicating if we're going to be working together in the future. Leave that to me as well. So pleased to be of service, Inspector. Goodbye."

Chatpati didn't like the sound of 'working together in the future' much, but he had far bigger fish to fry and precious few cooks

In Cloud24's restaurant, Nair was holding court,

everyone paying rapt attention except for Seema and Hemanth, who were monitoring the drones.

"And then," Nair said, pointing an imaginary gun at Aramada, "the Inspector said—" He broke off as Chatpati walked in. Nair grinned. "Just filling the troops in."

"What's Shaji up to?" Chatpati asked. The view on screen showed the top-down view of a warehouse set in a walled compound.

"Gone in there. Warehouse in Peenya industrial estate. Just off Temple Road." Hemanth replied. "He took a couple of jerry cans with him from the trailer. He's been in there for a while."

"What is that place?" Nair asked. "Who owns it?"

"I'll have a look," Raj said, powering up his computer. "Give me the co-ordinates."

"I don't think you need to bother," Chatpati said. "Look who's here."

A white sports car was driving up the approach road. The gate guard ran to open the gate. The car drove in without stopping.

"The guard didn't even stop it to check who was in it. Someone important, judging by the guard's haste. Can we get faces, Hemanth?"

"Not from this angle," Hemanth said. "I'll need to get lower. It's risky. They might see the drone."

"Do it," Chatpati said. "We'll take the risk. We need to know who they are. Withdraw the drones once you're done, somewhere close but out of sight."

"CH4NDR4 JR on the car's licence plate," Hemanth read. "Look familiar? Whoops, they've spotted us."

Two men had just got out of the car. The driver was wearing a green baseball cap. He looked up at the drone, then said something to the man getting out of the passenger side. The passenger looked up. With the zoom maxed out, the faces were clear.

"Well, well," Raj said. "Mr. K. Chandra, CEO, and Mr. Santosh Shetty, Director of Marketing. Of bloody Coco2Go!"

Chandra and Shetty ducked their heads and ran for the warehouse. The last thing they saw before the drone spun away was Shetty raising a phone to his ear.

CHAPTER 32

THE DEATH BERRY

Chatpati paid for lunch. The Inspector had been unrestrained in his ordering, his relief at the morning's turn of events materialising as meat. There was mutton biryani and chicken kebabs. There were fish pakoras and seekh kebabs. Nair had not been forgotten either.

"What are we celebrating?" Hemanth asked as he emptied a foil bucket of kebabs onto a Cloud24 serving dish in the kitchen. "Is that it? Is the case done?"

"Not quite," Chatpati replied, removing plates from the dishwasher. "We still have much to do, but we're a lot closer to the endgame than we were a day ago."

The working lunch took place at a loose horseshoe of tables arranged on the dance floor. While the rest of the team seated themselves, Chatpati brought up the map of Bangalore on the giant display, along with the overlay of red dots showing the poisoning cases.

"We know now why the cases appeared one after another at these three locations," Chatpati began.

"Ooot," Nair said, his mouth full. He swallowed. "Sorry. Route. I meant."

"Exactly," Chatpati nodded. "Shaji's route. From his chemistry lab in that bungalow. Starting at St. Gregory's, then west to Cubbon Park and finally north to Russell Market. And the cases only happened on particular days of the week because that was when he went round the vendors."

"But why only one case at each site per day?" Raj asked. "I don't understand that."

Chatpati looked at Nair. "Vasanth, you're the coconut expert here. Care to demonstrate?"

Nair set his plate down. He fetched the sackcloth package and unwrapped it on a desk. He selected a machete and felt its heft in his right hand. Nair walked to the centre of the floor, looking like an urbane butcher. Chatpati tossed him a tender coconut. Nair caught it deftly in his left hand.

Using the edge of the blade, Nair hacked off the top of the coconut in three strokes. Chunks of shell spattered the parquet. A thin remnant layer of husk was all that contained the coconut water within. Nair adjusted his grip and used the curved tip of the machete to pierce it. A few drops of coconut water spilled out of the hole in the shell onto the floor.

There was a brief round of applause. Nair bowed, laid the blade on the console, then returned to his table.

Chatpati took centre stage again. "Any ideas, anyone?"

Seema raised a hand. "The blade was poisoned. With the chemical in Shaji's trailer. But surely any poison would have rubbed off the blade as it cut through the shell. The poison would have been transferred to the husk. Which is now on the floor."

Chatpati nodded. "Correct." Chatpati picked the blade

up. "You use the edge to chop the husk away. There's no poison left on the edge by the time you're done. It's been wiped off, as you say, through contact with the husk. But it's the point of the blade that you use to make the hole. That the customer drinks from." He tilted the blade towards them. "There's poison left on that."

Everyone had stopped eating, all except Nair, who was laying into another cauliflower floret.

"The tip of the blade pierces the coconut," Chatpati said. "The poison on the tip gets into the coconut water."

"Brilliant," Raj said. "And when the blade is used a second time, there is no more poison left on it. Or very little."

"Which means there are no more poisonings," Chatpati said. "The next time the blade is used, it's clean. One case a day, that case the unfortunate person who drinks from the very first coconut cut open with Shaji's poisoned blade. And because the poison takes some time to work, the unfortunate victim makes it some distance away before they suffer any ill-effects."

Seema asked the next question."Why did the first three cases die, then? All the others only got sick."

"For that," Chatpati said, "I hand over to our resident botanist."

Nair plugged his phone into a socket on the console, then swiped at it. The picture that appeared on the display was of the upright trunk of a tree. Entwined around it was a creeper, with clusters of crimson berries and broad, heart-shaped leaves.

"*Anamirta cocculus*," Nair said. "Commonly known as the fish berry and the crow berry. Native to South-East Asia. Notionally a medicinal plant but used, historically, to kill fish. And crows. And head lice. Swallow three pretty little berries and you're as good as dead. The active agent is picrotoxin. The symptoms, I hear you ask? Headache, delirium, seizures, diarrhoea, vomiting. And paralysis. Exactly what the victims suffered."

They applauded again. He bowed theatrically.

"Good job," Chatpati called from the sidelines. "Now where did Shaji get the know-how to extract the poison? Who taught him?"

"Oh, I can answer that," Nair replied. He looked like a small boy caught with his fingers in the cookie jar. "I made some enquiries. My contact in Cochin identified Shaji from his fingerprints. From the brochure he gave me at the coconut yard. I processed the prints myself." He glanced at Chatpati. "Sorry. I should have told you, but I didn't want to lead us on a potential wild goose chase without being sure."

There was a sudden hush as Chatpati glared at Nair.

"Bravo," Chatpati said finally, meaning it. "Bravo, Vasanth."

"Oh, really?" Nair brightened. "Thanks."

Chatpati waved it away. "You still haven't answered Seema's question. Why did the first three cases die? And not the rest."

"A question of dose," Nair replied. "I'm not an expert, but that's what I think. Extracting alkaloids, chemicals, from plants is technical. Some berries have more poison, some less. The poison content depends on many variables: species, sunlight, water. If we were extracting a herbal compound from a plant as a medicine, say, we would need a properly equipped lab to purify and standardise the extract."

Nair paced along the floor. "I think Shaji got the first dose wrong. I don't think the intention was to kill. But it did. Which led to a bit of a delay because he realised he couldn't just boil the bloody thing up in a vat and expect it not to kill people. He got it right the next time. And the time after."

"Of course," Hemanth said, slapping his head. "The warehouse. In Peenya."

Raj broke in. "It's a beverage processing plant. With labs. ISO-certified labs. Belonging to—"

"Coco2Go," Hemanth said. "It all makes sense."

"Shaji Tharakan," Nair continued, "is actually Shyju Thomas. He's a trained organic chemist. He used to cook amphetamines for Tablet Thomin's gang in Cochin. The gang got busted, but Shaji disappeared before the Drug Squad could nail him. I knew he looked familiar. His police record says he has a wife and two children. A few weeks after Shaji disappeared, the wife and children disappeared from the wife's mother's house. I'll bet the family is in that rather pleasant villa in Cox Town. And I'll bet I know who's paying the rent."

"No one's taking that bet, Sub-Inspector," Seema said.

"The evidence is good enough to take Shaji down," Chatpati said, "but not Coco2Go. Or Chandra. Or Shetty. A good lawyer might get them off. And Chandra can afford good lawyers."

Raj looked surprised. "Really? The case seems water-tight to me."

Nair shook his head. "The boss is right. All we've got is Shaji. We can link him directly to the murders, no problem. But Chandra? Coco2Go? The only thing we have is overhead footage from a drone of Shaji's bike parked at the ware-house. And Chandra arriving at the same time."

"Exactly," Chatpati said. "Shaji will keep his mouth shut. If Shaji's going down, he'll want to make sure his family is looked after. Chandra will do that. As the price for Shaji's silence. No, we need more. We need a definite link between Shaji and Coco2Go."

"How?" Raj said. "They must suspect something's up. They saw the drone."

"I have an idea," Chatpati said. "I don't like it. Neither will you. But it's all we've got."

They were just about to leave when the driver arrived. The driver's uniform bore the Falcon logo emblazoned on one breast.

The man nodded at Chatpati. "Sir. From Falcon Travels. With Madam's compliments."

Chatpati took the folder. "Your Travel Itinerary" it said on the cover. Chatpati flipped through it.

"Everything satisfactory, sir?" the driver asked. "Any message by return?"

"Please thank Madam very much," Chatpati said. "And tell her I'll be in touch." The driver touched his cap and left.

"Anything interesting?" Nair asked as they stepped into the lift.

"Oh, yes," Chatpati nodded. "Very interesting indeed. I'll fill you in when we get back."

CHAPTER 33

SWALLOW A SPIDER TO CATCH A FLY

They parked up just after they turned off Webster Road. It was late afternoon. Bloody Shaji's road was lined with elegant houses, all in good repair, many with fine front gardens and lush lawns. It took a lot of money to waste scant metered water on a lawn.

Shaji's villa was the very last on the left, the road ending just beyond at a row of trees. The villa's wall was ten feet high, crowned with barbed wire. Through the leaves of the trees in the garden, the windows of the upper storey were visible. The curtains in the windows were drawn.

"Affluent neighbourhood," Raj remarked. "Lots of schools. Parks. Tennis club. Gymkhana club. I counted at least three pedigree dogs as we passed."

"Nice and expensive," Chatpati returned. "I don't think you or I could afford to live here, not even if we invited the Sub-Inspector to join us."

"Terrible idea," Raj replied, shaking his head. "You weren't there, boss. The driving. On that Bullet. Terrible."

Chatpati patted Raj's shoulder. "Trust me. I've been there."

Seema spoke over the radio. "He's moving. Heading back into town. I've had to pull the drone back. He keeps looking up. I think he's on to us."

"Chandra or Shetty must have told him to watch out. Think he's seen it?" Chatpati asked.

"Maybe," Seema replied. "Hemanth and I are going to leapfrog ahead of him. We'll have one drone over the next junction, then, depending on which way he turns, deploy the other near the junction after. That way, there's nothing obvious overhead."

Nair broke in. "I hope he doesn't head down some side road and leg it. Or leap onto a Metro train. We could lose him." Nair was on the Bullet, parked under the Cox Town flyover a few streets away. "I should have followed him in."

Chatpati considered it and had to admit Nair was right. They might have overplayed their hand. In his eagerness to wrap things up, Chatpati had revealed his only face card. That had been a mistake. The criminals must now know that they were being watched.

"You're right," Chatpati replied. "We got that one wrong. I got that one wrong."

Confirmation came ten minutes later.

"We've lost him," Hemanth said. "He's driven into the underground parking lot of the Mantri Square Mall in Malleswaram." Hemanth paused. "There's a Metro station right next to the mall. He can get to it undercover. The drones are no use. Sorry."

"Not your fault," Chatpati said.

"I could try to get CCTV," Seema broke in. "From the Mall cameras. And the Metro stations along the route."

"No point," Chatpati said. "We'd have to watch, what, forty cameras for hours. We don't have the manpower. Damn."

"In hunting," Aramada said, "you either chase the prey. Or you lure it in."

Chatpati turned to him. "What do you mean?"

"We've lost the chase," Aramada said, "but we have a lure." He gestured at the villa. "There. His family. He'll come for them."

"Not necessarily," Nair replied. "The last time he disappeared, he left his family behind. He sent for them later. Weeks later. He may not come to them today. He might disappear again. We can't wait here for weeks. Aramada's right. We need to bring him here now. I have an idea."

Chatpati nodded. "It's all we've got, I guess. The Civil Nuisance Unit might not exist in days, let alone weeks. What do you have in mind?"

Nair explained. Chatpati didn't like it at all, but time and circumstance conspired against them.

"Are you sure you're up to this, Vasanth?" he said. "You might give the game away."

"Trust me," Nair replied. "I used to do this all the time when I was chasing smugglers. They never saw through me. Until I wanted them to."

Chatpati had serious doubts about the quality of Cochin's smugglers. "Alright," he said. "Go on. But avoid speaking Kannada at all costs!"

A few minutes later, Nair sauntered past the van, as cool as you please, heading for the villa. He gave the van door a knock with his elbow as he passed. "Idiot!" Chatpati growled.

Nair bade "good afternoon" to a lady in her garden watering her roses with a hose. He nodded to an aged man walking an aged Alsatian. Nair looked, for all the world, like a man completely in his element. Chatpati watched through the binoculars. He saw Nair ring the bell at the gate of Shaji's villa. Nothing happened. Nair rang again. Chatpati saw the curtains on the upper floor part, then close. Nair rang once more, then began hammering at the gate.

Chatpati spoke into the radio. "Vasanth! Enough of that. There's someone upstairs. That's enough. Come back before you give the whole thing away!"

Nair made as if he hadn't heard. He knocked again, then paused. The gate opened slightly. There was someone standing just within. Nair seemed to talk a lot, pointing this way, then that. Nair nodded, listening, said something else, then fished a pen out of his pocket and scribbled on a bit of paper from his wallet. He handed it in, then raised a hand and walked back towards the van. The head that popped out to watch him go was that of an old woman, silver-haired and rheumy-eyed, much too old to be Shaji's wife.

Nair walked past the van and turned the corner. The old woman's head receded, and the gate closed. The curtains on the upper level parted briefly, then closed again.

"Their maid," Nair said over the radio. "Not Shaji's wife. But there are children in there. I heard voices shouting 'Daddy! Daddy!'"

"I hope you stuck to English," Chatpati said.

"I chanced it," Nair replied. "I spoke Malayalam. The servant looked like a Malayali[1]. She was wearing a pavada[2] and blouse and those gold hoop earrings old Malayali grandmothers favour. I guessed right. They must have brought her with them to help look after the children."

"What did you say?"

"Oh, I said I was Sam Kandathil, a friend of Shyju's from Cochin. Kandathil and Shyju were both part of Tablet Thomin's gang, before that operation got closed down. Kandathil is still in jail, but I said I'd just been released early. For good behaviour. I said I'd heard from an old work associate that Shyju was in Bangalore. I said I'd just arrived in town, that I was looking for work. The old girl wasn't for letting me in the house, though. She was quite suspicious to start with, but I softened her up with a few familiar names and places. I gave her my number and asked her to tell Shyju to call me."

"Bit of a risk, Vasanth," Chatpati said.

"I don't know, boss," Raj replied. "The maid will tell Shaji's wife. His wife will ring Shaji. It's got to alarm them, some figure from the past turning up on their doorstep unannounced. That might bring Shaji here. And that's all we need. One chance."

Chatpati had to admit that the idea had some merit.

"OK," he said. "Seema, withdraw the drones from the shopping mall. Deploy all four on the approach roads to Cox Town. Let us know if you see him. All we can do now is wait."

And wait they did. It didn't take long. Half an hour later, the radio buzzed.

"Villain's inbound," Hemanth said, relief in his voice. "He's back on the bike. Stopped at traffic lights on Pottery Road, just before the Cox Town flyover. Sub-Inspector, he should be approaching from your right."

Chatpati felt his heart leap. The chase was on again.

"Got it," Nair said. "I'm going to duck behind a pillar. I'll call it in when he passes."

A minute later, Nair called back, his voice taut with excitement.

"Plan's a go. He's just passed me. I'm going to follow behind. I'll give you sixty seconds. Starting now."

Aramada started the van and swung it left across the road so it lay diagonally across the tarmac. With the rain-water gutters on either side, there was no way past. They got out, Chatpati and Raj staying on the right side of the van, concealed from Shaji's approach. Aramada lifted the hood and stuck his head under.

Less than a minute later, the trailer bike swung round the bend and stopped. Chatpati could see Shaji's reflection in the left wing mirror. He was wearing sunglasses and a denim shirt. Shaji shouted at Aramada.

"Hey! Move your van, fool! I want to get past!"

Aramada didn't look up. "It's stalled," he called back. "Sorry. Just give me a push and I'll steer it out of your way, OK?"

Shaji looked annoyed. "Bloody nuisance," he muttered, as he got off the bike. They could hear Nair's Bullet approaching in the distance.

Aramada went round to the driver's side, keeping his face from Shaji's view.

"Just putting it in neutral," Aramada shouted back. "Lean on the rear door so it doesn't roll back when I take the handbrake off. When I say push, push!"

Aramada put the gearstick into neutral, released the handbrake, then leapt out again. Aramada leant against the doorjamb, his left arm through the open window, left hand on the steering wheel. "OK, push!"

They put their backs into it, and the van moved. Chatpati and Raj walked back as the van rolled forward, emerging round the back of the van just as Nair turned into the road behind Shaji's bike. Shaji glanced back at the noise of the Bullet, saw Nair, started and straightened up. The next thing he heard was the click of Chatpati's revolver, pointed at his face.

"Keep your mouth shut, idiot." Chatpati said. "Open the door. Climb in. Lie on your front, arms behind your back. One move, Shaji or Shyju or whichever idiot you are today, and you'll have a sizeable hole in your stupid head."

Raj leapt on Shaji, now face down on the floor, and handcuffed him. Nair was already wheeling the trailer bike back around the corner as Chatpati closed the van's rear doors. Raj and the Inspector got in. Aramada started the engine and reversed out, before putting it in first gear.

Aramada's grin was as wide as the horizon.

"Inspector," he said, as they moved off, "I never thought this Civil Nuisance stuff would be so much fun!"

"Bloody hell!" Chatpati said. "I hope this is the last."

The curtains on the upper storey of Shaji's villa, Chatpati noted, had parted again.

CHAPTER 34
FOUL IS FAIR

The Inspector didn't want to take any chances of being recognised by the demonstrators at the Utilities Building. The last thing they needed was for the demonstrators to stop the van and recognise their fearless leader trussed up in the back. It might turn into a bloodbath.

He had Aramada drop him off at the rear entrance to the Utilities Building then take the van around to the loading ramp. Chatpati went up to the 24th floor ahead of his men. He sent the freight elevator back down, shifting from foot to foot, as he watched it creak its way up again. When the doors opened, all three officers were in it. And Shaji, with a sack over his head.

They dragged Shaji through into the restaurant and sat him down on a chair before they took the sack off.

"Got him! Yes!" Hemanth shouted, giving a little leap. It was the most excited anyone had ever seen him. Seema shook her head in disbelief, hands clasped to her chest.

Shaji's sunglasses had fallen off somewhere. He didn't

look so cool with cabbage leaves stuck to his boot-cut jeans. Shaji craned his neck, scanning the room for exits.

"Forget it," Chatpati said, pulling a chair up. "There no escape for you, Shaji Tharakan or Shyju Thomas. Whichever idiot you are, we've got you."

Shaji chewed at his lip, weighing up his odds. Before Chatpati could react, Shaji jerked up out of the chair and ran for the open door to the balcony. Chatpati leapt for him but missed. If it hadn't been for Raj, Shaji would've been out on the decking before they could've got to him. And over the railings, plunging headlong to earth. Twenty-four floors down.

As it was, the chair Raj shoved into Shaji's path was Shaji's undoing and the CNU's salvation. With his hands cuffed behind his back, Shaji's attempt to leap the obstacle failed; he went down with a clatter, ending up on his face under a dining table

Aramada hauled him back up again by the wrists.

"Argh!" Shaji screamed. "Stop! You're hurting me! My arms! Stop!"

Aramada paid him no heed and dragged him back to the chair. Raj was ready with another pair of cuffs. They clicked into place around Shaji's ankles.

"You'll have to hop out of here now, Bugs Bunny," Aramada said into Shaji's ear.

There was blood on Shaji's face, dripping down from his split lip onto his denim shirt. Raj found a rag and pressed it to the wound until the bleeding stopped.

"Damn, you must be pretty desperate," Raj said to Shaji. "What were you trying to do? Kill yourself?"

"For a chemist, you're pretty stupid," Chatpati said. "The difference between a competent criminal and an amateur criminal is that the good one knows when the game is up. Yours is. There's really no escape. Your best bet is to tell us what we need to know."

The muscles in Shaji's temple worked as his teeth clenched. He looked away.

Chatpati continued. "You can try to ignore me, but it's no use. We have the picrotoxin. We have the knives with the toxin on them. We filmed you making up your poison. We know where your little chemical factory is. Your criminal record and fingerprints are in our possession. There's enough evidence here to charge you with three murders and six attempted murders."

"Murder is still a capital crime," Raj said. "You'll get the death sentence, no doubt about it. Ever seen anyone dangle from a rope? It's not pretty."

Shaji said nothing.

Chatpati scratched his chin. "You might think that silence is your best chance. That Chandra might get you a fine lawyer. In which case, it might be just a life sentence. Either way, you're not seeing your family again."

Shaji had started at Chandra's name. "Oh, yes," Raj said. "We know about Chandra."

Chatpati shook his head. "Such a shame. Your young children growing up without a father. Your young wife with no one to look out for her. Wicked world out there. And a lot of powerful criminal associates who will be furious at all the money they've lost. Because of you."

"It's all in here," Chatpati said, lifting the Falcon folder. "StreetEatz. Your supposed charity. All the money flowing into your bank account. From your 'American donors', actually just shell companies, set up by shell companies, set up by shell companies. Subsidiaries of subsidiaries. It's a complicated network, but we've traced it. All the way back to one Santosh Shetty, Marketing Director of Coco2Go."

Shaji glared at them. "So?" he grunted. "So what? You say you've got it all. Arrest me and get on with it, then. Spare me all this Bollywood hero talk."

Aramada was on his feet, fists bunched. He stalked across the floor towards Shaji. Shaji squirmed and twisted away from Aramada's approach. The giant Coorgi stopped a breath away from Shaji, grabbed him by the hair and turned Shaji's face towards him.

"You just shut your mouth," Aramada growled, "and listen to the Inspector. That's a good Bugs Bunny."

Chatpati tapped Aramada on the shoulder. Aramada stepped back.

"Constable Aramada goes hunting in his spare time," Chatpati said. "I wouldn't annoy him. And the Bollywood hero talk was just the preamble. You know how it is. The hero has to start with a big dialogue about justice and fair play and all that. That was it. There are usually some violins in the background, but the budget wouldn't extend to that. Now, it gets real. And dirty."

"What do you want?" Shaji said through gritted teeth.

"A confession. You tell us all. From start to finish. In exchange, we'll look at getting you a deal. You'll go to jail, but your wife and kids will be in protective custody. They'll still have a life."

Shaji's eyes darted around the room. His mouth worked. "I can't," he said. "They'll know. They'll kill me. I can't."

Chatpati shook his head. He'd hoped it wouldn't go this way.

"Final answer?" he asked. "Before you reply, consider who you're dealing with. We might just **not** let it be known that we cracked this case without your help. What would your criminal associates do, I wonder, if they thought you'd turned informant?"

Chatpati got down on one knee so he could look Shaji in the eye. "You saw how easy it was for us to get to your family. You think they can't? They might send a wicked man to knock at your gate. Your wife is worried. She hasn't heard from you for days. The wicked man says you've had to go into hiding. The wicked man says he's come to help your family get away. Your wife might let him in. Who knows what might happen once the gate closes behind the wicked man?"

Shaji stared at the Inspector, transfixed. Chatpati continued, all thoughts of mercy long dispelled.

"There are places in this city for bones. Dark places. Under bridges. Under culverts. Places people throw their rubbish. Places dogs roam. The bodies are usually dead. But not always. Sometimes, they're incapacitated instead of killed. Alive but unable to move. We sometimes find them with their faces chewed off. Do you really want that to happen? To your wife? Your children?"

Terror wracked Shaji's face. His eyes bulged. Tears ran down his cheeks.

"What will the wicked man do, Shaji? You decide. Because it's your choice."

"Stop!" Shaji wept. "Stop! Please! Enough!" His head lolled. Snot dripped into his lap. "I'll talk! I'll do whatever you want. Just please keep them safe!"

It didn't take long for Shaji to give his first brief confession on camera.

It had been Shetty's idea. Chandra's first plan to recruit vendors as franchisees had been a failure. The company had been losing money hand over fist. Chandra's rich father was not about to throw good money after bad. Desperate,

Chandra sought investment from the criminal fraternity in Dubai, Shetty's so-called 'venture capital' firm. Shetty and his colleagues had pumped money into Coco2Go. Shetty got a seat on the board. With so much at stake, Coco2Go couldn't afford to fail again. So Shetty hit upon the plan to discredit the street product.

A contact of a contact had recruited Shaji. They set StreetEatz up as a front, allowing Shaji access to the street product. The first trial run had not gone exactly to plan. People had died. However, over the next few weeks, Shaji had standardised the poison and the next two trial runs produced the desired effect.

All that remained was to instil fear in the public. The interview with the Inspector had been a godsend to the criminals. All it took was the right word in the right ear.

"What about the attacks?" Chatpati had said, when Shaji had finished. "The attacks on the markets? Was that also part of the plan?"

Shaji had shaken his head. "I know nothing about that," he replied, his eyes on his feet. "I was just told to make sure that, going forward, there were cases of poisoning every day. The pressure had to go up, Shetty said. I don't know why."

They saw to Shaji's wounds as best they could and locked him in the makeshift cell.

"What about his family?" Nair said. "Should we get them out? It's late, but we could head over there now. Bring them here."

"Not yet," Chatpati said. "So far, no one knows anything's amiss. Shetty & Co think Shaji's on the run. They won't expect to hear from him. We'll attend to Shaji's family later. Once we wrap this thing up. If we're quick, it'll be over before the villains can react."

"That was pretty horrible, Inspector," Seema said. "Having to make those threats." She shuddered. "Horrible."

Nair snorted. "He killed three people. I don't think any of their relatives would have any qualms about our methods. It's not nice, but it's just."

Chatpati shook his head. "Sub-Inspector Nair, I never thought I would hear you say something like that."

Nair shook his head back. "I never thought I would see Inspector Chatpati do something like that. Justice is not pretty."

"No," Chatpati replied. "It's not."

"Inspector!" Hemanth called out. He was on his feet, pointing at the display. "It's starting! It's starting!"

Chatpati turned towards him. "What? What's starting?"

"Riots! They're rioting! Look!"

CHAPTER 35
CRY HAVOC

The riots that started that afternoon ran on until darkness fell. It began in Hosur to the south-east as sporadic attacks on coconut vendors. Before long, there were reports of the same at the satellite towns of Magadi, Kombalgodu and Doddaballapura. The pattern was the same: gangs of masked men on motorcycles, beatings with blunt weapons and petrol bombs.

The images of burning stalls and panicked people looped endlessly on BTV News, Nita Singh's breathless voice-over detailing fresh statistics.

"Fifteen hospitalised!" became "Twenty-seven wounded!" then "forty-four with minor and major injuries!"

The police were caught unaware. The outlying districts called for help and help was despatched, arriving too late to do anything except attempt to re-establish order. The criminals were long gone, leaving devastation in their wake.

The social media frenzy ramped up several notches. #BadCoconut was rapidly out-trended by #BadPolice and #PoliceIncompetence. @BangPoliceOff gave up on responding to five thousand expressions of outrage and merely cycled through a series of banal admonishments to "Keep public order!" and "Don't spread rumours. It's a crime!"

ACP Srinivasan appeared on the BTV evening news. Chatpati watched from a dining chair in the restaurant, his team similarly distributed.

Nita Singh was frothing with indignation. Srinivasan had barely acknowledged her introduction before she laid into him.

"So what exactly are the police doing?" she asked. "Days of unchecked violence! Fifty people hospitalised! Markets in flames! People terrified of going out to buy their daily essentials! And the police do nothing!"

Srinivasan shook his saggy jowls. He dabbed at his forehead with a handkerchief.

"Not true! Not true, Nita," Srinivasan said. "The police are responding. We've scrambled all available forces to the scenes of the crimes-"

"Scrambled?" Nita returned. "A great word. For eggs! Hasn't your whole handling of this been nothing but a big, yolky mess?"

"That's very unfair," Srinivasan said. "The fact is, these attacks today are happening outside Central Division jurisdiction—"

"Oh? So because it's not in your patch, you're not concerned? Is that it? If my neighbour is being battered by hooligans in his backyard, I hide in mine? Because it's not happening in mine? Is that your approach?"

Srinivasan had a hand up. "No, no. You're not letting me finish. What I meant to say is that we are helping our colleagues, but we also have our local policing priorities to keep in mind. Our approach has to balance resources against need."

Nita nodded. She had the look of a headsman listening to her victim's last defence.

"Right," she said sarcastically. "Of course. I let my neighbour get battered to a pulp because I have to water the roses right now. That's your approach?"

There were damp patches under Srinivasan's arms. His collar was wilting.

"No, that is not what I am saying—"

"That's all we have time for," Nita snapped as the axe fell. "ACP Srinivasan, we're so pleased you could join us to tell us what the police plan to do. Perhaps you should have spent that time actually doing it!"

She turned to the camera. "Are the police just sitting back and waiting for things to happen? Should the police be more pro-active? What's being done to anticipate these threats? Is this the new 'intelligent' policing the Justice Minister spoke about? You decide. Join the discussion on our social channels."

NAIR TURNED to Chatpati with a smile on his face. "It couldn't have happened to a better Assistant Commissioner."

Chatpati was about to reply when his phone buzzed. It was the ACP's PA.

"Inspector," she said. "I have ACP Srinivasan on the phone. Please hold."

"Sorry," Chatpati replied. "Tell the ACP I have more important things to deal with. You can use those exact words." He ended the call.

"Not so *persona non grata* now, eh?" Nair said. He rose to

his feet, arms raised to the ceiling. "Oh Fortune! Fortune! All men call thee fickle!"

Chatpati got up. "Alright, Mr. Shakespeare, let's call it a day. Tomorrow, we make our move on Coco2Go. Bring your machetes."

As he made his way to the Metro station, Chatpati couldn't help but notice that there was nary a street vendor to be seen. The usual office crowd, spooning chaat into their mouths from the vendor on Residency Road, was conspicuous by its absence. There was no sign of the chaat[1] stall or its owner. The orange juice man on Church Street had disappeared. Even the paan[2] vendor outside the string of restaurants had gone.

Many of the shops had already downed their shutters, he noticed. They had taken in the goods that were usually displayed on the pavements in. Even the Metro was quiet – there were vacant seats. The passengers all seemed to be plugged in to the unfolding violence on their screens, their faces flickering with the flash of pixel-rendered flames.

He called Avicenna as he closed the front door of the apartment.

"Another practice run?" he asked without preamble.

"Maybe the real thing," Avicenna said. "Who knows?"

"What's the word on the streets?"

"The streets are silent, Inspector. The city is shutting down. Russell Market is inhabited only by ghosts. There are all kinds of rumours floating about. People are scared. This is a bigger thing than any of us know how to deal with."

Chatpati nodded. "I've let the right people know what might be happening. Keep in touch if anything new develops."

"I will, Inspector. Though if the last few days are

anything to go by, we civilians had better prepare to look after ourselves."

Inspector Chatpati slept soundly that night. So soundly that he woke up an hour later than usual. In his hurry to get to work, he didn't watch the news until he got to the Metro station. He knew then that something wasn't right.

The station concourse was deserted. It should have been thick with bodies, so densely packed that the floor was invisible. They should have been shoulder to shoulder on the escalators leading up to the platforms. Instead, a few handfuls of the bewildered stared up at the departures board. Every other train had an 'X' next to it, alongside the word "Cancelled". He accosted a Metro official who merely shrugged.

"No drivers, sir," the official replied. He shrugged again, as if that were an explanation.

The teenagers manning the Coco2Go stall were nowhere to be seen. He ordered a tea at the tea shop while waiting for the next train and was told that there was no milk.

"No supply today, sir," the stall owner said. "Only black tea. Or coffee."

"What's going on?" Chatpati said.

"Supply problem, sir," the man replied. He had the look of someone who had been asked the same question count-less times already.

The train, when it arrived, was hardly half full. There was no pushing or shoving to get on it. Again, there were plenty of seats. Chatpati checked the date on his phone to make sure he hadn't missed some new public holiday. He hadn't.

He swiped across to BTV News. Anchorman Prashanth

was in the last few minutes of his night shift. He looked careworn and dishevelled.

"There have been major problems in Bangalore overnight, stemming from the unprecedented attacks on produce markets over the last two days. Movement of fresh produce into the city's markets from farms and warehouses in the countryside has ground to a halt. Fear of attacks has led many distributors to shut down their facilities."

"Yesterday evening, many shops in the city had run out of essentials, like milk, cooking oil and flour. There were scenes of chaos as shoppers scrabbled for the remains. A wave of panic buying grips Bangalore."

"Overnight, there were two further attacks at satellite towns in the north, one not five kilometres from the International Airport. Fire crews from the airport were called to the scene of one attack because civil units were overwhelmed dealing with the other. Arson is suspected in both cases. If true, this represents an escalation of disorder to a dangerous new level."

"Several private schools near major markets in town have announced that they are not opening today. This has led to a domino effect as people stay away from work to look after their children. We're awaiting confirmation from the Education Minister whether government schools will remain open."

"There is a pall of fear across the city. Traffic levels are half of what they would be on any weekday. Many businesses have not raised their shutters this morning. Police are stretched thin dealing with the fallout from the past several days, giving rise to concerns that they cannot react to any fresh attacks. Let's hope it doesn't come to that."

CHATPATI ALMOST RAN down the escalator at the MG Road station. His phone buzzed as he stepped off it. It was the Minister.

"Hari," the Justice Minister said. "Can you talk? Have you seen what's going on?"

"Yes, sir," Chatpati said. "It looks pretty bad."

"I'm flying back from Delhi shortly on an Air Force plane. Our mutual friends conveyed your message to me. I've spoken to the Commissioner. They're assembling the BSF[3] Riot Squad. All police units are being redeployed and I've agreed for your team to join the effort. You can decide on how best you can help."

"Of course," Chatpati replied. "I'm on my way to the CNU now. Can I call you back once I have an update on the current state of play?"

"Do," the Minister replied. "I've asked our mutual friends to help as well. You may hear from them. Work together on this."

It had already started by the time the Inspector made it in to the Civil Nuisance Unit.

"Three more attacks, sir." Raj said without looking up. The map of Bangalore was on the screen. "All close together. Magadi Road, Banshankari and Adugodi. Central Division is scrambling to those sites. There's a lot of radio chatter."

Chatpati frowned. "There are no produce markets in those areas. Are you sure?"

Raj looked up, his face drawn. "It's not markets, sir. It's stations. Police stations. Two of them are on fire."

They watched the police stations burning on the news. With the police deployed all across the city and beyond, there were only a few gate guards on duty at each of them. The petrol bombs had been launched at close quarters. Footage from a bystander's phone showed masked men climbing back out over the walls into the street as smoke rose behind them.

By mid-morning, the vegetable market in Halasuru had been hit. An hour later, Johnson Market, a kilometre to the south, was reported to be in flames. Chatpati felt a growing sense of powerlessness, a contagion that spread among the team. They sat and watched the incidents bloom on the map in silence.

Chatpati walked out into the open-air lounge. He could see the smoke rising to the south. The air was sharp with its taint. There was a distant sound of sirens. He called Mary D'Souza. She sounded preoccupied.

"Have you got anything for me?" he said.

"Not yet," D'Souza replied. "We've just started working on these attacks. We don't really have a handle on key targets, so we're collating cell phone traffic data around the three police stations. The numbers need time to be crunched. I'll get back to you when we do." She paused. "It may not be today, though."

"That may be too late," Chatpati replied. He sounded grim. "This looks organised. Guerrilla warfare. I think it's meant to stretch us."

"Well, they're succeeding," D'Souza said. "Most of the police were out overnight patrolling the satellite town-ships, anticipating another attack there. They'll all be rushing back into town now."

"To nothing," Chatpati replied. "We'll be chasing the criminals all day, but by evening, the gangs will melt away."

"What's your thinking about this?"

Chatpati thought for a moment. "We need to meet them head-on. Rather than running after them."

"Where? And when?"

"I don't know. I need to think about it."

"Well, let us know when you do. We'll do what we can to help. You should know that the tone of the social media discourse has changed radically in the last twenty-four hours. It's gone from #GoodCoconut versus #BadCoconut to something else entirely. Calls to anarchy. Incitement to violence against the instruments of the state. Most were from new social media accounts created in the last week. Faceless and nameless."

"Meaning?"

"Meaning, I agree with your assessment. This is more than just a handful of street gangs. It's organised. On a large scale. I'll call you when we have more."

Chatpati went back in and studied the red icons on the map. The city was ringed and impaled, each glowing red icon a wound. Wounded everywhere, he noted, except in its aged, tattered heart.

He called the Justice Minister.

"I have an idea and a plan," Chatpati said, "but I'll need some backup. What can you spare?"

The Minister asked a few questions before he rang off.

"I'll call the necessary people," the Minister said. "Make your way there. You have full authority from me to take whatever action necessary to prevent damage to property and loss of life. You'll have that in writing in ten minutes."

"Unnecessary, sir," Chatpati replied. "Your word is enough."

"Fine." The Minister paused before asking the next question. "How sure are you about this?"

"Not sure at all," Chatpati said, "but there's only one

potential target that is conspicuous by not having been attacked so far. The biggest market and distribution centre in the city. Russell Market. I think that will be their end-game. And it will happen today."

"Not another police station?"

"No," Chatpati said. "That was a feint. As all the other attacks have been. Their actual target is the one that lies wide open and undefended. The market's cheek by jowl with high-density housing. If they set fire to it and the fire spreads, it will be a disaster. We need to act."

"Do what you must," the Minister said. "As will I."

The squad had assembled on the dance floor. Their eyes were on him as he approached.

"Anyone fancy a spell in the Riot Police?" Chatpati asked. "Not you, Hemanth. You're private. That's beyond the call of duty. You co-ordinate. We'll need the drones."

Chatpati turned to face them. "We're going in. The police are stretched thin and we can be of better use on the streets. A battalion of BSF Riot Police is going to be dispatched to the sports ground of the High School opposite the Traffic police station just north of Russell Market. We're going to join them. We will deploy the drones over the market. First sign of trouble, we go in. The aim is to deter and disperse. Necessary force has been authorised."

Nair raised his hand.

"No, Vasanth," Chatpati said. "You can't have a revolver. There's only one in this Unit and I'm keeping it."

Nair lowered his hand.

Chatpati looked at Seema. "You might want to sit this one out."

It was the first time Chatpati had seen Seema look annoyed.

"Why?" she replied. "Because I'm a woman? I'm a police officer too. I'm going."

Chatpati nodded. "Fair enough. You're right. Excuse me if that sounded patronising. I was only concerned about your safety. If you get captured—"

Seema shook her head. "Thank you, Inspector, but I'm a woman who's grown up in this city. I can look after myself."

"Don't need guns," Aramada said. "A lathi will be good enough. Good solid bamboo. One blow to the head. Or the groin. Or a jab to the neck. Just a matter of timing. I'll show you how it's done."

Seema glared at Aramada. "I might be the one showing you!" she shot back.

"Enough," Chatpati said. "Go get ready. Two Hoysalas will be here in ten minutes."

Chatpati found Avicenna's phone and rang the only number on it.

The Hoysalas sped through the streets, sirens howling. Traffic was thin. The odd auto-rickshaw puttered past. The pavements were empty. Even the beggars seemed to have made a run for it.

The media spread the message, Nita Singh particularly strident in her declarations.

"Stay off the streets, Bangalore! This is a dangerous time for civilians! There have been another cluster of attacks at the vegetable market in Halasuru and Johnson Market just a kilometre from the city centre! More people have been taken to hospital. One market is on fire. Emergency services are scrambling, but they're overwhelmed. Help them out and stay at home!"

"THAT'S south and east of us," Raj said. Raj, Chatpati and Nair were in the lead Hoysala, Seema, Aramada and Singh following behind. "There's only one other likely target left."

Chatpati nodded. "They'll be concentrating their forces on this last skirmish. They'll be expecting the police to have run to the sites they've already attacked, leaving the field free. But, if I'm right, they're in for a surprise."

The Riot Squad were waiting in the shade of the blue police bus parked next to the goalposts of the High School playing field. There were only twenty-four of them, all members of the Provincial Armed Constabulary, not the crack BSF team Chatpati had expected. The BSF had tear gas, smoke shells and dog squads. They were trained to deal with large-scale public disorder and counter-insurgency. The PAC, by contrast, was only ever meant to deal with lower order student or labour unrest. All they had were helmets, shields, and lathis.

The unit commander approached and saluted.

"Head Constable Ismail, sir," the officer said. "Pleased to meet you. Sir."

"Where's the BSF?" Chatpati asked, dismayed. Their numbers were too small. Even with the CNU team, there would only be thirty policemen against an unknown number of street-hardened thugs. "I was told they would be here."

"Diverted, sir," Ismail replied. "ACP Srinivasan's orders. He feared the attackers might target Central Division HQ, so the BSF has been deployed there. We were sent instead." Ismail ventured a nervous smile. "We are ready, sir."

"Bloody idiot," Chatpati growled. Srinivasan, covering his own arse. "Not you, Ismail."

Chatpati wondered whether he had enough time to ring the Justice Minister. The Minister might be airborne. By the time he got through, and the Minister made the order, and the BSF arrived, the whole thing might be over. They would just have to make do.

He turned to the CNU team. "Suit up. It's just shields and lathis. No dogs. No tear gas. It's going to be very old-fashioned."

"Just the way I like it," Aramada said.

Chatpati's radio buzzed. It was Hemanth.

"Inspector, lots of motorcycles converging on the Russell Market area. They're coming through the minor roads and alleyways in ones and twos. They're taking care to avoid the main roads. I make nearly thirty vehicles, each carrying two."

Bad odds, Chatpati thought. Sixty rowdies. Against half that number of policemen. They would need back up but he couldn't rely on the ACP.

Chatpati rang Avicenna again. "We're on," he said. "Are you ready?"

"No problem, Inspector. Sultangunta is ready to welcome the invaders. You just do the necessary, as we discussed, and leave the rest to us."

Chatpati mounted the steps of the blue police bus and turned to face the assembled officers.

"Listen up," he said. "We have one chance at this. The odds are not great. Two to one, not in our favour. We will not win a frontal assault in the market square. They can surround us, flank us, attack us from all sides."

There was dismay on some faces.

"But," he continued, "what we have is the element of surprise. It may be enough."

He stepped down and chalked a sun on the side of the bus with five rays radiating out.

"The market square is the centre. There are five narrow alleys leading off the square. We approach down these lanes. With luck, they won't know we're there until it suits us. On my command, we rush them."

"I'm hoping we'll drive them off. If they come at us, don't fight back. Just retreat the way you came. Back into the alleyways. Keep your shields up, form a wall and back away. The alleys are so narrow that they cannot get around you. Provided you maintain your formation. Stick together."

"Help will arrive. When it does, do not intervene. Do not save the criminals. Do not arrest them. Just keep the shield wall up and hold your ground. Clear?"

There were some nods.

"Alright, divide into five teams of six each. Team leaders are Ismail, Nair, Raj, Seema and Aramada. Singh and I will co-ordinate. Leaders, set your radio channels, listen for my instructions and stick with your teams. Remember your orders. Ready?"

They nodded en masse.

The radio buzzed. "It's starting, Inspector," Hemanth said. "They're demolishing the market. I've already requested help from all available units. Good luck, Inspector."

"Thanks, Hemanth," Chatpati said. "We're going to need it."

CHAPTER 36

THE BATTLE OF SULTANGUNTA

The police bus dropped them off in their groups, making a wide circle around the outer fringes of the market area. Chatpati and Singh joined Seema's group, the last to decamp just east of the market square.

"You're in charge, Seema," Chatpati said. "You lead. Singh will back you up. I will command from the rear. OK?"

Seema nodded. "Got it, Inspector. I'm ready. Let's go."

Chatpati led them down an apparent dead-end street, then pushed open a door. They were in a narrow alleyway, the rough walls of houses on either side. Clothes line was strung across the gap above, between the narrow balconies three floors up. The sky above was a bright blue slit. The house doors were all shut. Even the motorcycles and bicycles had been taken indoors. Faces peered at them from barred windows. A toddler, perched on her mother's lap, waved at them as they passed. No one waved back. Their eyes were on the danger ahead.

The alleyway was barely wide enough for three to walk abreast. They proceeded in two ranks. They turned another corner, then another. There was light at the end of the alley, the flicker of fire and the sound of shattering glass. They stopped just short of the alley's mouth.

The rowdies were on a rampage. They were a motley crew, their T-shirts and vests stained with their fresh sweat and the dried blood of others. Most wore face-coverings, either surgical masks or scarves knotted behind their heads. Hockey sticks and crowbars had already rendered several produce stands into so much timber.

The market square was a battlefield of fractured cabbages and shattered marrows. A stack of cooking oil barrels had been overturned and set alight. The flames were yellow, tinged with soot. A cargo auto-rickshaw lay on its side. One rowdy lit a petrol bomb and tossed it at the vehicle. The bottle exploded with a thump as the flames spread.

"All units," Chatpati said. "Confirm your positions when ready."

"Ismail. Ready."

"Raj. Ready."

"Bullet One. Ready. Sorry. I mean Nair ready."

"Aramada. Ready. To crack some heads."

"On my command, deploy," Chatpati said. "On my second command, retreat to your alleys and form your walls. Acknowledge."

Four acknowledgements followed.

Chatpati took a deep breath. He cast a prayer heavenward.

"Engage!"

They surged out of the alley. Chatpati's team took the nearest pair of thugs by surprise, knocking them over with their shields. One went flying into the oil drums, disappearing in a tangle of limbs. The second tumbled end over end before sliding to a stop. He jumped to his feet. Half of the skin on one cheek lay on the tarmac underfoot. His eyes were wide with astonishment. He turned and fled.

Chatpati saw Seema swipe at the legs of another rowdy, felling him. Jaswant Singh followed up with a kick in the face.

Two constables to Chatpati's left surprised another pair of hoodlums, charging with lathis raised. The gangsters turned to meet them. They fought back, hockey sticks raining down on the policemen's shields. One constable lost his footing in the oil slick and fell. His partner held his ground against the two rowdies as the fallen constable struggled to his feet. The blows rained down upon the defending policeman from all sides.

Seema hooked in from the side and hit one thug in the ear with the end of her lathi. There was a crunch of cartilage and a starburst of blood. The thug howled, dropped his stick, and ran. The odds were reversed. Seema and the two policemen knocked the remaining thug down with a shield blow to the face and a swipe at his kneecaps. The thug screamed as he crashed to earth. He kicked himself away from them, scrambled to his feet, and stumbled away.

Chatpati looked around. The other four teams held their ground around the perimeter of the square, the entrances to the alleys at their backs. They stood on clear ground, their targets either floored or fleeing.

Raj's crew stood stock still, as if on parade, shields up, lathis upright. Aramada, towering like a mythical giant over his men, shouted abuse at the retreating thugs. Nair stood at the head of his team, waving his lathi over his head. Ismail's team was a narrow, still huddle.

The gangsters fled to the centre of the square. There had been a solitary tree there ever since Chatpati could remember, perpetually leafless. The thugs clustered around its trunk in frank disarray. Many were bleeding from scalp wounds. Some limped. A few had broken wrists or fingers clutched to their chests. They pressed together for safety, clearly unsettled. Their faces registered shock. Only a handful still carried their weapons. They had abandoned the unlit petrol bombs where they had fallen.

Chatpati identified the leader straight away, a short, thickset man with a black bandanna over his face and a gold chain around his neck. As the policemen waited and watched, the leader kicked and pushed his men into some sort of order, administering a slap or two where required.

In a few minutes, the rowdies had reformed into a rough circle, facing out, the tree at their backs. A few braved the no-man's-land between the police and their rallying point to retrieve their discarded weapons. Others, not so brave, unfolded long knives.

Chatpati could feel the mood change. He could see it in the set of their shoulders and their jaws.

"They're about to come at us," Chatpati said into his radio. "Some have knives. The moment they move, form your shield wall and retreat. Do not stand your ground or engage! Move back!"

He had barely finished when a roar filled the square. The gangsters surged forwards, running at the police like demons whipped them.

Chatpati cast a glance back. Too far! They had strayed too far! The safety of the alleyway seemed a mile away.

"Run!" he shouted. "Quickly! Run!"

They turned and ran, making it in between the narrow walls just as ten gangsters closed in on them.

"Lock shields!" Chatpati shouted. The policemen skidded to a stop and spun to face their attackers, Seema in the front row. They brought their shields together just as the gangsters crashed into them. Chatpati felt more than heard the crunch as the policemen rocked back, a jarring that he felt in his teeth. He leant his shoulder to the press.

"Walk back!" Chatpati shouted. "Keep together! Shields up! Walk back!"

They retreated down a ravine of brick and mortar. The gangsters' faces behind the transparent shields were full of incandescent rage, their teeth bared. They had murder in their eyes.

The gangsters swung at the shields with their hockey sticks, but the alley was too narrow. The blows ricocheted off shields into the faces of their fellows. They kicked out, but their kicks caught on the shield edges. They thrust their knives at the policemen, but the hardened plastic thwarted the thin metal.

The policemen had retreated halfway down the alley when the doors of the narrow houses opened. The gangsters were so intent on their retreating quarry that they did not notice the men trotting quickly up the alley behind them. The new arrivals were armed with cricket bats, lengths of iron, mallets, and staves. There was even a pair of dumbbells.

Without preamble, the men of Sultangunta fell upon the gangsters from behind.

"Halt!" Chatpati shouted to his team. "Stand your ground!" The shield wall stood, bearing witness to the carnage.

The gangsters' bodies thudded against the shields as the blows rained down on them from behind them. Blood spattered the clear plastic. A tooth flew over the Inspector's head. He heard the crunch of bone. The howls of rage had turned to squeals of pain, of calls to mothers long departed, of invocations to Gods never before invoked.

It was no use. In less than a minute, the residents of Sultangunta had rendered the rowdies into a single untidy tangle of sagging limbs in pools of gore.

Avicenna Yousuf nodded to the Inspector from beyond the bodies, a rusty, iron dumbbell in one hand. Avicenna was panting. There was a patch of denim stuck to the dumbbell.

"The leader," Chatpati said. "Get that one. Black bandanna. Gold chain. Alive if you can."

Avicenna sketched a salute and called a word to his men. They turned as one and ran back out to the square.

Chatpati keyed his radio. "All units, check in!"

"Aramada. We're fine. They're not."

"Nair. No problem. Will need to dry clean this uniform, though. Can I claim that?"

"Ismail. All fine, Inspector. We're safe."

"Raj here. Were we meant to take them alive, sir? Just asking."

"We're meant to disperse them, Raj." Chatpati replied. "I think we're done."

Raj replied. "Well, dispersal suggests movement, sir. There's few moving."

"Too bad," Chatpati said. "Head back the way you came. The bus will pick you up. Let's leave Sultangunta to clean up its own mess."

Sirens sounded in the distance.

"Central Division boys are here, boss," Hemanth said over the radio. "Late. As usual. And ambulances. The dispatcher wants to know how many we'll need. Ambulances, that is."

"Lots," Chatpati replied. "Tell them to send lots."

CHAPTER 37
DIAMONDS AND CLUBS

Inspector Hari Chatpati had never expected to set foot inside the Richmond Club. He'd peered through its gates several times, though, while stalled in traffic on Richmond Road.

The Club's whitewashed colonnades seemed unblemished by engine heat. Its soaring hedges were immaculate, its sweeping driveway weed-free. The British had built it for the officers of its Empire. That Empire had decayed, but a new one had sprung up in its place. The Club was now the province of by India's New Emperors, its billionaires and its plutocrats, those who favoured dress codes and the exclusivity of a men-only lounge bar. Admittance to membership was by proposal. Chatpati had no one to propose him, even if he could have afforded the yearly fee, that the price of a new car. Chatpati couldn't even afford the price of an old car.

It was late evening, two days after the Battle of Sultangunta. There had been much comment on social media about whether or not it was insensitive to host a gala re-launch of packaged coconut water so soon after the Coconut Wars, as the media were now calling it.

The tides of commerce, however, swell to the lunar pull of lucre. And there was plenty of lucre to be had.

It wasn't necessary, Chatpati supposed, to do it this way, but the thing had a natural justice about it, a thumbing of the nose at the old order, that sat very well with the Inspector. The Justice Minister had agreed.

It hadn't been necessary to ride up on a Bullet either, but his mode of arrival had attracted the necessary attention, once Nair had convinced the gate guard, in Nair's customary fashion, to raise the barrier.

"Vagrant! Unfurl thou yon drawbridge! Dost thou not see the justiciary approach! Expedite, rascal, or feelest though mine hand the back of!"

The Bullet's unsubtle thunder echoed down the Club's grand corridors, bringing uniformed men scuttling, like so many penguins to a feast of fish. Nair pulled to a halt under the portico, revved the throttle twice for good measure, and turned the key. Chatpati climbed off.

A gaunt, bald man in a baggy tuxedo appeared at the top of the marble steps.

"You can't park there!" he wailed at them. "Parking is around the corner. You must move! There will be other vehicles arriving."

"Verily?" Nair said, taking off his helmet. "Thinkest thou so?" He looked back. "Ah! Thou hast the boon of prescience!"

The Hoysala pulled up behind them, flashers on. Raj and Aramada got out.

The Duty Manager gawked at them, mute.

"Ha!" Nair said, taking the stairs in twos. "Methinks thou gaspest. Like a mackerel!"

"Police," Chatpati said to the Manager. "Get out of the way."

"But you can't," the Manager gasped. "You can't. The Club is closed to non-members. For a private function."

Nair scowled. "Vagrant. Pay thou good heed. It is for that very purpose that our forces are arrayed. Now, dissipate thyself."

"Or feel his wrath," Chatpati said. "Seriously. I wouldn't."

They proceeded down the corridors, Raj marvelling at the extravagance.

"Is that a chandelier? So many bulbs. On just one! More light bulbs than in my entire house! And there's another one! And the floors! Like a chessboard! Is that a deer's head? Why is it on a wall?"

All play in the Billiard Room ceased as the convoy passed through. Drinking slowed in the Mixed Bar and ceased altogether in the Men's Bar. Perturbations marked their passage, like the distant strike of artillery shells, the sight preceding the sound. Eyebrows rose before murmurs followed.

Chatpati strode, the Manager at his shoulder. The Inspector noted they had gathered a tail of followers. Heads popped out from archways and doorways, swivelling as if on ball bearings. So much the better, he thought.

"Never in a hundred and fifty years," the Manager wailed. "We've never had the police! Never! The Commissioner is a Member! Do you know that?"

"I know," Chatpati said. "He told me."

The archway guarding the Mysore Room was the height of an elephant and finished in teak. The double-headed eagle crest of the Maharajah of Mysore glinted at its apex. Beyond, the ballroom had been decked out for a grand occasion. Crystal chandeliers cast a gracious amber light onto polished hardwood floors. The walls were the colour of ripe corn, the columns the same except for pearl-grey capitals supporting soaring arches. Heavy gold brocade hung around the windows. The tables were dressed with starched linen and floral centrepieces.

Such finery was as nothing before the accumulated splendour of the audience: gold ringed fingers, platinum encircled wrists, diamonds embraced necks. Downmarket silver was reserved for the cutlery. Silk and sequins shimmered in the gentle draft of flitting waiters bearing champagne bottles on salvers. The soundtrack was the clink-clink of rich people having a rich old time.

At the far end, Santosh Shetty stood poised behind a lectern on a dais. A video screen behind him displayed a giant, grinning coconut. Shetty wore a dark silk three piece suit. He positively glowed as he spoke.

"Friends," he began," thank you for coming tonight to celebrate the re-launch of Coco2Go." There was a small cheer from the audience. "It's so great to have so many friends and well-wishers and, most importantly, investors from Bangalore and abroad who could join us this evening. Tonight marks the end of that great journey that began two years ago when my colleague and dear friend, Mr K. Chandra, made the brave decision to enter the tender coconut water market."

There was more applause.

"That foresight has been rewarded. We're poised to go public. It's a great thing for a small private company. To list itself on the stock market. It proves that from tiny acorns grow mighty oaks. It's the way elite companies all begin. General Electric. Apple. IBM. And we're going to join them!"

Applause again, embellished with a few whoops.

"And now, it's my pleasure and privilege to introduce a man who needs no introduction. A man of vision. A man of character. A man of ambition. Ladies and gentlemen, your host. Mr. K. Chandra!"

Chandra hopped onto the dais. He looked a million dollars in his designer sherwani[1]. The effect was discounted twenty per cent by the now-familiar luminous green baseball cap.

"Thanks, friend, thanks!" Chandra said into the microphone. "It's so great to be here, after such a long, hard struggle. It just shows perseverance pays off!"

Another round of applause. Chandra waved them to silence.

"Before we begin, though, I think it is only right that we remember those who suffered in the recent riots." He paused, face sombre. "It's at times like these that we can come together as a family. Coco2Go is a family. We care for others. Which is why I'm proud to announce our Corporate Adoption Scheme. This company will automatically adopt all tender coconut vendors throughout the City who have lost their means of earnings. They will become our franchisees. We will pay their salaries. The uniforms will be free. We will train them, also for free. And we will send them out into the world to spread the word of Coco2Go! For these people, the future is bright—"

"The future is coconut!" the audience sang back.

Chandra laughed, delighted. "Fantastic! But now, before we begin the night's festivities, let's have a moment of silence to remember those who came to harm in the rioting of the last few days."

The clinking stopped and heads bowed.

Chatpati bore three seconds and no more. He strode

forward, Nair at one shoulder, Raj at the other. Their shoes clacked on wood underfoot, the sound of cavalry cantering to a charge.

"Mr. K. Chandra," Chatpati said in the silence. "Mr. Santosh Shetty. Bangalore Police. You are both under arrest."

The consternation was immediate. Chairs tipped to the floor, the sound like firecrackers, as people leapt to their feet. Someone dropped a bottle. It shattered.

There were cries of "What?", of "No!", of "Outrageous!", of "Security!"

Disbelief battled with discord. Discord won.

Aramada had Shetty bent over the table as Raj slipped the handcuffs on. Shetty's tie was in his champagne glass.

Nair hauled Chandra off the dais by his collar and spun him round. The baseball cap tumbled to the floor.

"Desist thine infernal grappling, vagrant," Nair said. "All is lost. The justiciary is victorious."

"How dare you!" the shackled Chandra roared. "Don't you know who I am? I'll have your badge, you—"

"Save it," Chatpati said. "I've heard it all before. Badge, then courts then lawsuit. Blah, blah, blah. You're charged with nine counts of conspiracy to commit murder, financial fraud, money laundering and incitement to riot. You're going to jail for a very long time. Or you'll hang. Save your breath. While you have it."

The green coconut on the screen did a jig as the policemen dragged the suspects out. They marched them through the Club and down the steps. Chatpati took some small pleasure from the shock on the faces of the assembled patrons. He looked them in the eye as they passed. You're not safe, his look said, your chandeliers and your dress codes won't protect you.

Producer Derek Mendes had acted on the Inspector's tip-off. There was a crowd of reporters waiting at the gate, jostling for room. A BTV News van was parked on the pavement, the cameraman on the roof, visible above the Club's boundary wall. The lenses tracked the arrest party as they made their way down the driveway to the waiting Hoysala.

Flashbulbs rent the evening darkness.

"Slow down," Raj said to the captive Shetty. "We want to make sure the cameras get an excellent shot. Marketing, right?"

"The future is bright," Nair said, behind him, turning Chandra to face the cameras, "but it's certainly not coconut!"

CHAPTER 38
HELLO, GOODBYE

I
t did not surprise anyone at the Bangalore Civil Nuisance Unit that the Tender Coconut Tamasha made headline news the next day.

"Astounding developments!" Nita had said, astounded. "Just days after the Bangalore Coconut Wars, police detained one of the city's financial Young Turks. K. Chandra, founder of the Coco2Go franchise, was arrested last evening at a star-studded event at the prestigious Richmond Club. They led away him in shackles, along with his Director of Marketing, Santosh Shetty. Both have been recent panellists on this very programme!"

"Chandra faces charges of murder, attempted murder, fraud and incitement to riot. The police allege that the riots three days ago were part of a cynical attempt by Chandra and colleagues to corner the coconut water market. The plan would have succeeded without the intervention of the Banga-lore Police and the personal intervention of the Hero of the Vidhana Soudha, Inspector Chatpati."

"Many had questioned the Inspector's fitness for his role as head of Bangalore's elite Civil Nuisance Unit, but recent events have shown those fears to be unfounded. We hope to hear from the Inspector himself in the coming week."

"The protestors outside the headquarters of the Civil Nuisance Unit have dispersed. Mr. Shaji, who represents the tender coconut vendors, could not be contacted for comment."

"Unsurprisingly, Coco2Go's much-hyped IPO is now not going ahead. The company is in crisis as investigators from the Fraud Squad trawl through their accounts."

"And, finally, street tender coconut operations have resumed all over Bangalore. The enthusiasm for the street product seems to have reached new heights, especially now that the State Government has banned sales of packaged coconut water, pending a review into the whole affair."

THE DEMONSTRATORS outside the Utilities Building had melted away. There was no sign that they had ever been there except for a few errant coconuts. The cinema re-opened. The CNU's star seemed to be in the ascendant again; the cinema manager sent up a roll of complimentary tickets for the latest Kannada blockbuster, with his good wishes.

Throughout the rest of the day, and the following one, the Utilities Building's elevators ran non-stop, ferrying gifts from well-wishers up to the twenty-fourth floor. There were stuffed toys the size of toddlers. There were enough bouquets to furnish a mass wedding. The disco ball disappeared behind squadrons of bobbing balloons.

"Where the hell do we put it all?" Nair said as he watched yet another floral tribute be wheeled through the saloon doors. "So undignified! This place looks like a children's birthday party!" Raj laughed and threw a teddy bear at him.

Inspector Chatpati bore all this with equanimity. Mostly. The absolute limit, though, was the arrival of a cartload of tender coconuts. The Utilities Building manager rang them from the loading ramp. It wouldn't fit in the elevator. Chatpati despatched Raj to the ground floor post haste.

"With regards from the vendors of Bangalore," Raj said over the phone. "That's what the card says. Shall I bring them up?"

"No bloody chance!" Chatpati replied. "Not a single tender coconut in this Unit! Ever. Get rid of it."

In the end, they redirected the consignment to the ground-floor restaurant, where it was put to good use.

ACP (Traffic) sent another card, this one the size of a newspaper, accompanied by a kilo of laddus.

"*Welcome back!*" said the panda on the cover. It held a bouquet and was poised on one leg, like a ballerina. "*We missed you!*"

"Shall I send a 'Thank You' card back?" Seema asked.

"No," Chatpati said. "Absolutely not. I'm confiscating those laddus." He looked around at his officers. Some looked disappointed. "You're all getting fat. Back to work!"

The requests for interviews with Inspector Chatpati and members of his team grew threefold. Seema despatched them with practised ease.

Raj reported that the drones now had their own Facebook pages. Garuda Two had the most Likes.

Avicenna called to offer his congratulations. Chatpati enquired after his health.

"Fine, fine," Avicenna said. "All our men are intact. Not

a single injury. It was a good plan, Inspector. The story of the battle of Sultangunta has spread far and wide. No one will ever dare to try their luck against us in our place."

Chatpati promised to leave Avicenna's phone under the tree that evening. Along with a kilogram of laddus for the small boy and his followers.

#BadCoconut had disappeared almost entirely from social media by the time the other special phone rang. Mary D'Souza sounded very pleased.

"Good morning, Inspector," she said. "So glad to see events have come to a satisfactory conclusion."

"Thanks to you," Chatpati replied. "We couldn't have done it without your help. I think we owe you one."

"Actually," D'Souza replied, "I think it may be the other way round. It may interest you to know that the travel agency, too, has profited from your excursion. Shetty is someone we've been looking for. For a long time. Except we didn't quite know it was him we were looking for."

The agency had been trying to crack open a major money laundering racket for months.

"Quite hard going," she said, "even with several agents working on it. We had the bones of it laid open. We had the bank accounts and shell companies, but we could link none of the activity to a single individual."

"Until?" Chatpati asked.

"Until you asked us to look into that coconut water company and the payments they made to StreetEatz. Two of the shell companies used in those transactions were ones we were already examining. That led us to look closer at Shetty. He seems to have been a key figure, not just in Coco2Go, but in the channelling of money towards other criminal activities. We'll be interviewing Mr. Shetty shortly. I expect he will be eager to co-operate."

"What does that mean?" Chatpati asked. "In real terms?"

"Oh, that we might crack open a major international money-laundering syndicate. It might even lead to a solution to the Humayun's Tomb Incident. That would be a genuine triumph. For travel agents everywhere."

D'Souza paused for a moment before continuing.

"Some of Coco2Go's money also went towards paying for Chinese 'bot farms'. Which we'd suspected, based on the social media activity during the riots."

"I don't understand," Chatpati replied. "What farms?"

D'Souza's reply had a trace of humour in its tone. "Bot farms. They're not farms at all. Rather, they're groups of computer mercenaries for hire. They post messages on social media for payment. Coco2Go paid for #BadCoconut. Many of those posts weren't even real people at all, just computer programmes pumping out disinformation."

"To what end?"

"To write a new truth," D'Souza said. "To control the narrative to their advantage. Painting organised attacks as a public backlash. Sow confusion, reap inaction. Clever, but ultimately unsuccessful."

"Control the media and you control the truth? Is that it?" Chatpati said.

"Not quite," D'Souza replied. "Control the media and you get to write the truth."

Chatpati nodded. "Your Director was right. About cross-pollination between domestic crime and international crime."

"He usually is, Inspector. He's also very pleased. The Director said to send you his regards. And to tell you we owe you one. As always, get in touch if we can help. Goodbye."

Nirmala returned from Madras that evening. Chatpati left the Unit early to meet her train at Central Station. The old lift operator was back, one eye now clear. The old man fixed Chatpati with his monocular gaze and gave him a small salute. Chatpati saluted back.

The Inspector surprised his wife by enfolding her in a bear hug as she stepped onto the platform. Nirmala's bags fell to the floor.

"Good heavens, Hari," she said into his shoulder. "If I'd known I'd get this kind of welcome, I'd have come home sooner." She rubbed his ear. "It's good to be back."

"It's good to have you back," he said. He released her and picked up her bags. "Ready for dinner? We're going out."

"Why, Inspector," she said, with a giggle. "Are there no minor crimes in Bangalore that need your attention? Are you sure the Civil Nuisance Unit can manage without you for one night?"

He gave her a smile. "They'll manage just fine. Right now, the only thing that's commanding my attention is you."

Early the next morning, Chatpati and Raj saw Nair off at Central Station. The platform was crowded with travellers, well-wishers and vendors. Bottled water and packed lunches changed hands all around them. They found a spot to wait at for Nair's train.

"So are you?" Nair asked.

"Am I what?" Chatpati replied, looking at the board. "Your train's on time."

"Are you appearing on BTV? For another interview?" Nair said.

"No chance," Chatpati said. "I'm not going near another TV camera again. How long are you away for, Vasanth?"

"Well," Nair said, "that rather depends on you. I was going to bring back some personal items, look for a more permanent place to say, but if I'm only staying for three months—"

Chatpati ignored him. "Oh, here's your train," he said. He turned to Nair. "What were you saying?"

Nair looked crestfallen. Chatpati slapped him on the shoulder. "I heard you, Vasanth. Bring back anything you like. We'd be happy to have you at the Civil Nuisance Unit. If you want to stay, that is."

Nair crushed Chatpati to his chest. "Thank you! Thank you! That's great! I will!"

"Wonderful," Chatpati said, almost meaning it. He levered himself out of Nair's grip. Raj was next to be so enfolded. Raj gave Chatpati a look over Nair's shoulder, the look of a pigeon in the jaws of a tomcat. Not quite dead and wishing he was.

The arrival of the train at the platform accelerated Raj's release. Nair climbed aboard and Raj handed his suitcase up to him.

"What about the ACP?" Nair asked from the vestibule as other passengers pushed past him.

"Sulking," Chatpati replied. "I haven't heard from him for days. He's not covered himself with glory. The Commissioner is furious. I imagine he'll get a serious dressing down."

"Any chance of the ACP's post suddenly becoming vacant?" Nair winked at him. "Perhaps someone could be promoted up? You know, from the Inspector of a certain 'elite Unit' to Assistant—"

Chatpati raised a finger. "Any more talk of promotions, Sub-Inspector Nair, and you needn't come back!"

The whistle blew, and the train moved off. Nair waved

madly from the door like a schoolboy. Raj waved back. Even Chatpati raised a hand. The two policemen made their way back through the throng to the exit.

"So what now, boss?" Raj asked as they queued for an auto-rickshaw.

"Now? Now we go to work. We're getting all our people back. We'll need them to clear out all the teddy bears and balloons. I have lots of new applications to join the Unit. Who new Civil Nuisances could be so attractive?"

"The future is bright," Raj began, "the future is—"

Inspector Chatpati's finger rose. "Not another word, Constable Raj. Not another word."

NOTES

2. NO HERO'S WELCOME

1. The building that houses the State Parliament.
2. (Hindu/Urdu) "Well done!"

3. ILL-MET BY AUTO-RICKSHAW

1. A tuk-tuk by another name.
2. The term used to refer to the century of colonial British rule, ending with Indian independence in 1947.
3. Translates as 'oppressed'. Term used by people belonging to the lowest
    Hindu castes to refer to themselves.
4. The Hoysala is Traffic Division's standard patrol vehicle. Named after the imperial dynasty that had ruled Bangalore six centuries ago, the Hoysala is a hulking SUV with three red lights, two different klaxon tones and a roof-mounted loudspeaker to harangue road users with.
5. Kannada is the official language of the state of Karnataka, of which Bangalore is the capital.
6. A neighbouring state.
7. A traditional form of theatre, often based on Hindu epics, involving face-paint, costumes, drums, declamation and grand conflict. Typically performed in the open air. Performances last all night.

4. CIVIL NUISANCES, ALL

1. A light two-wheeled horse drawn carriage, like a cabriolet.
2. Tonga driver.
3. A customary Hindu greeting. The gesture involves hands pressed together, palms touching, fingers upward. Literally means 'I bow to the divine in you.'
4. A sarong. A length of cloth wrapped around the waist and extending to the ankles.

NOTES

5. VIEL UNKLAR

1. A city located in north-west Karnataka.

6. THE PERILS OF TOURISM

1. A savoury rice crepe peculiar to South India, with diverse regional variations. The 'benne' or butter dosa involves liberal amounts of ghee and is unique to the state of Karnataka.
2. A steamed rice cake, another breakfast staple.

8. ALL'S WELL THAT BEGINS WELL

1. Indian cottage cheese.
2. A legendary bird from Hindu mythology, ever watchful, with the power to go anywhere. Garuda is the vehicle of the Hindu God, Vishnu.
3. For over 600 years, the Kingdom of Mysore was ruled by a single dynasty until it was absorbed into the Indian Republic and became the state of Karnataka.

9. COMETH THE HOUR, COMETH THE NAIR

1. A lakh is one hundred thousand.

10. CASE HISTORY

1. Fried balls of sugary dough, steeped in sugar syrup.
2. Another Indian sweet, made of condensed milk and sugar.

11. A FALCON IN TIME-

1. A state to the north of Karnataka and formerly a Portuguese colony.
2. The enclave in New Delhi that houses the embassies and seats of the Central Government.
3. One of Bangalore's oldest districts.

12. FIRST INFORMATION RECEIVED

1. Short for First Information Received, an FIR is a document prepared by police when they receive information about the commission of a cognisable offence. The police must register an FIR before they can investigate.
2. The Royal Enfield Bullet is a single cylinder four-stroke motorcycle, originally made by Royal Enfield in Worcestershire, now produced in Madras. It has a cult following. It guzzles fuel and is very loud.
3. The prototype dish of Chindian (Chinese-Indian) cuisine, a distinct culinary form created by the Chinese community in Calcutta a hundred years ago.

13. LIFE INTERRUPTED

1. (Hindi) Villain.

14. PARK LIFE

1. Non-Governmental Organisation, usually used to mean charity or social enterprise.

15. BUBBLE, TOIL AND TROUBLE

1. Tea vendor.
2. The Hindu Hell, presided over by Lord Yama, the God of Death.

16. MORE HEAT THAN LIGHT

1. Member of the Legislative Assembly (equivalent to a Member of Parliament).
2. An elaborate vegetarian affair involving several courses, typically served on a banana leaf. Followed by the loosening of belts.
3. Lime juice and soda water. Served sweet or salty.
4. Three lentil-based accompaniments served with all vegetarian meals.
5. A legendary warrior and prince, Bhishma was renowned for his pledge of celibacy. He was also given the gift of being able to choose

the time of his death, remaining immortal until that point. He chose to die on a bed of arrows.

6. A Sanskrit epic, the longest epic poem known, depicting the war between two royal families.

17. THE FUTURE IS BRIGHT, THE FUTURE IS COCONUT

1. A sun hat made from the pith of the stems of sola plants.

18. TENDER COCONUT TAMASHA

1. There are one hundred paisa in a rupee, like cents in a dollar.

19. OF KINGS AND SAMARITANS

1. The language of the state of Kerala.

23. AN ABSOLUTION FOR SINS

1. Meaning 'service', seva refers to the Sikh ideal of good work done under God's will, without expectation of reward.

2. A hunter-warrior tribe with its own culture, language and traditions, whose homeland lies in the forested hills of Coorg.

24. CRUISING UNDER THE STARS

1. Spirit beings, often depicted as a woman at the foot of a tree, guarding buried treasure.

25. ENDINGS AND BEGINNINGS

1. Indian Police Service, specifically that cadre of officers selected by competitive examination to provide command and administrative leadership. Considered the upper echelons of the police service.

2. Central Reserve Police Force, an armed police unit functioning under the authority of the Ministry of Home Affairs under the

Government of India.

27. SPLINTERS AND THUNDERBOLTS

1. A long, heavy iron-bound bamboo stick.

33. SWALLOW A SPIDER TO CATCH A FLY

1. A native of Kerala.
2. A traditional Keralan pleated skirt.

35. CRY HAVOC

1. Savoury Indian street snacks.
2. Betel nuts and lime wrapped in a betel life and chewed for hours on end.
3. Border Security Force, an armed paramilitary police force administered by the Central Government.

37. DIAMONDS AND CLUBS

1. A long coat, elaborately hand-embroidered, worn as formal evening wear. Traditionally worn by aristocracy.

AUTHOR'S NOTE

Reviews are the life blood of the independent author's career. Positive reviews tell me I'm on the right track. Negative ones tell me to think again. Both are welcome.

I'd be grateful if you would consider leaving an honest review wherever you bought this book. I read, and value, every one, even those that question my competence! They are (sometimes) on the money.

Thank you for reading.

ACKNOWLEDGMENTS

'Acknowledgements' seems too narrow a word to encompass all those who've helped the Civil Nuisance Unit reach its audience. Nevertheless, that is convention, so, onwards.

My wife is a force of nature. If it wasn't for her encouraging me to sign up for a writing competition, this journey would never have begun. She has been companion, advocate, critic, editor and inspiration. I could not do without her.

Saina Jayapal is the 'go to' person if you want to find the best places for *'bene dosa'* (and for that matter, anything else in Bangalore).

Glenn Jones is a gifted artist. He whipped up a great cover in very short order. A true professional. Anyone who can reconcile coconuts and drones on a single cover can't be anything but.

ABOUT THE AUTHOR

Joe Chacko lives in Scotland. He works as an anaesthetist at a rather large, rather ugly hospital. He likes growing vegetables and plays bass guitar, but is very bad at both.

He's currently working on the next instalment in the Inspector Chatpati mysteries and a dark hospital-based crime thriller.

Find out more at www.joechacko.co.uk.

If you enjoyed this book, please leave an honest review wherever you bought it.

ALSO BY JOE CHACKO

THE REALLY HIGH TEA

The Prequel

Join Sub-Inspector Vasanth Nair as he navigates the steamy by-ways of Fort Cochin in this solo adventure novella, a prequel to The Tender Coconut Tamasha.

Get a FREE ebook copy by signing up to the author's mailing list.

http://bit.ly/3HXQ8DL

THE DISAPPEARING DHOBI

Book 2

Release date: early 2023

The CNU investigates the theft of dirty laundry. Why has the *dhobi* disappeared? And why do the residents of Regal Inheritance Apartments deny all knowledge of the *dhobi's* existence? It's a grand conspiracy of the unexpected.

Read an extract on the following pages.

THE ARMS OF DURGA

Book 3

Release date: mid-2023

Inspector Chatpati faces his greatest challenge as a series of gruesome ritual murders plague Bangalore. Is it the work of human hands? Or has the Hindu warrior goddess Durga really returned to the world to deal justice on the wicked?

THE CASE OF THE DISAPPEARING DHOBI

AN EXTRACT FROM THE NEXT IN THE
SERIES

.

1: A MATTER OF LIFE AND LAUNDRY

After it was all over, Mrs. Sarojini Hegde ('Saro' to her
friends, 'that cow' to her enemies) would have to admit
that it might have been better if she had learned how to use
the washing machine after all. It's not that she feared technology, it was just that she had a clear sense of its limita-
tions. The raising of children, the chopping of cabbages, the
rolling out of chapatis-all of these matters required the
considered application of the human hand. No machine
could do any of these things.

The same was true of fabric. There was nothing quite
like being pummelled on a stone, rinsed in a bucket, wrung
out, then finally hung out to dry on a line to teach recalcitrant textile who was boss. A white box with a spinning
drum could not, by any means that she could see, expunge
grime better than human endeavour. Endeavour was the
iron with which Mrs. Hegde beat the reluctant world into
her preferred shape, and it was endeavour that would deal
with her laundry.

Which was why she was taken aback when Flora D'Cruz, her neighbour across the hall on the first floor of Regal Inheritance Apartments, had snorted at what Mrs. Hegde had thought was a reasonable question. Ms. D'Cruz ("Call me Flora, darling.") wore far too much makeup for someone her age and spoke in English, rather than Kannada. She was also fifty, if a day, and unmarried. It was all highly suspect. Mrs. Hegde would never have lowered herself to ask such a woman such a question, except that the situation was desperate. The pile of dirty linen grew by the day, and there was no washerman in sight.

"*Dhobi*?" Ms. D'Cruz had said, pointedly, in English. "Who uses a *dhobi* these days, my dear? Buy a washing machine. It's the modern way."

Mrs. Hegde's reply rang out across the hall from the threshold, where Mrs. Hegde guarded her front door.

"I have a washing machine, Mrs. D'Cruz! But I want a *dhobi*. Man power is better than electric power!"

Ms. D'Cruz had made a face and continued down the stairs, her manservant in tow.

Mrs. Hegde had complained about Ms. D'Cruz' calculated disregard to her husband, but Mr. Manoj Hegde had been unsympathetic.

"Look, just use the infernal thing, Saro," he'd said from the breakfast table. He waved at the washing machine. "It's not a *rakshasa*. It's a device. Think of it as a servant, but without the disadvantages of having to be paid. Or fed. Or harangued."

That last word had been ill-chosen—Mr. Hegde sensed the tremors, but too late. He tucked the last idli into his mouth with haste and leapt to his feet.

Mrs. Hegde had been rinsing the idli steamer at the

sink. She froze as the last word hit home. The steamer flew into the sink with a clang. She spun to face her husband and raised the sponge.

"O-ho!" she began. "As if it wasn't bad enough that you have dragged me here from my native place in the peaceful countryside to this smelly, filthy city. Never mind that I had to leave my sisters and my ageing mother behind, abandon my family, our ancestral home, our fields, to come and live in this concrete chicken coop, surrounded by nasty, sniping women. No servants. No help. Not even a husband who cares!" Suds ran down her arm as she wrung the life out of the sponge.

Mr. Hegde paled. "Now, now dear," he said, raising an arm and taking a backward step out of the kitchen. "Don't get excited. Saro. Don't. Remember your blood pressure!"

He fled as the sponge hurtled towards him.

This was why, when, later that day, Mrs. Hegde spied the van (marked with the words 'Super Volcano Traditional Dhobi Laundering') pull up across the road, she leapt out of her seat in the wicker chair on the balcony. This was why, when she saw the dhobi walk through the gates of the apartment complex bearing paper-wrapped packages, her heart leapt. This was why she had accosted the man on the ground floor while he waited for the lift. This was why, despite the man's protestations about being overburdened with work, she had dragged him into Apartment 12 and stood over him, arms crossed, while he gathered up her laundry. And this, too, was why, when next she saw Ms. D'Cruz, she had given that woman a triumphant look, and waved the laundry chit at her.

All of this was also why it would be several weeks before she saw her husband's underwear again. The dhobi would disappear, and with him, her linen. It would take no less than the reluctant intervention of Inspector Chatpati and the infamous Bangalore Civil Nuisance Unit to restore order to laundry. And turn her world upside down in the process.

2: THE UNWELCOME IGNITION OF ECSTASY

As it happened, it was the state of his underwear that preoccupied Inspector Hari Chatpati on that fateful morning when it all began. He emerged from the shower with a towel wrapped around his waist. Nirmala, his wife, had already laid his uniform out on the bed. All that remained was for the Inspector to select his undergarments. That should not have taken much time-the Inspector's tastes in undergarments were spartan: one colour, clean, Y-fronts, not boxers.

He slid open the drawer in question. And stopped short. He could barely believe what he was seeing.

"Nirmala!"

The shout made its way into the kitchen, loud enough to be heard over the sizzle of dosa batter crisping up nicely on the cast iron *tawa*. Nirmala cast a glance over her shoulder, shook her head, and turned her attention back to her husband's breakfast.

"Nirmala! What's happened to my underwear?"

She stifled a chuckle. She slid the tip of the steel spatula under the dosa and lifted the edge up. Browning nicely. Just right. With a flick of her wrist, she lifted the dosa onto a waiting plate, then stepped out of the kitchen just as the third hail sounded.

"Nirmala!"

Her husband awaited her in front of the dresser, his stance that of a mildly enraged sumo wrestler. He pointed at the drawer.

"What. Is. That."

Nirmala made a show of glancing in, though she knew full well what lay within.

"Organisation," she replied. "Stop making such a fuss and put one on, will you? Your breakfast is getting cold." She glanced at his nether regions. "As are other things."

It amused Nirmala to find that her husband got dressed in record time; usually, there would be some meandering through the text messages on his work phone before he arrived at the breakfast table. The Inspector entered just as Nirmala ladled the steaming spiced potato filling into the dosa. She placed a dollop of hot onion chutney on the plate and placed it in front of her husband.

"Organisation," she said to Chatpati. "Home organisation. That is the correct way to fold underwear. No need for so much outrage."

Chatpati dug into the dosa. He considered a reply, then thought it best to remain silent.

"Nothing to say?" Nirmala asked. "Unusual for you, Hari."

"Nice dosa," Chatpati ventured. "Very nice. Hot. It's usually just warm."

"Thank you," she replied. "And it's usually your fault that it's not hot. Any other observations?"

"Chutney's spicy."

"I'll tone it down next time. That it?"

Chatpati tried a quick glance up. She was watching him like a hawk.

"About the underwear," he began.

"Yes?"

He frowned. "It seems an odd way to fold them. They look like, well, like dumplings."

"As long as they look after your dumplings, my darling, why do you care?"

There was no discussion to be had-he knew he was on shaky ground. The home was very much Nirmala's domain, and she ruled it with the same exactitude that Chatpati ruled his Civil Nuisance Unit. His authority and jurisdiction ended at the threshold, where hers began. That had always been the way of things.

"Fair enough," he said. "I suppose it's that Chinese lady, is it? From YouTube."

Nirmala sniffed. "Hmph. Chinese lady! What an insult. I bet you wouldn't describe Albert Einstein as that German fellow. And she's not Chinese, she's Japanese. The name is Miko Chan. And she's an Organising Consultant. The world's best."

Chatpati nodded and set his head back down. He'd been vaguely aware of a gathering orderliness in the flat they'd lived in for just under a year now. Things that he had left in one place, intending them to be retrieved later, disappeared. He had to ask Nirmala for them, that resulting in instruction as to "where things should be kept". It was all very well, if slightly humiliating. Chatpati belonged to a different school of philosophy. The motto of that school was not "Everything in its place. And a place for everything."

"It's called ChanMiko, Hari," Nirmala said. "It's not just about tidying, it's about mindset, outlook, attitude. It's a way of organising everything: underwear, home, work, life. Even the world. It's about 'Igniting Ecstasy' through organisation." Nirmala took a breath. "I think she's just brilliant."

The ringing of his mobile phone cut inspector Chatpati's further participation in the ignition of ecstasy short. Chatpati leapt to his feet.

"Well, that'll be the driver," he said. He washed his hands in the sink, gave Nirmala a hug with his forearms, and dashed out of the kitchen. Nirmala cocked her head. And waited.

The Inspector's head reappeared in the doorway.

"Hat," he mumbled. "Where's my hat, please?"

3: RELAXATION IN CHAOS

The driver that Traffic Division had allocated to ferry Inspector Chatpati to and from work was a thoughtful man. Narayan had been driving the Inspector for three months now and had gotten to know what the Inspector liked, and did not like. The Inspector liked to listen to the news on the radio. The Inspector did not like idle chatter.

The Inspector could not abide rapid acceleration or deceleration, which meant that Narayan could not exploit gaps in traffic. Which translated to a pedestrian rate of progress through rush hour traffic.

Narayan had found that odd. Driving a police Hoysala gave him a distinct advantage over other road users. Civilian drivers reacted to the Hoysala much like civilians reacted to the proximity of the police on foot. Civilians moved to one side, tried to become inconspicuous, hung back. Civilian drivers did the same—they gave the Hoysala space. It was foolish not to take advantage, Narayan thought. But the Inspector was not a man to use his advantages. That much was clear.

Narayan was, therefore, taken aback when, ten minutes

in, the Inspector turned the radio off. And asked him a question.

"Narayan," Chatpati said. "Have you heard of MikoChan?"

Narayan cast a sidelong glance at Chatpati, then fixed his gaze on the traffic light. It was still red.

Narayan nodded cautiously. "Um, I think so, sir," he said. "That new Chinese restaurant? In the Pentagon Hotel. I hear it is very expensive."

Chatpati shook his head. "No. It's a way of organising things. House. Clothes. Life. Japanese, apparently."

Narayan shook his head. "That is very good, sir, but this is Bangalore." He pointed with his chin.

The traffic light had turned green, but the flow of traffic had stalled. A rather large cow had settled down in the middle of the junction. A pumpkin lay there in pieces, no doubt fallen off a truck, and the cow, being a Bangalore cow, was not one to miss an opportunity. Motorcycles zigged and zagged around it, causing cars to brake in their wake. The air rang with the clamour of horns.

"Yes," Chatpati said. "This is Bangalore. And India. Not Japan. Organisation is not in our makeup."

"Over-rated, sir," Narayan offered. He cast the Inspector another glance. The comment did not seem to have offended. He waved at the snarl of cars in front of them. "Organisation. It is over-rated. How to organise things like that? Better to let things happen as they must and make our way around."

"Hmm," Chatpati said. "I wonder how it is abroad."

"I have been abroad," Narayan said. "UK. England. We went once on an organised tour. London, then the country-side. Spotless. Roads are straight. Everyone obeys rules. No horns. Very different. But-"

"But?"

Narayan sucked his teeth. "Britishers become furious very quickly, sir. On the surface, very proper and polite, but underneath? Bubbling! One fellow in front does not put on an indicator, everyone behind is straight away annoyed. If you don't join the queue, the insults start. Very peaceful and straight, but everyone is very angry. That is why they look so pale and unhealthy."

The Inspector glanced over at his driver. "Are you saying chaos is preferable?"

Narayan shrugged. "Better relaxation in chaos than anger in order. Sir."

A man had gotten out of his car and was now trying to wave the cow on with his hands. The cow got to its feet and shook its horns at him. The man retreated. The beast settled back down again.

"Well," Chatpati said, "you'd better radio that cow in to Traffic HQ. Whether it's the natural order of things or not, we'd better try to lessen the bovine risk to public safety. And soothe a few tempers."

The rest of the drive was uneventful, giving Chatpati time to consider Narayan's pronouncement.

'Better relaxation in chaos than anger in order.'

The thing had some merit to it, he decided. It would be an injunction he would be hard pressed to follow in the days to come.

4: Huddles and Muddles

All seemed in order when the Hoysala pulled up the loading ramp of the Public Utilities Building. The goods entrance was Chatpati's preferred route of entry-it avoided encounters with members of the public, who came to the Utilities Building for its single cinema or vegetarian restaurant or shops.

Chatpati waved Narayan off and threaded his way between the usual riot of handcarts being pushed and cartons being heaved. The shouting of the labourers abated to a degree when they saw the Inspector, but resumed its customary volume as Chatpati stepped into the freight elevator. Chatpati felt strangely comforted by this; however serene the unloading of cargo might be in Japan, in Bangalore it was a distillation of chaos and there was some comfort to be found in the usual disorder of things.

The Civil Nuisance Unit occupied the twenty-fourth floor, the very highest. This had once been the premises of a fabulous nightclub and restaurant called Cloud24. After a spectacular opening and six months of success, Cloud24 began to flounder. The state government eased liquor licensing laws and pubs became all the rage. The restaurant had closed down. The twenty-fourth floor's destiny, of being a repository of cobwebs, had changed when the CNU sprang into being.

The Utilities Building was government-owned and government-run, which was why there were relics of the former restaurant still in view. Getting things done was a constant challenge; the building manager was either absent or short-staffed. Besides, there was no good way to remove the defunct neon sign above or the gilt revolving doors ahead. Ripping out the chandeliers to fit strip lighting was beyond the budget. So these embellishments stayed, and the CNU tried to distract attention with noticeboards featuring the latest 'Most Wanted' and posters exhorting good citizenship.

The reception area had served as Cloud24's sports bar. Constable Jaswant Singh was in charge. He was a reliable, athletic sort of fellow, always neatly turned out in uniform, turban, and beard. Singh was one of those officers Chatpati regarded as part of the Civil Nuisance Unit's trusted core. When Chatpati had been suspended months earlier and the CNU temporarily disbanded by Assistant Commissioner of Police Srinivasan (Chatpati's unsworn nemesis), Singh had been one of a handful of officers that had defied the ACP's edicts and stayed on. The CNU's unofficial investigation of what would later be known as "The Tender Coconut Caper" had led to Chatpati's reinstatement, the CNU's fame and Srinivasan's ignominy.

Chatpati would normally pass a few moments with Singh to get a feel for the flavour of the morning but, on this occasion, Jaswant Singh was paying serious attention to a short, plump woman in a rich floral sari who was waving a slip of paper at him. The lady's speech was animated, her arm movements no less so, both of which Jaswant Singh countered with studied immobility.

Chatpati sensed customer dissatisfaction. It was too early in the day for complaints, so Chatpati sped up and slipped through the saloon doors before Singh could turn his gaze away from his interlocutor.

Cloud24's restaurant and discotheque occupied most of the remaining floor-space, that the size of three Olympic swimming pools. There was another bar in the corner, and three private suites, two of which had been repurposed into holding cells. When the CNU had started off, they had had to make do with restaurant tables and chairs, but now they had proper office furniture, desks and filing cabinets arrayed in an open-plan layout. The floor-to-ceiling windows had, at last, been cleaned and natural light suffused the room.

A casual visitor might have been taken in, but the appraising eye would detect the sprung dance-floor in the centre of it all. And the silvered, still glittering, disco ball that spun from the rafters.

At least the abstract artwork had been removed and replaced with portraits of great figures, living and deceased, but the cheesy neon frames remained. Chatpati thought the pink glow rather enhanced the Chief Minister's rather plain features, but he was alone in that opinion. Chatpati had permitted a single snooker table to remain, with strict instructions that no cues were to be wielded during working hours. SubInspector Vasanth Nair had made a case for keeping it, citing workplace policies at Google and Apple, where such things were usual. Or so he said. Chatpati hadn't thought there was much prospect of the Civil Nuisance Unit becoming as global a phenomenon, but he'd agreed, and hadn't, as yet, had cause to regret it.

Usually, the CNU would have been a hive of noisy activity, but today, the Inspector found his officers clustered, all quiet silent, on the dance floor, all facing the central Command Console that was the electronic brain of the operation.

The Console had three operators, all women. Constable Seema was in charge of these, she another of Chatpati's trusted few. The console operators were to the CNU as air traffic controllers to an airport: they took calls, registered cases onto the PoliceNet database and updated the status of ongoing investigations. All these were displayed, in real time, on the huge flatscreen display that hung down from the ceiling on steel wires. At the moment, the display showed an overhead satellite map of Bangalore, with dots and flags representing crime, traffic and deployed resources.

Chatpati cleared his throat. There was a start, and the ranks of khaki-clad backs opened up before him like the Red Sea before Moses. There, in the very centre, stool Constable Raj.

Raj was as spick as ever in his khaki uniform. That was usual. What was unusual was that he was holding a clipboard. Barely twenty-three years of age, and the first of the CNU's recruits, Raj belonged to that generation who could type with their thumbs into their phones. Chatpati had attempted it once and shattered the screen. Chatpati preferred paper -at least you could crumple it up and throw it away without incurring a hefty bill- but Raj was rarely seen anywhere near stationery. Today, though, Raj was holding a clipboard.

A salvo of salutes marked Chatpati's passage between the ranks.

"Raj," Chatpati said, without preamble, "you're holding a clipboard."

"Morning, sir. Yes, sir," Raj said, flashing an anxious grin. "It is a clipboard."

"Why?"

"Why?"

"Yes. Why?"

Raj looked left and right for help. None was forthcoming.

"Huddle. Sir." Raj said, with some reluctance.

"Huddle?"

"Huddle."

"What is a huddle?" There was a trace of impatience in Chatpati's tone.

Raj blanched. Seema, who shot to her feet, saved him.

She removed the headset and gave the Inspector a salute, which he returned. Seema was quite the handsomest of the three female constables, and even Chatpati was not immune to her natural charm.

"Sir, good morning, sir," she began. "What Raj is trying to say is that today is the first day of the Morning Huddle."

Raj broke in. "Yes. And the Evening Huddle."

Seema nodded. "Yes. There is an Evening Huddle as well." She paused, blinking at the expression on Chatpati's face. "It was in the memo, Sir." She paused again and bit her lip. "From Central Division HQ."

The silence was almost palpable, interrupted solely by the brisk chatter of the other two console operators talking to callers.

"I see," Chatpati said, slowly. "What memo? Why didn't I know about this? Raj?"

Raj paled. "Sir, I left it on your desk. Two weeks ago. When it came in."

"Where did you leave it?" Chatpati said.

"On the right, sir. Next to the table lamp. Just in front of the two stacks of files."

"I see," Chatpati said. The memo was now, undoubtedly, under a third stack of files, all of which Chatpati had placed on the floor. Chatpati hated paperwork; he subscribed to the school of workplace productivity called Purposeful Procrastination. It was a technique that mostly worked-important things inevitably rose to the surface, at which point they would be dealt with. The irrelevant things just went away. Every few months, Chatpati would clear the lot out and await the next incursion. Occasionally, the odd elephant would rumble through and catch him unawares. Like today.

"I have a copy here," Raj said, in a rush. He held out the

clipboard. "If you care to read it. To, um, refresh your memory."

With some unwillingness, Chatpati took the thing and read.

MEMORANDUM

Distribution List: All heads of police stations and Divisions, Bangalore

You are hereby notified that, with effect from the date below, the WorkPlace Improvement Micro-Strategy Bi-Daily Huddle will be implemented at all workplaces. This has been authorised by the Commissioner of Police and the Productivity and Innovation Steering Sub-Group.

The Huddle is a short, informal but official meeting that takes place twice a day. Huddles have been proven to improve Workplace Productivity, generate Shared Vision Thinking and Big Picture Visualisation.

Guidelines for the conduct of Huddles follow. These are non-negotiable.

1. The Huddle shall take place at the beginning and at the end of every shift.

Regularity is order.

2. The Huddle shall take no longer than fifteen minutes. Any longer and a Huddle Exception Report must be filed in triplicate.

Time is the lifeblood of work.

3. All officers and constables shall attend, except if on active duty or sanctioned leave. Breakfast, lunch, dinner, tea, cigarette breaks, and toilet needs are not valid exemptions.

Delayed gratification strengthens character.

4. Any officer absent will file a valid excuse in writing, in triplicate, and a Huddle Exception Report, also in triplicate, before the next Huddle. The only valid excuse is being on active duty.

Duty is discipline.

5. The senior-most officer present will lead The Huddle. If no officer is present, the senior-most constable will lead. In this situation, a Huddle Exception Report should be filed in triplicate.

Leadership is presence.

6. There will be no sitting. All will stand. Sitting leads to laziness. Standing focuses the mind.

The chair is death.

6. The Huddle will cover, as a minimum,

a. An update on all cases still active since the last Huddle

b. An update on all cases closed since the last Huddle

c. An update of all fresh cases since the last Huddle

d. Any expected or foreseeable challenges to the closure of active or new cases before the next Huddle.

Order is rigour.

7. On completion of the Huddle, the senior-most officer will complete the Huddle Bundle Checklist, to be filed in triplicate, at Central Division HQ within five working days.

Punctuality is politeness.

8. Compliance with the Daily Huddle and the Huddle Bundle Checklist will be audited by the Huddle Bundle Checklist Audit Working Group. Failure to achieve 95% compliance every quarter may trigger a spot audit by the Huddle Bundle Checklist Audit Working Group Adhoc Enforcement Unit.

Regularity is religion.

9. Serial under-performance on key performance indicator metrics will lead to scrutiny and, where necessary, disciplinary action including, but not confined to, reduction in pay, suspension and/or

dismissal.

Failure is found out.

A Weekly Huddle Improvement Tips Newsletter will be sent out to facilitate the smooth running of this Quality Improvement. All officers are required to read the Newsletter. It is to be displayed on a special Productivity Noticeboard (to be requisitioned as per usual channels—quote reference 'NotHDL33').

Questions not dealt with in this memorandum should addressed to the Huddle Governance Team at Central Division HQ.

-Assistant Commissioner of Police Srinivasan, Central Division
Acting Head, Quality Improvement

"Bloody hell!" Chatpati almost spat. "Srinivasan! Now in charge of Quality Improvement. It's another scheme to drown us in paperwork." He suppressed the urge to say more because all eyes were on him. And all ears.

He exhaled. "Right. Fine. We do this Huddle." He flipped over the memorandum. There was a checklist underneath. "Who's got a pen?"

"Excuse me, Inspector." A small voice sounded from somewhere beyond the ranks of constables. Chatpati looked up and saw a single hand raised above the khaki-clad shoulders. The intervening policemen stepped to the side.

The raised arm belonged to Hemanth Sachdev, the CNU's part-time IT contractor. Hemanth had helped to set up the CNU's electronic infrastructure. Although the CNU was now running independently, Central Division still contracted Hemanth to work one day a week on site. When present, Hemanth operated out of the former DJ booth at the far end of the dance floor.

Hemanth's premature male pattern baldness had progressed, Chatpati noted-there was even more glistening pate on view than earlier. He was also looking rather more prosperous-there was a bulge around Hemanth's collar that Chatpati attributed to Hemanth's recent entry into married life. Hemanth's wife was clearly a capable cook.

"Yes, Hemanth?" Chatpati said. "Your question?"

"Am I meant to be present? At the Huddle, I mean. I'm a private contractor, not an officer-"

Chatpati considered this. "Good question. Strictly, no, but I think we would appreciate your expertise if you attended. When you are here, of course." Chatpati frowned. "No one expects you to attend on other days. I mean, it's going to be bad enough one day a week."

A few of the constables grinned. There was a general murmur of assent.

"Any other questions? No? Everyone here?" Chatpati looked around. Raj looked even more uneasy. "Well," Chatpati said, "what is it, Raj? Speak up."

Raj opened his mouth, but before he could say a word, the saloon doors clattered open. As a man, the officers' heads swung to see.

SubInspector Vasanth Nair sauntered into the CNU HQ, motorcycle helmet swinging from one arm. Nair was not in uniform. He wore a checked shirt tucked into khaki slacks. Polished Oxfords encased his size 12 feet. Nair was whistling a tune, but stopped short when he saw he was the object of attention. Nair reached up with his free hand, and, with a finger and thumb, smoothed his moustache.

Raj spoke up. "I was about to say, Sir, that we're missing one."

Dhobi: A traditional washerman, typically a 'collect and deliver' cottage industry for dirty laundry, now under threat from washing machines.

Rakshasa: A Hindu demon

Printed in Great Britain
by Amazon